Well Met

Well Met

Jen DeLuca

JOVE
New York

A JOVE BOOK
Published by Berkley
An imprint of Penguin Random House LLC
1745 Broadway, New York, NY 10019

Library of Congress Cataloging-in-Publication Data

Names: DeLuca, Jen, author.
Title: Well met / Jen DeLuca.
Description: First edition. | New York: Berkley, 2019.
Identifiers: LCCN 2019001004| ISBN 9781984805386 (paperback) |
ISBN 9781984805393 (ebook)
Subjects: | BISAC: FICTION / Romance / Contemporary. |
FICTION / Contemporary Women. | GSAFD: Love stories.
Classification: LCC PS3604.E44757 W45 2019 | DDC 813/.6—dc23
LC record available at https://lccn.loc.gov/2019001004

First Edition: September 2019

Printed in the United States of America
1   3   5   7   9   10   8   6   4   2

Cover art and design by Colleen Reinhart

Dedicated to the memory of my mother,
Jane M. Galbavy.

Thank you for bringing the love of books and
Shakespeare into my life. I spelled "sleep" right this time.

One

I *didn't choose the* wench life. The wench life chose me.

When I pulled into the parking lot of Willow Creek High School on that late-spring morning, I had very little on my agenda. No doctor's appointments for my big sister, no school obligations to shuttle my niece to. The only thing I needed to do was get my niece to the sign-ups for the Renaissance faire. We were five minutes late, so it was going great so far.

Caitlin huffed from the back seat as I threw my little white Jeep in park. "Em, we're late!" She managed to stretch both my name and that last word out into at least three syllables. "What if they don't let me sign up? All my friends are doing this, and if I can't, I'll—"

"They'll let you sign up." But of course she was out before I'd even unbuckled my seat belt. I wasn't going to call her back. I didn't have that kind of authority over her. At barely ten years older, I was more a big sister than an aunt. When I'd first come to stay with my older sister and her daughter, April had tried to get Cait to call me "Aunt Emily," but that was only a short hop away from Auntie Em and Kansas jokes so we'd abandoned it quickly. My relationship with the kid had settled into more of a friendship with overtures of Adult In Charge.

This morning, Adult In Charge was kicking in. No way was I leaving a fourteen-year-old by herself in a strange situation, even if it was her high school. I grabbed my coffee mug from the cup holder and started after her. She couldn't have gone far.

My cell phone rang from inside my purse when I was halfway across the parking lot. I fished it out and kept walking.

"Did you find it okay?"

"Yeah, we're good. Hopefully this won't take too long."

"Oh, God, you don't have to *stay*." April sounded slightly horrified by the prospect. "You just need to drop her off and come back home."

I held my breath and tried to analyze her tone through the crappy cell phone connection. The past few days had been rough as she'd started weaning off the pain medication. "Everything okay?" I tried to sound as casual as possible. "Do you need me to come home?"

"No . . ." Her voice trailed off, and I stopped walking and listened harder.

"April?"

"No, no, Emily. I'm fine. I'm right where you left me, on the couch with coffee and the remote. I don't want you to feel like you have to . . ."

"It's fine. Really. Isn't this why I'm here, to help you out?"

Another pause. Another sigh. "Yeah. Okay . . ." I practically heard her shrug. "I feel bad. I should be doing this stuff."

"Well, you can't." I tried to sound as cheerful as I could. "Not for another couple months at least, remember? Doctor's orders. Besides, this 'stuff' is what I'm here for, right?"

"Yeah." A tremble in her voice now, which I blamed on the Percocet. I'd be glad when she was off that shit for good. It made her weepy.

"Drink your coffee, find something awful on television, okay? I'll make lunch for us when we get home."

I hung up, shoved my phone back in my purse, and once again cursed out the driver who had run the red light that night. A vision of April's SUV popped into my head, that twisted lump of silver metal at the junkyard, and I pushed it aside. Caitlin had been asleep in the back seat, and somehow she'd walked away with nothing more than some bruises and a sprained ankle.

My sister hadn't been so lucky. Mom had stayed with her while she was in the ICU, and by the time April was home from the hospital a week later I'd moved in, so Mom could go home to Dad in Indiana. My older sister needed a caregiver for a while, and my niece needed an Adult In Charge who was mobile, so I was here to stay.

As for me . . . I needed a change. A couple weeks before the accident I'd lost not only my boyfriend and my apartment, but all my plans for the future. Willow Creek, Maryland, was as good a place as any to lick my wounds while I took care of April and hers. Smack in the middle of wine country, this area was all rolling green hills dotted with small towns like this one, with its charming downtown storefronts and friendly people. Though I hadn't seen any willows yet and as far as I could tell there weren't any creeks, so the name remained a mystery.

I picked up the pace and pushed through the double doors, finally catching up with Caitlin outside the high school auditorium. She didn't look back at me, running down the aisle instead to join a handful of kids roughly her age clustered in front of the stage, getting forms from a guy with a clipboard. The auditorium was filled with clumps of kids embracing like long-lost relatives who hadn't seen each other in years, even though they'd probably sat next to each other in class the day before. There were adults around too, sprinkled here and there, but I couldn't tell if they were chaperones or participants. Then one of the adults turned around and his black T-shirt said HUZZAH! across the front in huge white letters, and I had my answer.

I took a long sip of coffee and sank into a chair in the back row. My job as taxi service was done. I checked the time on my phone. One hour until I needed to be back to pick her up, which wasn't enough time to go home. Willow Creek was a small town, but April lived on one end of it and the high school was on the outskirts at the other. I pulled up my list-making app. I'd picked up refills of April's meds the previous day, and this Renaissance faire tryout was the only other thing on my list. Was there anything else I needed to get done while I was on this side of town?

"Are you here to volunteer?"

One of the adults I'd spotted before—cute, blond, shortish, and roundish—had splintered off and now hovered at the end of the row where I was sitting. Before I could answer she took a form off her clipboard and pushed it into my hands.

"Here. You can go ahead and fill this out."

"What? Me?" I stared at the form as though it were printed in Cyrillic. "Oh. No. I'm just here to drop off my niece." I nodded toward the group of kids at the front.

"Which one's your . . ." She looked down the aisle. "Oh, Caitlin, right? You must be Emily."

My eyes widened. "Yeah. Good call. I keep forgetting how small this town is." I'd come here from Boston, and had grown up outside of Indianapolis. Small towns weren't my thing.

She laughed and waved it off. "You'll get used to it, trust me.

I'm Stacey, by the way. And I'm afraid you kind of have to volunteer." She indicated the form still in my hand. "It's a requirement if a younger student wants to be part of the Faire cast. Anyone under sixteen needs a parent or guardian in the cast with them. I think April was planning to volunteer with her, but . . ." Her sentence trailed off, and she punctuated it with an awkward shrug.

"Yeah." I looked down at the form. "You can't call it volunteering, then, can you? Sounds more like strong-arming." But I looked over at Cait, already chatting with her friends, holding her own form like it was a golden ticket. I read through the form. Six weeks of Saturday rehearsals starting in June, then six more weekends from mid-July through the end of August. I was already playing chauffeur for Caitlin all spring and summer anyway . . .

Before I could say anything else, the double doors behind me opened with a bang. I whirled in my seat to see a man striding through like he was walking into an old-west saloon. He was . . . delicious. No other way to describe him. Tall, blond, muscled, with a great head of hair and a tight T-shirt. Gaston crossed with Captain America, with a generic yet mesmerizing handsomeness.

"Mitch!" Stacey greeted him like an old friend. Which he undoubtedly was. These people probably all went to this high school together back in the day. "Mitch, come over here and tell Emily that she wants to do Faire."

He scoffed as though the question were the stupidest one he'd ever heard. "Of course she wants to do Faire! Why else would she be here?"

I pointed down the aisle to Cait. "I'm really just the taxi."

Mitch peered at my niece, then turned back to me. "Oh, you're Emily. The aunt, right? Your sister's the one who was in the crash? How's she doing?"

I blinked. Goddamn small towns. "Good. She's . . . um . . . good." My sister hated gossip in all forms, so I made sure not to contribute any information that could get around.

"Good. Yeah, glad to hear it." He looked solemn for a moment or two, then brushed it aside, jovial smile back on his face. "Anyway. You should hang around, join the insanity. I mean, it's lots of work, but it's fun. You'll love it." With that, he was gone, sauntering his way down the aisle, fist-bumping kids as he went.

I watched him walk away for a second, because, damn, could he fill out a pair of jeans, both front and back. Then what he said registered with me. "I'll love it?" I turned back to Stacey the volunteer. "He doesn't know me. How does he know what I'll love?"

"If it helps . . ." She leaned forward conspiratorially, and I couldn't help but respond with a lean of my own. "He carries a pretty big sword during Faire. And wears a kilt."

"Sold." I dug in my purse for a pen. What was giving up my weekends for the entire summer when it meant I could look at an ass like that?

What the hell, right? It would be time with Caitlin. That was what I was there for. Be the cool aunt. Do the fun stuff. Distract her from the car accident that had left her with nightmares and weekly therapy sessions, and left her mom with a shattered right leg. When I'd arrived in Willow Creek, gloom had hung low over their household, like smoke in a crowded room. I'd come to throw open a window, let in the light again.

Besides, helping out my sister and her kid was the best way to stop dwelling on my own shit. Focusing on someone else's problems was always easier than my own.

Stacey grinned as I started filling out the form. "Give it to Simon up at the front when you're finished. It's going to be great. Huzzah!" This last was said as a cheer, and with that she was gone, probably looking for other parental-type figures to snag into this whole gig.

Oh, God. Was I going to have to yell "huzzah" too? How much did I love my niece?

The form was pretty basic, and soon I followed the stream of volunteers (mostly kids—where were all the adults?) to the front of the auditorium, where they handed the papers to the dark-haired man with the clipboard collecting them. Simon, I presumed. Thank God, another adult. More adultier than me, even. I'd rolled out of bed and thrown on leggings and a T-shirt, while he was immaculate in jeans and a perfectly ironed Oxford shirt, sleeves rolled halfway up his forearms, with a dark blue vest buttoned over it.

Despite his super-mature vibe, he didn't look that much older than me. Late twenties at the most. Slighter of build than Mitch, and probably not quite six feet tall. Well-groomed and clean-shaven with closely cut dark brown hair. He looked like he smelled clean, like laundry detergent and sharp soap. Mitch, for all his hotness, looked like he smelled like Axe body spray.

When it was my turn, I handed the form in and turned away, checking to see where Cait had wandered off to. I couldn't wait to tell her I was doing this whole thing with her. That kid was gonna owe me one.

"This isn't right."

I turned back around. "Excuse me?"

Simon, the form collector, brandished mine at me. "Your form. You didn't fill it out correctly."

"Um . . ." I walked back over to him and took the paper from his hand. "I think I know how to fill out a form."

"Right there." He tapped his pen in a *rat-a-tat-tat* on the page. "You didn't say what role you're trying out for."

"Role?" I squinted at it. "Oh, right." I handed the paper back to him. "I don't care. Whatever you need."

He didn't take it. "You have to specify a role."

"Really?" I looked behind me, searching for the desperate volunteer who had coerced me into this gig in the first place. But she was lost in a sea of auditionees. Of course.

"Yes, really." He pursed his lips, and his brows drew together over his eyes. Dark brown brows, muddy brown eyes. He'd be relatively attractive if he weren't looking at me like he'd caught me cheating on my chemistry final. "It's pretty simple," he continued. "Nobility, actors, dancers . . . you can audition for any of those. You could also try out for the combat stuff, if you have any experience. We do a human chess match and joust."

"I . . . I don't have any experience. Or, um, talent." The longer this conversation went on, the more my heart sank. Now I was supposed to have skills? Wasn't this a volunteer thing? Why was this guy making it so freaking hard?

He looked at me for a moment, a quick perusal up and down. Not so much checking me out as sizing me up. "Are you over twenty-one?"

Jesus. I knew I was on the short side, but . . . I drew myself up, as though looking a little taller would make me look older too. "Twenty-five, thank you very much." Well, twenty-five in July, but he didn't need to know that. It wasn't like he'd be celebrating my birthday with me.

"Hmmm. You have to be twenty-one to be a tavern wench. You could put that down if you want to help out in the tavern."

Now we were talking. Nothing wrong with hanging out in a bar for a few weekends in the summer. I'd worked in bars before; hell, I worked in two of them until just recently. This would be the same thing, but in a cuter costume.

"Fine." I plucked my pen back out of my purse and scribbled the word "wench" down on the form, then thrust the paper back into his hands. "Here."

"Thank you," he said automatically, as though he hadn't admonished me like a child thirty seconds before.

Gah. What a dick.

As I headed up the aisle toward the back of the auditorium, it didn't take me long to spot Caitlin a couple rows away, talking to her friends. A smirk took over my face, and I scooted down the row in front of her, maneuvering around the folded-up seats.

"Hey." I gave her a mock punch on the shoulder to get her attention. "You know you need an adult to volunteer with you, right?"

"I do?" Her eyes widened, and she looked down toward Simon with alarm, as though he was about to throw her out of the auditorium. Well, he'd have to go through me first.

"Yep. So guess who agreed to be a tavern wench this summer. How much do you love me?" I held my breath. Most teens wouldn't want to be caught dead with a parental figure within a five-mile radius, much less want to spend the summer hanging out with them. But Caitlin was a good kid, and we'd developed a rapport since I'd stepped in as her Adult In Charge. Maybe she'd be cool with it.

Her look of alarm turned to surprised joy. "Really?" The word was a squeak coming out of her mouth. "So we both get to do the Faire?"

"Looks like it," I replied. "You owe me one, kiddo."

Her response was more squeal than words, but the way she threw her arms around my neck in an awkward hug over the row of seats told me everything. Maybe that was the advantage to being a cool aunt as opposed to a mom. This new family dynamic took some getting used to, but I was already starting to like it.

"We talked you into it, huh?" Mitch was waiting for me at the end of the row when I scooted back down to the aisle.

I shrugged. "It's not like I have much of a choice." I looked over my shoulder at Caitlin, giggling with her friends over something on their phones. "Doing this means a lot to her, so here I am."

"You're a good person, Emily." He squinted. "It was Emily, right?"

I nodded. "Emily Parker." I moved to offer a handshake, but he came back with a fist bump instead, and what kind of idiot would I be to not accept that?

"Good to meet you, Park. But trust me. You're gonna have a great time at Faire."

I blinked at the immediate nickname, but decided to roll with it. "Well, I have been promised that there are kilts involved, so . . ." I did my best to let my eyes linger on him without being some kind of creep about it. But Mitch didn't seem like the type of guy to mind a little ogling. In fact, he seemed to encourage it.

"Oh, yeah." A grin crawled up his face, and his eyes lingered right back. A flush crept up the back of my neck. If I'd known this was going to be a mutual-ogling kind of day, I would have done more this morning than wash my face and put on some lip gloss. "Believe me," he said. "You'll have a great summer. I'll make sure of it."

I laughed. "I'll hold you to that." An easy promise to make, since I was already enjoying myself. I headed back up the aisle and plopped into my vacated seat in the last row. Down at the front, Simon collected more forms, probably criticizing applicants' handwriting while he did so. He glanced up at one point like he could feel my eyes on him, and his brows drew together in a frown. God, he was really holding a grudge about that form, wasn't he?

At the other side of the auditorium, Mitch high-fived a student and offered a fist bump to Caitlin, who looked at him like he hung the moon. I knew which of these two guys I was looking forward to getting to know better this summer, and it wasn't the Ren Faire Killjoy.

I'd always been a little in awe of my older sister. Married young and divorced young from a man who'd had little interest in being a father, April had raised Caitlin on her own with an independence that bordered on intimidating. We'd never been particularly close—a twelve-year age difference will do that, when April was off to college right around the time that I was starting to become interesting—but I'd always thought of her as someone to emulate.

Which was why it was so hard to see her in her current condition.

When we got home from auditions, I opened the front door to find a crutch in the middle of the living room floor. I followed the line of the crutch, which pointed directly at my big sister on the couch. She looked like a dog who'd been caught going through the trash.

"You tried to get up while we were gone, didn't you?" I crossed my arms and stared her down. It was hard to look threatening when you were barely five foot three, but I managed pretty well.

"Yeah." April sighed. "That didn't go well."

Caitlin didn't notice our little standoff. "Hey, Mom!" She dropped a kiss in the vicinity of April's cheek before running off to her room. She could text more efficiently in there, probably.

I picked up the fallen crutch and propped it against the arm of the couch next to the other one. "BLTs okay for lunch?"

"Sure. Everything go okay?" April craned her neck to the side and tossed the question over her shoulder as I went into the kitchen to get the bacon started. "Did Caitlin get signed up for the cast?" Shifting noises on the couch, punctuated by some swearing under her breath. Yeah, she was definitely cutting back on the pain medication. The next few days would be bumpy.

"Everything went fine. They said they can't take everyone, but they're sending out an email next week to everyone who made the cast."

"Next week? Oof. I don't know if I can live with her long enough for her to find out if she's in."

"She'll get in." I punched down the bread in the toaster and started slicing tomatoes. "If they don't let her in, they don't get me. Thanks for that, by the way. You totally set me up."

"What? No, I didn't. I told you not to go in there. All you were supposed to do was drop her off."

"Yeah, well." I got down three plates and started assembling sandwiches. "Caitlin can't be in the cast without a parent volunteering. They said you were going to volunteer, you know, before . . ." There was no good way to end that sentence.

"What?" April was repeating herself now, and it had nothing to do with meds. "I . . . oh." Yep. There it was. She remembered now. "Shit." I glanced through the pass-through to see her sag against the back of the couch. "I did set you up. I completely forgot."

"Don't worry about it. I have it on good authority that it'll be fun." I put the plates on the pass-through and tossed a bag of chips up there beside them. I thought about Mitch and his promised kilt. That would certainly be fun. Then I thought about Simon and his disapproving face. Less fun. I brought lunch out to the living room, and we ate on TV trays so April wouldn't have to get up. I left the third plate on the counter; Caitlin would be along for it eventually.

"Fun," April repeated as she reached for her sandwich. She didn't sound convinced. She took a bite and shrugged. "I guess. I mean, what else have you got going on, right?"

I crunched a chip and half squinted at her. She couldn't be serious. I had a list-making app completely dedicated to their schedules. Surely she remembered what a nonstop life she and her kid had before one guy ran a red light one night and changed everything.

She met my gaze and squinted back with an exaggerated face. She wasn't serious after all. I wasn't used to a sister who joked around with me. But she was trying, so I played along, throwing a chip at her. "You're right. In fact, I picked up a box of chocolates so we could lie around all weekend and watch television."

"Good plan." She leaned forward and snagged the bag of chips. She shook her head at me. "You're too defensive. That Jake guy did a number on you, huh? You know, when Mom told me about him I said he was no good. You broke up, what, a couple months ago?"

"Yeah." I sighed. Of course Mom had told her. April and I had always gotten along fine, but the age difference, plus all the moving away from home and starting our own lives, had kept us from being as close as sisters usually were. Hence Mom acting as a kind of conduit between us, filling us in on each other's lives. It was a weird system, but it worked for us. "Yeah, it was a week or so before your accident. So you know, good timing."

"Well, it saved you from being homeless."

"I wasn't homeless." But I frowned into my sandwich because she was right. When Jake had left for his fancy lawyer job he'd not only dumped me like unwanted baggage (which I guess I was), but he'd canceled our lease on the way out the door. I'd been panicked, scrambling to find another apartment I could afford with my two part-time jobs, when Mom had called from the hospital about April's accident. It'd been a no-brainer to throw my stuff into storage, drive the four-hundred-something miles from Boston to Maryland, and transfer my panic away from myself and onto them.

But I didn't want to talk about Jake. That wound was still too fresh. Time to change the subject. "Stacey says hi, by the way."

"Who?"

"Stacey?" Had I gotten the name wrong? "Blond hair, about my height, big smile? She acted like she knew you. She knew Caitlin, anyway, and she knew who I was."

"Ugh." April rolled her eyes and took a sip of her Diet Coke. "That's the one thing about living in a small town. Everyone knows your business. Even people you don't know that well."

"So . . . you don't know Stacey?"

"No, I do. She works at our dentist's office, and we say hi every time Cait or I have an appointment. Nice, but . . ." She shrugged.

I got it. ". . . But not someone who should know that much about you."

"Exactly."

I thought about that, considered my next question. "I don't suppose you know a guy named Mitch, do you?" Now, there was someone I wouldn't mind knowing a little better.

"Mitch . . ." April tapped a chip on her bottom lip. "No . . . Oh. Wait. Kind of a big guy? Muscles? Superman jaw?"

"Looks like he can bench-press a Volkswagen." I nodded. "That's the one."

"Yeah, I've seen him around. Nice guy. I think he teaches gym? Hey, Cait?" April leaned back on the couch and called toward the hallway. I turned to see my niece had come out in search of lunch.

"Ooh, sandwich. Thanks, Emily." Caitlin grabbed her plate and perched on a stool. While she chewed she raised her eyebrows at her mother. "What's up?"

"That guy Mitch . . . doesn't he teach gym at your school?"

"Mr. Malone?" She swallowed her bite of sandwich. "Yeah. And coaches something. Baseball maybe?" Caitlin wasn't into sports. None of us were, so she came by it honestly. "He was hitting on Emily today." She reached over and dug a handful of chips out of the bag.

"No, he wasn't." Was he? Maybe a little. The back of my neck prickled with heat.

"Don't get excited," April warned. "From what I hear, he hits on everyone."

"Damn. So I'm not special?" I tried to look upset, but being teased about a guy by my big sister was something that had never happened before, and it made me grin. I shrugged and handed Caitlin the chip bag. "That's okay. I'm not planning on marrying the guy. Maybe just objectifying him while he wears a kilt."

The more I thought about it, the more this summer was starting to sound like fun. And I needed to have some fun. Put Jake in the rearview. I still remembered the look on his face when he told me he was moving on without me. His face had looked like . . . well, his expression had reminded me of Simon's. The form-police guy from this morning. I'd gotten serious Jake flashbacks from him, and I didn't like the way that made me feel. Embarrassed and small.

Right now, guys like Mitch were much better for my sanity. Guys like Mitch offered the possibility of a quick, fun hookup at some point during the summer, with no complex emotions or perceived inadequacies to get in the way. I could use someone like that in my life right about now.

After cleaning up the kitchen, I pulled up my calendar app again. My afternoon and the rest of the weekend were pretty much an open book. Much like my entire future. I didn't like it. I liked plans.

With Jake I'd had a plan. We'd met my sophomore year in college at a fraternity party, two like-minded intellectuals that were too good for beer pong. We'd talked all night, and I thought I'd found my soul mate. He was smart, focused, driven. I'd liked that streak of ambition in him that matched mine. For years I'd stuck with both him and our plan. Get him through law school. Once he'd set himself up in a career we'd be an unstoppable team. It was going to be us vs. the world. Jake and Emily. That was the plan.

But Jake was gone. What I hadn't realized was that, while my ambition had been for us both, his was only for himself. When he got that high-powered job he'd been shooting for, he left old things behind. Like our place, which he left for a high-rise apartment downtown. And me, the would-be fiancée he no longer needed. "It doesn't look good," he'd said. "I can't have a wife who works in a bar. You don't even have a bachelor's degree." It was like he'd forgotten all about our plan. And maybe he had. Or maybe he'd gotten what he'd wanted out of it and didn't need me anymore.

So here I was in Maryland. I'd arrived without a plan, but my sister needed me. That was enough for now. The thing was, I needed her too. I needed to feel like I could help. Make a difference in someone's life. Fixing things was what I did.

Two

And just like that, I was a tavern wench. The email arrived on Wednesday afternoon, sending Caitlin tearing into the house after school.

"Did you get the email, Em? Did you get it? I'm in the Ren faire cast—are you in? Did you get in?"

She finally took a breath—did she run all the way home from the bus stop?—while I pulled up my email on my phone. Sure enough, there was a message from the Willow Creek Renaissance Faire, welcoming me to this year's cast. Caitlin gave me a quick hug of excitement and grabbed a soda from the fridge, then she was off to her room and I went back out to the car for the last bags of groceries.

I finished putting the groceries away, checked on the chicken slow-roasting in the oven—yep, it was still there—and looked in on April. She'd gone to her room to take a nap before I'd left for the store. Yep, she was still there too, just stirring from sleep.

"Did I hear Cait come home?"

"I think the whole neighborhood heard her come home." I handed April the bottle of water on her nightstand and perched on her bedside. "Looks like us Parker girls are doing the Renaissance faire. You sure you don't want to sign up too? I don't want you to feel left out. Crutches are period. You could be an old beggar woman."

"Funny." She took a sip of water and struggled to sit up. I took the bottle from her and offered a hand for balance, but she didn't take it.

"Oh, Marjorie came by just now." Ambushed me when I'd pulled into the driveway more like, but April didn't need to know that.

She groaned. "Oh, God. Did she bring another casserole?"

I nodded. "Mac and cheese this time. It'll go with the chicken, so that saves me some work. I'll make a salad."

"Thanks."

"It's no trouble." I shrugged. "Caitlin needs a vegetable in her life."

April gave a thin smile at that. "No, I meant for running interference with Marjorie."

"She seems nice," I said tentatively.

"She is. It's just . . ." She sighed. "This neighborhood has a lot of families, and that's great. Kids for Caitlin to play with, you know? But the moms do things like get coffee together on Tuesdays."

"Hmmm." I nodded solemnly. "They sound like monsters."

She whacked me on the arm. "They get coffee on Tuesdays at ten in the morning." She raised her eyebrows at me in meaning, and then it clicked.

"When you're at work."

"When I'm at work. I don't think they do it on purpose,

but . . ." She shrugged. "I'm the only single mom on the block. I'm sure Marjorie's perfectly nice, but I'm also sure that she wants to know how I'm doing so she can tell the other moms. It's like the whole town wants to micromanage my recovery. She wants gossip, and she pays for it in casseroles."

I thought about that for a second. "You want me to give it back? I could make some mashed potatoes."

"No, that's okay. I mean, it is mac and cheese."

"The kind with the crunchy topping," I said. "I peeked at it."

"Oh, we're keeping it then."

"Yeah, we are." I stood up. "Don't worry," I said. "I'll take care of it. Caitlin, Marjorie, the town. All of it." I put the bottle back on the nightstand and stood up. "Light on or off?"

"On, please. I think I'll read for a bit." She settled back against her pillows. I lingered for a moment, but she was already lost in her e-reader so I went back into the kitchen and read the email on my phone again. First rehearsal was Saturday morning, dress comfortably. I made a note in my calendar app and went to make sure Caitlin had started her homework.

"Hey." I knocked on her bedroom door before bumping it open with my hip. "Dinner's ready at six." I leaned against the doorjamb. "Got a lot of homework?"

"Not really." She looked up from her textbook-scattered desk. "I think they're being nice to us since finals are coming up in a couple weeks."

"I don't miss those days. Let me know if you need help studying, okay?"

"Well . . ." She glanced down at her books, then back up at me. "How good are you at geometry?"

I winced. "Not very. Let me amend that. Let me know if you need help with, say, English or history, okay?" Those subjects were more my speed, and Cait's grin said she knew it. She was messing with me. Smart kid.

"Hey, Em?" Her voice stopped me as I started to head back to the kitchen. "Thanks."

I shrugged. "No problem. Sorry I can't help with the geometry, but I know more about—"

"No." She turned in her chair, sitting sideways to face me head-on. "I mean thanks for signing up for the Renaissance faire with me. So I could do it." Her face fell a little and she cast uncertain eyes toward the hallway. "Mom wouldn't have."

"Sure she would. She just can't because of the accident."

She shook her head, her brown curls—so much like her mom's, so much like mine—bouncing around her face. "I don't think she knew. About having to volunteer with me. And if she had, she would have said no."

"I don't know about that." I came into the bedroom, quietly pushing the door closed behind me, and sat down on the edge of Cait's bed. "Stacey said at tryouts that your mom was going to volunteer. So I think she was really planning to before all this happened."

But Caitlin looked skeptical. "She would have changed her mind." She looked guiltily toward the bedroom door and lowered her voice. "Mom doesn't like doing stuff, you know? She doesn't volunteer."

I tried to think of something comforting to say, but the truth was she was right. April wasn't a joiner. She hadn't needed me to take over anything extracurricular for her while she was laid up, and she wasn't terribly involved with Caitlin's school. Just as she didn't want people knowing her business, she didn't really care to know anyone else's. My sister seemed to live a pretty lonely life. But she also seemed happy with it for the most part, so who was I to judge?

I took Cait's hand and gave it a reassuring squeeze. "Well, I'm here now, and apparently I do volunteer. So I hope you're ready for this." I looked back at her when I reached her bedroom door. "Come help me set the table about five thirty?"

"Yep." But she was already frowning over her geometry textbook, and I hurried out of there before she could ask for help again.

Saturday was, in a lot of ways, a repeat of that tryout morning. We pulled into the parking lot five minutes late. Caitlin zipped ahead to find her friends who had also made it into the cast. I hung out toward the back of the auditorium, because I had no friends to find. Yeah. This wasn't awkward at all.

But to my surprise, the awkwardness didn't last.

"Hey, there you are!" The chipper voice made me look up from my phone, and I smiled at Stacey, the volunteer who'd gotten me into this mess in the first place. "Why are you all the way back here?" She hooked a hand around my arm and gave a tug. "Come on, you need to join the rest of the group."

I wasn't used to this kind of aggressive friendliness, but I let her drag me down toward the front of the auditorium to mingle with the rest of the cast.

"I'm in charge of the wenches, by the way," Stacey said. "And since you're the only other one who signed up, that'll be an easy job for me this year."

"Only two of us?" I remembered my days of tending bar, the panic when coworkers called off on their shifts, leaving me to do the work of two or three people at once. My feet started to hurt from the memory. "Can we do that?"

She waved off my concern. "Oh, easily. We're not really tavern wenches. I mean, yeah, we'll be serving drinks and flirting with patrons and speaking with an accent. But there will be plainclothes volunteers doing most of the actual work. We're there for color. You know, to look pretty."

I wasn't entirely convinced, but I let Stacey lead me toward a seat in the third row, introducing me to people along the way. I didn't have a prayer of remembering any names, but I did my best. We'd barely settled in the third row before we were all told to stand up again and sit in a giant circle on the floor of the stage.

Oh, boy. My anxiety shot up again. I'd taken a few theatre classes in college, but stage fright had driven me away from performance and back to the books and my English major. I wasn't worried about role-playing the part of a tavern wench on a one-on-one basis, but the second I was asked to get in the center of the circle and say or do something with lots of people staring at me, things were going to get ugly. Projectile-vomiting kind of ugly.

My anxiety wasn't alleviated by a woman stepping into the middle of the circle almost immediately. She was definitely one of the older adults of the group. Her hair could have been light brown, dark blond, faded gray, or a combination of all three. She wore it in a long braid down her back and was dressed in well-worn jeans and a faded T-shirt but carried herself with an authoritative air. She had the look of someone who could be anywhere from twenty-seven to fifty-five.

"Good morrow, everyone! And well met!" Her voice had a cheerful lilt to it, and when she spoke, a smile lit up her face like sunshine. A chorus of *good morrows* answered her back, my voice included. "Great, everyone knows that first phrase, that's not a surprise. But the other greeting we'll be using a lot at Faire is 'well met,' which can be a simple 'nice to meet you,' but it can also mean you're particularly pleased to see that particular person at that particular time. This is a good meeting, so we are well met. Got it?" Her smile stayed in place throughout the entire speech, which was an impressive feat unto itself.

"I'm so glad to see everyone here," she continued. "Welcome to the tenth season of the Willow Creek Renaissance Faire. Ten years! Can you believe it?" This sparked a small round of applause, and I clapped too because I wasn't an asshole. "I know I say this every year, but I'm excited about this year's Faire. For those of you who are new or might not know me . . ." She looked right at me as she said this last bit, and good God, was I the only stranger in this town? "I'm Christine Donovan. Most people call me Chris, or Miss Chris, or Your Majesty." She shrugged through the friendly laughter. "Which is my subtle way of letting you know that yes, I will be your Queen again this year. The year is 1601, and Elizabeth is still on the throne."

I did some quick math in my head and then leaned over to Stacey while Her Majesty continued her welcome speech. "Elizabeth was pretty old by then, right? Chris looks good for someone pushing seventy."

She shushed me through a grin. "We take a little dramatic license around here."

I got the message and settled down, crisscross applesaucing my legs in front of me as Chris finished outlining the rehearsal schedule, stressing how important it was we not miss too many of them. We'd be learning about the history of the period—apparently the more purist of the patrons made a day out of quizzing the cast as to their religious preferences and hygiene habits. We would also spend time working on costuming and in our various groups. Singers had songs to rehearse, dancers had dances to learn. And the fighting cast had to, well, learn how to fight.

Next up was . . . I groaned, but covered the sound by taking another pull off my iced coffee. Simon. Form-police guy. The one dull spot in this whole experience. As he took his place in the center of the circle I noticed he looked as put-together as he had the last time I'd seen him. How early did he wake up to get ready? I was only marginally sure I was wearing clean clothes, while it looked like both his jeans and his light blue button-down shirt were freshly ironed. He handed a stack of papers to someone in the circle to pass around, and I stifled a sigh. Great. Homework. That did absolutely nothing for my opinion of him.

"Chris already welcomed all of you, so I won't do that again." He gave a small smile, and some people chuckled. "For those of you who don't know me, I'm Simon Graham, and I've been with this Faire since . . . well, since the beginning, like Chris. She and my older brother, Sean, started the Faire ten years ago." He smiled again, but this time it didn't quite reach his eyes. "And yes, I'm back again this year too, doing my best to fill Sean's shoes." His smile fell fast, and he ran a hand over his close-cropped brown hair. "If you have any questions about how things are run, or what you need to be doing, you can always come to me. I'll be glad to help you out."

Ha. Fat chance. He'd be glad to tell me what I was doing wrong, more likely.

"This morning I'm going to talk about names."

Names? I tilted my head like a cocker spaniel.

"One of the first things you'll do as a cast member is decide on your Faire name. This is a very important decision for each and every one of you." He turned in a slow circle as he spoke, never standing still, making fleeting eye contact with everyone in the group. This guy wouldn't projectile-vomit in front of a crowd. He was used to talking in front of people. "You already know what part you're playing: nobleman, merchant, dancer. But your name is your identity. Names are important. Names have power. Names are one of the things that tells you who you *are*." He tapped the knuckles of his closed fist against his chest.

I still didn't like this guy, but that made an odd kind of sense. I didn't realize I'd leaned forward to listen, my elbows on my crossed knees, until Stacey nudged me and handed me the diminished stack of papers. I took one and passed the rest to the teenager on my left.

"Now, Shakespeare disagrees," Simon continued. "In *Romeo and Juliet*, he said 'a rose by any other name would smell as sweet,' implying the essence of a thing doesn't change just because it's called something else." He shrugged. "He makes a good point. But we humans are easily persuaded. We see commercials all the time. We buy the brand name of something instead of a generic, thinking it'll be better quality, right?"

Something about the cadence of his voice was both familiar and comforting. He had a voice I wanted to keep listening to. That, combined with his obvious comfort in talking in front of a crowd of both teens and adults, not to mention the bit of Elizabethan literary criticism thrown in on a Saturday morning, made a lightbulb click on in my head.

I nudged Stacey again and nodded in Simon's direction. "English teacher?" I kept my voice a low murmur; I didn't want to distract him while he was on a roll.

She gave me a lopsided smile back and a confirming nod. "How'd you guess? The Shakespeare?"

"Kinda gave it away."

"Did you have a question? Emily, right?"

Oh, shit. I turned innocent eyes at Simon, who faced me now, arms crossed over his chest. "Sorry," I said. "I didn't mean to—"

"No, please." Yep, he was definitely a teacher. He had a full-on why *don't you share with the rest of the class* attitude, as though I were one of his students he'd caught passing a note. "What was your question?"

"Oh." I thought fast. "I was wondering who's playing Shakespeare. You?"

A couple people in the group tittered, but Simon looked like he was about to scowl. "No. We don't have a Shakespeare in the cast."

"But we could," I argued. I don't know why I let this guy get under my skin. Thirty seconds ago, I didn't give a damn if we had a Bard of Avon wandering around or not, but the idea of it seemed to annoy Simon, so now I was all for it. "You said 1601, right? He was giving command performances of his plays for Queen Elizabeth around that time. She was a big fan, so it would stand to reason—"

"We don't have a Shakespeare in the cast." And the subject was closed. I was impressed; he had a grade-A Teacher Voice. But instead of giving me detention, he went back to addressing the rest of the group as though our conversation had never happened. "Most of us who are repeat offenders here have our names and identities pretty well established. But for those of you joining us for the first time this season, or if you thought your name last year didn't fit, you've all got a list of names that fit the time period. Take a look, see if anything looks right. Feels right."

Jeez. This whole thing took a quick left turn into culty. I'd been planning to coast through this: wear a cute costume and hang out in a bar so Caitlin could participate. I hadn't intended to spend the next few months in some kind of live-action method-acting exercise. I stifled a sigh and looked down at the paper in my hands.

Thankfully, Simon didn't make anyone stand in the middle. Instead, we went around the circle, where we each introduced ourselves by our real name as well as our chosen Faire name. The point of the exercise was probably for everyone to start to get to know each other. Instead, my blood pressure rose with every new voice that spoke, as my turn to talk inched closer and closer and I had no idea who my character was besides someone who served beer. The paper crumpled in my hand as I focused on Caitlin across the circle from me. She giggled at something one of her friends said, and seeing her that relaxed made something inside me relax too. I could do this.

Next to me on my right, Stacey spoke up. "Hey, everyone! I'm Stacey Lindholm, and this is my . . . oh, God, eighth year doing the Faire. Is that right? Can that be right?" She moaned dramatically. "Anyway, I started when I was in high school, as a singer, but now that I'm an adult—" A snort came from a few people down to my left, and Stacey tsked in that direction. "Shut up, Mitch. Now that I'm an adult, or once I hit twenty-one anyway, I moved over to being a wench. There are two of us this year." She nudged me with her shoulder, and oh, shit, it was my turn.

But she wasn't done yet. Simon cleared his throat. "I assume you're keeping the same name?"

"Oh! Yes. Of course." Suddenly Stacey slipped into a pretty good English accent and she drew herself up into a straighter posture. Before my eyes, she became a completely different person. "If you want to find me in the tavern, ask for Beatrice. That'll be me."

Would I need to have an English accent too? But I didn't have time to worry about that, because it was my turn to speak.

"Hi!" I tried to smile, look friendly, and wave all at the same time. My smile came out as a kind of nervous exhale, probably showing too many teeth, and my wave looked like a dorky muscle spasm. "I'm Emily. Emily Parker. I'm new in town, so I've never done this before."

"Don't worry, Park. We'll be gentle." Mitch laughed at his own joke, and I snickered a little too, but my laugh was shut down by a forbidding-looking Simon.

"As Beatrice said, you're a wench this year as well, right?" His question prodded me along, and I got the message. *Stay on topic.* I'd already pissed him off with the Shakespeare thing; I needed to behave.

"Right. Sorry. Yes. Yes, I am a wench with Stacey."

"Beatrice." He repeated the name, as though I were slow in understanding, and good Lord, I had no idea plain brown eyes could look like lasers. But Simon's stare was about to burn a hole in my forehead.

"Yes," I said. "Beatrice. Sorry. Again." What was with this guy?

"And your name?"

"Emily."

He sighed. "Yes. But your Faire name."

"Oh . . . It's . . ." I smoothed out the wrinkled paper in my hands, stalling for time. "I guess Shakespeare's out, huh?" I chanced a look up at him, but the thunder in his expression told me that my jokes weren't welcome here. "Fine, okay. I'll be . . . ummm . . ." My eyes landed on a name. Easy. "Emma."

"Emma." His voice was flat.

"It's period." I pointed at the paper. "See, right there on the list. And I'll remember to answer to it."

Another short sigh. "Glad to see you're putting a lot of thought into this."

I opened my mouth to retort, but Simon turned to the teenager immediately to my left and made clear I had ceased to exist to him.

I leaned back on my hands and sighed. Dick.

Stacey nudged me. "Don't worry about him," she whispered. "Your name is fine."

"Are you sure?"

She nodded. "Don't let him bother you."

I blew out a breath. "I'll try." I turned my attention back to the circle, where Mitch was up next.

"Mitch Malone." His voice exuded confidence, and why not? Look at the guy. Someone like that could be conceited about himself, and for all I knew he was. But the way he smiled, not only at me but at the kids in the circle, told me there was more to him than how much he could deadlift. "And I've been doing Faire for, what, about as long as you, Simon, right?"

Simon nodded. "You started the year after me. So the second year of Faire."

"Yeah, that sounds right. Your big brother bugged me for, like, half of senior year in high school to join up. Said he needed more big strong guys, and not scrawny little guys like you."

"I was not scrawny." Simon huffed, but a smile played around his mouth too. This was obviously an old, toothless argument.

Mitch waved a dismissive hand. "Whatever. 'Scrawny' is a relative term, right?" I wasn't sure if he consciously flexed his pecs at that point or what, but there was definite movement under his tight gray T-shirt, and it was a beautiful thing to watch.

Simon sighed again, but unlike when he expressed his disapproval of me, this sigh came out as more of a laugh. "Okay, whatever. I assume you're bringing the kilt again this year, right?"

"Oh, aye, lad. Marcus MacGregor rides again!" Mitch's slip

into a Scottish brogue made my eyebrows shoot up. I'd dismissed him as a meathead, with the tight T-shirt and high-maintenance physique. But the meathead had hidden depths. He was friends with an uptight intellectual like Simon and could affect an accent on command.

As we kept going around the circle, I found my attention wandering back to Mitch and that tight T-shirt. To my horror, Mitch caught me looking at one point and sent a wink my way, along with finger-guns. Ah, well, he was still kind of a meathead after all. I snorted, which I tried to cover with a cough, but Mitch laughed anyway. Simon cleared his throat, shooting a dirty look to the both of us, and I looked away, my cheeks burning.

"I'm Caitlin Parker." My niece's voice was like a cool, deep breath to my soul, and I looked to where she sat across the circle from me with a gaggle of her friends. "I'm new this year—hi!" Her dorky wave was so much like mine I couldn't help the smile that broke across my face. The Parker DNA was strong in that one. But how would her natural dorkiness play in this room? I bit my lip and glanced around, but everyone looked welcoming and accepting. My heart softened. Maybe there was something to it all, cultiness aside.

"I'm a lady-in-waiting to the Queen," Caitlin continued, pride in her voice, and was it weird that I felt kind of proud too? Like she'd landed a really good job or something? You go, kiddo. "And . . . um." She looked down at the paper, then back up at Simon. "I want something fancy, Mr. G. Since I'm a noble, right? What about Guenevere?"

I narrowed my eyes at Simon while he considered. If he threw a barb at her like he had at me, I was going to come at him, right in the middle of that circle. But to my surprise, he nodded.

"I don't see why not." He talked to her in a gentler version of his Teacher Voice. Not condescending, but still authoritative. "Now, you're young, though, remember. So the other ladies-in-waiting will most likely call you a diminutive."

Her face screwed up. "A what?"

"A nickname. Like Gwen, or Ginny. But merchants, or anyone else of a lower status, will call you Lady Guenevere."

"Okay." Her smile widened. "Hear that, Emily? You're lower status, right?" A few people chuckled when she yelled across the circle at me.

"Yes indeed, milady!" I called back. More chuckles. I leaned back on my hands again as Cait and I grinned at each other. Yeah. I liked these people. Then I glanced up at Simon again. Okay, I liked most of these people.

The rest of the rehearsal was a basic rundown of the schedule, and then those in the more specialized small groups—singers, dancers, fight crew—split off to talk further. Wenches and ladies-in-waiting weren't needed anymore, so Cait and I got to leave.

About halfway through the drive home, Caitlin put her phone into her pocket and leaned between the front seats. Ever since the accident she'd refused to sit in the front seat of any vehicle. Since she'd been in the back at the time of the crash, it made sense. It was going to be tricky when it was time for her to learn to drive, though. "Do you think we can watch some Harry Potter tonight?"

"Um . . ." I glanced at her in the rearview mirror. Where had this non sequitur come from? "Sure . . . ?"

"Mr. G said it was a good way to work on our accent. You know, for Faire. Watch a lot of Harry Potter movies and, like, soak up the accent."

"Mr. G said that, huh? I must have missed that part." My estimation of Simon went up one very small notch. Give a kid a homework assignment like that and it didn't feel like home-work. "So was Mr. G one of your teachers this year?"

"No." She snorted, like that was the stupidest question I could have possibly asked. "He teaches juniors and seniors. Honors-level, college prep stuff."

"So you'll get him in a couple years then, right? Your grades are good enough." I had no way of knowing if that was true or not, but I'd always been a smart kid, and I'm sure April had been too. Caitlin had to take after us. Parker DNA and all.

"Oh, yeah," Caitlin said quickly. "I'll get him for AP English both junior and senior year." I liked her confidence.

"Good." I hazarded another glance at her. "How's your mom feel about Harry Potter movies? And maybe ordering pizza?"

That got me a grin as we pulled into the driveway. "She likes 'em. Both."

Three

Faire rehearsals became a part of our little family's routine. Early every Saturday morning Caitlin, along with me and my very large travel mug of coffee, tumbled into the white Jeep and drove to the high school. These mornings were called "rehearsals," but at first they were basically crash courses in Elizabethan history. We learned the hierarchy of nobility and how to address everyone around us. How low to curtsy to the Queen as opposed to a merchant. What kinds of things a tavern wench might discuss with a town crier.

It still had its culty moments, but I was getting into it. Those Saturdays were packed, but I loved it all. The history lessons, which reminded me of my European history classes back in college. The snatches of song starting and stopping from out in the vestibule, where the acoustics were better, as the singers rehearsed their harmonies. The bits of costumes appearing. As the weeks went by, it became normal to see a girl running down the aisle wearing a bodice over a sundress, or the guy who had worn the HUZZAH! shirt walking around in a jerkin and jeans. Rehearsals were a lot of fun.

Well, mostly. There was one big exception. It seemed like every time Stacey said something to make me laugh a little too loudly, Simon noticed and shot a glare my way. Having too much fun must have been against his rules. He also noticed those couple of times I paid more attention to my phone than a history discussion. That usually earned me another glare. I did my best to not shrink under his gaze, reminding myself that I was a volunteer and these people were lucky to have me.

After rehearsals we went home, and at night, we ordered pizza and practiced our accents.

Okay, we watched Harry Potter movies. And Jane Austen adaptations. And more Harry Potter movies. And talked to each other with exaggerated English accents. But we got better at it as time went on. April even joined us, even though she had no accent to work on. So of course she picked it up faster than we did.

One night, after we'd watched *Shakespeare in Love*, I noticed Caitlin watching the closing credits with a thoughtful look on her face.

"We just studied *Romeo and Juliet* in school this year," she said. "Ms. Barnes didn't say anything about any of that stuff happening when Shakespeare wrote it."

I fought against a smile and lost. "That's because it didn't. Dramatic license, kiddo."

"Oh. Yeah." She looked at the screen again. "So what's the play he's writing at the end?"

"*Twelfth Night*. Have you read that yet? They don't teach it in high school as much." She shook her head. "You might like it," I said. "Mistaken identity; everyone falls in love with everyone else. It's pretty fun." I thought for a moment. "We can't talk about it at Faire, though. For one thing, I don't think tavern wenches can read. For another, isn't it 1601 at Faire? It was written around

1601 or 1602." We couldn't risk anachronism, even if it was only a few months' overlap. Simon would probably give me detention.

Between accents and history lessons, time passed in strange ways over the next few weeks. I stopped paying attention to the Monday-through-Friday of things, since school let out in early June and for the first time in ages I didn't have an actual job. Taking care of April and running her house—without making it too obvious that I was doing all the things she couldn't—was a job in and of itself. With Faire obligations on top of everything else, I had plenty on my plate.

Instead, we marked the passage of time by April's appointments. Follow-up appointments gave way to physical therapy sessions, all marked on my calendar app. After dropping her off for her first physical therapy appointment in a small building downtown, I wandered the block in search of a cup of coffee. I found something better: a bookstore called Read It & Weep.

A bell chimed as I pushed the door open, and as soon as I stepped inside I felt like I'd come home. I hadn't had a lot of time for reading in the past two or three years, and I hadn't realized how much I missed it. The smell of the books, the promise in the shelves of printed pages . . . I loved stories, and always had.

I took my time exploring the shop. There was a section up front with new titles, giving way to shelves and shelves lined with used books. It didn't take long for me to find a used copy of *Twelfth Night* in the classics section, and I snagged it to read with Caitlin. When I reached the back I discovered the world's smallest coffee bar: basically an espresso machine, a coffeepot, and a few platters of pastries wrapped in plastic. The owner met me behind the counter and I wasted no time in ordering a latte from her.

"There you are, Emma." She slid the coffee cup across the counter in my direction with a smile.

I shook my head. "Emily. My name's . . ." Then I took a good look at her for the first time. I was an idiot. I'd just bought a coffee from Chris Donovan, our Faire's Queen, and I hadn't even noticed. In my defense, though, it wasn't like I talked to her much during rehearsal. She was one of the ones in charge, so something always had her attention. Also, she looked different in this light, not to mention more professional; here she wore her blond-white hair up in a twist and had on a twinset and pearls instead of a faded T-shirt.

I smiled as I took the coffee. "Thank you, Your Majesty." I bobbed a quick curtsy, which made her laugh.

"I'm just Chris here." She took my money and made change from a small cashbox under the counter. "You're April's sister, right? How are you enjoying Faire so far?"

"It's . . ." I dropped the change into the tip jar while I struggled with this question. The people who were into it were very into it, I'd noticed, and I didn't want to insult her by telling her that deep down, I still thought it was a little silly. "It's interesting. Just seems a little intense."

"What do you mean?"

"Well, it's a fund-raiser, right? But we're spending a lot of time getting accents right, learning history . . . are people going to care that much?" I held my breath, waiting for her to frown and tell me I didn't understand. She wouldn't be too far off the mark.

Instead she considered my question. "Short answer? Not really. But at the same time, yes. It's a fund-raiser, sure, but it's grown over the years into a pretty big event. We have talent coming from all over the country to perform. It's not one of the big Faires by any means—we certainly have nothing on the Maryland Renaissance Festival."

My eyes widened. "There's another one?"

Chris laughed. "Oh, honey, there's tons of them! Maryland's one of the biggest in the country; they even have permanent structures they keep up year-round. We're small potatoes—tiny potatoes, even—compared to them. But we do our best and take it seriously, and so we've gotten a reputation as a solid smaller Faire. And of course there's the educational aspect. The kids participate in a living history project where they can demonstrate their knowledge to paying patrons while wearing period costumes, and it doesn't feel like learning."

"Wow." I took a sip of coffee. "I have to say I didn't think of it like that."

"It's all right." She shrugged. "Not everyone does. And you're new around here, so you haven't seen it grow gradually like we have. Sometimes I remember the early years, when the whole thing took place on the high school football field." The bell over the front door chimed, signaling a new customer in the shop, and she came out from behind the counter to head to the front of the store. "Very different than being out in the woods." She continued our conversation as she walked, so I followed.

"The woods?" I remembered now how Stacey had mentioned the site at one rehearsal, and I had no idea what she was talking about, or where I was going to be spending the rest of my weekends this summer. "We're going to be in the woods?"

"Ohhhh. You haven't seen the site yet?" Chris chuckled when I shook my head. "Can't wait to see what you think."

"What who thinks?" A new voice came from the front of the shop and as I rounded the corner behind Chris I bit back a sigh. Simon. Great. I took in his jeans and button-down shirt and wondered if he owned a pair of shorts. Unlikely. He didn't even dress down at rehearsals on Saturdays. But he wasn't wearing a vest, so this had to be a casual day for him.

He blinked when he saw me, his dark brows drawing together in a frown, so he was obviously as thrilled to see me as I was to see him. His green shirt was open at the throat, and I could see the neckline of a white undershirt in the V. This man wore a lot of layers. Clothing as armor. What was he protecting?

If Chris noticed any tension between us, she blissfully ignored it as she gestured in my direction. "I was telling Emily about the site. She didn't know we were going to be out in the woods."

"Oh." He raised an eyebrow. I hated people who could do that. Mostly because I couldn't. "What do you think?"

"I think it sounds great." I would have crossed my arms, but there was a very real danger I'd spill my coffee if I did. "I was a Girl Scout. Camping was my favorite. I don't have a problem with the outdoors." Why? Why did I say that? I was a Girl Scout, sure. But I'd faked having the flu to get out of going camping, because the idea of sleeping on the ground, where there were bugs . . . I suppressed a shudder. But Simon had challenged me, and if he thought I was going to back down, then he didn't know a thing about me.

He nodded once. "Good." A slightly awkward silence stretched between us, and he opened his mouth as though he were going to say something else, but instead turned to Chris.

"I wanted to make sure you had everything I ordered. For the summer reading lists?"

"Oh. Yes." She moved behind the front counter and woke up her laptop. "I placed the order last Monday, and I got about half of them in yesterday. Should be getting the rest . . ." She tapped a few keys and squinted at the screen. "Looks like tomorrow. So I'll get the display up by this weekend." She shrugged. "No one's asked about them yet, so you should be okay."

"I'm not surprised." He shook his head with a rueful smile.

"The school year just ended. The last thing these kids are think-ing about is next fall."

"You've always got one or two overachievers in your AP classes, though." She tapped some more keys, bringing up another screen. "Oh, wait. They sent a different edition of *Pride and Prejudice* than the one you asked for. Let me go get it and make sure it'll work. I can exchange it if you need me to."

She bustled into the back room of the shop, and Simon and I stood in silence for a few excruciating moments. I searched des-perately through the corners of my brain for something to talk about, before settling on the most obvious.

"What are you assigning the kids to read? I mean, besides Austen."

Thankfully he seized on the topic. "Mostly classics. But at-tention spans are short in the summer, so nothing too taxing. I also throw in one or two more recent books, so they don't think I'm stuck in the nineteenth century." He offered me a tentative, closed-mouth smile, and I grabbed it like a lifeline.

"So what's this year's modern book? *Nineteen Eighty-Four*? That's always a safe choice."

"It is." He nodded. "But I went even more modern. Have you read *Station Eleven*?"

His tone of voice said that he expected me to respond with a confused look and shake of the head, so it was nice to surprise him. "I have. I read it in college." Back when I'd had time to read for fun, which felt like a hundred years ago. I shook off the thought. "Huh. That book's about Shakespeare too, in a way. Sort of a theme with you, isn't it?"

Simon's brow furrowed. "Not that I'm aware of. I just . . ."

"You just like Shakespeare. It's okay, you can admit it." My heart beat a little faster as I ribbed him. Was he the kind of guy who could take a little joking around? Jake had always gotten surly and defensive, but maybe Simon was different.

"You should talk." He nodded at the copy of *Twelfth Night* in my hand. "You knew off the top of your head what Shakespeare was doing in 1601; you rattled it off like it was nothing at rehearsal." There went that eyebrow again, but this time it wasn't as annoying. Weird. "Seems I'm not the only one with a mild Shakespeare obsession."

He remembered that? "Guilty. He's always been my favorite." But now that he mentioned it . . . "Are you sure we can't have someone playing Shakespeare at this thing? Wandering around, maybe reciting sonnets at people?"

"That . . . no." The furrow in his brow deepened, and he frowned. This was not a man who was open to new ideas. Yet his eyes remained bright, negating the severity of his expression, so maybe he was still open to *me*. That idea thrilled me more than it should have.

"No, you're right. I have a better idea." I clapped my hands together as the brainstorm took hold. Oh, it was terrible, and I almost laughed. "What if you have multiple Shakespeares?"

"What . . ." He shook his head. "Why would you . . . That makes even less sense."

"Now hear me out. You have four or five guys in costume, each one saying he's Shakespeare, right? And the patrons have to figure out which one is the real Shakespeare, and which ones are only poseurs like Francis Bacon or Christopher Marlowe."

"Marlowe . . ." His confused expression cleared up in a snap. "Are you talking about the *authorship question*?" A look of horror spread across his face, and the laugh that threatened now bubbled out of me.

"Well, sure." The more I grinned, the more dismayed he looked. "It's educational, right? You could teach people about multiple historical figures in one story line."

"Except it's a load of crap." He crossed his arms over his chest, but there was a spark in his eyes, and his lips pressed together in a thin line to hide a smile. He was enjoying this as much as I was. I liked this side of the Ren Faire Killjoy. "Shakespeare wrote Shakespeare. Please tell me you don't think someone else did."

I didn't, of course. I thought the so-called authorship question was a bunch of garbage. One of the world's oldest conspiracy theories, and a mystery that might never be completely solved. How do you prove definitively who wrote something over four centuries ago?

But Simon seemed so horrified that I might actually believe it, like I might pluck a tinfoil hat out of my purse, that I couldn't let on. It was fun, and I hadn't had a lot of fun lately. Not to mention that if you squinted, this conversation could be considered flirting, and I hadn't had a lot of that lately, either. So of course I had to keep needling him. "You can't deny there's some pretty compelling evidence. I mean, if you look at the life of Edward de Vere alone, you have to admit the Earl of Oxford had the requisite background to—"

"No." He closed his eyes, pinched the bridge of his nose. "God, this is worse than I thought." He peeked at me through his fingers. "Are you seriously an Oxfordian?"

"No." I couldn't hide my laugh anymore, so I let him off the hook. "Not really. But I had a very open-minded Shakespeare professor. Class discussions were interesting." I hadn't thought about those classes in years. Or Shakespeare. Or poor Edward de Vere. I didn't realize until just now how much I missed the intellectual side of myself. It was nice to see her again.

Simon cracked a smile, and although he immediately swallowed it, there was still interest in his eyes. I felt like I'd scored a point. "So you have an English degree?"

"Oh." My smile slipped. "Well, no. I have most of one."

"Most of one," he repeated. He gave a little shake of his head like that didn't make sense.

"Yeah." All the levity of the past few minutes drained out of me like a punctured balloon. "I ended up leaving my junior year." It wasn't something I was proud of, but it wasn't a shameful secret, either. However, admitting it out loud to this man made me feel about two inches tall.

"Really." His expression fell, and while he did his best to not let it show, his disappointment was clear.

"Yeah." I studied my feet, flexed my toes in my sandals. I needed a pedicure; the pink polish was looking pretty chipped. It was easier to think about the state of my toes than about my life and its aborted plans. Why should I care what Simon thought of me? I didn't even like this guy, remember?

"What happened? Why did you—?" He stopped speaking abruptly as I looked up at him. I couldn't imagine what emotions were playing across my face, but they must have been bleak enough to stun him into silence. "I'm sorry," he said. "That's really—"

"No, it's okay . . ."

"None of my business. It's none of my business." A painful silence stretched between us that I didn't know how to break. He stuck his hands in his pockets and looked down at the counter, at the floor, over his shoulder to where Chris had disappeared. How long did it take her to find a book back there? Neither of us spoke, and I desperately wanted to rewind the last few minutes, and go back to the two of us laughing about crazy Shakespeare theories. What was worse in his estimation: that I didn't have a college degree, or the act of dropping out before finishing it?

He was right. It wasn't any of his business. But he was someone who appreciated scholarship, and my confession probably told him that I didn't give a damn about education. But the truth was I did. I'd cared so much about it that when Jake had gotten into law school I'd put his education above my own, working two jobs so he could have the extra time to study. He was supposed to reciprocate, and I'd trusted him.

That wasn't how it had gone. Not even close.

"Here we are!" We both jumped, startled out of our uncomfortable reveries as Chris emerged from the back room with a small paperback in her hand. She looked from Simon to me and back again closely before handing him the book. Simon frowned as he took it.

"You're right, this isn't the right one. I wanted the annotated edition of *Pride and Prejudice*." He turned the book over in his hands before giving it back to her. "How long would it take to exchange them?"

She waved a hand. "Not long at all. I already ordered the replacements. I just wanted to make sure you didn't want these for some reason before I sent them back."

He shook his head. "No. I don't need these."

"The annotated one is good," I said. I'd relied on it pretty heavily when I'd studied Jane Austen. "It's smart to assign that one. The explanations give the kids a good start to understanding the text better." I faltered as he turned to look at me again. That spark between us had gone, and I could see myself reflected in his brown eyes. Small. Worthless.

Well, fuck him.

Chris turned back to me after Simon had left. "Did he annoy you?"

"No." *Yes*. I took a swig of my coffee, which had started to go cold.

She took in my expression and frowned. But where Simon's frown had made me feel inferior, Chris's was more concerned. More motherly. "He can sometimes come across a little . . ." She screwed up her mouth and made a face that perfectly described how I felt about Simon at that moment. Then she shook her head. "Don't worry about him. Stacey was telling me the other day how glad she is you've joined us for the summer, and I couldn't agree more." She placed a hand on my shoulder. "Welcome to the family."

I turned those words over in my head as I finished my coffee and browsed the new arrivals section. *Welcome to the family*. Why did those words fill me with excitement and dread at the same time? I had no idea what I'd gotten myself into when I'd signed on to volunteer. Simon made me want to spit nails, but Chris made me feel like I'd joined an exclusive club. I looked at the cardboard coffee cup in my hand, where she'd written *Emma*—my Faire name—in cursive with a small heart at the end. The sight of it made me feel warm inside, banishing the rest of the chill I'd felt when Simon had looked at me like I was nothing more than a college dropout.

My phone buzzed in my pocket. April was ready for her ride home.

Home.

I meditated on that word as I pulled up to the doctor's office to pick up my sister. Her house wasn't my home. This town wasn't my home. Yet when I looked at the coffee cup again, that warm sense of belonging lingered. I wanted to hold on to that feeling. But I didn't trust it, either. Not as long as people like Simon Graham were out there judging me.

I glanced at April quickly before pulling out into traffic. "How was therapy?"

"Painful." Her sigh was tired, but there was a note of hope in her voice I hadn't heard since I'd moved in. "I think it's really going to help, though. I can do this."

"Of course you can." I allowed a small smile to show, but mostly masked the thrill flaring in my heart. My sister was confiding in me, and that wasn't something that had happened much when we were younger. Mostly because we hadn't been young together. But now that we were adults together, maybe things would be different. Sure, we weren't braiding each other's hair and confessing the darkest secrets of our hearts quite yet, but it was a start.

"What's new in the world of the Renaissance faire?" Another surprise. While April was supportive of our Harry Potter nights and Caitlin's endless lectures on the various forms of curtsies she'd learned, she hadn't expressed much interest beyond that.

Where should I start? "Well, apparently this whole thing takes place out in the woods. That's not new per se, but it was certainly news to me when Chris told me."

"Chris," April repeated blankly. "Oh, do you mean Christine Donovan? She owns the bookstore, right?" She smiled at my nod, like she'd caught me out. "So you found something to do while I'm at therapy."

"Yep. What can I say, I miss books."

"You were an English major, right?" After I nodded, April fell quiet as I pulled into the driveway and shut off the car. "Are you thinking about going back to school? You don't have much left on your degree, right?" I came around and opened her door, but she didn't take the hand I offered. Instead, she levered herself out of the Jeep.

"Right. I don't know. I haven't thought that far ahead yet." That was the truth, at least; the end of the summer was as far as I could see right now. The month of September may as well have been a sign that said *Here Be Dragons*. Right now it was easier to think in terms of what I could do for April or Caitlin than what I wanted to do for myself.

I closed the passenger door once she'd cleared it, and I caught up to her as she worked her way up the front walk. I offered my arm and she managed to take it without making it look like it was necessary. She didn't need my help; my help just happened to be there, so she took it.

"Why don't you order your transcript? We could see how many more credits you need."

I considered it. "That's not a bad idea. Maybe I should. You're getting better every day, so you won't need me much longer."

April's laugh was a little strained. "I wouldn't say that." She gripped the railing and pulled herself up the stairs, one slow step at a time. She was making progress; she couldn't have done that two weeks before. Physical therapy was going to be good for her. "But let me know if you want any help. I started looking at college options for Caitlin when she was eight, so I have plenty of sites bookmarked."

I grinned, because that sounded like something I would do. Maybe April and I were more alike than I'd realized. "I'll do that. Thanks." I was warming to the idea of having a plan again.

"Maybe not the fall semester, though. Since you're spending the summer in a corset and all. That's going to keep you pretty busy."

I waved a hand. "Nah. Corset'll be a piece of cake."

I was wrong. I was so, so wrong.

Four

"C ostume day today!" Caitlin practically vibrated in the back seat of the Jeep on the way to rehearsal.

"I thought you already had your costume. Pink, right?" I could have sworn I'd seen her in a hoopskirt and elaborate over-dress a couple weekends back, wandering the aisles of the auditorium.

"Yeah, I tried it on, but it was way too long. They had to hem it up."

"Ah. Well, you can thank your grandma for that." Mom was not a tall woman, and consequently neither was April nor I. And Caitlin seemed to be following in our footsteps: short Parker women.

She shrugged; her height didn't matter to her at all. Good kid. I'd let that bother me for way too long. "But it's supposed to be ready today for a final fitting, and Miss Chris is going to show me how to do my hair too."

"That's great." I couldn't help but notice she hadn't taken her phone out once on the drive to rehearsal this morning. We were talking a lot more on these Saturday drives, and while I still felt a little roped into this whole thing, I liked that it was bringing Caitlin and me closer.

As we pulled into the parking lot, I noticed Stacey pulling shopping bags out of the back seat of her car. "Huh," I said. "Looks like it's costume day for me too."

Caitlin followed where I was pointing and her eyes widened. "How many costumes are you wearing?"

"One, I hope." Stacey had taken my measurements the weekend before, promising to pull some potential costume pieces for me from the collection the organizers had amassed over the years. "Those of us long-timers end up buying our own stuff," she'd told me then. "But there's no reason for you to do that yet. There's plenty to borrow." Thank God. I didn't have a job and was mooching off my sister as it was. I didn't have the money to blow on an elaborate costume.

I caught up with Stacey and took one of the bags out of her hands while Caitlin, true to form, ran inside the school building.

"What's all this?" I tried to peek in the bags and walk at the same time.

"Options." She bumped the door open with her hip and eyed my yoga-pants-and-tank-top ensemble as we walked through. "Good, you wore tight clothes. We should be able to put this stuff on over what you have on now."

In the organized chaos of the auditorium we found a quiet corner in the back of the house. Stacey dumped all the bags on the floor and crouched down to start sorting through them. She passed me a large swath of white fabric that looked like a bedsheet. "Put this on."

"This?" Once I had the bedsheet in my hands I saw it had

sleeves, as well as a neck hole. I pulled it over my head and stuck my arms through the voluminous sleeves. The sleeves ended in elastic cuffs that wrapped around my elbows and gave the whole thing a tiny bit of structure, but overall I was wearing a tent that had been made into a granny-style nightgown that brushed my ankles.

"This can't be right." I tried to adjust the neckline, which kept slipping over one shoulder or the other, like a bad eighties sweatshirt. "Didn't you bring my measurements with you when you pulled costumes?"

She clucked her tongue at me. "It's fine. You'll see." She squinted up at me and shook her head. "Lose the tank top. Bra too. They're both going to show."

"What? Out here in front of everyone?" I darted my gaze around the auditorium. My scandalized indignation faded fast once I realized absolutely no one was paying attention to us. I sighed and pulled my arms back through the sleeves of the giant nightgown and maneuvered my top and bra off underneath the tent of fabric, letting them both drop to the floor at my feet. "Happy?" I held the ridiculous neckline closed with one hand so I didn't flash anyone while I scooped up my clothes and balled the bra inside the top.

Stacey eyed me again as she stood up, holding more bundles of fabric. "Okay, overskirt next. Put this on over the chemise." She handed me a long deep-blue skirt that went over my head easily. I pulled on the drawstring and cinched it securely around my waist. At this point I was drowning in fabric. Did wenches dress like this? This couldn't be right.

Stacey regarded me for a long moment then nodded. "That's a good color on you. The blue matches your eyes. I think this outfit will work."

I looked down at myself. I was wearing a poofy grandma-style nightgown with a blue skirt tied over it. "I . . . I don't see how."

"Patience. Here's your bodice." She handed me what looked like a vest in the same color blue as the skirt. I put it on and my skepticism only grew.

"Um . . ." I pulled on the edges of the bodice, which didn't close across my chest. "Did this shrink in the wash? Or was it made for an eight-year-old?"

She snorted. "Neither one." She produced a long piece of black cord, which she proceeded to stick through the holes in the front of the bodice, lacing the garment up like it was a tennis shoe going up my chest. Things got a little personal as she tightened the lacing from the bottom, but to my surprise the bodice closed most of the way.

I put my hands on my much flatter stomach and breathed. Thank God it fit. "This isn't so bad. I can breathe and everything."

"Oh, we're not even close to done yet!" She sounded way too cheerful. "But we need to adjust everything while it's still loose." I wasn't sure what that meant, but I followed directions pretty well, holding up the outer blue skirt while Stacey tugged down on the white chemise. My neckline got lower in front, but the blue bodice held the top of the chemise in place, so it didn't slip off my shoulders anymore.

"We'll pin the blue skirt up here in the front so the white shows underneath. That gives everything a little more fullness too." She produced some safety pins and showed me what she meant, gathering up the front of the blue skirt in a few different places and pinning the fabric up by each hip. Then she pulled the bodice down a little more snugly around my hips to cover the pins.

She stepped back to survey her progress. I was starting to feel less like a person and more like a doll she was putting into a costume. Ren Faire Barbie.

"Okay, let's tighten this for real now. Hold up the girls."

"The . . . what? Hold up the what?"

"The girls." Stacey cupped her own breasts over her T-shirt, hiked them up dramatically. I let a nervous giggle slip out because wow, she was not a bit self-conscious. "They're gonna be on display for six weeks this summer, we have to strap 'em in properly."

"Okay." My dubiousness showed in my voice. "You know there's not a lot here to work with, right?" Hell, most days it was a toss-up as to whether I felt like wearing a bra or not. It wasn't exactly necessary.

"You'll be surprised. Now, hike 'em up and brace yourself!"

"Yes, ma'am!" I snapped to attention at her commanding voice and reached down into the bodice, under the chemise. Treating my palms like a push-up bra, I pushed my breasts together and up, and Stacey started tugging on the laces again.

Everything got tighter. So. Much. Tighter.

"Jesus, Stacey!" I planted my feet a little wider. I couldn't exactly see what she was doing because the whole process hiked my boobs higher up my chest and those things were pretty opaque.

"Nope!" Her voice was far too chipper, but she wasn't the one getting all the oxygen sucked from her body with each pull of the strings. "Not Stacey, remember? We have to start using Faire names!"

Another pull, and I grunted again. "Right, sorry, Beatrice." Did it really matter? Apparently so, since everyone had started using their character names in conversation a week or two ago.

Which frankly sucked, since I'd just started learning people's real names. So I was going to be lost all over again.

"Thank you, Emma," she replied. Then she sighed. "You put so much effort into picking a name."

"I'm guaranteed to answer to it, at least." I'd made that joke more than once whenever anyone called me on my uncreative Faire name. She snorted in reply and pulled on the strings again. I *oof*ed again.

"Almost done here . . . one more good tug . . ." I couldn't tell if Stacey was talking to me, to herself, or to my bodice. But sure enough, she tugged once more and then I felt her fiddling around with the front of it, tying the strings in place. I didn't want to move my hands yet; better to wait until she was done before making sure I was, well, tucked in properly.

While she finished up, I looked down to the front of the auditorium, where a clump of high school kids sat on the floor in a rough circle, their skirts billowing around them. Caitlin, resplendent in pink brocade and elaborately braided hair, giggled at something one of her friends said, and her hand flew to her mouth to cover her toothy smile. She was like me in that respect: a girl who laughed with abandon. Except she was also like April, slapping her hand over her laugh, stifling it to not stand out as much.

But she was having a great time, and that was all that mattered to me. That was why I was here.

I was so distracted looking at my niece I didn't notice Stacey and I were no longer alone until I heard a voice behind me.

"Wenches. How are the costumes coming?"

Fuck. Simon had joined us, and I was standing there holding my breasts in my hands like some kind of pervert.

To his credit, he froze when he came around to where he

could see me properly. His mouth closed with a snap, and the tips of his ears got red fast.

"Um," I said.

"Sorry." He immediately spun around, turning his back to me, even though I was completely covered.

"No, no, we're good here." Stacey stepped back. "How does that feel?"

I extricated my hands from inside my dress and made sure I was tucked in before taking a breath, but it stopped about halfway through. Deep breaths were apparently off the menu. I tried smaller sips of air, breathing from the top half of my chest instead of from my diaphragm. Much better. I gave her a thumbsup before adjusting the chemise until it sat even in a ruffle over my breasts.

And damn, said breasts looked pretty good. The tight lacing of the bodice had sucked everything in and pushed it all up, and ... damn. I should look into wearing these all the time. Well, maybe not all the time. Breathing once in a while would be nice.

Stacey tilted her head to the side and surveyed my completed costume. "I like it. Just need to get some boots. What do you think?"

"I don't know." I tried to look down at myself, but all I could see was cleavage cushioned in blue and white. "It feels okay. Kind of tight, but I think I can get used to it." I looked up at her again and realized she wasn't talking to me at all. Her gaze was to my right, where Simon turned back around to survey my completed outfit.

While he inspected me, I inspected him right back. He was usually so put-together, not a wrinkle in his clothes, a hair out of place. Not a single muscle relaxed.

Today he looked ... slovenly. Instead of the meticulously put-together guy I was used to, he looked like he'd woken up late and thrown on the first clothes he'd found in the dark on the floor. Leather boots under faded black pants that had seen better days. They looked like sweatpants cut off at the ankles so they hung loose around the tops of his boots. A heathered gray-green T-shirt hung untucked over the pants. There wasn't a neatly ironed garment or a vest to be seen. His hair seemed longer too, or maybe it was just a little mussed, and he had a few days' growth of stubble on his face. For a split second I wondered if he was okay—had he been sick? I shook off the thought before I did something stupid like ask.

He chewed on his bottom lip and narrowed his eyes on my bodice, and I was starting to feel insulted. Couldn't he drool over my cleavage a little bit? But I wasn't a person to him. I was a cog in his Ren faire machine. We'd hardly spoken since that day in the bookstore.

Finally he nodded, a short jerk of his head. "It all looks fine. Hair?"

"Yes. This is my hair." I gestured to the wavy brown mess in its usual ponytail, and Simon didn't smile. Did he know how to joke? At all? "Okay, sorry. We haven't talked about hair, but . . ." I pulled the elastic out of my hair and shook it out. "It's long enough to pull back; I figured something like . . ." I gathered it all into a sort of knot at the base of my skull in illustration.

He nodded again, his eyes lingering on my hair for an extra moment or two. "That works." He turned to Stacey, and I was dismissed in that moment. "How about you? Same costume as last year?"

"Yep, I haven't had time to get anything new. Oh, but I bought a necklace from a vendor at the end of Faire last year. I was planning to add it."

"What kind of necklace?" He looked skeptical, because jewelry was apparently a crime. "Wenches aren't flashy, you know."

"Aren't flashy?" I would have laughed out loud if I'd had the lung capacity. But my laugh came out more like a wheeze. "I've got my boobs out for everyone to see. How is that not flashy?"

Simon kept his attention on Stacey, who answered his question as though I weren't there. "It's a pewter Celtic knot on a cord, nothing fancy." Her fingers went to the base of her throat and tapped her collarbone. "It feels like I should have something here, you know? Like Emily says, we're kind of out on display here, and it feels like a blank canvas."

He cracked a smile, but only for a second. "I see your point. That's fine. Names are finalized, right? Not changing them?"

"Of course not." She smiled at him. "Sean gave me that name. I'm not changing it."

"I didn't think you would." By the time he turned to me his smile had vanished, which was too bad, because he looked much better when he smiled. "How about you?"

"Still going with Emma." For the first time, I sort of regretted my flippant response to this assignment. But I squared my shoulders and owned it. The girl who wore this outfit was Emma, and if he didn't like it he could suck it.

He didn't like it. His mouth twisted. "Are you taking this seriously at all?"

His vitriol was startling. "What do you mean?"

"Did you put any effort into picking out a name?"

This again? When Stacey had said it, it had been kind of funny. But she had been teasing. Simon sounded like I was working his last nerve by choosing a name that was so close to my own.

But now rage bubbled in my chest. "Not taking it seriously?" I spread my arms. "I'm standing here with my internal organs squeezed together. I'm pretty sure I can't bend enough to sit down. And you're going to give me shit about picking out a name?"

He practically flinched when I cursed, and his eyes darted around us. Ah, crap. I'd forgotten we were in a room full of kids.

"I mean honestly." I pitched my voice lower, even though I wanted to yell at him. No one was paying attention to us yet, and I wanted to keep it that way. "How am I not taking this seriously? I show up every weekend, almost always on time."

"You're on your phone during most of the history discussions. You can't brush up on Elizabethan history if you're scrolling through Instagram."

Oh, the nerve of this guy. "I listen plenty, even though I can't imagine needing any of this information. I mean, I'm a tavern wench, right? Is a patron going to give me a pop quiz while I'm selling them a beer?"

"They might!" My rage was apparently contagious, because he glared at me with stern eyes and a set jaw. "You never know when a patron is going to ask you about the time period. You're going to want to know what religion you're allowed to be then, and who supports and opposes the Queen, right?"

I rolled my eyes. "I know all of that. You know why? Because I've been here: Every. Damn. Weekend." His eyes flared at my repeatedly foul mouth, but I'd stopped caring. "Don't you think I'd rather sleep in on Saturdays, instead of setting my alarm clock to come here?"

"If this is such a waste of time, why are you here? No one's forcing you. You can quit anytime." He raised an eyebrow, and I knew he had me. If I wasn't a part of this, Caitlin couldn't be a part of this. I looked over at her again. There was no way I could quit, and he knew it. Asshole.

I tried a different tack. "Is Emma a period-appropriate name?"

He narrowed his eyes, and his only response was a nod.

"Then what's the problem?" I met his eyes and he met mine, and we had a staring contest of hate for a good ten seconds. But I was too tired to fight. Not to mention too oxygen-deprived. "Look. I'm living in my sister's guest room, taking care of her and my niece until she's able to do it on her own. When I'm on my phone, it's because I'm checking my schedule to make sure I'm not missing anything. My sister still can't drive, so I try to consolidate errands, getting her stuff done as well as mine." *Shut up,* my mind screamed. *Shut up, shut up. He doesn't need to know any of this.* But to my horror my mouth kept going. "I don't have a job. I don't even know where I'm going to be living or what I'm going to be doing six months from now. I have a lot on my mind. So when I had to pick out a name for Faire, I took a shortcut by using something I can remember to answer to. Okay?"

I didn't back down from his gaze. It was just him and me and his muddy brown eyes, but then he blinked, and something in his expression flickered. "Family's important." His voice was softer, kinder than I'd ever heard it before.

With those two words all my rage dissolved, and a warmer feeling bloomed in my chest. It was like we understood each other, finally. "Yeah," I said. "It is."

He watched me for another moment, then the moment passed and he was back to the same disapproving Simon he'd always been.

"It's fine," he said, his voice clipped. "The name is fine." And with that he was gone, moving on to the next clump of cast members to terrorize. Probably to give them a pop quiz about their diets and their opinions of the Queen.

"Ugh." I turned to Stacey. "Is he always that unpleasant?"

"No, you seem to bring it out in him. Good going." She watched him walk away. "The thing about Simon is that Faire's just . . . it's his thing. He's very protective of it. Everything has to go right."

"Really?" I turned back around to see where he had stalked off to, but I'd lost sight of him. "Then why doesn't he look like he's having fun? Shouldn't he be having fun?"

Stacey shrugged. "It's a lot of work, I bet. I mean, he used to help his brother when Sean used to run things, but I'm sure it's a lot harder when it's all up to you."

I shook my head. "Then he should learn to delegate." No wonder he was a dick. I thought he and Chris jointly ran this thing. Was he responsible for everything? That was a lot for one person to take on. "Besides," I said, "if he cares so much, then why does he look like he just rolled out of bed? The guy's wearing sweatpants."

Stacey chuckled. "I think they have extra fight rehearsal today. They usually do those on Sundays, separately from the regular rehearsal. But we're getting close to opening now, so they're probably doing an extra run-through of some of the fight choreography."

"Oh, really?" So he wasn't coming off a bender. He was wearing comfortable clothes he could move in. I couldn't picture Simon fighting. That would require emotion, and he was one step removed from being a robot. "Who does Simon fight?"

"Looking good, Park!"

Oh, good. Mitch was here. He always entered rehearsal the same way: booming voice announcing his arrival, gym bag slung over one broad shoulder, passing out fist bumps to kids like they were candy.

Now that we were a few weeks in, I was used to Mitch. God

bless his collection of tight T-shirts, and if his hair was dyed black he could cosplay Superman any day of the week with that chiseled jaw. But he had some annoying habits too. The unironic fist bumping. The nicknames. No one had ever called me Park in my entire life. But God help me, I answered to it. Every damn time.

But today, when I laid eyes on him, every negative thought about the guy flew out of my head. Because today, Mitch wasn't Mitch. Today, Marcus MacGregor had come to play. Mitch was wearing the Kilt.

The Kilt. The kilt I'd been promised when I'd agreed to this whole shebang in the first place. It had slipped my mind with everything else going on in my life. But suddenly, volunteering for this Faire was the best damn idea I ever had.

Don't ask me what clan the tartan was, I didn't care. That wasn't important. What was important? Those legs. In a kilt, Mitch transformed from goofy jock-douche to a man. A man who didn't skip leg day. A man with calves that could have been carved from marble. There were muscle and power in those legs, and I'd never wanted to touch a guy's legs the way I wanted to put my hands on Mitch's.

But then he strutted over in our direction, his eyes focused about six inches south of my chin, and I bit back a sigh. Yes, the boy was hot. But, much to my libido's chagrin, looks weren't everything.

"Thanks." I straightened my chemise a little, even though I'd just finished doing that. "You don't look so bad yourself." I gestured to his kilt. "So this is the famous kilt, huh? You wear that every year?"

"Sure do. The kilt's been a thing for a while now," he said to my tits.

"Oh, it *haaaaaas*." Stacey turned to me with a grin. "I'm telling you, Em, this is my favorite part of rehearsals. I like to think of it as Kilt Day."

I snorted, a little awkwardly in the costume, while Mitch dragged his eyes upward; he shrugged and tried to look self-deprecating, but he was far too pleased with himself to pull it off. The guy practically preened. "The girls love it."

"I'm sure we do. Er, they do. I'm sure they do." But there was no saving it. I flushed bright red while Mitch laughed. And when the man laughed, he *laughed*. Loud. And long. Heads turned in our direction, and most of them turned away again with a be-mused smile at Mitch being Mitch. But Simon, standing at the lip of the stage, frowned before shaking his head and going back to whatever he was saying to Chris, turning a black hat with a giant red feather around and around in his hands.

"Good job," I said. "Because the boss isn't mad at me enough."

"Who?" Mitch followed my gaze and scoffed. "Oh, the Captain? How'd you piss him off?"

Mitch had a nickname for everyone, apparently; even the head of this whole operation. "Captain" was probably a better nickname than "Dickhead." "Who knows? Showing emotion? Having a good time?"

"I'm telling you," Mitch said. "That guy seriously needs to get laid."

I choked. "Ugh. Who the hell would volunteer for *that*?" I couldn't imagine a worse way to spend a night. And I'd worked closing shift in a bar on St. Patrick's Day.

"You'd be surprised," Stacey said. "There was that one girl, re-member, Mitch? A couple summers back? She was what, a dancer? Something? I remember her being . . . limber."

Mitch snorted. "Fight crew. They lasted all of a minute." He shook his head. "Doesn't count."

"Well, yeah, but that was . . ." Stacey trailed off like she was looking for the right word. "It was a couple years ago. His head wasn't in the game."

"Is it ever? The guy's been like a monk ever since Sean's been gone."

I blinked. What did his brother leaving town have to do with Simon having a girlfriend? It must have made sense to Stacey, though, since she tsked at him. "Can you blame him? It's not really fair to . . ." She trailed off again. Why couldn't she find the words when it came to Simon?

But Mitch must have understood; part of that small-town shorthand that I wasn't privy to yet. "Yeah, you're probably right." He sighed. "Still think it would be good for him." With another exaggerated eye roll, he wandered off down the aisle, giving out more fist bumps and posing, basically working the kilt as much as he worked the room.

Stacey shook her head as we watched Mitch go. "Y'all really should be nicer to Simon. He'll grow on you, I promise."

I snorted again. It was easier to do this time, but being strapped in took getting used to. It was rigid. Even though my body moved inside it, the bodice itself had steel bones running through it so it didn't bend much. It was like a cage around my torso. I'd adjusted to surviving on sips of air, but I already felt like I hadn't taken a good deep breath in years. Now that it was on my mind, panic rose in my lungs. I was suffocating. I wanted to tear off the fabric and metal cage around my ribs and *breathe*.

By force of will I calmed myself down. I wasn't suffocating. I was wearing a tight bodice. That was all.

Stacey noticed my distress. "Hey. You're okay. I know, it's weird at first, but don't worry. It gets easier. How about we go outside and watch the fighting? You need to move around some, and get used to wearing it."

"So Mitch is fighting? While wearing that kilt?" That would be enough to distract me from this suffocating death trap I was wearing.

"Oh, yeah. Why do you think I keep coming back every year?" She didn't have to ask a second time.

Outside, the heat of the late-June morning had started to kick in. I followed Stacey out of the auditorium, past the singers harmonizing in the foyer, then out the double doors and around the side of the building. There was a pavilion about fifty yards away with picnic tables, probably a popular place for students to eat lunch when the weather was nice. Some of the picnic tables had been commandeered by the tech crew, where they cut and sanded various lengths of lumber, while others were busy with paintbrushes.

Stacey waved at one of the techs, who waved a greeting back in our direction. Past the tables, in the center of a field, a group of men and women milled around in twos and threes. Most of them were armed in one way or another, with everything from convincingly real-looking swords to throwing daggers. One young man wielded a quarterstaff easily twice his height. They conferred in small groups, and occasionally one would brandish a weapon and attack at a ridiculously slow speed, working on the timing of the fight. My theatre classes in college had included stage fighting, so the sight stirred a memory in me.

"So what is this exactly? It's not the joust—that's on horses, right?"

"Yeah." Stacey looked amused. Okay, maybe Simon had a

point. Maybe I could be a little more informed. "Yeah, that's on horses. No, this is the human chess match."

"Okay . . ." That didn't clear things up. What did fighting have to do with chess? I wanted to ask, but I'd already used up my stupid question quota for the day with the one about the joust.

Then I spotted Mitch. Green and blue plaid kilt, gray T-shirt, heavy Doc Martens–looking boots strapped over his calves. He'd been wearing running shoes earlier. He stood with his back to us, eclipsing whoever he was talking to from my view. Then they separated, and started circling each other slowly with swords drawn.

He was fighting Simon. That hardly seemed fair. Mitch had almost half a head on the guy. They didn't seem evenly matched for a fight of any kind.

They moved in slow motion, talking to each other as one thrust, one parried. Mitch leaned in with his sword, Simon blocked it with an exaggerated motion as he spun away. Then they stopped moving, went back to talking for a few moments before they dropped their swords and Mitch went in for an upper-cut that Simon caught in both hands, twisting both their bodies as he turned the defensive move into an elbow to the jaw (well, about six inches from the jaw; none of their blows were even close to landing on each other).

My skepticism must have shown on my face, because Stacey leaned in. "It'll look a lot better when we're at Faire and they're doing it in real time and in full costume."

"Man, I hope so." Because right now they looked like two drunks trying to remember how to fight. The fact that they were armed, albeit with ancient weapons, made the prospect even more frightening.

Stacey squinted at me. "You feel okay?"

"Sure." But once she mentioned it, I had to admit I felt a little off out here in the sun. Not sick, not dizzy, just . . . off. I moved my arms experimentally. "Are my hands supposed to feel tingly?"

"No. You're laced up too tight." She tugged the bow on my bodice loose and pulled on the strings. "It's been long enough, let's go ahead and get this off." I gasped as it loosened a fraction, and I was able to take a deeper breath. It was delicious. "We'll make sure to cinch it a little less next time. Don't want you passing out."

"That would be bad," I agreed. The relief as the garment came off, the rush of blood back to my extremities, the relaxing of my flesh, the ability to take a good deep breath again, all felt better than the best orgasm I'd ever had. Not that any of mine had been particularly great. Or plentiful, especially in the past couple years. Jake had been busy in law school, then studying for the bar, then dumping my ass and starting his new life . . .

Focus, Emily.

I held the bodice in front of me like a shield, suddenly feeling naked in only the chemise up top, even though you could fit a whole soccer team under my skirts. But I couldn't deny I was much more comfortable as we settled down in the grass at the top of a small hill that gave us a great vantage point to watch the fighting.

After a few minutes the group of teenage singers from the front hall had wandered outside to join us. By the time the fighters started running through the choreography in real time, we'd all woven a six-foot chain of dandelions like we were in grade school, and I wore a crown of them in my hair. We made a motley group of Renaissance-era cheerleaders, wearing half period costume and half street clothes.

The *huzzahs* started when two sword fighters got into it. I didn't know a rapier from a saber, but these two looked impressive, whipping the sharp metal at each other and punctuating their swordplay with a well-placed fake punch. When one fell to the ground, Stacey called out "Huzzah!" in a clear, loud voice, and the singer girls around us picked up the call. So what could I do but follow along? I remembered the first day, hoping to hell I wouldn't have to speak with an accent or yell out anything weird and period-sounding. Now I sat shoulder to shoulder with my fellow wench with flowers in our hair, cheerfully calling out encouragement to the fighters, sounding completely unlike myself.

Because I wasn't myself. The girl who wore chemises and sat in the grass was Emma, not Emily. And I was starting to like her.

In the field, it was Mitch and Simon's turn to run through their fight, and I had to admit it did look pretty amazing sped up. They started out with blades, taking turns having the advantage, until they'd disarmed each other and sent each other sprawling with punches to the jaw and jabs with elbows. Simon was smaller but he proved to be more than a match; the sleeves of his T-shirt strained against biceps I didn't realize he had. He wasn't built like Mitch—he was more lithe, almost wiry—yet he was still able to flip the larger man over his shoulder, kilt flying. Dammit, Mitch was wearing bike shorts.

I turned to Stacey, betrayed.

"I know, I know." She shook her head in sympathy. "It's a disappointment, right? But this is a family show."

I grumbled under my breath, turning back to watch as Mitch landed on his feet and spun, throwing a punch that Simon easily blocked. But Mitch used the twist of his body to conceal the action of pulling a dagger from his boot. I heard myself cry out a warning before realizing I'd made a sound. Mitch backhanded Simon, who went to his knees, and the fight ended with Mitch holding his dagger to Simon's throat. The two men froze in that tableau for a few beats as we all erupted in applause: the other fighters, the girls in the grass, all of us.

"Huzzah!" My hands stung from clapping, but the guys deserved it. That had been an incredible show.

They broke the pose, and Mitch extended a hand to help Simon up. They were both sweating, chests heaving from exertion, and they turned to acknowledge our applause with grins and waves. Mitch noticed Stacey and me sitting on the hill and pointed his massive sword at us in acknowledgment. He leaned over to Simon, saying something, pointing in our direction, and when Simon looked at me the force of his smile hit me in the chest. I smiled back at him in a Pavlovian response. But his grin faltered, as though he didn't know what to do with mine. He made a gesture that seemed to start as a wave, but at the last second he changed his mind, pushing his hair off his forehead instead.

"So what did you think?" Stacey nudged my shoulder as we walked back into the high school auditorium. "Pretty cool, right?"

"Yeah." The fights had been incredible to watch, and cheering them on with the girls had made me feel like I was a part of something. But I glanced back over my shoulder at the field, watching Simon talk to a couple of the others. The knowledge that he didn't want to share his joy with me rankled. What was I going to have to do to prove I was worthy of that smile?

More importantly, why did it bother me so much?

Five

The next weekend's rehearsal took place at the actual Faire site. Only two more weeks until we were up and running. And while that was exciting, this new meeting location threw off my routine. After all these weeks, I could practically drive to the high school on Saturday mornings with my eyes closed. Now my Jeep and I had to shift gears, and while Caitlin read to me off some emailed directions (apparently the place didn't show up on GPS), we ended up in a field-turned-parking-lot at the edge of a forest.

"The hell?" I got out of the car and squinted toward the trees. "We're going in there?" This was exactly how stupid white girls died in horror movies.

"Come onnnn." Caitlin hadn't watched the same horror movies as me, and she tugged on my arm and led me toward a path snaking into the trees. I sighed and followed her. What the hell. By now April was mostly mobile. She'd be able to take care of herself if I was hacked to pieces by a serial killer in a hockey mask out here.

The wide, well-trod path opened up almost right away into a clearing, with multiple smaller paths forking out in all directions. A few stages were constructed within sight of the clearing, and other wooden structures dotted the distance. It was like a whole civilization hidden inside the outer ring of trees.

Caitlin, with the confidence of an excited kid, led me down a path on the right winding through full green trees that acted as a filter for the early-morning sunlight. When I glanced back over my shoulder the parking lot wasn't visible at all. It was a little unsettling, but as I turned back to the path, the sun and the trees had a calming effect. I already liked it here.

The rest of our people were gathered in a clearing with a sign nailed to a tree: CHAUCER STAGE. There was no stage. There was half a platform and a stack of planks ready to be made into the rest. Chris sat on the edge of the finished half of the stage, holding up a pearl-encrusted bodice and talking to one of the other adult volunteers.

Costume. Right. I stuck my sunglasses on top of my head and fished in my backpack while I walked toward her. I'd brought my boots today for final approval. If Chris okayed them now, I wouldn't have to talk to Simon unless it was absolutely necessary. Everyone would win.

Chris looked them over. "No zippers or modern ornamentation. Looks good to me." She handed them back to me. "I didn't see you at the bookstore this week."

"I know." I smiled; it was nice to be missed. "April's down to physical therapy every other week now."

"That's great news! So she's getting better?"

"Much." My smile widened. "Thanks for asking."

"Of course! Tell her I'm thinking of her." Chris placed a hand on my shoulder and gave a gentle squeeze. I was dismissed, but not rudely.

My smile remained in place as the rest of the cast gathered around the half-finished stage for our morning briefing. I liked these people; I liked this town. Why didn't April? I could see her valuing privacy, but no one was trying to meddle. So far, everyone I'd met in Willow Creek was *nice*.

Then I spotted Simon. Okay, almost everyone. I looked him over and frowned. It wasn't like him to be at the back of the crowd like this, but there he was, leaning against a tree, fiddling with something in his hands. Sunlight flashed off silver, and I squinted when I realized he was holding a flask, turning it over and over, tossing it lightly from one palm to the other.

What was with this guy? The day we'd met he'd been the straightest of straitlaced people, but lately it was like he'd been letting himself go. His hair was massively in need of a trim, and if I'd thought he looked scruffy the weekend before, now he looked like he'd given up on shaving entirely. And why was he skulking in the back with booze? He was a teacher, for God's sake.

He looked up and our eyes met. I started like I'd been caught at something, which I guess I had been. He frowned at me and stowed the flask in the back pocket of his jeans. Then he folded his arms firmly over his chest, his gaze more of a glower in my direction. I quickly turned back around.

The energy in the group was charged with excitement, and it was easy to see why as I looked around. Wearing long skirts and practicing accents in a high school auditorium felt like planning an overly elaborate Halloween costume. But here in the woods, away from traffic noises and the hum of industrial air conditioners, the only sounds were the chatter of the kids around us and the wind rustling in the treetops. It was easy to imagine we'd stepped into another century.

"Different kind of rehearsal today!" Chris's voice rang out in her usual sunny tones, and everyone quieted down and turned their attention to her. "This is going to be our home from now until the end of the summer." She threw her arms wide as if she could embrace the trees. "We open in two weeks, and we have volunteers working hard to put this place together. So what we're going to do today is take a walk around the site and get to know it. It's all basically one big circle, with lots of side paths. Feel free to explore for a little while, and then we'll get to work."

"Work?" I turned to Stacey, my eyebrows raised. She bumped me with an elbow and directed my attention back to Chris, who was still smiling, way too pleased with the idea of work on a Saturday morning.

"We leave the heavy lifting—literally—to our stage techs and volunteers, but there's plenty we can get done this morning. A couple of the sets are constructed and ready for paint; that's why we asked you to wear old clothes today, remember!"

I had forgotten about that, but thankfully it was laundry day, so I was wearing a stretched-out T-shirt and an old pair of jeans. I craned my head around for my niece. What had she worn to-day? God, I'd be useless if she ever went missing. I spotted her curly brown hair toward the back with the usual friends, and thank God she was actually wearing paint-appropriate clothes. She'd listened better than I had, apparently.

Once the meeting broke up, we split into smaller groups of five or ten to explore the paths snaking through the forest. Time to see where we were spending the rest of the summer.

Simon didn't join any of the groups. He slipped out of the clearing as soon as the meeting was over, striding with intention down a side path. Off to drink probably, judging from the flask. I frowned again as I trailed after Stacey. Simon and I weren't friends. I didn't know him well at all. But something seemed so off about him today I couldn't help wondering if he was all right. And why no one else seemed to notice. He seemed relatively well-liked among cast members who weren't me. Why wasn't anyone checking on him?

I shook off the thought as we moved deeper and deeper into the woods. The main trails were paved for the most part, but halfheartedly so, like roads that had been abandoned long ago. Side paths weren't paved, but a thick layer of mulch had been laid down. I coughed as our footsteps stirred up dirt and dust.

"That'll get better," Stacey said after I coughed for the third time. "It's always a little dusty when they first put a new layer of mulch down. But by the time we open, especially if we get some rain, everything will be tamped down pretty well." She twisted her mouth up a little. "Be prepared, though. Faire is really dirty. The long hot shower at the end of the day is going to be your best friend for a long time."

"Along with taking off that outfit." Because I couldn't imagine anything in the world feeling better than that.

Stacey laughed. "That too." She led me off the main path, and somewhere in the middle of the woods, she threw her arms wide at the edge of a clearing. "Here's the tavern!"

I turned in a slow circle. "Uh-huh." I probably looked as unconvinced as I sounded. It was a clearing in the woods. Nothing else. "Where exactly is it? Don't tell me we have to build it ourselves."

"God, no. The guys are coming in over the next few days to build the bar. They'll put in the tables a day or two before we open."

"So people hang out and drink?" What were open container laws like out here in the forest? I'd spent most of Jake's law school career working as a cocktail waitress and backup bartender, so now that the talk was turning more toward the tavern part of tavern wench, I felt a lot more in my element. "So what are we serving? Beer, wine? Liquor?"

"Not liquor." She shuddered. "Believe me, beer and wine are enough. I don't want to imagine shots."

"But we're gonna have all this cleavage." I gestured at my T-shirt, which currently contained nothing of the sort. I needed the outfit to make cleavage happen. "I figured body shots were a must."

Stacey giggled. "This is a family-friendly Faire, remember?" She gestured again toward the invisible bar. "We'll have kegs with some beers on tap. Some bottled imports, usually some ciders and mead too to mix it up a little. A few kinds of wine. That's about it. We try to keep it pretty simple."

I nodded while I took mental inventory. "Food?"

"Not here." Stacey gestured in a *waaaaay over there* motion. "Food vendors are that way. Typical outdoor Faire stuff."

"Turkey legs?"

"Hell yeah turkey legs." She grinned, and I did too. Because what was a Renaissance faire without turkey legs? Nothing, that's what. I may have been a newbie, but even I knew that.

I put my hands on my hips and surveyed our little clearing. I tried to picture it decked out as a tavern, with the tables and bar the way Stacey described. I didn't love the idea of working in a bar again, but at least I'd be outside in the fresh air instead of cooped up in a sweaty dark box with lots of twentysomethings wearing too much cologne.

"I like it," I finally said. "What do we need to do? Obviously there's nothing to paint yet."

"Today?" She shrugged. "Nothing, really."

"So why am I here, exactly?" I hoped my smile took the malice out of my question.

It obviously did, because Stacey answered me in kind. "Because you had to drive your niece here?" She laughed at my sigh of mock defeat. "Come on. I'll show you where the food vendors are going to be, and then we'll swing back over toward the front and do some painting."

We took a path that led deeper into the woods. The trees got thicker, but it never seemed to get darker. The path stayed wide and well trod, and for a few fleeting moments I could ignore the paved part of the path and feel the time period we were going to be portraying. Even with the distant sounds of hammering and voices calling to one another, everything felt simpler out here. I took a few good deep breaths. Even the air seemed cleaner.

Stacey showed me the food vendor area—a much larger clearing than our tavern area. Beyond that was the jousting arena, a giant field at the very back of the grounds. I had to admit my inner fourteen-year-old was very excited at the prospect of seeing a real joust, on actual horses.

"Will I have time to see it at some point?"

"Oh, yeah," Stacey said. "We won't be chained to the tavern. The volunteers can handle things by themselves if we take off for a bit. Last year we were able to do some walking around, interacting with patrons. Watching the shows."

She pointed down a hill to an area she called the Hollow. She explained it was our backstage area, with a couple of changing tents and some tables and chairs, away from the rest of the action, where we could do emergency repairs to costumes and snatch a break here and there.

I squinted down the hill. "And why do we call it the Hollow?" It sounded like fairies should be living there, not a bunch of weary Faire folks.

"Sounds better than 'backstage' if someone says it out loud, basically."

I couldn't argue with that.

"And then this path takes us back up to the front." She shrugged. "It's pretty simple."

"Simple," I repeated. If she left me here right now, I would die of exposure before finding my way to the front again.

"Believe me, after a weekend or two you'll know this place blindfolded like the rest of us."

Since part of me was still looking for an ax murderer behind a tree, I wasn't sure how much I believed her. "I'll take your word for it."

"I'm going to head back up to the front and help put benches together. Why don't you explore a little more. It might help you get a better handle on things. Then you can come find me and I'll stick a paintbrush in your hand."

"Thanks, I think I will." I watched Stacey stride up the path leading to the perimeter of the grounds and tried not to panic about being left alone. Once she disappeared into the trees I took a different path, not going anywhere specific, just wandering, and the panic faded pretty quickly. There was something about the setting, the way the sun came in through the trees, the way my footsteps rustled on the path, that made me feel more content than I'd been in a long time. Tension I didn't even know I'd been carrying melted away, and the sun warmed my soul as much as it warmed my skin. Even though it was almost July, it was still early enough that it hadn't gotten too hot yet, and all the bullshit of the past few months felt as though it were long in the distance.

I was so intent on the trees around me that I didn't hear the footsteps, and didn't register someone was approaching until we almost collided. I jumped a step backward with an "Oh!"

Simon had appeared out of nowhere, from a small side path that wound deeper into the forest. He stopped short when he saw me, frowned a little, but didn't say a word.

"Sorry," I said. "I guess I wasn't paying attention to where I was going."

He squinted at me, as though my voice reminded him who I was. His eyes seemed to be rimmed with red. He scrubbed a hand over his face and sniffed. "What are you doing over here?" His voice was rough and rusty sounding, as though he hadn't used it in a while and wasn't quite sure how it worked.

What was his problem? Then I remembered the flask I'd seen before. Whatever he had in there must have been strong; he looked pretty rough. But his eyes were clear and he was standing straight. So, probably not drunk. Allergies, maybe? There had to be a crap-load of pollen in these trees. "Just wandering around," I finally said. "Stacey was showing me where everything's going to be."

He made a show of looking behind me, even leaning a little to his right. Then he straightened up and trained those laser-like eyes on me. "I don't see Stacey."

"No, well, she went up front to help the others. I'm going to head up there too, I just . . . wanted to get a little more of a feel for the place." The more I talked, the more annoyed I got, which seemed to be a trend whenever I had a conversation with Simon. Why should I feel defensive that I was walking around the site instead of helping up front? After all, he was walking around out here too. I couldn't shake the feeling he'd caught me doing something I shouldn't, and that irritated me even more. Simon was a vicious circle of annoyance.

He sniffed again and shifted from one foot to the other. He glanced over his shoulder the way he'd come, and then it clicked: It wasn't that he'd caught me. I'd caught him. Now I leaned to my right, an echo of his previous movement. "What's down there?"

"Nothing," he said quickly. But he glanced over his shoulder again.

"Nothing?" I crossed my arms over my chest. "So why's there a path going that way?"

"A lane."

I blinked. "What?"

"A lane," he repeated. "They're called lanes at a Faire."

"Oh. Okay." Was he trying to distract me or was he being his normal nitpicky self? So hard to tell with Simon. "Then why's there a *lane* going that way if there's nothing there?"

"Well, there's nothing down there now." His sigh was short and exasperated. "It's where some vendors are going to be set up. It's nothing you need to worry about."

"Okay . . ." I had no idea why he was trying to keep me from going down that side path—sorry, *lane*—but he sure as hell wasn't going to confide in me. Maybe it was where all of his drug deals went down. It was always the quiet, clean-cut ones. The ones you didn't expect to be kingpins.

"So you're going back up to the front? Where Stacey is now?" His voice didn't sound friendly, but he didn't quite sound like he hated me, either. This apparently was Simon making an effort. Now that I saw him up close, I noticed I'd misjudged his slovenliness this morning. The scruff he'd been cultivating recently had been tamed into a neatly trimmed beard that framed his jaw. Out here in the woods, the sunlight threw flashes of burnished red into his brown hair. He looked . . . better out here. "You're going to want to take this lane back around, and where it curves to the left, there's a side lane that goes . . ."

"I know." I sounded more petulant than I wanted, but he wasn't subtle about wanting me gone. "I can find it, thanks. I don't think I'll get lost in a couple acres of woods." He didn't need to know I'd been worried about that exact thing five minutes ago.

But I didn't leave and neither did he, so we looked at each other uncomfortably until he finally sighed again. "Why are you here?" He sounded tired now, not exasperated.

"Um." I looked around, as though maybe the answer were somewhere in the trees. "We're all supposed to be here today, right?"

"No. Why are you here? At the Faire? Why haven't you dropped out yet?"

I narrowed my eyes. "Because I committed to it. If I don't do Faire, my niece can't do Faire."

He gave a long-suffering sigh. "We don't actually hold people to that. It's just a way that we make sure that the younger kids who sign up really want to do it. Surely you've noticed a bunch of parents have dropped out already."

I had noticed that, but doing the same hadn't even crossed my mind. I wasn't about to admit it to him, but I was actually having fun. "Well, you know me." He didn't, but that to me made it even more passively-aggressively bitchy. "I like to help out my community."

"But it isn't." He ran a hand over his jaw again, rubbing at the bristles on his cheek as though he could scrub them out. "This isn't your community. You don't live here."

Those words were a dart, and they hit the bull's-eye. To my

horror, my eyes started to sting. "Excuse me?" I blinked hard. I was not going to let this asshole see he'd made me cry.

But he noticed. "I mean . . ." He had the grace to look a little ashamed and started to backpedal. "You're not staying, right? I thought you were only here short term to help out your sister."

"Well, I hadn't thought about it yet. I'm . . ." I put up a hand, stopping the thought. Stopping him from saying anything else. "You know what? My future isn't any of your business. What is your business is I represent fifty percent of your wenches, and Faire starts in two weeks. Do you really not want me here?"

Simon's mouth compressed into a thin line, and instead of backing down I held his stare. We looked at each other for a good solid minute, which doesn't sound like long until you're in a staring contest with someone and you don't want to lose.

Finally he sighed. "You're right."

"And?" It was nice to have won, but I still didn't know what exactly I was right about.

"And we only have two wenches this year, so we can't afford to lose you. I . . ." He looked over his shoulder one more time. To see if he had stalled long enough, and his drug contact had ske-daddled by now? When he turned back to me, something in his face had changed. "Sorry," he said, and I almost fell over back-ward to hear him apologize. "This time of year is hard. And this year is . . ." That was all he said, but I watched his face. He looked tired, maybe a little sad. Why did he do Faire every year if it made him look like this?

But I didn't ask. Because that was the kind of thing a friend would do, and we weren't friends. I was starting to regret that.

"Anyway." I half turned away from him, pointing up the lane. "This way back to the front, right?" I knew it was, but something in me wanted to defer to him this little bit. Like a peace offering.

"Yeah." His voice had gone all rusty again. He cleared his throat. "That way, and it curves around to the left." He pointed halfheartedly, and I made a little show of watching where he indicated, like he was being helpful.

"Thanks." I started down the lane, but before the curve I ducked down a side lane. I peered around a tree and watched Simon walk the same main lane as me, heading up to that curve to the left, and as soon as he had disappeared I doubled back the way I'd come. I was better at figuring out these woods than I thought, and it didn't take long to find the clearing where he and I had been talking. I followed the side lane where Simon had appeared. There was something down here he didn't want me to see, so naturally I had to find it.

I followed the lane until I came across another intersection. Nothing. There was nothing here. No key to why Simon was the way he was. I stepped onto the lane, the one that was paved, when a flash on the ground caught my eye. It was sunlight, glinting off metal. Off silver.

It was the flask. The one Simon had been playing with during the morning briefing. Now it lay under a tree. He must have dropped it, and I bent to pick it up, but my hand stopped. The flask hadn't been dropped, it had been deliberately laid down; it stood on its end, leaning against something.

Simon hadn't been back here for a drug deal. He'd been back here for a tree. A very specific tree.

I crouched in the dirt on the side of the path, and my fingers reached out to the raised plaque resting at the base of the young tree. My fingertips grazed over the largest two words on the plaque: SEAN GRAHAM. Beneath the name was a set of dates, and my breath whooshed out of my body.

Sean Graham. Simon's older brother, the founder of the Faire.

People talked about him in the past tense, but the stories were always fond, and everyone had a smile on their face when they spoke about him. I'd convinced myself Sean had left town, maybe gotten married or something, and simply wasn't part of Faire anymore. It hadn't even crossed my mind that he was dead. Simon had lost his brother. I looked at the dates again and did the math in my head. Sean had died three summers ago, at the age of twenty-seven. No one should die that young.

Beneath the dates was one final line. *Bring me that horizon . . .* My lips quirked up. I'd seen the *Pirates of the Caribbean* movies more than once. I recognized the line, spoken by Captain Jack Sparrow at the end of the first film before embarking on an unknown voyage. It was a fitting farewell to someone who had spent his summers creating and running a Renaissance faire. Simon's flask leaned against the plaque, and if I had to guess I'd have said there was rum inside.

This time of year is hard, Simon had said. Well, of course it was. This was obviously a ritual he had followed these past few years, saying hi to his brother on the first day the cast came here for the season. This whole morning snapped into clearer focus, and I burned with shame, remembering the assumptions I'd made. His thunderous face during the meeting this morning, his red-rimmed eyes, his clear discomfort and insistence that I not know what he was doing back here. Of course he didn't want me to know. Like I said, we weren't friends. I hadn't wanted to confide in him. Why would he want to confide in me?

Now I understood the past few months more than I ever had. Every disparaging thing I had said about Faire, every flippant comment I had made about my character or my costume, and every stiff response from Simon, down to his disapproval of how I'd filled out the audition form. Simon was carrying on his brother's legacy; of course he'd be protective of it. Of course he wanted everything to be just right.

"I'm sorry," I said to the plaque, to the tree dedicated to the memory of Sean Graham. "I'm sorry I didn't know you, it sounds like you were a pretty cool guy. But I promise, despite what your brother thinks, I do take this seriously. I'm gonna be the best damn wench he's ever seen."

I turned and headed back up the side lane, back to the main one that curved to the left. Stacey was waiting at the front with a paintbrush for me. I had work to do.

Six

When the *Fourth* of July rolled around, April had no interest in the festivities, so I dragged Caitlin with me to the town center to see how Willow Creek celebrated. The downtown area was practically awash in bunting, the perfect backdrop for the parade strolling through the main street. We kept running into people we knew from Faire, making me feel even more welcome in this small town. The whole day was like something out of an old movie: high school marching band, Boy Scouts riding on red fire trucks waving little American flags, a hot dog–eating contest (that Mitch won, to no one's surprise), and a modest but delightful fireworks display after dark.

In mid-July, I turned another year older. My birthday was the Thursday before Faire opened, and I woke up to a reminder to pick up Caitlin's costume from the dry cleaner's after I dropped April off at her physical therapy appointment. I didn't expect anyone to acknowledge my birthday, so I wasn't disappointed when no one did. April had never been one for something so demonstrative; birthday greetings usually came from our mother.

But even those weren't forthcoming. Mom didn't call all day, and there wasn't a card from her when I checked the mail. Which was . . . weird.

So after dropping off April, finally returning Marjorie's casserole dish (and fending off her politely probing questions about April's recovery), and picking up the dry cleaning, I headed for Read It & Weep. I deserved a book for my birthday, at the very least. Not to mention Caitlin and I had finished Twelfth Night a week or two before. We'd had a lot of fun reading it out loud together, pausing every so often if she needed something explained. I wanted to keep the momentum going with a copy of A Midsummer Night's Dream. If she was picking up my Shakespeare nerd gene I wanted to encourage that as much as possible.

I strolled the stacks for a little while before Chris realized I was there, and by the time she waved me over to make me a coffee I'd picked out three new books I couldn't live without. Screw it, you only turned twenty-five once, right? I headed for the back of the shop, where she had coffee waiting for me, with half-and-half the way I liked it, as well as one for herself. I reached for my wallet to pay, but she waved it off.

"My treat," she said. "Books too. Happy birthday."

My jaw dropped. "How did you . . ."

"It was on the audition form, remember?"

I didn't, but she did. A few months ago I might have muttered something about "goddamn small towns," but now I thanked her with a grateful smile and shoved the books into my messenger bag.

"How's April?" She pushed my coffee cup toward me as she picked up her own.

"Good. She's good." I took a tentative sip; it was still hot. "The doctors all seem to be impressed with her progress, and with how fast she's healing. But they don't know her. She's pretty determined." I tried not to wince, both from the hot drink and from my own mouth. Was I talking too much? Giving away too much of April's private information?

"So what does that mean for you?"

"For me?" I tilted my head.

"Well, sure. You've been her caretaker for, what, about four months now? If she's mobile again, what does that mean for you? Are you heading home?"

"Oh . . ." I took a long sip of coffee to avoid answering right away. Mostly because I had no idea what I'd say. Or where home was. "I haven't thought that far ahead yet. I'm here for the next six weeks at least, since Faire starts in two days."

"Two days. Finally." She shook her head. "Every year I think we should make the rehearsal period shorter. I worry about the kids burning out, you know? What do you think?"

I had to laugh. "Caitlin couldn't be more excited. Especially now that it's all coming together and we're spending more time out in the woods." We'd been back a second weekend for more painting and more exploring. It still looked pretty bare-bones out there, but Stacey assured me that I'd be amazed this coming Saturday. I took her word for it.

Talking about the woods reminded me of something else I wanted to ask her. "I didn't realize Sean was . . ." I didn't know how to finish that sentence. "Dead" sounded too heavy, like the word would flop on the counter between us and lie there, staring at us. I started over. "I saw his memorial. At the site."

"Oh. Yes. Poor Sean." Her smile grew sad as she took a sip of coffee. "Of course you wouldn't have known about him, but Sean Graham was an institution around here. It was such a shock when he . . ." She pressed her lips together and didn't finish the sentence. We both had the same problem with finding the right words.

"I've never met anyone like Sean. He was good at everything. One of those boys in high school who was both the star quarterback and the lead in the spring musical. Basically the opposite of his brother."

I choked on a laugh. "Yeah. I don't see Simon on the football team."

"Definitely not." Her expression turned thoughtful. "I don't think Simon did any sports in school. He didn't crave the spotlight like Sean did. Sean loved the attention; he soaked it up like sunshine. And that boy could sell a cheeseburger to a vegan. He had a gift for getting people to do what he wanted." She shrugged. "Like dress up like Queen Elizabeth every summer."

"So this Faire wasn't your idea?"

She laughed. "Oh, no! That was all Sean. His high school class went to the Maryland Renaissance Festival on a school trip one October, and that was it. He had to put one together himself, even though he had no idea how to do it. He got the school on board by pitching it as a fund-raiser. No one could say no to him and he knew it. We had a couple summers on the football field until his ideas got too big for it. Then he talked someone into letting us use those woods, and it became what it is now. Even when he got sick, he was part of things, telling us all what to do, bossing his little brother around."

My mouth curved up at that; I couldn't imagine Simon being bossed around. But the picture of Sean started to come together in my head, and the saddest part stood out. "He was sick?"

She nodded. "Non-Hodgkin's lymphoma. Simon moved back home after Sean's diagnosis to help with things, and he hung on for a couple years. We were all sure he was going to beat it, and then . . ." Her light blue eyes shone with unshed tears. "That last summer, he was too sick to be part of things. Simon and I took over everything in the spring, though Sean still had some good ideas that we implemented. The joust was all his doing; he'd hired a touring company and planned out where the joust field would go. By that point, Simon and Mitch worked so well together that Sean talked them into putting together a full-on show, which became the human chess match. But by the time Faire opened that summer . . ." Her words thickened and she cleared her throat hard. "Simon shot some video with his phone. Showed it to Sean in the hospital. But three weeks into Faire he was gone."

"Right." I had to clear my throat too. "The date was on the plaque." I hadn't made the connection that Sean Graham had died while the Faire was underway. The more I heard, the more my heart ached for Simon, which was the last thing I wanted. Feeling sorry for him would lead to actually liking him, which might actually lead to being friends. No, thank you.

"We put that plaque up the last day of Faire. So he would always be a part of things. But over the winter, I started to think we should hang the whole thing up. I hadn't talked about it with Simon, and he was . . . well, he wasn't in any shape to talk about much of anything for the first few months. But you should have seen his face when I suggested we cancel Faire. He was determined to keep it going. I think working on it, all the organizing, helped him keep his mind on something else. And he's run it ever since. He loves it."

I nodded while I listened. But at the same time I thought about Simon, serious to the point of joylessness most of the time during rehearsals, then with red-rimmed eyes in the woods. Did he honestly love it? Or had it become an obligation? I knew a little something about taking on obligations, and how it was a great way to hide from things in my own life I didn't want to face. Could the same be true of Simon? What didn't he want to face? Maybe we had more in common than I thought.

Then again, Chris knew him better than I did. If she said he loved it, she was probably right. I was probably reading him all wrong.

"More coffee?" Chris moved behind the counter to the coffee-pot, and I pushed my mug toward her. I stretched a little; we'd been leaning on the counter at an awkward angle while we'd been talking. My back cracked when I stretched it. Wasn't I too young for that kind of thing?

I looked around while she poured the coffee. "You know, if you moved some of these shelves, you could fit in a few small tables. Maybe a comfy chair or two and turn it into a kind of gathering place." The more I talked, the more the idea of a little café in the back of this bookstore bloomed in my mind. Then I looked over at Chris, watching me with a smile, and my face flushed with embarrassment. It was her bookstore, not mine.

"When I first opened this place, everyone thought I was crazy. Small businesses don't last, and everyone buys their books on-line, right?" She gestured back to the front of the shop, where her laptop was set up. "But the great thing about small towns is people here want you to succeed. So I have enough loyal customers that they'll make the effort to order through me. I mean, I'm not retiring to Jamaica anytime soon, but I'm able to stay afloat.

"But a café . . ." She sighed. "After I got divorced, I decided to renovate my kitchen. New appliances, floors, granite counter-tops. But I ran out of steam before I got to the walls and the backsplash. The holidays were coming up, and I told myself once the new year came, I'd get back to work on it." She took a long sip of coffee. "That was almost four years ago, and I still don't have a backsplash."

My eyes widened. "That's a long time." I hated the idea of leaving things unfinished, but I had no room to criticize, given my academic background.

"This store is kind of the same." She put her mug down and leaned her elbows on the counter. "The bookstore side of things is doing great. But my original plans for this place were almost exactly what you described. I've got it all lined up: permits, food service license. This could be a coffee shop if I'd just get off my ass and do it. It always seemed like a lot to take on all by myself."

I tried to make my shrug casual, my voice unconcerned. "You wouldn't have to do it by yourself. You know, if you wanted help . . ."

"I'd love help." The front door chimed, and she turned her attention to the front of the shop. "Let's survive this first weekend of Faire, but why don't you come by on Monday. We can talk more about it then."

"Hello in there!" April's voice filtered back to me from the front door. "Anyone around?"

I grabbed for my phone in my back pocket. Had I missed her text? I was the worst sister ever. "I'm sorry!" I called. "I didn't hear my phone. Did you get a ride or . . ." But there weren't any texts. I hadn't missed anything.

I followed Chris to the front of the store, where April leaned against the counter, her face flushed and a little tight with discomfort, but mostly triumphant. I stopped short when I got a good look at her.

"Where the hell's your boot?"

"I don't need it anymore!" She swung her right leg to and fro, still clinging to the counter, like a ballerina at barre practice. "It feels amazing, Em! I can *walk* again!"

"So you walked *here?*" I was going to kill her. "What the hell's next, you doing a 5K this weekend?"

"Har." She pushed off the counter, and while she had a little bit of a limp, she was steadier than she'd been since . . . well, since the day I'd come to Willow Creek. "It was only half a block. I wanted to surprise you." Her face fell a little, the triumphant smile dimming under my scrutiny.

"You did." I rushed to her, not sure if I wanted to hug her or hold her up. I'd been holding her up for months now. It had become a habit. I settled for hugging this time. "You really did."

"So were you surprised?" April asked as we left the bookstore and started down the sidewalk to where my Jeep was parked.

"Of course I was. You scared the shit out of me."

"Good. That's what I was hoping for." Her voice was cheerful, but her smile was tight, and when I glanced at her I noticed her limp had become pronounced very quickly.

"Okay, you're trying too hard. Here—" I ushered her to a nearby bench and made her sit. "Stay there, I'll get the car."

"I'm sorry." She pressed her lips together hard; I could see white around them. "I thought I could make it."

"You could," I said. "And you did. It's just making it back that's the problem. Now wait here." I jogged down to get the Jeep and drove back to where she sat. I threw the Jeep into park and got out to help her in, but she waved me off.

"I can do it myself."

I recoiled a little at her snapping tone. "I know. I'm just—" But I stood aside and let her get in on her own. I bit back a sigh as I got behind the wheel, and we drove off in silence. Same as ever.

"Sorry," she finally said about halfway home. I glanced over in time to see her hunch forward, burying her face in her hands. Her dark brown curls cascaded around her head. "God, I can be a bitch, huh?"

"It's okay. You just overdid it. Don't worry. I won't tell your PT. Or your doctor."

"God, please don't. They'll make me put that damn boot back on." She was quiet for a moment, and I almost reached over to turn on the radio when she spoke again. "I've been meaning to thank you."

"For what?" I kept my eyes on the road. The air between us was too charged for me to look at her.

"For everything. Moving in, helping out. You've been here almost four months, and I haven't thanked you nearly enough. You dropped everything for Cait and me."

I shrugged. "There wasn't much to drop. Besides, that's what I do, isn't it? Drop everything. Help people. Fix things." My laugh was a little more bitter than I wanted it to be. "At least it was for family this time, instead of a guy."

"Hey." She reached out and laid her hand over mine on the gearshift. Squeezed a little, and I felt that squeeze in my heart. "What he did was shitty. An absolute douche move. That's not . . ." She blew out a breath. "You shouldn't be treated like that. Ever. Not by that dickhead you lived with, and not by me. I'm sorry."

"It's okay." It was a good thing we were almost home because I had to blink hard to see the road.

"It's not," she insisted. "You've done so much for us these past few months, and you don't know how much I appreciate it. And that's my fault." She waved off my protest before I could even voice it. "These appointments are kicking my ass, but I'm doing my best. The sooner I'm better and back to work, the sooner I can get my life back. And then maybe we can figure out yours."

"Trying to get rid of me, huh? I guess you want your guest room back." I was joking, but my stomach dropped as soon as the words came out of my mouth. Maybe she did want me gone. Wanted her life back. "I'll figure something out. I can probably get an apartment or something. I don't have much saved yet, but hopefully soon I can . . ."

"Are you kidding?" April cut through my babble. "Stay as long as you want."

I kept my eyes on the road. "You mean that?"

"Of course I do. You're here through the end of the summer with Faire anyway, right? And Cait loves having you around. There's no rush."

"Okay." I sighed and turned into our neighborhood. Not just April's neighborhood. Ours. I liked the sound of that. "Okay. You're right. Things are going to get pretty busy soon."

There was a pink balloon tied to the mailbox. I registered it out of the corner of my eye as I pulled into the driveway. I wanted to turn my head to look back at it, but I also didn't want to ram into the side of the house. "What the hell is that?"

"What is what?" April looked over her shoulder and shrugged. "Oh, probably something Caitlin's doing. Can you come help me out of the car?"

I narrowed my eyes as I walked around the front of the Jeep. She never needed help out, and if she did she never admitted it, even when she was back in her hard-cast-with-crutches days. But I forgot about the balloon as I helped April out and we hobbled up the front walk together.

"Okay," I said once I'd unlocked the door. "Let's get you inside and on the couch, and I'll get dinner started—what the hell?"

The dining room looked like it was on fire: all the lights were on, and multicolored, while flames blazed merrily. But then I realized the colors were from balloons tied to the chandelier over the dining room table. The flames were birthday candles on a cake sitting beside a pizza box. Dinner had been taken care of. And my birthday hadn't been forgotten. Next to a small pile of inexpertly wrapped gifts—probably by Caitlin—were a handful of birthday cards in colorful envelopes.

"Surprise!" Caitlin jumped out from the kitchen.

"Yeah, surprise." April wrapped an arm around my shoulders as I turned to her with wide eyes. She laughed at my stunned expression. "Did you really think we'd forget your birthday?"

"Well . . ." I opened my mouth, closed it again. "Yeah." I peered closer at the cards on the table. "That's from Mom. You stole my birthday card from Mom out of the mailbox?"

"It was part of the surprise!" Caitlin said.

April clucked her tongue. "Sorry. That was my idea. We didn't get you a lot for your birthday, so I wanted the table to look as full as possible."

I tried to glare at her, but it turned into a teary laugh instead as she pulled me into a hug. The second one that day. "Remember what I said about appreciating you? I meant it." While I was surprised at this new show of affection, I went with it. It felt nice. Like I had a real big sister.

"Come on, Em! Blow out the candles so we can eat!"

I laughed and dashed away the tears that had gathered in the corners of my eyes.

"Yes, ma'am." I bent over the small round cake, letting the flames dazzle my eyes as I contemplated a wish. I wanted a home. I wanted a place where I could build a life. And someday, I wanted someone who would love me. Not for what I could do for them, but for who I was to them. Seemed like a lot to wish for at once, but it was my birthday. Birthday wishes were allowed to be lofty. I blew out the candles and let those wishes fly away with the wisps of smoke. The ones that were meant to be would come back.

"Were you surprised?" Caitlin flipped open the pizza box and started tearing off slices, distributing them onto plates.

"I was." I took a bite of pizza. "Though the balloon on the mailbox made me wonder what was up."

April shook her head. "Yeah, maybe leave that off next time."

"Ugh." Caitlin gave a dramatic face-palm. "I was trying to be festive."

"You did a great job." I gestured around the room. "This is festive as hell."

"Oh, did you pick up my dress? For Faire?"

"Yes. Whoops, I left it in the back of the Jeep. You can go grab it after dinner. After you wash your hands." I looked pointedly at Caitlin, and she licked pizza sauce off her fingers and nudged her crust to the edge of her plate before grinning at me.

"I'm so excited! Faire is going to be so much fun."

"Are you two all ready for it?" April asked.

"Oh, yeah," I said. "Costumes are all set, accent's as good as it's going to get at this point." I reached for a second slice of pizza, because I had two more days until I was getting laced into a tight bodice. "Should be a fun rest of the summer."

I always had been good at understatements.

Seven

Saturday morning in mid-July. Opening day of the Willow Creek Renaissance Faire. Caitlin and I were ready. We weren't fully awake, but we were ready.

We hit the road at oh-dark-thirty while I sipped my second cup of coffee from my travel mug. I was dressed in the absolute minimum—my loose chemise/nightgown and a pair of spandex shorts—while Cait sat bleary-eyed in the back. Her costume rode shotgun next to me in a garment bag, in an effort to keep it wrinkle free for as long as possible.

I felt more human once I pulled into the field designated as cast parking and grabbed the wicker basket containing the rest of my costume. Cait trooped behind me like a sleepy kitten, but the morning air was good for the both of us. I wasn't scared of these woods any longer, and by the time we got to the Hollow, that backstage cast area set at the bottom of some hills, my coffee had kicked in and Cait had run ahead to meet her friends. Pretty much back to normal.

I let her go—she had all her stuff, and could get dressed on her own time—and started getting ready myself. Since I'd driven there wearing basically my Renaissance faire undies, I dumped the rest of my outfit on an outdoor table and started covering myself in the layers that composed my wench costume.

Hose first—basically long socks that went up over my knees. I pulled the blue skirt on over my head and swam through the fabric until I got it settled around my waist. I tugged the white underdress down, then put on my boots. Boots first, then corset—that was the most basic costuming rule for a Renaissance faire player. All that was left was the bodice. I set it aside: not yet. Instead, I opened up my compact and did a quick eyeliner job, followed by a berry-colored lip stain—a natural enough shade even Simon couldn't argue with. While I tugged my hair back into an artfully artless knot, I watched the sun come up through the trees around us and soaked in the sounds of teenage chatter around me. At the next table, Chris sat patiently while the head dancer braided her hair into an elaborate, queen-appropriate coif. She winked at me and waved hello, careful not to move her head too much.

I spent so much time on my hair that I still hadn't put on my bodice when the morning's briefing started. Like we had during the rehearsal process, we took attendance every morning and had a quick meeting. Last-minute instructions, schedule changes, that kind of thing. I looked around while lacing Stacey into her corset and wow, we looked like a professional operation. Costumes were all on point, down to hairstyles and hats. People I didn't know lingered on the edge of the meeting, but since no one else seemed alarmed I decided not to be, either. They must be the talent. Musicians and other touring acts had been booked by the Faire (well, by Simon and Chris) to play with us and for us for the next few weeks. Most stayed only a weekend or two at a time, so the briefings would also let us know who was playing at what stages.

This kind of information was lost on me, so I listened with one ear while I tucked the blue skirt up in front and secured it with pins. Then I tugged down my chemise and tugged up my breasts while Stacey finished tightening me in. As the meeting broke up, I stashed my empty coffee mug in the bottom of my wicker basket and covered it with a tartan scarf I'd borrowed from April. Together, Stacey and I started up the hill away from the Hollow and toward the grounds themselves. Some of the kids ran ahead of us, swirls of color and skirts and hats with feathers in them.

Stacey sighed, a wistful sound. "I remember being young and having that much energy."

"Come on, Grandma." I elbowed her in the side, which she probably couldn't feel through her corset. "You're the same age as I am, right?"

"Twenty-six in October. But this early in the morning? I feel about a hundred and four."

I couldn't argue with that.

We were almost to the top of the hill when an outburst of male laughter from behind us startled me. I looked over my shoulder and spotted a group of pirates about halfway down the hill, huddled together as they walked, sharing a joke of some kind. One of them had his back to us, walking backward up the hill, telling a story I couldn't hear but that made the other guys laugh uproariously.

Walking backward. Up the hill. Did I mention he was wearing leather pants?

I couldn't tell who the pirate was from the back. He was

dressed all in black, with a hat with a large red feather. The hat looked familiar. While half of my brain melted at the sight of what a pair of leather pants did to a man's ass while he walked backward up a hill, the other half wondered who the hell he was. I'd spent two months of weekends with these people, and knew most of them well enough to stop and chat at the grocery store if we ran into each other. I thought I was becoming part of this community, but if that was true then why didn't I recognize this guy?

Then Leather Pants turned around and our gazes collided. The smile on his face slipped a fraction, and I almost swallowed my tongue.

Leather Pants, whose ass I'd just been ogling, was Simon Fucking Graham.

Life wasn't fair sometimes.

He didn't look like himself at all. Was it because he was smiling? The only other time I'd seen him smile—like, a full-on, with-teeth-and-everything smile—had been an accident too. Those smiles were never meant for me.

But now, he held my gaze in a way he never had before, and his faltering smile rallied into a broad grin. He nodded in my direction, touching his fingertips to that ridiculous hat in a kind of salute. Not only was he not avoiding me, he was flirting with me!

Well. This was new. I whipped my head around again, breaking eye contact. But it was too late. The image of him was already seared in my brain.

And what an image. Black, billowy shirt open about halfway down his chest, bracketed by a deep red vest the color of blood, showcasing a sprinkling of dark hair across an unexpectedly defined chest. Now his longer hair made sense; his former shorter cut would have been completely hidden under his hat.

Oh, no. The Ren Faire Killjoy was *hot*. Even his stupid hat couldn't dim the wattage of his smile, and my heart still pounded in reaction to the sight of him.

"Jesus." I'd meant to mutter the word under my breath, but it came out as more of a wheeze, and Stacey turned to me.

"You okay?"

"Yeah. Just . . . Simon is a *pirate?*"

She glanced back over her shoulder at the pirates behind us and grinned, nodding a hello in their direction. "Oh, yeah. Captain Ian Blackthorne. He's been a pirate since the early days. Him and his brother, Sean." Her grin transferred to me. "I forgot you haven't seen him in costume yet. He said he was a pirate, don't you remember?"

I searched my memory. I really didn't. But I hadn't cared much about details, least of all related to Simon, those first few weeks. He could have said he was playing a dragon and I wouldn't have given a shit.

But now . . . All this time I'd been wondering why Simon did Faire every year if it was so stressful. I was pretty sure I had my answer. He'd slid into this new identity like a second skin and he wore it now with ease. It wasn't just about carrying on his brother's legacy. It was because for a few weeks every summer, he could put on that getup and become someone completely different. Someone who didn't have to worry about summer reading lists or losing a brother to cancer.

I looked over my shoulder again. Yep. Still hot. He was talking to the pirate next to him, but looked up as though he could feel my eyes on him. The flirty grin came again to his mouth as though he wore it every day. His smile sent a tingle across my skin, and to my surprise and horror I felt an answering smile come to my own face. I couldn't help it. His eyes flared in response, and his grin widened, all straight white teeth.

I took a shuddering breath as I faced forward again, stunned by this new realization. Emma the Tavern Wench was turned on by Captain Blackthorne, Pirate.

This could be a problem.

"Well met, ladies."

My attention snapped forward again at the sound of the deep voice in front of us, and a smile broke across my face. This smile made a lot more sense.

Mitch Malone stood at the very top of the hill, in the middle of the lane, backlit by the morning sun. Knowing him, he probably consulted the *Farmers' Almanac* to determine the exact place to stand so the sun would halo his head, making him look like a golden god. In his kilt, boots, and sporran, shirtless, with his hands on his hips, he should be obnoxious as hell. But I'd grown used to smiling at Mitch. Just as I'd grown used to Mitch and his insanely ripped physique. Gorgeous as it was, it didn't thrill me anymore. I wanted to turn around and look at Simon again. The leather, the open shirt . . . now, that was a revelation.

But I kept my eyes forward, and my mind on task.

"Well met, good sir!" I dropped into a short curtsy as Mitch stepped forward to offer me a hand as I rose again. For all his obnoxiousness, when Mitch turned his attention to you it was like getting the full force of the sun. I was going to need a stronger SPF if I was going to make it through August.

"Good morrow, ladies." He tucked my hand in the crook of his elbow and offered his other arm to Stacey. Could a girl ask for a better escort on the first morning of Faire?

When we stepped onto the main lane, my jaw dropped. We'd

spent the past two Saturdays in what was basically an empty forest. I'd helped place what felt like ten thousand benches at each of the performance spaces, but the stages had still looked desolate, like something you'd stumble across in . . . well, a deserted forest.

But now . . . now I stood in an Elizabethan village. Or a reasonable facsimile thereof. Brightly colored flags hung from poles at certain intervals along the lane, and there was activity everywhere. The lanes were lined with stalls, and merchants in period dress set out their wares for the day. Leather goods in one stall, hammered silver jewelry in another. My steps slowed as I found myself window-shopping while we walked. One large stall had outfits, and I practically drooled over an intricately embroidered corset, even though my wench's mind dismissed it as far too elaborate, given my status.

We passed one of the performance spaces, where musicians lounged center stage, acoustic instruments at their side. If I squinted and knew where to look, I could spot the sound equipment, discreetly placed to the sides of the stage and covered with fabric. But most of the musicians didn't need amplification. The stages were rather intimate, after all, and sound carried out here in the forest.

Then we made it to our tavern, and I couldn't keep the grin off my face. Our blank clearing had been utterly transformed. Colored banners wove through the trees to form a kind of canopy above our heads, making it easy to spot. We had a real canopy as well: an open-sided tent, which gave the tavern an actual roof, and under the tent was the bar itself, with a few tables and benches scattered in front of it. It was weird to see a bar in the middle of the woods—the right thing in the wrong place, like seeing your teacher at the grocery store. As we approached I could see it was an actual, proper bar, with a particleboard surface and tip jars already placed. Behind the bar was a cooler that housed the beer kegs. The taps were already hooked up, judging from the red-shirted volunteer who stood behind it, a plastic cup half-filled with a dark beer in his hand.

"Jamie!" Stacey broke away from Mitch and me and hurried to embrace the volunteer. Her exuberance knocked his baseball cap askew and he laughed as he straightened it. "Emily, this is Jamie. He's one of our best volunteers. I'm so glad you're here again this year!" She punched him in the arm. "The man actually knows how to pour from the tap, unlike some of the volunteers we get."

He shrugged. "That's why they keep putting me here, I guess."

"Jamie, this is Emily. She's our other wench this year, and she's new, so be nice."

"I'm always nice." He extended his hand across the bar and I shook it. His eyes didn't immediately drop to my cleavage, so he went up a little in my estimation. "Great to meet you, Emily. What's your Faire name, so I know what to call you?"

"Emma." I bit down on the inside of my cheek, waiting for the usual *boy, you didn't think too hard about that one* response, but to my surprise all he did was nod.

"Emma," he repeated. "Well, the setup's pretty simple. We've got coolers at each end of the bar with the bottled drinks. Openers here by the cashbox. I'll pull the beers from the tap while you serve the customers who want the bottled stuff or wine. Oh, and there are coolers under the bar here with water. It gets crazy hot later in the day, so you'll want to hand those out to cast members or volunteers who come by." Jamie nodded behind me to Mitch. "Marcus, good to see you, sir." His Scottish accent was terrible, and his smile said that he knew it.

"Oh, aye, and you, sir." Mitch's accent was much better. In an instant, the good-natured jock had transformed from a dude in a kilt into Marcus MacGregor, Scotsman. So many sudden changes today.

"Want a beer? We have some this year."

Mitch/Marcus laughed and Stacey joined in, but I looked at the three of them in confusion. "Okay, I'm missing the joke." I hated that I was missing the joke. At what point would I truly be a part of this place?

"It's something we say every year now," Stacey said. "Ever since . . ."

"Ever since Sean forgot to pick up the beer for Faire one year, so we had taverns with no beer in them." Mitch finished the story for her.

I blinked. "He forgot the beer? How did he . . . What the hell did you do?"

"We closed all the taverns but this one," Jamie said. "Then we all went and bought a few cases of beer each—those of us who were old enough, anyway. That's why there's only one tavern now."

"Believe me, it was a mistake he only made once," Mitch said.

Jamie scoffed. "Oh, he made plenty of others."

The three of them laughed again, but I still felt a little left out of the joke. Not for the first time, I wished I'd known Sean, just so I could really understand what the fuss was about. He must have been charismatic as hell. There was no way Simon would forget to order beer for the tavern. I couldn't imagine Simon forgetting a thing. The man probably made lists in his sleep.

"So." Jamie raised his plastic cup in Mitch's direction. "Too early for a beer?"

"Never too early, but I have two fights today, I should keep me wits about me." He unsnapped a pewter tankard from the belt around his waist and pushed it across the bar toward Jamie. "I'll take some water, though, if you don't mind."

Jamie filled the tankard, then pushed it across the bar to Mitch. He took it, saluted us, and sauntered away. I'd like to say I didn't watch him walk away, but that would be a terrible lie. I had no idea backs even had that many muscles.

"So." Stacey waved me to join her behind the bar. "Here's where we live for the next six weekends. What do you think?"

I looked around from the canopy banners waving in the light breeze to the tables that would soon be filled with customers to the hip-height boxes filled with ice and chilled beverages. "I love it." I'd never meant something so much in my life. After all, I'd tended bar before. I'd waited tables. But doing it in the fresh air, with the sights and sounds of a Renaissance faire coming to life around us? This was going to be fun.

Several hours later, I revised my definition of "fun."

It had started slowly. The gate opened at ten in the morning, and not a lot of people immediately sprinted to the bar to start drinking that early. There were a few, of course, mostly dads who looked like they could use a beer already as they herded little girls in princess dresses. But for the first hour or so I looked around, feeling a little awkward. Maybe people didn't drink much at these things? Maybe it was more about the music and the atmosphere, and getting that turkey leg or funnel cake?

But as the hour crept toward noon, the crowds picked up, and things got chaotic. Time passed in a blur of popping bottle caps. Of making change. Of grabbing a rag and wiping the bar down as it got wet from the bottles being hauled out of the cooler. I poured wine. I called orders to Jamie, who pulled beers at record speed. Somewhere in there, a band at a nearby stage started playing, guitar and fiddle and hand drums with a rhythm that echoed with a thud in my chest. The sound filtered toward us through the trees, not enough to hum along with a melody, but enough to serve as background music to my day.

Across from the tavern a crowd had started to gather on the benches lining the perimeter of a nearby field. I peered in that direction and could barely make out one of our cast standing in the middle, saying something to the patrons, but I was too far away to make out the words. I nudged Stacey.

"Beatrice, darling, what's over there?" I had to admit, my accent was pretty damn good.

She followed my pointing finger, squinting like I did. "That's the human chess match. Remember? We watched them rehearse."

"Oh, the fighting?" I remembered now. The sword fighting that became fisticuffs. Simon flipping Mitch over his shoulder. Mitch winning the fight. The moment I'd first caught the full force of Simon's smile.

"The fighting." She nodded in confirmation. "There are two different matches today. We should try to watch one of them."

I turned to her in confusion. She had to be kidding. "When on earth will we have time?"

"It slows down at certain times of the day, believe me." She patted my arm. "We won't be far off. If Jamie starts drowning in patrons we can come running back."

"Yeah," Jamie chimed in. His regular voice with its modern American accent suddenly sounded weird and flat against our faux-English lilts. "This isn't my first rodeo. Since you're new to all of this, you should definitely check out some of the shows when we slow down."

After a little while, I started to see what they meant. People showed up to the tavern in waves. As shows finished, crowds would filter away from the stage area and flow our way. The main appeal seemed to be that they could take a drink to go, and wander the lanes with a beer in hand.

As one of those waves finally thinned out, I caught a flash of pink brocade out of the corner of my eye.

"Milady!" I bobbed a quick curtsy to my niece, then bent to grab a bottle of water from the cooler. Her cheeks were flushed—I didn't want her getting overheated and keeling over on my watch. April would kill me.

She took the water gratefully and poured it into the glass bottle I'd gotten her for this very purpose. "I'm supposed to get you, actually."

"Me? What on earth for?"

Cait nodded vigorously. Not something a well-bred Elizabethan lady would do. Ah, well, it was still the first day; she'd get used to it. "We need you at the jousting field."

"Uh." I looked in that direction, as though I could see that far. "Why? I know nothing about jousting." If someone wanted me to get on a horse I was out of here. "My assigned place is here. You're the one who's supposed to float around."

"I dunno. They just said I should come get you." She came around the bar then and grabbed my arm.

"Okay. This isn't period at all." I dropped the accent as I pulled myself free.

"Come on! They're waiting."

I glanced over my shoulder at Jamie, who shrugged. "Go ahead," he said. "I've got it here. Stacey will be back from the bathroom soon; she can help me when the show gets out."

I hated abandoning my post, but Caitlin looked like she was going to pop a blood vessel from stress, so I followed her out of the tavern. We tripped our way down the main lane that wound through the trees and led to the jousting field. In the distance cheers rang out for the knights on horseback, loud and sustained. "What are we doing? It sounds like the joust is almost over." My heart pounded from our sprint across the grounds and a slight lack of oxygen.

"Yes, but the handfasting is next. And they don't have enough people, so . . ."

I stumbled over a root and barely managed to recover before I fell on my ass. "Handfasting?" I yanked my skirt up so I wouldn't trip over it. "I don't know anything about the handfasting ceremony. I didn't rehearse it." How could we be short on people? Everyone was at the morning briefing in the Hollow.

The handfasting was a cute little ceremony for the patrons, which took place after the joust. Couples signed up ahead of time to pledge themselves to each other for a year and a day. Flowery words were spoken, and a golden cord bound their hands together. I was told it was a popular attraction, especially for older couples who wanted to feel young again. But my place was at the tavern, on the other side of the grounds. This was something for the ladies-in-waiting, and other people in the prettier costumes. Not a tavern wench who probably smelled like beer.

We arrived at the clearing to the left of the jousting field. The joust had just ended, and patrons filtered out around us. As we got closer to where the handfasting took place I realized I'd misunderstood Caitlin. We weren't short on cast members to perform the ceremony. We were short on actual participants. Two couples, in shorts and T-shirts, stood among the cast, looking as awkward as they probably felt, wondering what they had gotten themselves into.

"Aye." Now that we were among others, Cait slid into her accent again. But she pitched her voice low. "It's only the first day, they said, so we have very few takers for the ceremony. But we could use the practice, so I was sent to get you, and some others are coming too."

"For what, an arranged handfasting? Who am I being married off to, then?" I cast my eyes around the field, trying to see who my intended was going to be. Mitch was there—I spotted his kilt right away—but one of the maids to the Queen was already giggling on his arm, so I guessed he wasn't for me. Dammit. So then who . . .

Then Chris the Queen and her gigantic dress moved about three feet to the left, and I stopped in my tracks.

"No."

Cait rolled her eyes. So much for staying in character. "God, I knew you'd react this way. Come on." She pulled on my arm, but I wasn't moving.

"You couldn't have said this from the start?" I yanked out of her grasp and crossed my arms across my chest.

She made a disgusted noise in the back of her throat and tugged at my elbow, and I allowed myself to be pulled forward. It was either that or make a scene, and as annoyed as I was, I wasn't going to do that.

Then a voice called out. A merry, jovial voice I wasn't used to, because I was used to nothing but criticism from him.

"Is this the wench you have brought me?"

Oh, Jesus Christ.

Eight

There stood Simon in full pirate regalia. But I couldn't call him Simon, of course. No one took this Faire more seriously than he did, so God forbid I fuck it up for him. Captain Ian Blackthorne. Pirate.

I was still getting used to this abrupt shift in Simon's character. He wasn't giving me his usual glare, or waiting to pounce and criticize me for something I'd done wrong. Instead he wore his Hot Pirate smile, which both dazzled me and propelled me forward. I remembered my etiquette just in time; pirates were roughly the same place in the hierarchy as tavern wenches, but women still gave deference. So I stopped in front of him and dropped into a practiced curtsy. I kept my eyes aimed at the ground, and the silver buckles on his boots winked at me as he stepped closer.

His outstretched hand appeared before my downcast eyes, and I looked up as he bowed slightly before me, as if we were in a dance. I rested my hand in his as I rose back to my feet. But he didn't let go. Instead, he held my gaze and brushed his lips across the back of my hand. I felt the contact as a jolt through my entire body, and every instinct told me to snatch my hand back. But I kept my composure; I hadn't taken three semesters of theatre courses for nothing. I could stay in character, even when noticing that this close, Simon's brown eyes were actually hazel; there were flecks of gold and green in them I had never noticed before.

"Captain Blackthorne." I quirked my lips in a smile that told him I'd play along, but I wouldn't make this easy on him. "I was told you sent for me? What is your will?"

Simon—no, in my mind now he was Captain Blackthorne, because Simon never looked this cheerful or laughed this easily— let my hand fall from his grasp and chucked me under the chin. If he'd tried that move at a bar, he would have earned a slap in about two seconds. But out here, with the sunlight filtering through the trees, I wasn't looking at the guy who had been a pain in my ass since the middle of May. Out here, I was looking at a pirate, all black leather and open shirt, with kohl smeared around his eyes, giving them a hooded bedroom look. Out here, the sun threw those glints of red in his brown hair, which matched the closely trimmed beard. To my utter shock, that same sun glanced off a silver hoop dangling from one ear.

This pirate was doing things to me I didn't want to admit to anyone. Least of all him. Or me.

At that point the Queen spoke, and we all fell in line. Ladies-in-waiting bustled around those of us who were being hand-fasted. With the two sets of patrons, Mitch and his girl, and Simon and me, we made four couples. I could see now it looked better to have cast members playing along, so the patrons wouldn't feel awkward or singled out. We made a comfortable crowd this way.

One of the ladies-in-waiting took my hand and put it in Simon's. His hand closed around mine, warm and dry despite the heat of midsummer. I'd held hands with my share of guys over the years; this certainly wasn't a new experience. But this was the first time I'd felt this: a sense of peace. Of protectiveness. The sense that this was the guy, and he was going to take care of me.

Take care of me? What century was my mind in, anyway? Maybe I was getting a little too into character.

"Groom and Bride," the Queen began, and my eyes widened. I hadn't heard Chris speak yet in character, and it was astounding. Her voice was deep and commanding. This was not a woman to laugh and share coffee with you. "I bid you look into each other's eyes." Her gaze flicked to each of us four couples in turn, to make sure we followed her command. "Will you honor and respect one another and seek to never break that honor?"

I looked up at my fake betrothed with what had to be horror. It was probably being called a bride and groom that did it, but this was all sounding far too real. Too official. But he stayed in character, regarding me with an affectionate smile as though we'd known each other for years. In the silence that followed, I realized we were supposed to speak.

"Aye." My voice came out scratchy, thick. I cleared my throat and tried again. "Aye." It was an easy thing to promise, after all. I may not like the guy much, but honor and respect? I could give him that. I knew how important this Faire was to him, and even though he got on my nerves I certainly didn't want to do anything to make his life harder.

"Aye." His response was firm, casual, almost amused. Did pirates honor and respect anyone but themselves? Gold, maybe? Rum? I made a mental note to ask him later.

"And so the first binding is made." The lady-in-waiting in front of each of us couples wound a golden cord around our joined hands, tying them together loosely. I could pull my hand out of his easily and break the connection. I should want to do that. But I didn't move.

"Will you share each other's pain, and seek to ease it?"

"Ummm." I glanced up at him again, but he immediately answered with a firm "aye," and so I did the same. Again, this wasn't such a terrible thing to promise, was it? That was a normal thing any nice person would do. Share pain, seek to ease it. I thought about the day I'd run into Simon here in the woods, the pain on his face. The memorial to his brother. I hadn't talked to him about that, told him Chris had filled me in a little on his past. Maybe I should.

"And so the second binding is made." Another loop around our hands, and he tightened his hand a little around mine. I squeezed back, but I had no idea why. In this moment, I felt closer to this guy dressed as a pirate than I'd ever felt to Jake. And I'd dropped out of college for Jake. I'd worked two jobs while Jake went to law school.

"Will you share the burdens of each, so your spirits may grow in this union?"

Sure, my smart-assed self wanted to respond. *Why not.* But it was a defense mechanism. This was getting more personal now. I couldn't laugh this off as something I'd promise any guy on the street. Now our union was being brought into this. My union. With a guy wearing leather pants who I barely knew and didn't really like. But he agreed with an "aye," his voice solid and sure, and what kind of asshole would I be if I didn't do the same?

"And so the third binding is made." Another loop. We were

well and truly bound together now, the gold cord practically covering our hands up to our wrists. Pulling away from him would prove difficult, so I didn't even consider it. Worse, I didn't want to consider it.

"Bride and Groom, as your hands are bound together now"—the Queen took her time and looked at each of us joined couples—"so your lives and spirits are joined in a union of love and trust." Mitch smirked and his girl barely stifled a giggle; I kind of wanted to kick them for not taking this seriously.

"Above you are the stars and below you is the earth." The two sets of plain-dressed patrons in between us only had eyes for each other, and when I looked at them I could see how affecting this ceremony could be for people who were deeply in love. Were they remembering their own weddings? Were these vows a reaffirmation?

"Like the stars, your love should be a constant source of light, and like the earth, a firm foundation from which to grow."

Then there was Simon and me. Captain Ian Blackthorne the pirate and Emma the tavern wench. The words were beautiful, but man, were they wasted on us.

"You are hereby bound for a year and a day," the Queen proclaimed. "At the end of this time, should you wish to remain so bound, you must appear before me and state your intention to remain so. Otherwise, at the end of that time you may go your separate ways."

In character, I nodded solemnly at this, but I also wondered how we—or any of the patrons—were going to be held to this. Were we supposed to mark a calendar? Buy a ticket for next year and hope Chris was playing the Queen again?

I was probably overthinking it. This was a fun tourist activity that resulted in a souvenir golden cord and nothing more. But

I'd never been bound to someone, even temporarily, and by royalty no less. This whole ceremony was messing with my head. But that was nothing compared to what came next.

As the ladies-in-waiting burst into delighted applause, my traitorous niece among them, the patrons directly to our right sealed the bargain with a sweet kiss. I grinned at the display of love between the middle-aged couple, a reminder that love was real, and it really did last for some people. Then the other pair of patrons got in on the act, followed by Mitch, who dipped his lady in a deep, probably not period-appropriate clinch, which they played for laughs. It was all very cute and very funny, till I realized Simon was about to kiss me and my heart dropped to my knees.

My gaze flew up to his, and seriously, when did he get those flecks of green in his eyes? His bound hand tightened on mine a little before he pulled me closer, his other hand coming up to cup my cheek. He barely touched my skin, but I repressed a shiver anyway. One eyebrow arched in a challenge as he bent toward me. Daring me to deny him, to break character and not let him kiss me.

Well, screw that. I made my eyes as limpid as I could while I gazed up at him, imagining how a tavern wench would feel bound to a pirate who looked like this. Pretty damn good, I'd imagine. I put some extra flutter in my eyelashes as I let my eyes fall closed a moment before his mouth touched mine. His kiss was firm but gentle; he didn't try to sneak in some tongue or force a passionate response. It was a brush of lips, followed by a settling of his mouth on mine. A perfect staged kiss.

So there was absolutely no reason for my heart to be thudding in my chest like that. There was no call for my senses to be filled with him, with the scent of leather and warm skin, the gentle rasp of his beard against my cheek and his fingertips skimming my jaw.

The kiss ended sooner than I wanted it to, though I'd never admit it out loud. My eyes slowly opened as his lips left mine, and for a moment nothing existed but his eyes gazing down into mine, brown and green and gold and what was happening here? For a split second he looked as rattled as I felt, but then he slid into character again, and his easy grin was back. With one last squeeze on my hand he disengaged; as we pulled our hands apart, the golden cord loosened and allowed the separation. I caught the cord before it could fall to the ground and wound it between my fingers. I already missed the heat of Simon's skin and cursed myself for it.

He turned to the people around us and acknowledged their cheers with another grin. I managed a shaky smile while I told my heart to stop pounding. I was also acutely aware of how long I'd been gone. I needed to get back to the tavern. I never should have left it in the first place.

I cut across the empty chess field on the way back, since the first match wasn't for another half hour. I was about halfway across when I got a good look. I couldn't even see Jamie in the throng of people under our little tent. Shit. I grabbed the front of my skirts and sprinted the rest of the way.

"Sorry, I'm so sorry!" As flustered as I was, I remembered to slip back into my accent and jump right into serving people, instead of my first instinct, to start swearing a blue streak.

"Hand me the chardonnay. Where were you?" To her credit, Stacey's question was just that; there wasn't a hint of accusation for me abandoning my post for what had to have been a good fifteen or twenty minutes.

I plucked the cold bottle of white wine from its bed of ice to my left and handed it down the bar to her. "Sorry." Ugh, that was three times now I'd apologized in the space of about thirty seconds. "I'll tell you later, I promise." It was far too busy for any kind of storytelling, and this one was a doozy. I could catch her up when the crowd thinned out.

Except it never did. The afternoon passed in a blur of serving drinks and counting cash and keeping a smile plastered on my face. Whenever we thought there was a break in the action, another show would let out and more people would stream over to the tavern. When I had a spare moment I scooped up my glass water bottle and took a good swig, wishing the clear liquid were vodka instead. I marked the passage of time by the show on the stage behind us, the hand drums thudding through my consciousness. At one point, I glanced across to where the human chess match was going on. I saw Simon in a flash of black and red, Mitch in a blur of green tartan. I heard the cheers of huzzah! from my vantage point.

Eventually, the crowd of drinking patrons slowed to a trickle, and I had never been so glad to see the end of a day in my life. I waved an exhausted goodbye, scooped up my basket, and stumbled back across the grounds and down the hill to the Hollow, searching for Caitlin. By the time I got there she had struggled halfway out of her outer dress, and I helped her peel the rest of it off. She unlaced my bodice and I took my first good deep breath since sunrise. Too tired to speak, we trudged to the parking lot and practically fell into the Jeep.

"Only five and a half weekends to go!" I forced cheer into my voice as I turned onto the road and toward home. Caitlin groaned a response from the back seat, and I couldn't blame her. How much was it going to hurt to walk when we got home? Were foot transplants an option?

After a long shower—amazing how much dirt was accumulated after a day spent outside, not to mention all the weird places you found said dirt—and a huge dinner, I dumped my basket out on the bed to set out my costume and accessories for the next morning. A long golden cord tumbled out with April's tartan scarf, and I wound the cord around my fingers. My mind was full of the memory of Simon's hand warm around mine, and how surprisingly soft his lips had been. I pushed those thoughts away, but then I remembered I had never told Stacey about my adventures in handfasting. Maybe she'd forget to ask about it.

I *should have known* better. Stacey didn't forget a thing.

"So what happened yesterday?" She glanced over at me as she opened a new bottle of white wine.

"Pardon?" I brushed my hands on my overskirt, which looked a little grubby on its second day of wear. I had a clean chemise for each day, but the outer parts of my costume had to last the weekend.

"Yesterday," she said patiently. "When you ran off, remember? Where did you go?"

"Oh, that." I sighed. "I had to go to the joust field and be married off."

"What?" Her laugh was a loud shock of sound, and the middle-aged patron she was pouring the wine for raised her eyebrows.

"I'm going to need to hear about this," the woman said as she slid the cash for her wine across the bar.

I shook my head and opened bottles of import beer for Jamie while he poured drafts for me. For the next few minutes the three of us worked hard serving everyone who had come out of the Celtic folk-singing show behind us. Once the rush was over, I grabbed a clean bar rag and wiped up the puddles on the bar.

"Don't think I'm going to let you forget." Stacey plunked the wine bottles back on ice and started taking note of any beers or ciders that needed restocking.

"Forget what?" I blinked innocently.

"The married thing," the wine drinker from earlier piped up from the other side of the bar. She had been sipping on her chardonnay the whole time we were working. "I mean, I know there's lots of authentic things going on at this Faire, but getting married off seems a little much."

"Exactly!" Stacey said triumphantly. "This is the Renaissance, darling. Not the dark ages. And it's not as though you have a vast fortune for a man to want to get his hands on. No offense."

"None taken." I loved that without even trying we were perfectly in character in this moment, gossiping in our accents, sounding like true barmaids. "All right, perhaps I exaggerated a little." But another group of patrons came in and I became too occupied serving them to finish my story. And another group after that. Now that afternoon had hit, we were going to be as busy today as we'd been the day before. Which was great, when it came to the bottom line and the whole fund-raising aspect of things.

Across the way the human chess match had begun its first performance of the day. The sounds of fighting and cheering filtered their way to us in our tavern. I had to admit there was part of me that had started to grow a little jealous of those ladies-in-waiting I'd been with during the handfasting, even my own niece. They all got to be part of Faire, to walk the grounds. They could watch the human chess match or listen to the Celtic folk singers. They got to interact with the patrons in a more meaningful way than handing them a drink and collecting their cash. Stacey had said this was a fun gig. Were we going to get any share of that fun? I couldn't imagine getting any less busy as the summer wore on.

About fifteen minutes later we hit another lull, and Stacey had run out of patience. "Finish your story!"

I traded an opened beer to a patron for a five-dollar bill and smiled my thanks before dropping it into the till. "There isn't much to tell." I turned my back to the bar and leaned my elbows on it. The stretch to my back felt good. "The wee Lady Guenevere was sent to fetch me to the handfasting ceremony, where I was promptly wed to a pirate." I narrowed my eyes at her, showing just what I thought of the pirate in question.

"Now, that's an exaggeration." I jumped at the voice behind me and whirled. Simon. No. The accent, the swagger, the cheerful expression. Captain Blackthorne had entered our tavern.

"Captain." I bobbed a quick in-character curtsy, and out of the corner of my eye I saw Stacey do the same. But as I reached my full height again I raised my eyebrows at him. "How do I exaggerate, milord?"

"We are not wed, we are simply pledged. For a year and a day, remember?" He nodded toward the golden cord, which I had found in my basket that morning. I wore it wrapped around my bodice like a belt and the ends dangled down among my skirts.

"Yes, of course." But I wasn't letting him off that easy. "And what is the difference?" It was so easy to slide into the bantery conversation with Simon-as-pirate, more than it ever was to talk to him when he was himself. I was even enjoying myself.

"The difference?" His smile widened; I'd said something either very, very wrong or very, very right, and he couldn't wait to take advantage of it. "Well, the difference is . . ." He shrugged, but the wicked grin remained intact. "I'm not sure I can say. This is a family-friendly Faire, after all."

I crossed my arms over my chest. Usually this would all but hide my inadequate cleavage, but in this outfit it highlighted it instead. I thought about dropping my arms, but screw it. Let him look. "This is a tavern," I reminded him. "Nothing family-friendly here."

To my horror, he took the dare. "Well, then . . ." He leaned his elbows on the bar, encroaching on my space. Patrons entered the tavern around us, and thankfully, Stacey and Jamie were able to catch them because neither Simon nor I was paying attention. For me, the world had narrowed to this black-clad man in front of me, and the impossible colors that sparkled in his eyes. "If we were wed, when night fell I would take you back to my ship, give the men a week of shore leave, and show you my appreciation very thoroughly, and in private. As it is, we are only pledged, and so I will show you my appreciation thus." He reached across the bar for my hand, and for some reason I gave it. Never breaking his gaze from mine, he bent over my hand and his mouth lingered this time, much longer than it had when we had been performing in front of the crowd. This kiss on the back of my hand was intimate, and his eyes promised even more.

This was all fake. I knew that. He wasn't a pirate. There was no ship to take me back to. He was a high school English teacher in a costume, and I was the snarky thorn in his side. He was probably doing all of this to make me uncomfortable so I would tell him to knock it off. Then he could later reprimand me for breaking character. Instead fire pooled low in my belly and my mind filled with the image of us in the moonlight on the deck of a pirate ship. The creaking of the wood, the breeze off the water. His hand touching my face, the warmth of his skin against mine.

"Emma?" Stacey's voice startled me, and with a blink I was back in the tavern. Which was full of patrons and a concerned-looking fellow wench. Shit.

I snatched my hand from Simon's grasp, and he started a little in confusion. Had he been on that pirate ship with me? "Excuse me, *Captain.*" My snippy tone covered up the mix of confusion, guilt, and arousal swirling inside me. "Some of us have work to do. I don't have time to play."

His face darkened as he took in the scene: a line of people waiting to buy drinks, and only three people to sell them. "Indeed." He doffed his stupid hat and his bow encompassed the room. "Ladies. Gentlemen. Enjoy the day." He sauntered out of the tavern, and I turned to the next waiting patron with a smile that shook only a little.

And the patrons kept on coming. I had originally thought people would cool it a little on the alcohol consumption on a Sunday afternoon, but apparently all bets were off when you were at a Renaissance faire. The familiar ache in my feet from the day before came back with a vengeance, and I longed for a break so I could snag a stool and sit down. Instead I opened cases of bottled beer while Jamie changed out a keg and Stacey handled cash. The three of us had become a well-oiled machine in only two days, but we were a woefully inadequate one. A single-cup coffeemaker for a party of ten. When the end of the day came I sank to the ground, not caring how dirty my skirts would get. We had five days until the next Faire day. Plenty of time for laundry.

Stacey counted down the cash while Jamie started locking up the stock, and with a whimper I hauled myself to my feet to help. I cleaned empty cups off the tables, and as I did so I realized we should have been doing that all day. We'd been so focused on serving people that the tables in our tavern looked like the overflow from the trash can: empty plastic cups stacked inside each other, some knocked over and lying in a puddle of hours-old beer dregs. I wrinkled my nose and made several trips to the nearest trash can, depositing plastic cups and paper cartons with a stray French fry in the bottom or a mostly gnawed turkey leg.

"People are pigs," I said after finishing my fourth trip. I wet a clean bar rag in melted ice and wiped down the tables. The ones in the back were neater, like they had hardly been used. As I wiped one of them I realized from this vantage point, I could barely see the main lane at all. These tables were pretty well hidden.

"Can we move some of these tables?" I asked.

Jamie shrugged. "I don't see why not. Right now?"

"God, no." I tossed the rag in the trash and reached for the bow tying my bodice closed. "This wench is done for the day." I loosened the laces and sucked in a grateful breath. "But maybe next weekend. People seem to be using the front tables as trash deposit, and no one's hanging out, which is kind of the point of a tavern, right? Maybe if people lingered, they wouldn't think of the place as a garbage dump."

He shrugged again. "Worth a try."

"We missed pub sing both days this weekend." Stacey's expression was mournful as she leaned wearily against the bar.

I shook my head. "What the hell's a pub sing?" We were already in a pub, and nothing was happening. Was I going to have to sing? My head was pounding, I could barely feel my feet, and I'd just taken my first deep breath all day. There was no way anyone could expect me to sing like this.

"Pub sing," Stacey repeated as though that explained everything. God, I was sick of being the newbie. I hated being told things with no explanation, as though I were supposed to magically know. My exasperation must have shown, because she hurried to explain. "It's a sort of farewell at the end of the day. Some of the entertainers and most of the cast members gather at the stage up front. We sing songs, give toasts, and generally thank the patrons for coming. And since it's up at the front, it's an easy step to usher the patrons out so we can close the gates at the end of the day." She pulled at her own corset strings behind her back and her sigh deepened. "I don't know what we're doing wrong this year that we can't get up front at the end of the day."

"I don't know, either." I moved behind her to help loosen her corset. "We'll do better next week, okay?" We had to. This pub sing thing was important to her, so it was up to me to figure out a way to make that happen for her.

"The two of you weren't at pub sing." My eyes flew up from where I'd been concentrating on unlacing Stacey's corset. Simon strode under the canopy and into the tavern, his hat in his hand. He didn't look like a pirate anymore, even though he still wore the outfit. He was back to being Simon again. He'd dropped the accent, and his regular voice made my blood pressure rise, and not in the fun way his pirate persona did.

"Brilliant deduction." I dropped my eyes again, dismissing him and getting back to unlacing Stacey, but she ruined my snarky effect by sighing.

"I know. I was telling Emily that we need to start getting over there at the end of the day."

"You do. And you need to get out from behind the bar more. Wenches are supposed to add color to the place. You should be interacting more with the patrons, enticing them in. As it is, all you're doing is acting like cashiers. You're hardly in character at all."

I breathed in sharply through my nose as Simon ended his

diatribe. I couldn't believe this. All that time he was kissing my hand and making me think indecent thoughts about moonlight, and he'd been critiquing my performance. How could he turn on a dime like that? Be fun and flirty with me all weekend, and then, as soon as the day is over—*bam*—back to his old critical self? I was getting emotional whiplash from dealing with him.

Stacey nodded along with him, but I wasn't going to take this criticism lying down. My feet hurt too much to not defend myself.

"I'd love to." I gave Stacey's laces a couple more good tugs and she was free. Then I gave Simon my full attention. "I'd absolutely love to spend more time talking to people, interacting, all of that. But instead I'm working my ass off for this Faire." Hands on my hips, I marched over to Simon until we were practically nose to nose. It was my turn to be in his personal space. "You were in here this afternoon. You saw how busy we were, right?" I barely gave him time to respond before I kept going. "You've got three people here, trying to do the work of at least six. There's no way you can expect us to sell drinks at the volume we're working here and be interactive at the same time. Unless you've got a cloning machine somewhere I don't know about."

My heart pounded against the walls of my bodice as I finished speaking, and I found myself wishing I'd taken it off completely before I'd lit into Simon. Loosened or not, I was a little light-headed from ripping him a new one.

He opened his mouth, closed it again. He looked from me to Stacey, then over to Jamie, who had locked up the cashbox and was leaving to take it up front, completely unconcerned about the costume drama happening in front of him. "See you next week," Jamie said with a little wave, rubbing in the fact that none of this shit concerned him. I envied him. Could we trade places? Could I wrangle him into a corset next week and take his red T-shirt? Probably not.

The three of us watched him walk away, then turned back to each other. But the moment had passed.

"Are we done?" Now the fight had gone out of me, leaving exhaustion in its wake. My feet were killing me from standing all day, and I wanted to go home. I wanted a shower, and I wanted my bed.

Simon wasn't looking at me. He was looking around the tavern as though he'd never seen the place before. "Yeah," he finally said. He rubbed the back of his neck, then ran a hand down one bristled cheek. "Yeah," he said again. "We're done."

"Good." Now that I wasn't actively angry at him, I could see he looked as tired as I felt. Of course he was—he'd spent the day performing, and he was also one of the point people for the whole event. Most of the Faire's success or failure rested directly on him. It was a heavy burden.

But he didn't have to carry it alone. I wasn't about to suggest anything to his face, because he'd probably shoot down any idea I had. But that didn't mean I was going to sit on my hands, either.

I turned to Stacey. "We'll get this figured out, okay? I promise, you're not going to miss pub sing for the entire summer." She gave me a tired smile in response, and that was good enough for me. "I have to go find Caitlin, but I'll think about it this week and figure out what we need to do better. I'll text you, okay?"

As I headed back to the Hollow to collect my niece, I wondered how this had happened. Of the three of us standing there in that tavern, I was the youngest. I was the stranger in town, and I was the newbie to the Faire. Yet somehow making the tavern run smoothly had fallen on my shoulders.

But I'd have been lying if I said I didn't feel a thrill in my chest at the prospect. Simon was overworked, and Stacey seemed to be in over her head. But me . . . my shoulders were made for this kind of thing. This was how I could contribute to the Faire, even more than wearing a spleen-squeezing costume and serving beer. I could do this, and maybe then I'd belong in Willow Creek too.

Ten

After a handful of Advil for dinner and a good night's sleep, I felt a lot more human by the time I met Chris at the bookstore on Monday morning. While I could walk without limping, I was still exhausted from two days of being outside in the woods and on my feet all day. But she had asked me to come to the shop on Monday, the day it was usually closed, so I figured she wouldn't say that unless she was serious. I arrived at ten in the morning with my trusty travel mug of coffee. When I got there she was just unlocking the front door.

"How do you stay open during Faire weekends?" It hadn't occurred to me until just now that she probably couldn't be in two places at once.

"My daughter's home from college for the summer. Nicole keeps the place running on the weekends so I can be Queen."

I followed her in, the bell over the door chiming in our wake. "That's a very understanding daughter."

Chris chuckled and flipped on some of the lights, enough that we could see, but not enough to signal that the store was open. "She has her moments." She put her purse down on the front counter and turned to me. "So let's get back to what you were saying the other day. About turning the back of the shop into a café?"

"Okay." I couldn't help the smile that came over my face. I was ready for this. "I have so many ideas."

I outlined them to her. A couple tables. Some cozy, comfy chairs designed to let people linger. An employee to man the counter and help in the store itself if the café wasn't busy. Start a book club to meet once a month, maybe a writers' group too. Maybe even a small menu: chicken salad, cheese and fruit plates. Simple food that wouldn't be a chore to make every day, and then she could still be creative with whatever desserts she felt like providing.

The more I talked, the more and more excited she looked. "Amazing," she said. "It's like you read my mind. That's exactly the kind of thing I wanted to do a few years back, but it seemed so overwhelming to do it on my own."

"You're not on your own now," I said. "You've got me through the end of the summer. What can I do?"

I'd always thought her smile was kind and genuine, but when it was aimed directly at me it warmed my soul. "Well, when you put it like that, I guess there's no time like the present." Before the words were out of her mouth she was halfway to the back room, and she returned a few moments later, juggling a handful of empty boxes. "There are more back there. Grab 'em and let's get started."

I knew better than to argue with the Queen.

My sore muscles groaned, but I did my best to throw myself into packing books into boxes and moving bookcases around. I couldn't believe how sore Chris didn't look by comparison. But then again, she was used to those weekends in the woods. Maybe in a few years I wouldn't be praying for death at the end of each weekend . . . that thought stopped me short. A few years? What was I thinking? I was only here for a few more weeks. Once Faire was over, I needed to start thinking about moving on with my own life. But that prospect gave me heart palpitations, so I concentrated on what was in front of me: hauling around bookcases with an ersatz Queen Elizabeth.

"How do we get the word out about a book club?" With her hands on her hips Chris surveyed the space we'd cleared out, but obviously she could think about more than one thing at a time.

"Oh, that's easy. We'll announce it on your social media pages. Create an event. Then post links to it in some strategic places . . ." My voice trailed off as she shook her head with a blank expression, and I bit back a sigh. "You don't have any social media pages, do you?" Now it was my turn to put my hands on my hips. "You have a website, at least? Right?"

"Sure. For online orders and such. But it's a small town. Everyone knows everyone anyway. So I always figured, what's the point of all that social media stuff?"

I inhaled through my nose, very slowly. "For starters, that's how you tell everyone about a book club." That came out a little snippier than I'd intended, but thankfully she laughed to concede my point. No big deal. I'd get those pages set up for her too.

At lunchtime we took a break to order some sandwiches from the deli down the street. By then, the space we had cleared out was huge. Maybe too huge.

"We can put some of these bookcases back, you know." I bit into my Reuben and closed my eyes in bliss. The guy down the street knew how to make a sandwich. "You don't need to keep this space completely empty."

She considered from her spot, cross-legged on the floor. I envied her. She was old enough to be my mother, but if I tried getting down on the floor like that I didn't think I'd get up again.

"No, but you don't want to hem people in, either. They should feel welcome to hang out, not feel claustrophobic." She gestured toward the front. "Those windows up front are so big and let in so much light, but the bookcases blocked all the light from coming back here. See how much more open it looks now?"

I had to admit, she had a point. "Just as long as you still have somewhere to keep your inventory. I mean, this is a bookstore."

"We could get some shorter ones, maybe bar height? Then they could serve a dual purpose."

"Now you're talking." I popped the last of my sandwich in my mouth and crumpled up the waxed paper it had come in.

"Speaking of bars, I meant to ask. How are you enjoying Faire so far?"

I groaned as I got to my feet. "I'm not sure if 'enjoying' is the word I would use." While I practically did a backbend to stretch out my back, I filled her in on the craziness of the past couple days, how I'd been run off my feet to the point of pain.

Her brow furrowed. "That doesn't sound right. You should be able to take breaks, walk around. See some of the shows and enjoy yourself."

"Stacey said that too, but I don't see how it's possible. I barely had time to eat something." Indeed, I had never wolfed down chicken fingers so fast as I had the previous day.

We moved over to a bookcase we'd emptied and together we started moving it toward the side of the shop. Without the books in it, the bookcase was . . . well, it was still heavy as hell, but the two of us were able to manage.

But Chris's mind was still on Faire. "I don't like the idea of you being worked to death like that. I mean, you're a volunteer. Hell, we're all volunteers. We do this because we enjoy it, you know? I wonder if Stacey . . . wait." She snapped her fingers. "It's just you and Stacey, right? Two wenches this year?" She smiled in triumph. "Well, there you go. Last year there were four."

I blinked. "Four?"

"Four. So you and Stacey are doing double the work of last year. No wonder you're frantic. You need more staff at the bar."

"Four." I shook my head in wonderment. So when I'd told Simon—well, bitched at Simon—we'd been doing the work of six people, I hadn't been far off. Go, me. "How did Stacey not notice this? Doesn't she do this every year?"

Chris pushed at one corner of the bookcase until it stood a little more at an angle away from the wall and nodded in satisfaction. "We can put the cookbooks and self-help back on this shelf, I think. Do you want to grab those?" As I went to retrieve the boxes she asked for, she raised her voice so it would carry to the other side of the shop. "Stacey's a great girl. She's fantastic in character, and she's so good at mingling with guests and being part of the whole Faire atmosphere. But she's less than fantastic at organization."

"That's putting it mildly." I stacked two boxes on the metal dolly and wheeled them back to the empty bookcase.

"So I have a feeling she didn't put it together that fewer wenches means short staff. Cookbooks on this side, self-help over there." She took the top box off the dolly and started unloading books. "I'll talk to someone this week. Maybe if they can move a few more volunteers over there, you'll be able to breathe more easily."

I wanted to make a breathing-in-a-corset joke, but I was too tired, and the offer made me too grateful. "That would be fantastic."

I stretched up onto tiptoe to place books, but even then I was too short to reach the top shelf. I needed a stool. "Anything that gets Simon off my back would be very much appreciated."

Chris laughed from the other side of the bookcase. "Trouble in handfasted paradise already? I thought you two crazy kids were going to make a go of it."

"Ha." I slapped two more books onto the shelf. "He dislikes me as much as I dislike him."

Chris hummed, a noncommittal sound. "I'm sure he doesn't dislike you. He's just . . ."

"An asshole?" But it was an automatic response. I was used to my knee-jerk reaction to Simon being irritation, but it had been a while since I'd truly felt that way about him.

The hum became a choked laugh. "Intense. Sometimes. Sean was the outgoing one, so Simon's always been a little quieter. I've known him for most of his life, so I'm used to him. He wasn't always this . . ."

"Intense?" I supplied her own word this time. She was right. That was a much better descriptor for Simon.

"Exactly. Especially when it comes to Faire. He's so protective of it . . ."

"Because of his brother." I finished the sentence for her.

"In any case," Chris continued. "Simon can be an acquired taste. Like strong espresso."

I liked strong espresso. It was dark. Rich. It exploded on your tongue and flooded your senses, waking everything up. Then I remembered Simon's kiss, the staged one at the handfasting. Followed by the kiss on my hand, when his eyes had shared unspoken secrets with me. The thought of espresso mixed in my mind with Simon, and I wondered how he would taste against my tongue instead. What would a real kiss with him be like?

Would his touch flood my senses? Could a buttoned-down guy like that overwhelm, overpower?

I suppressed a shiver and grabbed more books. But I blew out a long, slow breath as I stacked them, willing my body to calm down. My thoughts had gone in a completely inappropriate direction, and I couldn't let that happen. I didn't have time to wonder about the Ren Faire Killjoy and what his kiss might taste like.

The next Saturday morning I rounded the corner to the tavern and stopped in my tracks.

Stacey stopped alongside me. "What the hell?"

What the hell, indeed. Instead of only Jamie as our red-shirt volunteer, we had two more. Three people in red shirts, setting up the bar and getting ready for the day. The tavern had gotten an upgrade.

"Chris." A wave of relief washed over me as I said her name.

Stacey looked behind us, around us. "No, I don't see her."

"I mean Chris did this." I gestured to the additional volunteers. "I told her this week how insane everything was, and she said you had a lot more wenches last year, and so we needed more volunteers to make up the difference."

"Oh, *yeaahhh.*" Stacey drew out the last word for about five seconds. "I didn't even think of that."

"She said she'd talk to someone, and I guess she did!" By this time we'd remembered to keep walking and made it the rest of the way to the tavern, stowing our baskets and introducing ourselves to our new staff.

Staff. We had *staff.* The idea was so delicious I didn't know what to do.

"Where do you want us?" One of our new volunteers, Janet, was all smiles, the stereotypical soccer-mom type with a blond ponytail anchored by a baseball cap. I could tell by looking at her that she made cupcakes for her kids' class and was damn good at it. And now she was ready to be damn good at serving beer to semidrunken Renaissance faire guests too.

"Well . . ." I cast a quick eye over the whole setup, remembering how busy we'd gotten, and where the logjams had happened. It didn't take long for me to assign everyone to duties that would streamline everything, keeping Stacey and me front and center, maybe even out from behind the bar if all went to plan. If anyone had a problem with me taking charge, no one said anything. In fact, Stacey looked relieved that I'd put a plan into place. After what Chris had said about Stacey not being too organized I felt bad for her. Since she'd been guiding me all this time, choosing my outfit and educating me in all things Faire, I'd assumed she was in charge. But that wasn't her personality. That wasn't the kind of person she was.

But it was the kind of person I was. I could organize. Putting the volunteers where they needed to be was easy; in my bar days I'd managed employees all the time. This was exactly the same, only in a flashier, less comfortable outfit.

Now that things ran so much more smoothly, Faire became a whole different experience for me. For both of us. We could actually breathe—as well as we could in our costumes. We greeted patrons as they ducked into our canopied tavern; we cleared cups from tables as soon as they left. When we spotted a minstrel wandering the lane between his scheduled shows, we coaxed him inside, and he led us and the patrons in a drinking song. I didn't know the words, but like all drinking songs they were easy to pick up, and by the end I was belting it out with the rest.

I wanted to see the Celtic music show that we could barely hear, but its start coincided with another show ending, so every time I was about to duck out to see it we'd get hit with a wave of patrons, making it impossible to get away. I reminded myself that we were only on the second week of Faire, and we had a full staff in the tavern. There was still plenty of time to see everything. Including the joust. Oh, I desperately wanted to see knights on horseback, charging at each other with lances. I knew it was all choreographed. I didn't care.

Despite the easier time we were having in the tavern, by the early afternoon my feet had already started to ache. But the way things were now, we could take the occasional break to sit, and that made a huge difference in my outlook.

During a lull, Stacey grabbed my arm. "Come on, they're about to start the chess."

"Are you sure?" I glanced around the bar, but Jamie waved us off.

"Go. We're good."

"See? They're good. C'mon."

"I still don't understand why it's chess," I said as we followed the path to the field. "There's no pieces, and it's just fighting."

Stacey rolled her eyes, but the grin stayed on her face. "Human chess," she said. "Human. Meaning the people are the pieces." We reached the field, which had been turned into a chessboard. Lines were painted over the grass in a square pattern, with every other one completely shaded in with white.

"I see the board. I get that people are pieces. Where does the fighting come in?"

"When they play. You know, rook takes bishop." She shadowboxed against nothing, her fists going *pow-pow*. "Then they fight."

I remained skeptical, but we found a spot to stand in the back behind the rows of benches for the patrons. A dais was erected at one end of the field, where Chris, in full regalia as the Queen, sat with a retinue of guards and ladies-in-waiting. I didn't see Caitlin among them, though; she was probably making the rounds with other noblewomen. Meanwhile, cast members worked the crowd, announcing the match was about to begin, beckoning people off the lane to come and watch. One of those cast members was Simon. All in black, as usual, but he'd taken off his vest—he probably didn't wear it to fight.

He turned his head as we arrived, and my heart skittered at his surprised smile. He was about fifteen times handsomer when he smiled, becoming a completely different person from the stern, rules-driven dickhead I'd gotten to know. Since I'd only really ever seen him smile when he was in costume, it was no wonder Emma the tavern wench responded so strongly to him.

But my smile back was tentative, because the last time we'd talked . . . well, it hadn't so much been talking as bitching at each other. So I didn't understand the feeling tightening my chest. Why was I so glad to see him?

"Emma, my love!" He closed the distance between us in a few strides—he wasn't a tall man, but he could command a space when he wanted to. He caught my hand and brushed his lips over my knuckles as I bobbed my curtsy at him. "Have you come to see me win against these rapscallions?"

"Oh, aye, Captain." I almost laughed at his turn of phrase, but I knew the choreography. He lost the fight every time. His confidence was contagious, though, and I couldn't help but play along. "I have come to wish you the best of luck."

One more dazzling smile, and he dropped my hand to join the rest of the cast on the chessboard. "D'you hear that?" He turned to one of the other cast members, a tall, slim, blond young man leaning on a quarterstaff. "Did you hear how she called me 'Captain'? I love it when she does that."

Stacey giggled beside me. "He's sticking with this whole handfasting story line, isn't he?"

"Apparently." I didn't know what he was getting out of pretending to be involved with me. Sure, it was a fun little bit of business, playing a love story as a sideline thing. But it wasn't like we interacted very often. Shouldn't he have picked someone he'd be able to banter with on a more regular basis?

Then the chess match started and I refocused my attention, glad to not be thinking about Simon and his confusing smiles.

Everything that had confused me about the concept of a human chess match evaporated about thirty seconds after the match started. The cast stood on the chess squares, while the two people who "played" the game called out directions in turn. When a piece was called, the cast member standing on that square moved to the designated spot. Pawns moved forward. Knights leapt two squares up and one square over. Rooks paced back and forth in short horizontal paths. It all moved kind of slowly, though. Where was the *pow-pow* Stacey had promised?

And then: "King's bishop . . . take the queen's rook, if you please," said the overly polite monk who ran the white side of the board.

The cast scattered from the field, leaving Quarterstaff Kid and a slender, dark-haired woman armed with a rapier. She shrieked in fury and launched herself at the rook, who blocked her attack with his staff. I didn't remember seeing them during rehearsal, but even if I had, a partially blocked, half-speed fight was nothing compared to the grace they fought with now. The fight flowed like a dance as they disarmed each other and moved to hand grappling. I assumed at this point that he would best her easily, since he was about a foot taller. But she jumped on his back, hanging from his neck and taking him to the ground. I found myself caught up with the crowd in cheering her victory, before Simon's raised eyebrow made me realize I was cheering for the wrong side. Oops.

But when I expected a frown and some kind of silent rebuke, instead he gave me a warm smile as he resumed his position on the board. So Captain Blackthorne liked me in public, despite my gaffes. I could get used to this.

Simon and Mitch's fight was last: the big showdown between the queen's knight on the black side and the king's rook on the white. There was something about Simon being the queen's knight, the way he blew a kiss to the cast member playing the queen on the board as he strolled to the middle, that made my eyes narrow and my jaw set. Then, to my horror, he sensed my eyes on him and looked in my direction.

"It's all right, love!" he called to me. "The queen and I have an . . . arrangement. She doesn't mind that you and I . . ." He gestured between us, letting his voice trail off.

Oh, God, he was making our fake relationship part of the show. Fine. I crossed my arms. "But you and I made no such arrangement!" I called back. "We shall discuss this later."

Ooooooh, went some of the cast members, accompanying his wincing expression. Some of the audience joined in, craning their heads to look back at me. Meanwhile, Simon maintained most of his swagger as he prepared to face off against Mitch in the center of the board.

"All right, then, MacGregor?" Face-to-face like this, their size difference was readily apparent. Simon practically had to crane his neck to look up at Mitch.

Mitch stared down at him, stone-faced. This was the most I had seen him in character since Faire had started, and it was unsettling to see. Mitch was the most cheerful guy on the planet, so this giant of a man, arms crossed over his massive chest and looking daggers down at the pirate, was a stranger I had never met before. A pretty scary one.

"All right." Mitch's response was a rumble of rolled *r*'s as he slowly drew his sword. Also massive. "Said goodbye to your girl, then?" He tilted his head. "Both of them?"

Simon never lost his cocky grin as he drew his own sword, a rapier as slender as he was. "No need. This will only take a moment."

For a few beats they circled each other, Simon with loose-limbed grace and Mitch with solid, slower movements. They took turns testing each other with experimental taps of the sword, a quick occasional thrust and parry. Then the fight started in earnest.

I'd seen this in rehearsal. I remembered how exciting it had been, how my heart had leapt into my throat. Compared to what I watched now, that had been nothing. Now, at true full speed and in character, it was breathtaking. A dizzying spectacle. These guys knew what they were doing. Swords went flying. Mitch went flying in a flip over Simon's shoulder, the physics of which I still didn't understand. Their hand-to-hand grappling ended in that final moment with Mitch standing over Simon, the blade of his dirk against Simon's neck. The pirate knelt in the grass, his arms outstretched in defeat, his head tilted back to expose his throat, leaning back on his heels away from the blade.

After a beat of silence Mitch (well, Marcus MacGregor) was declared the winner, and the audience burst into applause. The two men broke the tableau, and Mitch took his knife away to offer his hand to Simon. It was a moment of breaking character as he helped him to his feet, but after the tension of the fight no one seemed to notice or mind.

I jumped as Stacey elbowed me in the ribs. "Good, right?"

I dropped my hands from where I had been holding them pressed to my mouth. "Yeah," I managed. "Yeah, that was pretty amazing. They do that twice a day?" I shook my head. I thought I was tired at the end of the day. At least I wasn't flipping people over my shoulder.

There was a bit of skit as the chess match ended; the two people who'd been calling the moves bickered over who had cheated and whether that checkmate was an illegal move. Then all the players came out for a curtain call, and the match was over. Patrons got up from their wooden benches and Stacey and I stepped even farther back to be out of their way.

But doing that put us in the path of the whole retinue of royalty, coming down off the dais. "Make way for the Queen!" The guards bellowed the command, and we all obeyed, patrons and cast alike, scurrying to the sides of the lane so the Queen and her ladies could pass by. Stacey and I dropped to the lowest curtsy possible. The Queen got the best, after all.

My eyes were still cast down, focused on the dirt about six feet in front of me, when the gold cloth of the Queen's skirts came into view. I waited for her to pass, but she stopped in front of me, causing me to look up.

"Ah, Emma." Chris as the Queen modulated her voice so that it was a smooth melody. I marveled again at how she sounded like a completely different person from the woman I'd spent the week with rearranging bookshelves. When I looked up, she looked like a different person too. Not only because of her makeup and elaborately braided hairstyle, but in the way she carried herself, the way she turned her head. She was regal with every inch of her being. And as a tavern wench, I was astounded she was calling me by name.

"Your Majesty." I met her eyes for a brief moment, then cast them back down again. Pretty sure wenches weren't supposed to make eye contact with royalty, much less make conversation, but speak when spoken to, right?

"I am glad to see you are out from behind the bar and enjoying this glorious day. Are you enjoying yourself, my girl?"

"Oh, yes, Your Majesty. Thank you." I chanced another look up at her. "Thank you," I said again, with a little more emphasis. I couldn't break character and thank her directly for getting those other volunteers to our tavern, but I did my best to get the message across. I think it worked. It was hard to tell; with another smile she was on her way, and Stacey and I headed back to the tavern. Extra volunteers or not, we still had drinks to serve.

The rest of the afternoon passed uneventfully, or at least as uneventfully as an afternoon spent in the woods at a Renaissance faire could pass. Patrons in various stages of costuming came through, and at one point I found myself kneeling in the dirt, marveling at a miniature knight wearing plastic chain-mail armor. He wielded a wood-and-foam sword with a lot of enthusiasm, if not skill.

"What's this?"

I heard Captain Blackthorne before I saw him. While Simon was pretty reserved in general, my pirate (oh, no, had he become my pirate?) easily made his presence known. Especially in a space like our smallish tavern.

I looked up from where I knelt, letting my eyes travel up from his silver-buckled boots, lingering on black-leather-encased thighs, wide belt wrapped around slim hips, and finally up to the billowy, loosely laced black shirt. I was in character; I was allowed to ogle. Once I reached his face, I took in his amused smile that said he knew exactly what I was doing. I should have felt embarrassed, but I didn't. Then I remembered he had asked me a question.

"This?" I rose to my feet as the small child in not-so-shining armor ran back to find his parents. "This good sir knight here was showing me his most impressive weapon."

"Oh?" His eyebrow arched, and I tried to ignore the way it sent heat speeding down my spine. "Are you seeking out others, then? Does my *weapon* no longer interest you?"

I had to bite down hard on my bottom lip to keep from laughing. We were blowing right past subtle innuendo today.

"Oh, Captain." I fluttered my eyelashes dramatically. "I believe you are quite aware that I have no complaints with your . . . weapon."

He choked for a split second, but covered it with a small cough before he leaned a casual elbow against the bar. "I hope not, love." His smile was as broad as ever. "I would hate to think I would have to duel with another for your affections."

"I hope not, as well, for your sake." I rounded my eyes in feigned horror. "I've seen you fight, sir. It typically ends on your knees in the dirt with a knife at your throat, does it not?" I shook my head, clucking my tongue. "Not a good ending." A nearby patron snorted, and it was all I could do to not turn my head. Great. Simon and I had turned into a show all on our own. Come for the beer, stay for the bad comedy.

"Odd." He tilted his head and considered me, his eyes doing the same slow travel mine had done on him. It took everything I had not to fidget under his gaze. "Typically women don't mind when I'm on my knees in front of them."

My gasp was drowned out by the laughter from a handful of patrons around us, and I dropped character enough to glance around to make sure there weren't any children who may have heard him. While I was thus flustered he stepped closer, reaching one hand up to catch a lock of my hair that had come loose from its twist.

"Besides . . ." He studied the way my hair curled around his fingers as though it was the most fascinating thing he'd ever seen. "This would be different."

"Would it?" I tried to maintain my air of nonchalance, but it was harder than usual to take a breath over the pounding of my heart.

"Aye." He leaned in closer, his eyes searching mine. What was it about that eyeliner that made his eyes look bolder, sexier?

"How so?" We had long since stopped performing for any kind of audience. My voice was little more than a whisper, and I was fascinated with the shape of his mouth, now a scant few inches from mine. I licked my suddenly dry lips and his breath stuttered for a split second.

"Well, love. I'd be fighting for you." His mouth was so, so close to mine, and his voice was low, almost gravelly, like he was telling me a reluctant secret. "That would be a fight worth winning."

Then he dropped my hair and straightened up, and with a tip of his hat he was gone.

I blew out a long, slow breath. Yeah. Quite an uneventful afternoon.

Eleven

As the end of the day approached, the crowd thinned out and we let the extra volunteers leave to help close up the ticket office. Stacey grinned at me as we cleared off tables. "Looks like we can make it to pub sing today!"

"Thank God for that."

My attitude must have shone through in my tone of voice, because Stacey rolled her eyes in response. "I know I won't shut up about it, but it really is a good time. You'll see."

"I'm sure I will." I was prejudiced against pub sing not because of Stacey's enthusiasm but because being there would make Simon happy, and apparently we all existed to make Simon happy. All memory of Simon-as-hot-pirate dissolved away as I remembered his diatribe at us the week before, when we'd missed both days. It made me want to skip it for the rest of the summer just to spite him.

But it didn't matter, because it looked like we were headed for the stage at the front, so I tried to let go of those prickly Simon thoughts. We hadn't had a customer for fifteen minutes, and Jamie had already locked up the cashbox and started stashing the alcohol away until the next day. We were all but dismissed for the night, so there was nothing left to do but—

I hadn't even taken a step out of the tavern area, following Stacey, when a banner fell on my head. The swath of fabric covered me like a bad Halloween ghost costume, and I stopped in my tracks because I couldn't see anything except purple. It took a little thrashing, but I fought my way out from under it, then I crumpled the fabric in my hands and looked up into the trees. It was one of the banners that formed a pseudo-canopy in the trees; I spotted the blank spot immediately. Apparently it had come loose and none of us had noticed it.

"Well, damn." I craned my neck and tried to figure out exactly how I was going to get it back up there.

"What happened . . . oh, no." Stacey followed my gaze up into the trees. "What did you do?"

I shot her an incredulous look. "Are you kidding?"

"Here." Jamie had the cashbox under his arm and he was already halfway out of there, but he stopped and put the box down on one of the tables. "I can get it back up there."

"No." I waved him off. "You need to go turn in the cash. I can do it." I eyed the tables underneath the trees. They seemed solid, and high enough that I could reach the branches without a problem. I could climb up there . . .

"But what about pub sing?" God, Stacey had a one-track mind.

I waved her off too. "You go. As long as one of us shows up it'll get Simon off our case." It took a little arguing, but within a few minutes I'd shooed everyone away and had the tavern to myself. After the bustle and chaos of the day, the quietness filled me with a sense of peace. I remembered that first day I'd walked the grounds. The sense of living in not only another place but another time. Now that I was here in costume, in a bodice that changed my posture and long skirts that brushed the ground, that sense was only heightened. Every once in a while it hit me in a wave: I wasn't Emily when I was here. I was Emma.

So Emma, not Emily, clambered up onto a chair, and from there to the top of the table. The top of my head almost brushed the lower branches of the nearest tree; I'd never felt so tall in my life. Still too short for what I needed to do, though. I stretched up onto my toes as far as I could and started threading the fabric around the branches.

It didn't take long for me to start cursing myself for my hubris. Would it have killed me to let Jamie help me with this? It was like trying to fold a fitted sheet with my arms over my head. The first attempts were failures, and my swearing intensified. I glanced around guiltily to make sure I was still alone; it probably wouldn't be good for patrons to hear me swearing like a sailor. Should I learn some period-appropriate curses? Would that be better? Doubtful.

Finally I got the hang of it, and the banner was back up in the trees where it belonged. I jumped down to the ground and walked out to the lane to make sure it looked all right. From my vantage point I surveyed the tavern as a whole. The way the tables were set up tickled at the back of my mind, bothering me again like it had the weekend before. It didn't look inviting. Drawing in more customers wasn't an issue, as busy as we were, but the setup looked more like a food court than a tavern. Sure, we were limited by the fact that the clearing was a pretty open area, but I wanted coziness. Seclusion. I thought of smoke-filled rooms, dark and lit by lanterns. Shadowy corners and places to hide. Places to linger.

No, I couldn't make it dark and shadowy here, under the

trees and in the sunshine. But what if the tables were arranged differently? Could I create those cozy hidden corners if I . . . ?

Yes. I could.

The hell with pub sing.

I pushed up my metaphorical sleeves and got to work.

The tables weren't that big, only made to seat four, and they weren't particularly heavy, but dragging them across uneven ground was a little awkward. I probably should have waited until the next morning, gotten Jamie or one of the other volunteers to help me. But I wasn't a hundred percent sure I was authorized to change around the layout of the tavern, and I was a firm believer in asking forgiveness instead of permission.

It took about fifteen minutes to make the changes I wanted. Tables were rearranged the way I'd envisioned, and as I stepped back onto the lane to check my progress I figured I could finish moving the chairs in the morning. I reached for the strings of my bodice as I stepped back under the trees again to get my basket from the bar. I probably should have loosened my laces, or taken the damn thing off completely, before I'd gotten started as it was uncomfortably tight now from all the exertion. Pub sing was probably close to over by now—maybe I should skip it, head straight for the Hollow to find Caitlin . . .

"What the hell are you doing?"

I jumped at the voice and dropped my hand from my bodice, as though Simon had actually caught me getting undressed. While the pirate wouldn't have minded and probably would have offered to help, the flat American accent told me Simon was out of character and back to being himself, and loosening my bodice out in public was probably a no-no. I let my breath out slowly and turned to face him. His arms were crossed over his chest as he glared at me. How could this be the same man who'd growled flirty secrets in my ear while playing with my hair just a couple hours ago? Once again, the change was startling, but I was getting tired of it.

"Hey, Simon." I gave a little wave as I scooped up my basket and set it on the bar.

He didn't wave back. "You're not at pub sing. Again."

"No. I'm not. Were you taking attendance?"

"No, I wasn't taking . . ." He tossed his hat with its stupid feather onto the bar, where it slid down to rest next to my wicker basket. "Where are the volunteers? I told them they needed to stay the whole day, help you out so you can do things like go to pub sing."

"We cut them loose a little bit ago, when things slowed down . . . wait a minute." I held up a hand. "You told them?" All day I'd thought Chris had gotten us the volunteers, based on our conversation earlier that week at the bookstore. But Simon had done it? Why?

"Yes, I told them. You needed them, obviously." But he answered the question absently; now he looked around the tavern with thunder in his eyes. "These tables are all switched around." He turned to me now, and I stiffened my spine against the force of that thunder aimed in my direction. "Why are the tables switched around? What are you *doing*?"

"Fixing the layout." I took hold of my basket, the wicker digging into my palm as I gripped it tightly. "It looks more inviting this way, doesn't it?"

He shook his head, like his brain was unable to comprehend something being different. "They've been arranged the same way for the past ten years. There's no need to change it now."

I sighed. "Okay. Look." I came around the bar and took his arm with the hand not holding a basket. I marched him back to the main path and pointed. "Look," I said again. "See how some of them are grouped together in little sections? People can gather. Congregate. And since Stacey and I have a little more free time, thanks to those volunteers, we can be out front more, like you said. Flirt. Play dice games. Maybe you can drop by again, in character, you know? Pirates hang out in taverns. If we add color to things, people might get a kick out of that. They'd stick around."

"And buy more drinks." The words sighed out of him, and I could see he understood my point of view now, even if he didn't want to.

"And spend more money," I clarified. "Isn't that what this is about? Bringing in more cash, raising more money?"

He nodded, but the nod turned into a shake of the head. "I don't know." He stalked back into the tavern to scoop his hat off the bar. "Some of the tables are all closed off." He gestured toward a grouping of tables off to the side. "Those don't look inviting at all. And what about all this empty space in the middle now? It looks like it's not planned out."

"I thought maybe we could get someone in." I shrugged as I followed him back to the bar. "I don't know, someone with a guitar or something. Entertainment."

"Entertainment?" He punctuated the word with a bitter laugh. "So, what, am I just supposed to pull an extra bard out of my ass now?"

"Not a bad idea," I shot back. "Maybe it would dislodge the stick that's up there." Oh, crap. I hadn't meant to say that.

He threw his hat back down onto the bar, and the thunder in his eyes turned apocalyptic. "Excuse me?"

Okay, maybe I had meant to say that. I'd had enough. "What is your problem? I'm just trying to help out here."

"I don't have a problem!" But the way he shouted it at me

belied that. "And I don't need your help! I just need you to be a tavern wench! Why do you want to change everything?"

"Why do you want to keep everything exactly the same?" I shouted back. "For God's sake, Simon, I moved a few tables around. It's not like I burned down the bar. Aren't you supposed to be a pirate? You sure are a stickler for the rules." I was done playing nice. I thought we'd been getting closer, with the banter at the chess field and the flirting in the tavern. I'd thought that maybe we were going to be friends. My heart sank as I realized I needed to let that idea go.

Simon didn't notice my emotional turmoil. "This is your first year here, and you think you know everything about how to run this Faire. You think—"

"Oh, I do not." I slammed my basket back down onto the bar, next to his hat. I was so sick of him that I wanted to burst into tears. I wanted to flee from this man who infuriated me so I would never have to speak to him again. But I was done dancing around our mutual dislike; better to get it all out in the open and over with. So I faced him, hands on my hips and not giving a damn about the green in his eyes anymore. "Why do you hate me?"

That shut him up. His rant stopped on a dime, and he blinked at me. "What?"

"Why do you hate me?" I hated the way emotion clogged my voice, anger and sadness mixed together. I'd seen the memorial to his brother; I saw how much it took out of him to keep this Faire going. All I'd wanted to do was help. But like he'd said, he didn't want my help. Any closeness between us was nothing but an act, brought on by costumes and accents and false personas. I should have known better.

"I don't hate you!" But he raked a hand through his hair, and the way he glared at me made me beg to differ.

"Everything I do is wrong," I persisted. "You hardly ever speak to me except to criticize something. I'm doing my best here, but to you it's not good enough." My voice faltered on those last words: *not good enough*. Jake made me feel that way. I wasn't about to let Simon do the same. Not without a fight.

"That's not . . . damn it!" He broke off with an inarticulate sound of frustration and he paced away from me a step or two, as though I annoyed him so much that he couldn't stand to be near me. "I didn't come here to fight with you!"

I had to laugh at that, but it sounded more like a scoff. "Of course you did. What else would you want to do with me?"

His eyes flared, and oh, no. I *really* hadn't meant to say that. Before I could blink he had stepped closer, impossibly closer, crowding me against the bar. I barely had time to draw a startled breath as he took my face between his hands and his mouth came down on mine.

Holy shit, Simon Graham was kissing me.

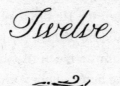

Twelve

This was nothing like the staged kiss we'd shared during the handfasting ceremony. This kiss was determined—hot and purposeful. Simon had run out of words for his argument and had decided to use his mouth in a different way. He kissed me like he had something to prove.

Just as my brain registered what was happening and I started to respond, he wrenched his mouth away. But he didn't go far; he leaned his forehead against mine, his hands still cradling my face. I dragged my eyes open but they were heavy, like I'd been drugged. I struggled to focus on him.

I wasn't the only one who seemed drugged. His eyes were hooded and half-closed, and his gaze stayed fixed on my mouth. "Emily." My name was a sigh, a low and desperate sound my body responded to in an instant. "I'm sorry. God." Even while he apologized he pressed his lips together, as if holding on to our kiss. Savoring it. He swayed into me and I caught my breath, anticipating another kiss, but he straightened up instead. He dropped his hands and I missed his touch immediately. "I shouldn't have—"

No. "Shut up." I didn't want him to say he regretted kissing me. I didn't want him to say anything at all. Talking made things go wrong between us, and his mouth was only a breath away. Now that the shock had worn off I wanted him back.

So I hooked my fingers in the open collar of his black shirt and tugged. I had just enough time to see his eyebrows swoop up in surprise before his mouth crashed onto mine again. This time I was ready, and I gave him a soft place to land. I opened my mouth under his, welcoming him, inviting him in. He sank into my kiss with a groan.

Simon kissed like a pirate. His lips were soft yet demanding, but his tongue . . . plundered. There was no other word for it. One hand cradled the back of my head, fingers anchored in my hair to better steer our kiss, while his other arm went around me, pressing me close. I loosened my grip on his shirt to slide my hands along the back of his neck. He was hot under my hands, but he shivered at my touch and kissed me harder. I was surrounded by him, by the scent of warm leather and warmer skin, and when his mouth traveled to my jaw, my throat, his tongue tracing a line that his lips followed, I pressed myself closer, eager for more of that heat.

He groaned again, and kisses became nips at the base of my throat as his hand tightened at the small of my back, pulling me into him. It was my turn to shiver at the rasp of his beard against my skin and the hard lines of his body against mine. Your typical English teacher shouldn't be this well muscled, but I was quickly finding out there was a lot about Simon that wasn't typical.

The world around me began to spin, and my chest felt tight. This was new; no man had ever kissed me until I swooned. It was a heady thing at first, but it became uncomfortable fast. My passionate grasp on the back of his head quickly became a desperate clutch of his shoulders as I tried to stay upright.

Simon noticed the change immediately, and when my knees buckled under me his embrace immediately went from amorous to supportive. "Whoa." He caught me by the elbows and held me up. "Hey. Are you okay?"

I nodded and tried to speak, but breathing seemed more important, and it was hard to do. His eyes turned assessing, sweeping up and down me.

"Shit. You're still laced up. Hold on." He tugged at my bodice with an urgency that had nothing to do with passion. Of course. It wasn't Simon's kiss causing me to swoon. It was lack of oxygen due to ten hours in this costume followed by some after-work making out.

A few more tugs and the garment loosened enough that my rib cage relaxed, and I sucked in a deep, sweet breath. Another couple of breaths, and the dizziness subsided. I sagged into him, resting my forehead on Simon's leather-and-cotton-covered chest, and his arm came around my back.

"Better now?" His lips brushed the shell of my ear and a thrill went up my back at Simon's voice, low and oh so close. How had the sound of his voice gone from annoying to arousing so fast? Maybe I was still oxygen deprived.

I nodded against his vest. "You're good at unlacing wenches. Very efficient. Do that a lot?"

"Well, I am a pirate, you know."

That surprised a laugh out of me, and his smile widened as I straightened up. "You're not, though." Being this close to him was making my voice low and throaty, and it was all I could do to not pull his mouth back to mine.

He raised his eyebrows—both of them this time; he wasn't showing off. "Not what?"

"A pirate." Because the whole time he'd been here, when he

was arguing with me and when he was kissing me, he wasn't speaking with an accent. And he'd called me Emily. Not Emma. So he wasn't Captain Blackthorne right now. This was Simon kissing me, not the pirate. Right?

"Aren't I?" He stepped closer, trapping me between the bar and his body. My heart pounded as the rough pads of his fingers stroked back up my throat, plunging into the tangled knot at the base of my skull . . .

"Emily? Are you still back here? You missed the whole thing!"

My head whipped around at the sound of Stacey's voice and Simon dropped his hand, backing up a step or two. By the time she appeared I was leaning on the bar, drinking a bottle of water, as though nothing had happened. Cool as a cucumber. Simon was a discreet distance away, cool as . . . well, cool as someone who'd been kissing a girl on a warm summer day. I took in his slightly flushed cheeks, his mussed hair, and the glint in his eyes and wished like hell that Stacey hadn't come looking for me.

But she wasn't alone. "Hey now, what's going on here?" Mitch looked from me to Simon and back to me again, taking in my loosened bodice with raised eyebrows and a cheesy grin. "Now I see why you weren't at pub sing. A little rendezvous with a wench, huh, Captain?" Now that he wasn't in character, Mitch was back to being a one-man innuendo machine.

I shot a wide-eyed look in Simon's direction. The three of them were established friends. I was the newcomer. What had happened between us was too new to give a name to yet, so I would follow Simon's lead on this.

"Oh, knock it off." Stacey dug an elbow into Mitch's side. Not that he felt it; it would have been like elbowing a brick wall. "Em stayed behind to fix a banner that fell. Simon probably ended up helping her."

I nodded at the half-truth. "Then I got distracted by moving the tables around." *And by being kissed senseless.*

Thankfully Simon jumped on the story. "And then her costume got too tight, so . . ."

"So I loosened it. Myself." That was a total lie, and the memory of Simon's hands on me, tugging at the strings of my bodice, sent heat coursing through me now, although at the time it had been an emergency situation. "I felt like an idiot—I almost passed out." I left out the fact that kissing him was the reason I couldn't breathe in the first place. Another glance in Simon's direction and I remembered the urgent press of his mouth. It became hard to breathe all over again. If Stacey and Mitch hadn't come along, how much more of my costume would have been in disarray by now? How much of his?

Simon's eyes went molten as his gaze met mine, and I knew he was thinking the same thing. I sucked in a shaky breath before I did something stupid like kiss him again. We had witnesses now.

"I'm just saying . . ." Mitch came closer, leaning an elbow on the bar next to me. "Next time you need your corset loosened, you can always come to me. I'm really good at that." He waggled his eyebrows in an exaggerated gesture that made me snort-laugh.

"Please." I echoed his stance and made a show of looking him up and down. "I know what's under your kilt. It's not that impressive."

Mitch barked out a laugh and slapped the bar with the flat of his hand. "Nice!" While Stacey and I shared a grin in response to my vague put-down, only half of me was paying attention. The other half was hyperfocused on the black-clad pirate in my peripheral vision.

"It's not a corset." Simon's voice had an unexpectedly ragged edge to it. The molten look in his eyes had gone as he looked from Mitch back to me. He looked like the normal critical Simon I was used to, and my heart fell. I could still taste his mouth, feel the weight of his kiss and the warmth of his touch. Simon, on the other hand, looked like our kiss had never happened. He looked like he hated me again. Damn, that was quick.

"What?" Mitch's brow furrowed. "She's wearing one right now. Kind of."

Simon gestured in my direction, the wave of his hand taking in everything I was. "She's wearing a bodice. Not a corset. And she had it laced too tightly." He turned his glare on Stacey now. "You shouldn't lace her up so tight."

"It was fine." I jumped in, wanting to save Stacey from his ire. "I just . . . overdid it." He looked back at me, and it was all I could do to not shrink under his glare. How had things changed between us so quickly, and then back again even faster? It was relationship whiplash. "It won't happen again." I was talking about my bodice, but I had a feeling I was also talking about kissing Simon. Which was a shame.

A muscle jumped in Simon's cheek. "Good."

The word was like a slap, and it stung. I felt vulnerable, and not only because I was standing there with my bodice half-undone. I smoothed a hand down my throat as though I could still feel Simon's mouth there. His eyes tracked the movement, the only outward sign of what had passed between us.

"Well, I'm sorry." Stacey scooped up my basket from the bar and handed it to me. "I'll make sure to be careful when I tighten everything up tomorrow, okay? Don't worry, no more passing out for you this summer!"

I forced a laugh. It even sounded genuine. "I sure hope not. Once was enough."

As I left the tavern with Stacey I looked back once, just in time to see Simon wipe his mouth with the back of his hand. He didn't see me, and I turned back around before he could.

Enough. I needed to track down Caitlin and go home. I'd had enough of pirates for one day.

The next morning, Stacey apologized for my near-fainting spell, even though she'd had nothing to do with the cause of it.

"I had no idea I'd laced you in so tight!" Yet she didn't change her routine. By the time she was done, everything felt as strapped in and hiked up as ever. I shifted around inside the costume, and while I was a little worried about getting dizzy again, I decided the best way to avoid that was to stop kissing pirates. I shifted around again when I discovered a new problem.

I had an itch.

Just under my rib cage and to the right of my belly button. This was bad news, since Stacey had already gone off to talk to someone else on the other side of the stage where we'd all gathered before the day started. And even if she was still around, it would be a ten-minute, pain-in-the-ass affair to loosen me up, scratch, adjust, and tighten me back in again. No, I was dressed for the day. I'd have to figure something out.

I tried ignoring it and turned my attention to the stage, but that didn't help. Simon hopped up there, ready to talk about something before we started Faire. So much for avoiding pirates.

"Some of you may have noticed we're missing some cast members." He adjusted one of the cuffs on his black shirt as he looked around the group. He avoided my eyes completely; he may as well have been looking through me. "I'm afraid we had to cut three people loose yesterday. We have some rules around here, and one of those is no cell phones during Faire." Some of the younger participants dropped guilty eyes to the dirt. I tried to peel up the bottom of my bodice so I could reach the itchy spot. No dice.

"I know you're tethered to your phones. We all are. But maintaining the illusion of the seventeenth century is the most important thing we do while we're out here. That's why we work so hard beforehand, learning about the time period, working on our accents. So when a patron walks by to see a cast member texting or Snapchatting"—he shrugged—"it breaks the illusion, and completely ruins everything we've created here." He shook his head, clearly disappointed, and I felt a prickle of guilt up my spine even though my phone was off and in the bottom of my basket. His Teacher Voice was back on.

I shot a look across the tent toward Caitlin, who shook her head at me emphatically. She patted the little leather pouch at her hip I'd gotten her the previous weekend. I raised my eyebrows in a silent entreaty that she keep her phone in there, and she nodded back in understanding. We were only in our second weekend of Faire, but we'd gotten pretty good at the whole communicating-with-our-eyes thing.

Meanwhile, this itch wasn't going away. While Simon finished up his lecture on the evils of cell phones or whatever, I tried shifting around some more inside my costume, but once again that did nothing. Annoyed, I slammed my closed fist into my side. That . . . that actually helped. I did it a couple more times, until I realized Simon had stepped off the stage and was staring at me while I stood there punching myself in the side.

"Everything okay?" The tremble in his voice said he was trying not to laugh.

I opened my fist and turned the last punch into a smoothing motion down my side, which fooled no one. "Fine," I said breezily. His eyebrows went up, and I sighed. "I had an itch."

He huffed out a laugh. "Well, that makes more sense than you being a masochist."

I gestured to my outfit. "I think wearing this all day qualifies me as a masochist all on its own."

"Hmmm." His hum in response was noncommittal, but the way he looked at me was more than assessing my costume for period-appropriateness. He stepped closer, and all my resolve about avoiding pirates melted away as I remembered the way his mouth had tasted. "Listen." His voice was pitched low, just for my ears. "Do you think—"

"Park! There you are, Park. Been looking for you!"

I jumped at the mention of my name—well, my nickname—and turned toward where Mitch bellowed at me from the other end of the tent. I threw up a hand to wave him over and he in turn threw an arm around my neck in greeting when he got to me.

"What are you doing tonight?"

"Taking a long hot shower and thanking my lucky stars I don't have to wear this costume for a week."

He shook his head. "Wrong answer. We're going to Jackson's tonight."

"What? Going to what?" Then it clicked. "Do you mean that pizza place, just before the highway?" I'd driven past the dingy, squat-looking brown building several times, but never felt like I had enough hand sanitizer on me to venture inside.

"Are we going out tonight?" Stacey had joined the party, which meant there was no getting out of it now.

"Oh, it's so much more than the pizza place just before the highway." Mitch didn't answer her question, choosing to rhapsodize on the qualities of Jackson's instead. "The food is good and the drinks are strong. The best part is that it's always happy hour."

"It doesn't look like much from the outside." Simon's reasonable tone cut through Mitch's enthusiasm. "But they make a good pizza and the drink prices are cheap." He shrugged. "A lot of people go there on Sunday nights after Faire." He wasn't extending an invitation the way Mitch was; he was imparting information. That was all. A feeling I didn't like prickled at the back of my neck.

"Exactly." Mitch pointed at Simon, who had already backed away a step or two from the group. It was like the sun going behind a cloud, and I felt a chill from it. "You're coming too, right, Captain?"

Simon shrugged a nonresponse, but I was still confused. "Why Sunday, though? Isn't Saturday night the party night?"

"Not on Faire weekends." Simon raised his eyebrows in rebuke. "Believe me, stage fighting in the hot sun with a hangover is something you only ever do once."

"Good point." The wisdom in that was obvious, and I was annoyed with myself for even asking the question.

"Besides, Simon and me"—Mitch gestured between the two of them—"a few others, we're teachers. It's summer, so we don't have to go to work on Monday."

"Chris doesn't open the bookstore on Monday, either." Suddenly that made a lot more sense.

"Right. See? Sunday is the perfect night for the Faire cast to blow off steam."

Wow. When I'd first met Mitch, I wouldn't have thought he was capable of putting together a cohesive argument, but here we were. Sure, said argument was about drinking, but still. I was impressed.

"Yeah, you should come, Em!" I knew enough about Stacey by now to know she was cut from the same cloth as Mitch—always up for a night out. "Come on, Simon, tell her. It's a good time, right?"

He shrugged again. "Yeah. I mean, if you want to." He sounded completely disinterested; he couldn't care less if I went out with them or not. He'd turned into the old Simon, the one who wanted nothing to do with me. He'd withdrawn from me in increments ever since Stacey and Mitch had arrived.

"Okay, so with Park and Stace, that's three, and you're coming too, Captain, so that's four. I'll work on the chess guys today, see how much of a party we can get out there tonight."

Simon's lips curled up in a smile that didn't quite make it to his eyes. "Sure. Yeah. Maybe I will." Everything in his body language said he was looking for a way out of this conversation. The prickling on the back of my neck intensified. Before Mitch showed up, he'd been about to ask me something, and I wanted to know what it was. Because if it had to do with kissing me again, I was all in.

"'Maybe.'" Mitch shook his head, clearly disappointed. "Yeah, I know what that means."

Simon took the rebuke with another limp smile and a wave of his hand. "I need to finish getting ready. See you out there."

No, I wanted to say. *Stay and talk to me some more. Or drag me behind a tent and kiss me again. Just do something so I know what's going on here.* Instead, I turned to Mitch after Simon walked away. "What does that mean?"

Mitch scoffed. "It means he's not coming. He says that to shut me up. Getting that guy to go out is like pulling teeth."

"Not everyone is as social as you are, Mitch." Stacey nudged him with a grin.

"Yeah, I know, but . . ." Mitch shook his head. "I thought he was a by-the-book nerd when we were kids, but it's even worse now. Like he's twenty-seven going on fifty."

I nodded in agreement, but my mind whirled. *Twenty-seven.* Something was important about that number, but I wasn't sure what.

"He is not." Stacey smacked Mitch on the shoulder, and the action broke my train of thought. "You need to stop."

"I thought that dude would lighten up once he went away to college, you know, out from under everyone's thumb." Mitch sighed. "But then he came right back. It's a damn shame." In Mitch's world, everyone should be having a good time at all times.

"It's not his fault," Stacey said. "You know how he gets. It's that time of year."

Something inside me stirred at her words, like a memory I couldn't quite catch. *This time of year . . .*

Mitch shook his head again before reaching up to pull off his T-shirt. "He needs to move on at some point." He stowed his shirt in his gym bag and picked up his claymore, indicating that he'd already mentally moved on from the conversation. "Okay, girls, time to start the show." He twirled the giant sword like it was a toy. "Break some hearts and fight some pirates."

I rolled my eyes and smiled, but as he left, my attention turned back to Simon, who was on the other end of the tent now. He chatted with some of the other cast members dressed as pirates, his little pirate clique, as he finished getting ready for the day. I whooshed out a breath as he buttoned himself into his vest, a black leather one today. How was I getting turned on by someone putting on *more* clothes?

His words echoed in my head. *Do you think . . .* Did I think what? There had been this split second of an almost-moment between us, before Mitch had interrupted. Like the ice had been broken by our kiss the previous day, and he saw me now as a person. Not just a wench in a corset—sorry, a *bodice*. But the moment hadn't lasted. As soon as we'd started talking about socializing outside of Faire he'd withdrawn completely, like my ex had. I knew the signs by now. I was an expert at *he's just not that into you*.

In a flash, I was back at the last party Jake and I had gone to together, sometime last fall. A networking event at his first firm, the small one where he'd been a promising new associate. He'd worked the room like the smooth attorney he was fast becoming, and it was there that he met the senior partner at the big firm that he left his first job—and me—to join. At that party, he'd hardly introduced me to anyone, and if he did I was "his friend Emily." Not *girl*friend, and certainly not fiancée. Friend. After an hour or so he'd abandoned me to make connections on his own, as I was clearly holding him back. I'd adhered myself to the open bar, nursing a cabernet and feeling about two feet tall.

Now I felt that way again, without the benefit of unlimited alcohol to drown myself in.

I probably should get the message: Simon wasn't interested. Besides, I shouldn't want him to be. I shouldn't want to be anywhere near someone who made me feel the way Jake had. That kiss had been an aberration, and I should forget it had happened.

"So you'll come out tonight, right?" Stacey asked as we walked up the hill toward the tavern.

"Yeah," I said. "Why not? It'll be fun."

Thirteen

I *t was not* fun.

Okay, the actual night out was great. Mostly. As promised, the pizza at Jackson's was good, and the drinks were better. For a place I had been actively avoiding due to its outside appearance, inside it was warm and friendly. Gleaming wood; a karaoke machine that worked a little too well once the pitchers of beer started flowing; dartboards and pool tables in the back. It had been a long time since I'd had a night out like that.

Which was why it had been a long time since I'd felt this shitty the morning after a night out like that.

Coffee was essential. Also a large glass of water. And a very dark, very quiet room where I could not talk to anyone all day. Thankfully, April was ambulatory, and ready to tackle the forty-minute commute to her office job for the first time since her accident. She hummed with energy while I sat at the kitchen table and stared into the cup of coffee in front of me. Would it be enough, or would I need another three or four?

"You didn't need to get up this early, you know." April stuck her earrings in and brushed her hair back over her shoulders. She'd blown it out; it looked sleek and smooth. Very professional. Mine was a frizzy nightmare that couldn't be contained.

My shrug was more of a slump from where I sat. "I didn't know if you would be up for driving yet. Thought I'd get up just in case." Physically she was in great shape; her limp was barely noticeable now. But she still tensed up when we went places in the car, and she hadn't yet been behind the wheel since her accident. So for her to think she could swan out the door like it was nothing was a little presumptuous on her part.

"Nah." She poured coffee into a travel mug and added a dollop of half-and-half from the fridge. "I'll be fine."

See? Presumptuous. But I sipped my coffee and didn't contradict her.

"Seriously, Em, go back to bed. There's no reason for you to be up at this hour. Especially since you were out so late last night."

"Ugh." My head thudded to the table. Ow. "Don't remind me. Mistakes were made." Mistakes of the multiple-tequila-shots variety. I wasn't a tequila girl, but Mitch could be very persuasive. That boy was something like ninety-eight percent muscle; he could drink. I shouldn't have even tried to keep up, but I'd been so discombobulated by the roller coaster of emotions that weekend at Faire. Simon was a dick. No, Simon was kissing me. No, he said he'd made a mistake in doing so. No, we were kissing again, and he was damn good at it. No, once other people were around he was back to acting like I was the living embodiment of gum stuck to his shoe. I'd hardly seen him all day Sunday, and while he'd shown up at Jackson's with everyone else, he looked like he hated being there and was gone after about fifteen minutes.

Which had left me with Stacey, Mitch, and his endless tequila shots. Mitch was genial. He was fun. He kept the booze flowing along with the jokes, and I didn't remember the last time I'd laughed so hard. When Stacey and I decided to split a cab home, he'd practically strangled me in a one-armed hug and smacked a kiss on the top of my head. "You're pretty cool, Park," he'd said, and that simple compliment had glowed inside of me all the way home. At least someone liked me.

That glow had long since died out by the time my alarm went off for April's first day back to work, and now I took another long sip of coffee.

"Did you have fun, at least?"

I contemplated that. "Yeah," I finally said. "I did. Some pretty good people live in this town."

"Yeah." April leaned against the counter and sipped from her travel mug. "I hate small towns, but I guess this place is okay."

I squinted up at her. "I don't get that. You've lived here for ages, haven't you?"

"Since Caitlin started the first grade."

"Why?" It was too early to do the math, but even I could tell that was a long time. "If small towns aren't your thing?"

"It's not for me. It's for Cait." She flicked her gaze to the hallway leading to her daughter's room. "If it were up to me, I'd be in one of those studio apartments in the city. I love the crowds, the noise. I like to blend in. You stand out too much in a small town." She studied her coffee mug as she spoke, biting her lip.

"You could have stayed in Indiana, though," I said.

"One town over from Mom and Dad for the rest of my life? No, thank you." She looked at me squarely and I had to concede her point.

"We moved out here when I got a job offer in Baltimore, and I never looked back. But then I had to think of the best place to raise Caitlin. The place with the best schools, the best environment for her to grow up. And that sure wasn't in the city. We were lucky to end up here." She looked at me appraisingly. "It's not a bad place to put down roots. You know, if you're feeling rooty."

"Rooty?" I snorted. "Is that even a word?"

She grinned back. "I have no idea. Maybe? You know what I mean."

I did. And while April wanted the anonymity of a big city, I wanted those roots. A home. A place where I belonged, with people who knew me, loved me, and wanted me around. It was the kind of life I thought I had been building with Jake, until he'd yanked those roots out of the ground and took them with him when he left.

For the first time, I considered staying in Willow Creek after the summer was over. Putting those roots down here. The bookstore café was coming together, and Chris seemed happy with our progress so far. The people from Faire had started to see me as less of a stranger in town and more of a friend, so now people said hi to me at the bank and the grocery store. Weirdness with Simon notwithstanding, I hadn't felt this comfortable somewhere in a long time. Which only made me realize how *un*comfortable I'd been the last year or so that Jake and I were together.

It had taken me some time to realize it, but maybe getting dumped by a successful, upwardly mobile attorney was the best thing that could have happened to me.

April waved goodbye on her way out, and a few seconds later the front door closed behind her. I sipped some more coffee and listened to her SUV start up. Then I listened to it idle in the driveway for about a minute and a half. Then it shut off, and while I took another sip of coffee the front door opened again.

"Goddammit." That was all April said, and all she needed to

say. I pushed my mug away and went out to the living room, where she leaned against the front door, her head bowed and her hair obscuring her face. I stepped into my flip-flops by the door and took the keys from her hand.

"It's okay." I threw an arm around her shoulders, and she leaned her head against mine for a long moment. I squeezed her shoulder and pressed a kiss into her hair. "Come on, let's get you to work."

"Goddammit." This time the tone was a flat sigh, but she didn't argue.

I didn't mind being chauffeur for a little while longer. I liked being needed. It made me feel like I was necessary. Part of something. Rooty.

Twenty-seven.

The number kept echoing in my head for no good reason, ever since Mitch had mentioned it on Sunday morning.

Twenty-seven.

Simon's age. And Mitch's too. But something else. I let it roll around in the back of my mind while I went through my regular week of non-Faire-related activities. Now that we were into week three a routine had set in, and my life was split neatly down the middle between the weekend and the week. Faire and mundane. Bodice and jeans. Tavern wench and bookstore. And while Chris and I took a little time on Tuesday morning to catch each other up on our weekend spent as our alter egos, for the most part those two distinct parts of my life didn't intersect. Once Faire ended on Sunday night, I went back to being April's chauffeur and Chris's barista/social media guru/bookstore minion until the next Saturday morning. So as I got busy with my weekday bookstore life, it was easy to let everything having to do with Faire fade into the background, and forget about one life while living the other.

But the number twenty-seven stayed in my head, and it wouldn't go away.

The number made me sad, I realized on Thursday afternoon. Something associated with grief, which made no sense, since Mitch was the most cheerful person in the world. And how could numbers be sad? At that point, I was tired of thinking about it, and hoped I'd either figure it out soon or forget about it altogether.

It all came together the next Saturday, in a place I'd almost forgotten about.

It had turned into a hot summer, so when Saturday dawned unseasonably clear and cool, we all rejoiced. My skirts didn't feel as heavy that day, and even my bodice felt less oppressive. That morning I took the long way out of the Hollow, wandering down some side lanes I didn't get to see much of during Faire, enjoying the early-morning sunshine. A few weeks back, these lanes had wound through empty woods, and now they were full of activity. Vendors were setting up their booths for the day. I window-shopped as I walked by, contemplating a pendant for my costume. Or a hand-tooled leather belt pouch, like the one I'd gotten Cait—okay, nicer than the one I'd gotten Cait. Maybe it was for the best I didn't come this way very often. April didn't ask me to contribute, but Chris didn't pay me all that much. I wasn't exactly swimming in cash.

Thinking about how empty the woods had looked without the vendors sparked a memory of running into Simon back here. The memory collided with the number twenty-seven in my head, and now I knew what I needed to see.

It took longer than I expected to find the young tree with the memorial plaque to Simon's brother—the lanes looked so different with the Faire set up around it—and when I did, I found crouching down to be problematic in this outfit. Instead I sat on the ground—thankfully the rain we'd gotten earlier in the week had dried by now, so my skirts wouldn't get muddy. It was almost like I was at a cemetery, and I wanted to say something. But I'd never met Sean Graham, and I didn't know what was going on between Simon and me, so I brushed the leaves away from the plaque and sat in contemplative silence.

"I think I understand." My voice was small, a secret whispered between me and a man who had died years ago.

"Understand what?"

I should have jumped, should have felt guilty that Simon had caught me here. He didn't know I knew about this place. I was prying. I had no right to be here, a thought that was only underscored when I craned my neck to look up at him. His jaw was set in a hard line as he looked past me to the plaque that held his brother's name, and his pirate hat with its ridiculous feather hung limply in one hand.

"Understand what?" He turned his eyes to me as he repeated the question, and I was surprised to see no hostility in them. Just curiosity.

I pointed at the plaque. "Of course you didn't want to go out last Sunday. That was the anniversary of his death, wasn't it?"

"Yeah." Simon exhaled in a sigh as he crouched down next to me. "Well, it was Monday, but close enough. Things always feel . . . kind of off this time of year, and the day itself . . . well, it's a hard day."

I looked back at the plaque because the sadness on his face was too raw, too intimate. I didn't have the right to share it. "And twenty-seven."

"Hmm?"

"He was twenty-seven. Same age you are now."

"Yeah. That's . . . yeah." He deflated the rest of the way, dropping from his crouch to sit cross-legged beside me in the dirt at the side of the lane. "Sean was . . ." He chuckled softly. "A force of nature. You would have liked him. Everyone did. He got all of this going by sheer force of will." He ran a hand over his cheek, down his jaw. "He was the one who made me become a pirate. He said I was too quiet, too serious all the time. Making me do this—he thought it would give me swagger." He shook his head and the tiniest smile played around his lips, but his eyes looked brittle. "I didn't want swagger, but you couldn't say no to Sean." He didn't look at me as he spoke. He looked at his brother's name, etched on the bronze plaque. "After he was gone I had three years. Three years of him still being my older brother. But this year . . ."

"This year you're twenty-seven."

"I'm twenty-seven," he repeated. "I caught up with him." He ran his fingers over the feather in his hat, pulling at it, his eyes fixed on the plaque. "And in September I'll hit an age he never did, and I don't deserve it. I shouldn't get to have years that he doesn't."

"Of course you do." Out of instinct I reached for him, placed my hand over his before he could shred that poor feather. "He wouldn't want you to think that."

"Maybe not." He turned his hand under mine and grasped it, and we were sitting there holding hands like it was the most natural thing in the world.

I tried for a happier memory. "Chris told me he was a football star."

Simon gave a ghost of a laugh. "He was an everything star.

Except track; that was what I did. You know, those long cross-country runs?" He wasn't looking at me, but I nodded anyway. "Not as flashy as football, no cheering crowds, but I didn't care about any of that. I actually think I liked it better that way. Measuring up to Sean was impossible, so it was better to not even try."

I frowned at this, because I wanted to disagree. From everything I'd heard about Sean, he seemed like a charismatic slacker who relished the spotlight, while Simon worked hard for little thanks. The dead are held in such high esteem that we only remember the good things, and we not only forgive their faults but we forget them. I thought about Mitch and Stacey, joking about the time that Sean hadn't gotten the beer for the beer tent. They'd turned a negative trait into a positive memory. Maybe if Sean hadn't died so young, Simon would see his own value a little more.

But I couldn't tell him that. Not now, and probably not ever. It wasn't even remotely my place to do so. Instead I steered the conversation another way. "What do you think he'd be doing now?"

Simon drew a slow, deep breath. "You know, I have no idea. Sean was amazing, but he didn't have a lot of . . . drive. So at thirty he'd probably still be getting his gen-eds out of the way at the community college. But being Sean, he'd somehow make it look like a stroke of genius." He shook his head. "Either that, or he'd have been elected mayor of Willow Creek by now." He smiled in response to my laugh. "After he died I started . . . I don't know, channeling him or something. I get to take the best parts of him, the parts I miss the most, and put them into the role I play here. These six weeks in the summer I get to stop being so serious, so responsible. I get to be more like Sean."

"Swagger," I said softly. The word was the last one I would use to describe Simon, but somehow it fit.

"Swagger." His chuckle was barely there, a mere exhalation of breath. "I feel close to him again. When I'm out here, in some ways it's like he's not really gone." His voice thickened on the last word, and he cleared his throat hard. "This Faire was so important to him. His pet project. He didn't care about much, but this . . . this he was good at. He worked so hard to expand it, to get more acts and then this space." He waved a hand around, encompassing the woods surrounding us. "The first summer we were out here in the woods was the last year he . . ." He had to stop and clear his throat again. He didn't finish the sentence.

I took up the thread of the conversation. "He'd be proud. I mean, look at this place. There's no way he wouldn't be proud of what you've done."

He dropped my hand abruptly, as though suddenly remembering that we weren't people who held hands with each other. "It's all I have left of him." He looked at me for the first time now, his eyes shining with tears that had gathered but he'd denied. "Sometimes I don't know what I'd do if I didn't have these summers. It's almost like he's still here. What happens if it changes too much, and it's not the way he left it? What happens if it ends? But then sometimes I don't . . ." Simon shook his head hard, dismissing that last thought before he could voice it. He ran a restless hand through his hair before clearing his throat and turning his attention to me. "You know what I mean, though, right? You have an older sister. I'm sure you feel the same way about her."

He looked so hopeful that I hated to disappoint him. "April and I aren't really like that." I shrugged. "I think it's the age difference. I was an afterthought baby, so she's twelve years older. By the time I was old enough to be interesting she was already out of the house. College, getting married, having a kid. She wasn't around to be a role model or anything. I mean, she's my sister and I love her, but growing up we were never particularly close."

His brow furrowed. "I don't understand. You've been here ever since her accident. Didn't you basically drop your whole life in order to help her out?"

"My whole life." I tried for a small laugh, but it came out much more bitter than I'd expected. "There wasn't anything to drop." I'd made the joke before to April, and making it again now didn't make it any funnier, or any less painful to say out loud. "The only thing I had going for me was my English degree, and . . ." I sighed. "You already know how that ended." I tried to sound casual, but the sting of our conversation from a few weeks back was still fresh. I could still see the disappointment in his face when he'd learned I hadn't finished college.

He nodded carefully. "You dropped out of school." His voice held no judgment, which surprised me. But he still didn't know the whole story, and since we were sharing confessions . . . what the hell.

"My boyfriend, Jake, had gotten into law school. But it's expensive, and it's hard. He had a lot of work ahead of him. Studying, clerking. So we made a deal. I'd drop out and support him, and when he passed the bar and got a job it would be my turn."

Simon had drawn back a little when I'd mentioned having a boyfriend, but something in my tone of voice must have alerted him that the story didn't have a happy ending, because his face darkened a little. "And what happened when it was your turn?"

My bitter laugh turned shaky, and even though I blinked hard a tear still hit my cheek. "Turns out a big-city attorney doesn't need a college dropout around anymore."

"So he dumped you? But he's the reason you dropped out in the first place." He put a hand to the ground like he was going to push to his feet, maybe go find Jake and give him a little talking-to. Maybe one that involved his fists. "He can't just . . ."

I reached out, put my hand over his but didn't let it linger. I couldn't bear it if he pulled away from me again. "It's okay." I considered that. "I mean, it's not okay, obviously. It was a shit thing to do. But I'm okay. At least I'm better than I was this spring." I remembered the girl who'd arrived in Willow Creek with everything she owned packed in the back of a white Jeep. I'd been worried then about my sister, sure. But I'd been worried about me too. "I was pretty lost then."

A clang of metal in the distance got our attention, and it brought us back to ourselves and to Faire. Time to start the day. Simon hopped easily to his feet and held a hand down to me. I gratefully took it, since getting up from the ground while strapped into this outfit was not a graceful endeavor.

Once we were both on our feet we made our way back to the main lane. I lingered at a jeweler's booth to examine a hanging display of crystal pendants. They caught the light and made rainbows on the tree behind the booth. When I glanced back again I saw Simon was waiting for me when I'd expected him to walk on ahead. But instead he was watching me watch the crystals, a thoughtful look on his face.

"How did you know?" he asked as I fell into step next to him again.

"Hmm?"

"How did you know I'm twenty-seven? I don't remember that coming up before."

"Oh. Mitch told me."

Simon's step faltered for a second, but he recovered smoothly. "Mitch," he repeated. All the life had gone out of his voice. "Right, yeah. Mitch."

"I'm sorry. Are you two not friends?" Had I said something wrong? I was getting that feeling again—like I was stepping into a web of long-term, intertwined relationships without a score-card, and I was blundering around making mistakes. "He said you'd known each other a long time."

"Oh, yeah. Since we were kids. I've known him forever." But his mouth twisted like he'd sucked on a lemon. "You two look good together."

"What?" I blinked at the non sequitur, but before I could ask what he meant we'd arrived at the tavern, where Stacey was set-ting up for the day with Jamie and the other red-shirted volun-teers.

Simon didn't continue our conversation. Instead he put on his hat and swept his arm in front of him in a gesture that was part bow, part ushering me to my station for the day. "Your tav-ern awaits, milady." The accent was back on, and he had changed personas again. Our heart-to-heart was over and he was gone, striding down the lane, without a care in the world.

"What were you and Simon talking about?" Stacey fished her pewter pendant out of her belt pouch and tied the black cord around her neck.

"Not much." I checked the wine bottles that had already been set up by the volunteer staff and tried to come up with some-thing else unnecessary to do. "We ran into each other on the way." Technically this was true.

"Well, you weren't yelling at each other, so that's progress. You might even like the guy by the end of the summer."

"Maybe." I forced a laugh I didn't quite feel. "I wouldn't count on it. You know Simon." She apparently knew him a hell of a lot better than I did. Everyone knew him better than I did.

Mitch and I look good together? What the hell did that mean?

I glowered at a bottle of chardonnay. Just when I was changing my mind about Simon being an insufferable dickhead, he had to all but dismiss me and toss me in Mitch's direction like an unwanted basketball.

I was so annoyed that it didn't hit me until an hour or two later, in the middle of opening a beer and handing it to a patron with a smile. I'd first signed on to Faire because of Mitch. I had made vague but firm plans of getting under that kilt before the summer was over.

When had I forgotten about that? When had my daydreams drifted away from the beefcake in a kilt and toward the slim pirate in black leather, with dark moods and perplexing smiles?

I made change for the patron as quickly as I could. Nothing about this summer was going the way I'd intended.

Fourteen

"*There she is.* The girl in blue."

I heard a giggle behind me as I cleared off one of the tables in the back, but I ignored it as part of the day's chatter. The band behind us had started their next set on the nearby stage, and I listened for my favorite song. Our third weekend was coming to an end. Halfway through Faire and I still hadn't made it to the show, but certain sounds filtered their way to me from the stage. While I'd never heard a song in its entirety, I always listened for favorite beats and moments that had developed into the soundtrack of my summer. A soundtrack that included the clash of steel on steel as the chess match played out, as well as cheers from the various shows around us.

Giggles like the one I just heard were also part of that soundtrack, so I didn't pay much attention as I gathered up the empties and tossed them in the trash. But when I turned to make my way back to the bar, there were three women eyeing me. I stopped moving for a second. Was I having a wardrobe malfunction? I felt as strapped in as ever, but had my bodice shifted and revealed more than it should?

A quick glance down confirmed I was intact, so I bobbed a quick in-character curtsy in their direction. "Miladies. What can I get for you this fine Sunday?"

"Ooh, wine." One of them caught sight of the bottle of white zinfandel on the bar. The other two nodded in agreement, and Janet started pouring for them while I moved back behind the bar to take their money.

"But we're here to ask you about Marcus." The tallest of the three leaned over toward me conspiratorially.

My brow furrowed. "Marcus?" They must mean Mitch, who was the only Marcus I knew. But why would they be asking me about him? I wasn't wearing a badge reading *Flirt with the shirtless guy in a kilt! Ask me how!* But I took a chance. "Do you mean Marcus MacGregor? Tall, muscled . . . ?"

"Kilt." She sighed with a smile. Yep, we were talking about the same guy.

I made change for their wine, then picked up a towel to do a quick wipe-down of the bar. "What would you like to know?"

"You know him pretty well, right? I mean, he was talking about you."

I dropped the towel. "He what?" From the other side of the bar, Stacey laughed in surprise.

"Oh, I need to hear this."

"Well, we were at the chess match, over there?" She pointed and we nodded, as though we had no idea where the chess match was located. "And Amber here was flirting with him—"

"I was not!" But the shortest of them, a blonde, blushed a little, making her protest invalid. "I was making conversation. Being friendly. I'm a friendly person."

"Mmm-hmm." The third one said this to her wine with a small smile.

"Anyway," Tall Girl continued. "He said he was glad we had come to the match, because not enough people were there to cheer him on. And then he mentioned you."

"Me?" I looked over at Stacey, who shrugged.

"He said his tavern girls hadn't been to see him fight in ages. And we should come here, get a drink, and ask you when you were coming back to see him. He said to look for the girl in blue."

"Did he." My eyes narrowed. It was impressive the way Mitch could flirt through third parties. Shameless.

"He has a point, though, doesn't he?" Stacey leaned on the bar and turned her full attention toward me.

"He does not," I said. "We were there last weekend; we saw the fighting then."

"But not this weekend. We should make our way there later today, what d'you think?"

Somehow the accent made it worse. Stacey's eyes were pleading, like I was some kind of fun police that never let us leave the bar. Like I was turning into Simon.

Well, screw that. "All right, then. The next match is at half past two, aye?" I picked up my towel and finished wiping down the bar. "We can go then."

Mitch and Stacey weren't wrong. I hadn't been by to see the chess match all weekend. I didn't want to see Simon any more than I had to. Since our talk in front of his brother's memorial the day before, things had been . . . weird. At the time, I'd thought something was happening between us, something that had sparked the previous week when he'd kissed me at the tavern. Our talk had been so frank, so open, more open than I'd been with anyone in a long time, and I'd thought that spark had been kindled into something more. Something I wanted to explore.

But it turned out to be nothing. Worse than nothing, Simon seemed to go out of his way to not see me. This Faire wasn't that big; it was hard to avoid someone around here. But since he'd walked me to the tavern on Saturday morning I hadn't seen him the rest of the day. He'd stayed on the other side of the stage as the group got ready this morning, and I hadn't seen him all day today, either. He was definitely avoiding me.

Emma the Tavern Wench missed Captain Blackthorne greatly. She wanted him to come by the tavern he'd been neglecting lately, because she thrilled to see him and lived for those moments where his attention was like the sun. But Emily the Regular Person wanted to give Simon a good shake and ask him what his problem was.

A little before two thirty Stacey and I left the tavern in the more-than-capable hands of our volunteers and trooped across the field to the chess match. Mitch greeted us with a large grin and a wave of his ridiculously large sword, and I couldn't help but smile back. The man was infectious.

"You're here!"

In response I dropped into a low curtsy, reflecting that even his Scottish brogue didn't do it for me as much as a pirate's quiet innuendo. What was wrong with me? "As requested," I said through my smile as I straightened back up.

He threw his head back and laughed. "I canna believe that worked! I should have plied you lasses with guilt long before this!"

Stacey giggled, and I joined in because why not? He bowed over each of our hands in turn, and it would be an absolute lie to say I didn't enjoy the attention. We needed to get out of our tavern more often; this was the fun part of Faire. I spied Simon on the other end of the chessboard, but he didn't come over to say hello or even look in my direction. Fine. Whatever.

The match was the same as it ever was. We'd seen it several times by now, but we cheered and reacted as though it was brand-new to us. At several points during the match my attention wandered to Simon, who always looked away when our eyes met. Finally it was down to him and Mitch, like always, and before he moved to the center of the board he circled the edge, coming toward us until he was in front of Stacey and me.

"A kiss for luck, darling?" He held out a hand toward me. I narrowed my eyes at him a little, but Emma the Wench missed her pirate, and I felt that side of me taking over. So my frown melted into a knowing smile and I slipped my hand into his. Instead of bowing and bestowing the kiss I expected, though, he grasped it tight and pulled, tugging me forward and stepping closer. Before I knew what was happening he was kissing me, not hard, not passionately, but a sweet brush of his mouth on mine. He took my startled gasp into his mouth like a prize he could claim and as the cast and audience whooped around us he grinned against my lips.

Two could play at that. As he started to lean away I reached for him, threading my other hand through his hair and pulling his head back down to mine for a better kiss. A real kiss. *Talk to me*, my kiss said. *I'm tired of playing. Is this real? How can we make this real?*

The whoops continued around us, and when the kiss reached its natural conclusion he pulled away and I let him go, looking up at him with searching eyes. I was breaking character in front of a crowd of people, but I didn't care. He looked back at me with a shaken expression, and I felt a jolt of guilt. He had to fight, a highly complex, choreographed routine with weapons.

Maybe telegraphing my confusion at our relationship via a kiss in front of a crowd wasn't the best plan at that exact moment.

"You ready, then, Blackthorne?" Mitch's easygoing demeanor had vanished into his warrior persona again, and his question was loaded with foreboding.

Simon cleared his throat and turned an easy smile in Mitch's direction. "Of course. Had to get a good-luck kiss from my girl first, you know."

"Your girl? Is that what she is?" Mitch raised an eyebrow. "You sure about that?"

Simon looked over his shoulder back at me, and his smile slipped a fraction. But he forced it on again for the performance. "Of course. You were there when we were bound, remember?"

Mitch shrugged. "And yet she came to watch the fighting at my request. Not yours." He twirled the claymore in his hand, the broad steel flashing in the sunlight, and Simon scoffed in response.

"That matters not, she came to see me."

Mitch pointed his sword directly at Simon. "I could take her from you without a thought."

Simon drew his own sword and slapped it against the claymore. "You are welcome to try."

I sucked in a breath; I didn't like the turn this had taken. My heart sank in my chest as they started their choreographed fight. I knew how it ended. Simon lost every time. That was the way they rehearsed it, the way they performed it. But now they'd added me to this fight, like a prize to be won. I watched the two men circle each other and tried to interpret Simon's expression. He said he was fighting for me, but he would lose. He knew that I knew that. Was there a deeper meaning there? Was he giving me the answer I'd asked for with my kiss? *None of this is real. I don't want you. Mitch can have you. I don't care.*

I knew every move of this fight, every step of it like a dance. But as I watched it this time, goose bumps rose on my arms despite the heat of the afternoon. Simon's face was ominous, angry. He'd completely abandoned the facade of the easygoing, rule-breaking pirate, and his attacks were harder than I'd ever seen. Mitch . . . well, Mitch was still built like a brick wall, so he moved through the steps of the fight like he always did. Except when Simon flipped him, he landed a little harder than he usually did, dropping to his knees instead of landing easily on his feet. He hopped up again in a smooth motion, but the fact that he had to do so at all bothered me. These guys knew what they were doing. Why hadn't that flip been timed right?

The rest of the fight went much the same way, especially as they fought unarmed. Simon's swings seemed wilder, a little more out of control than they needed to be. I was almost relieved when it ended and Simon was defeated without either of them being injured. He knelt in the grass, chest heaving with exertion, Mitch's knife at his throat. Fight over, Mitch stowed his knife and reached down a hand to help Simon up, like he did every time. But this time, instead of taking it, Simon slapped it away and got to his feet on his own. Then he stalked off the field, without a word or look to me, Mitch, or anyone else.

Mitch looked over his shoulder at me, his eyes wide, and I'm sure I looked exactly the same way. Then Mitch slipped back into character, and the chess match concluded. Simon didn't return to the field. He didn't come out for the curtain call. I wanted to look for him, make sure he was okay. But I had a feeling he didn't want to see me. Not then, and maybe not ever.

Stacey and I walked back to our tavern in an odd silence until I couldn't stand it anymore. "What the hell was that about?"

She looked back over her shoulder at the chess field, like she could see an answer there. But she shook her head. "I don't know. I haven't seen him act like that in years. Since . . ."

"Since . . . ?" I was well and truly sick of this. What tragic backstory was I missing here? Would I ever catch up, and stop feeling like the new girl?

She shook her head like I'd woken her from a trance. "Oh, nothing. The two of them weren't exactly best friends in high school. Mitch was, well, Mitch." She waved a hand, illustrating height, breadth, and I got the picture.

"So they fought over girls a lot?"

"No." She chewed on her bottom lip. "They didn't have to. Girls liked Mitch, you know. Varsity football and all that. All he had to do was wink and he had a new girlfriend. Simon . . . wasn't like that."

I sighed heavily. "Okay. But this isn't high school anymore, right?"

"You'd think so, wouldn't you?" With one last shake of her head, Stacey walked a little ahead of me to the tavern, while I turned to look back at the chess field. The audience had emptied out, and a few cast members still milled around. I didn't see either Simon or Mitch. I didn't want to. I wanted to go back to my tavern, where it was safe.

The end of the day couldn't come soon enough. Once the last patron was gone, I yanked at the strings of my bodice and tore it off before unpinning and stepping out of the overskirt. The white underdress was stuck to my torso and I peeled it away as I collected Caitlin. As we trudged to the back of the parking lot, she loosened the front laces on her bodice as she walked, while I fished my phone out of my basket. By the time we got to the Jeep we both looked pretty bedraggled, but this had become our daily post-Faire routine. We dumped our baskets and extraneous costume pieces into the back, I swapped out my boots and hose for flip-flops, and we hopped in for the drive home.

We were barely out of the parking lot when April called. I put her on speakerphone and handed my phone back to Cait.

"Hey, I called in Chinese food if you can pick it up on the way home."

"Umm . . ." I thought fast. I didn't have a change of clothes in the Jeep, and I was currently wearing basically a nightgown with no bra underneath and flip-flops. The people at the take-out place were gonna love me. But the thought of not having to wait for dinner won out over a little temporary embarrassment. "No problem. That sounds great."

"You got sweet-and-sour, right?" Caitlin always asked the important questions. She also yelled a little too loudly into the phone, and I winced on behalf of April's eardrum.

"Of course I did. I'm your mother, aren't I?"

It was a testament to how much this whole town knew about and supported the Renaissance faire when no one seemed to notice how I was dressed when I waltzed in to pick up our order. They'd probably seen worse.

Once we got home Caitlin carried the food inside while I got everything out from the back of the Jeep. The smell of my sesame chicken made me want to drool on my skirts, but I forced myself to put my underdress in the washing machine and get in the shower before eating. No matter how hungry or how tired I was, I couldn't do anything before washing off the day's accumulation of dirt.

I never felt particularly dirty while I was at Faire. It wasn't like I was walking through clouds of dust, or spent the day being pelted by handfuls of dirt. But by the time I got home my skin practically itched for a shower, and I couldn't wait to strip down and scrub. I loved watching in bemused disgust as the water swirled down the drain in a dark brown stream. But after shampooing my hair twice and basically loofah-ing off a layer of skin, I felt cleaner than I ever had in my life. Stacey had said at the beginning that a long hot shower at the end of the day would be my new best friend, and she was right.

When I made it back out to the kitchen, April took in my outfit: yoga pants and a stretched-out T-shirt. "Staying in tonight, huh?"

"Yep." I'd had enough of the men of Willow Creek for a while. I reached for a plate and the carton of sesame chicken, which was thankfully still warm. Across the table Caitlin was finishing up her sweet-and-sour pork.

"Can I have my phone back?" No phones at the table, that was the rule.

April shook her head. "Dishes in the sink first."

Cait huffed a little, then brightened. "They were fighting over Emily today."

I dropped a chopstick.

"What?" April asked.

"Nothing." I looked daggers across the table at Caitlin, who gleefully refused to get the hint.

"At the chess match." She got up to clear her dishes and grinned as she walked by me. "Coach Malone and Mr. G."

"Oh, really?" April turned to me, a slow smile crawling up her face.

I turned in my chair to watch my niece take her dishes to the sink. "You weren't even there!"

"I heard about it!" she called over her shoulder, and I slumped in my chair. Great. I was officially part of Faire gossip.

"Here." I scooped up Caitlin's phone from where it sat next to April's plate and tossed it to her. Cait caught it neatly. "Why don't you go play on your phone. Somewhere that isn't here."

"Don't think you're getting out of it that easy." April turned back to me as Caitlin all but skipped out of the room. "Why are men fighting over you? Something you're not telling me?"

Oh, God. I hadn't talked to April about any of this—Simon's hot-and-cold actions, Mitch's easygoing if meaningless flirting—and now I didn't know where to start. Instead I stared hard at my sesame chicken. "It's nothing," I finally said. "It's a bit. A little sketch we've been doing at Faire. Simon plays this pirate character who's in love with me . . ." *And he's kissed me. More than once. But it isn't real. None of it's real.* The thought made me sadder than I expected. "Mitch has been getting in on it lately, so they did this whole thing today . . ." I shrugged. "It was silly."

"Mmm-hmm." April crunched on an egg roll, and she sounded so much like our mother that I knew I hadn't fooled her a bit. "So this has nothing to do with why you're staying in tonight."

I had to laugh. "Oh, it's got everything to do with it." I pushed my food around on my plate a little before tossing down my chopsticks. I'd lost my appetite. Which was a shame, because I loved Chinese food. I reached for the fortune cookies in the middle of the table and cracked one open. *Tell me what to do, fortune cookie.* I unrolled the little slip of paper inside: *Ask the right question.*

Hmm. Adding "in bed" didn't make it much funnier, so it was kind of a bummer of a fortune as far as I was concerned, but at the same time it had a point. I'd been doing a lot of going along with things since I got to town, and hadn't asserted myself. I needed to ask more questions. Maybe it was time to start.

I looked up at April again. No time like the present. "How did you do it?"

She raised her eyebrows. "Do what?"

I gestured around. "All of this. After you got divorced. How did you pick up and keep going? How did you move on?" I held my breath. Was this too personal a question? We didn't talk like this. We never had. This may have been the first time I'd asked my big sister for advice.

April blew out a long breath. "Wow. Well . . ." She looked around the kitchen, as if seeing it for the first time. "I mean, 'all this' took a really long time. When Robert and I first got divorced, it was pretty much me, a baby, and a tote bag full of diapers."

"He really didn't help you at all? No child support, nothing?" I'd never known the details of April's divorce. I'd been younger than Caitlin when it had happened, after all.

"Nothing," she said. "My lawyer tried to call his bluff. Told him that if he didn't want to pay child support, he wouldn't have any parental rights. Turned out he was fine with that. I mean, I could have fought it. Tried harder to get him to step up. But I was so . . ." She sighed a long sigh. "I was so *tired*, and I was too young to feel that tired, you know?"

"Do I ever." I was thinking about Jake and me now. About how I'd come home one night last year from my second job, realizing I was twenty-three and my soul was exhausted. That night I'd felt much older than I had any right to. Yeah, I knew exactly what April meant.

"I figured the best way to stop feeling that tired was to stop fighting losing battles. Stop banging my head against a brick wall, trying to get him to do the right thing. I focused on what I had. Caitlin. Mom and Dad. You."

"Me?"

"Yeah, you. You know what I did? I wised up and went home.

I leaned on family. I was there with you for a long time, re-member?"

"Kind of?" I fiddled with my mostly dry hair, searching my memory for the time she came back home in the early days of her divorce, baby Caitlin in tow. I'd come home from school and there they were in the kitchen with Mom. I'd helped Dad get my old crib down from the attic and set it up in the guest room. I couldn't remember exactly how long they'd lived with us. "It felt like a while."

"A year, almost."

"A *year*? Was it really that long?" While in some ways it seemed like they'd stayed for ages, it felt like a blip in time in my mem-ory. Even when we'd lived under the same roof, April and I hadn't talked much, not the way sisters were supposed to. But I'd been busy being a kid, with lots of extracurriculars after school, and April had been a new mother trying to get back on her feet. We'd both been busy with our own stuff.

"I didn't want to be there that long, but you know Mom. She insisted. Helped me get enrolled in those accounting classes, made you babysit Caitlin while I was in class or at home studying."

"Is that what I was doing?" I remembered pretending Caitlin was my baby sister. I'd been so sad when they'd left again. At the time I hadn't paid attention to what April had been up to. I didn't remember college textbooks, or her studying. She was just . . . there. Funny how age gives you a change in perspective. I slumped a little in my seat with a mock pout. "Probably should have gotten paid if I was babysitting."

April cracked a smile. "Talk to Mom about that. See if you can get back pay." My smile in response matched hers; Mom was a skinflint through and through. Good luck getting cash out of her. "My point," she continued, "is those months living at home helped me get back on my feet. Get an accounting degree, a good job, and eventually this house in this town. But it didn't happen all at once. Starting over, especially that young and with a baby, was the hardest thing I've ever done. I felt so alone. Probably like you did when Jake left."

I nodded. "We had plans. Everything was figured out and then he . . ." My throat closed. I needed to talk about this, but I didn't want to talk about this. It was hard to admit out loud how worthless someone made you feel. I glanced down at the fortune in my hand again. *Ask the right question.* The right question. A stone settled in my chest when I realized I hadn't done that yet. I was asking her about herself, when I wanted to ask about me.

"How do I know if I'm worth it?" I barely got the words out before my throat clogged with tears. That visceral response told me that yes, this was the right question.

"Worth what?" But April's face softened, and she reached across the table to lay a hand over mine. "Oh, you dummy. Of course you are."

I shook my head, unable to speak as the hurt came flooding back. The feeling of being abandoned after everything I'd done for my ex. Everything I'd given up. Of my best not being good enough. Jake's face blurred in my memory, his hair suddenly dark, his eyes hazel and smudged with kohl. He looked like Simon now in my mind—another man who didn't think I was good enough.

"I know it's hard." April's eyes were patient. Kind. Something in her expression filled me with love, and a sense of belonging. "So do what I did. Lean on family. On Caitlin and me. Let us love you, and remind you that you're worth it until you figure out what you're going to do next."

I looked down at our joined hands and blinked back the tears pooling in my eyes. I wasn't used to showing emotion in front of my sister, and I certainly wasn't used to the kind of conversation we were having.

"What I'm going to do next," I repeated, still looking at our hands.

"Weren't we talking about you going back to school? Finishing your degree? Let's look into that more. Mom and Dad helped me get back on my feet when I needed it. I bet they'll help you too."

"Yeah. I could do that." I tried to work some enthusiasm into the idea, but it wasn't coming. That English degree wasn't as shiny and exciting as it had been a few weeks ago. "But . . . what if I don't do that?" I looked up at my sister again.

She frowned. "You don't want to go back to school? But I thought . . ."

"I did too. I mean, that's been my plan for . . . well, forever. But I don't know if I need it. What if what I want to do next is what I'm already doing? This town, you and Cait, Faire, the bookstore . . . I like it here." I hadn't thought about it in those terms before, but without my actively seeking it out or realizing it, Willow Creek had started to feel like a place where I could make a home.

April's frown smoothed into a smile. "Well, that's great too." She squeezed my hand one more time before she let go and sat back in her chair. "I mean, the last few months have been . . . well, okay, they've sucked. But having you here has been . . ." She blinked hard, and I willed her to not cry. I was barely holding it together as it was. "It's been nice having a little sister around."

"I know what you mean. Why haven't we done this sooner?" I gestured between the two of us. "Why did it take you getting in that accident and me getting dumped to bring us together? We wasted so much time, not being close."

She sighed. "Maybe we did. But it's okay." She reached for a fortune cookie of her own and cracked it open. "We're doing it now, right? That's what matters."

"You're right." If I was staying in Willow Creek, we had all the time in the world. I popped half of my fortune cookie in my mouth and crunched down on it. In these few minutes my worldview had altered. All this time August had been an end date. I'd be leaving town once Faire was over and I was no longer needed. But what if I stayed? Not because I was needed, but because I wanted to? "I should probably get the hell out of your guest room at some point, though, right?"

April snorted. "At some point. But no rush. I like having my own private driver."

A surprised laugh bubbled out of me, clearing away the remnants of my tears. "We need to work on that. Maybe you could try driving to work tomorrow. I'll go with you, to make sure you can do it."

"Maybe." She blew out a long breath. "Yeah. Maybe I can do that." She got up and started clearing away take-out containers. I looked at the little slip of paper with my fortune on it. *Ask the right question.* Maybe it was time to start applying that advice to other parts of my life too.

"You know, I think I'll go out to Jackson's for a little bit after all. You want to come?"

April shook her head. "On a Sunday night? Some of us have work tomorrow. Maybe another night. I'd like to see what all the fuss is about."

"It's a date," I said. "You need to get out of the house more. You know, now that you're ambulatory."

"Speaking of . . ." April leaned in the doorway to the kitchen to talk to me. "Marjorie came by today."

"What? Why?" I searched my memory. "I swear I brought all her casserole dishes back."

"It wasn't that. She's starting a book club in the fall, and wanted to know if I was interested."

"Another mom-gathering thing? When does this one meet, Thursdays at two in the afternoon?" I rolled my eyes. "But if you want to do a book club, Chris and I were talking about starting one at the store."

"No, it wasn't like that. She said she realized that all of their plans conflicted with my schedule." April's expression softened. "She came over to apologize for that. And to see if I'm free on the first Thursday of the month. In the evening."

"Wow. So do you think you'll go?"

"I might." She sounded surprised to hear herself say it. "As long as they have good taste in books." Yep, that sounded more like her.

"Well, you know someone who works in a bookstore. I can probably help you with that."

"I bet you can."

"Are you sure, though?" I studied her face. "I bet they'll want to know more about you. You'll have to socialize."

She shrugged. "Yeah. But it's not really gossip if I'm talking about myself, right? Maybe it won't be so bad."

I pushed back from the table. "Are you sure you don't want to come out with me tonight?"

"Nah." She waved a hand. "Let's save that for the fall too."

It didn't take me long to get ready. I put on my favorite sundress for confidence: a bright sunshine-yellow that made my skin look warmer and my eyes look bluer, with a halter-style top that tied at my neck and left my back relatively bare. May as well show some skin that had been covered up all summer by long skirts and chemises. I was sick of wearing my hair up all the time, but I hadn't done anything with it while it air-dried, so it was too frizzy to leave down. I wound it into a loose twist and stuck a clip in it before lining my eyes and applying some lip gloss. Good enough.

Before I left the house, I stuck the fortune-cookie paper into the pocket of my dress. I needed the reminder tonight.

Fifteen

ey, you made it!"
Mitch waved to me with his beer bottle, and when faced with a smile like his, I had no hope of hiding my own. I ordered a beer before meeting up with him. I was suddenly very glad I'd come out tonight. I'd had enough of games, of second-guessing, of wondering how I fit in with these people. I was armed with my fortune-cookie fortune, and I was going to do what it said. Ask questions. Get answers.

Jackson's wasn't crowded; despite Mitch's assertions, going out after Faire was apparently unnecessary to all but the most dedi-cated. What did that say about me? I slipped through the people gathered in various clumps and peered into all the dark corners, but didn't see Simon anywhere. I masked my frown with a swig of beer and nudged Mitch when I got to his side of the bar.

"Not many people out tonight, huh? Is Stacey here?"

He shook his head. "She said she had plans."

"Plans?" I raised my eyebrows over my beer. "More important than us?"

"Apparently." His eyes scanned the crowd absently as we talked. The familiarity of his expression hit me with sudden clarity. He was looking for a hookup; this was his normal Sunday night routine, Faire or no Faire. I couldn't believe it had taken me this long to put it together. He had never been flirting with me. Or if he had, it hadn't been because I was special. It was because flirting with girls was what he did.

But still . . . ask the right question. I drank some more beer for courage.

"We're not a thing, are we?"

Mitch paused in his scan of the room, then blinked down at me. "What?"

"This." I gestured back and forth with my beer bottle. "You're not, like . . ."

"Hitting on you?" He looked mildly horrified. "No. Oh, damn, Emily, I'm sorry. Did you think . . . ?"

"No!" Now that I had my answer, I wanted to shut down the conversation as fast as possible. "No, I didn't. I wanted to make sure you didn't . . ."

"No. No, not at all." Neither of us seemed keen on letting the other finish a sentence in our haste to get our own words out. He ran a hand through his hair and put down his beer. I'd never seen him look so serious before. "I like you, Emily. You're fun to hang out with. Stace and I thought . . . I dunno, you've been doing a lot to take care of your sister, and we wanted to make sure you had some fun."

My heart skipped an unexpected beat. "That's . . . that's nice of you. Of both of you. Thanks."

He picked up his beer again and clinked the neck of it against mine. "Of course. That's what friends do."

Friends. Yeah. I'd spent the past few years in a whirlwind of multiple jobs, taking care of an asshole of a law student, keeping my eyes on the future. I hadn't had a lot of time for friends. For hanging out. I didn't realize how much I'd missed it until this moment, when the feeling of belonging warmed my chest and I knew what I'd been missing for a long time.

Mitch looked me up and down. "You look cute tonight, though." He shrugged. "We could make out if you want."

I choked on my beer and concentrated on not letting it spew out of my nose. "No," I finally said after my coughing fit had subsided. "Thank you. Tempting offer, but no, thanks." I looked up in time to catch his smirk.

He shrugged around another sip of beer. "Just as well. I don't want to get between you and your pirate."

"My . . . what?" My heart froze, and every nerve ending came alive at the oblique mention of Simon.

Mitch scoffed. "Please. You two have been dancing around each other since day one. Has he seriously not done anything about that yet? Faire's half over. I thought he'd make a move by now."

"Um." I wasn't sure if I wanted to talk about my love life with Mitch Malone in the middle of a bar. Especially since I didn't have a love life. "I'm not sure there's been any . . . dancing . . ."

"Oh, I am. I've known Simon since . . ." He thought for a moment. "I don't actually remember meeting him, that's how long it's been. I know when he's smitten. Believe me, he's got it bad."

"Really?" I narrowed my eyes, and not only because Mitch didn't seem like the type of guy to use the word "smitten." "Then why did you just hit on me?"

His grin was slow and lazy. "I had to make sure you felt the same way about him."

"So that was a test?" I shook my head. "You're a weirdo."

"Guilty," he said with a grin. "But I think you knew that before now."

My chuckle died off as nervousness overwhelmed me again. "So you really think Simon . . . ?"

Mitch shrugged, clearly already bored with the conversation. Probably because it didn't involve him hooking up with anyone. "You should go ask him."

My heart froze in my chest, and I looked around the bar. Had Simon come in while we were talking? Worse, had he seen Mitch and me standing together? Even worse than that, had he heard us talking about him?

But no. If he were going to be here, he would have shown up by now. "Go ask him," I repeated. My hand wandered to my pocket, and the fortune therein. Ask. "Yeah. I should do that."

"Here." Mitch held out his hand. "Give me your phone." He pulled up the maps app, entered in an address, and handed the phone back to me.

I looked down at the address he entered. "So this is . . ."

"Yeah. He's lived in the same place since we were kids. I know exactly where it is."

I raised alarmed eyes to Mitch. "Wait. He lives with his parents?"

Mitch barked out a laugh. "No! No, his parents left town a couple years ago. Not long after Sean died. But Simon already had the teaching job, so he stayed behind. Plus I don't think he wanted to leave the Faire. It was like he had an obligation to keep it going."

The word "obligation" hit me in the heart. "That's what I thought too." Hadn't I almost said something to Chris? Wondered if Simon worked so hard every summer because he wanted to, or because he felt like he had to? "Does anyone else see that? Has anyone said anything to him?"

"I doubt it. I mean, I figure he doesn't mind so much. If he did, he'd just stop doing it, right? Simple." He shrugged, but I frowned. I was pretty sure it wasn't that simple. Mitch took another swig of beer. "The thing about this town is . . . well, it's a small town, you know?"

"Yeah." I nodded even though I really didn't get where he was going with that.

"I mean . . ." He picked at the label on his beer bottle. "When you live in a place like this, like when you grow up and then you stay, who you were in high school is who you are now. I mean, I'm cool with that because . . ." He spread his arms in a well, look at me gesture. "But Simon? When we were kids?"

A corner of my mouth kicked up. "Lacked your confidence?"

Mitch snorted. "Something like that. Nah, he's a great guy, but he was too busy following his brother around to realize it. To be, like, his own person. Then his brother died, you know? But he's still the same Simon he's always been. So busy paying attention to other people and what they need from him that he doesn't go after what he wants for himself." He sent me a pointed look. "I don't know. Maybe you know what that's like."

"I . . ." I cleared my throat. "Maybe a little." My mind reeled. Mitch was way more astute than I'd given him credit for. What happened to the goofy meathead that was supposed to be a fun, mindless hookup for the summer? I'd misjudged him from the beginning.

Just like I'd misjudged Simon. I'd thought he was just like Jake: judgmental and dismissive. I thought he'd never want someone like me. And I'd never want him. I was wrong about that too, wasn't I? I looked down at my phone again. At Simon's address. Suddenly I yearned to be there with all my heart. Was there a teleportation app I could download?

Mitch noticed where my attention had gone and glanced down at my phone too. "Look. What I think is, Simon's in a rut. And he needs to be shaken out of it." He looked up at me with a sidelong smirk. "I bet a cute girl in a yellow sundress will do the trick."

My face heated. "Maybe." A few months ago, I would have loved knowing that Mitch thought I was cute. But every cell in my body had come alive when he'd called Simon *my pirate*, and I couldn't downplay how I felt anymore. Not just about the pirate, but about the man who played him. Mitch thought Simon was smitten? Well, so was I. A few months ago, Simon had been the last man I'd wanted in my life. Now he was the only one.

"Well, you've got his address. He's in the same house he's always lived in, just by himself now." Mitch tilted his head back, finishing his beer, then he pointed the empty bottle at me. "You should go check on him."

"Yeah. I think I will." I clutched the phone tighter in my hand. I'd come to Jackson's tonight to get answers, but the answers weren't here. The good news was, I had turn-by-turn directions to where I'd find them.

Dusk was already streaking the skies when I left Jackson's, and I made a stop on the way, so by the time I pulled into Simon's driveway it was nearly full dark. I didn't knock on his door immediately. Nerves took over and for a minute or two I sat in the driver's seat, taking in his house, too scared to move.

I'd never thought much about Simon's life outside of Faire, especially where he lived. I'd certainly never pictured him in a two-story Colonial at the end of a quiet street. Mitch said he lived alone, and from the outside the house looked far too big for only one person. But the white picket fence and well-tended lawn gave the impression of an idyllic family home, and I pictured Simon as a child here, running around after his big brother in that yard. It made my heart ache with nostalgia for something I'd never actually seen.

Finally I shook it off and headed up the front walk. When my foot hit the porch a light came on, so he'd either seen me lurking outside or there was a motion sensor. I hoped for the latter.

My hand shook as I rang the doorbell, but I pushed the button before I could lose my nerve, then struggled to take a breath over the pounding of my heart. What was I doing here? Taking advice from a random piece of paper in my Chinese takeout? This was crazy.

Nothing happened at first, so for the space of a few heartbeats I was awash with relief. He hadn't seen me lurking after all. Then a few more heartbeats, and the door still didn't open, and the relief drained away, replaced with dread. He knew I was there and he wasn't going to let me in. How long should I stand on the porch like an idiot, hoping he'd come to the door? Should I ring a second time? Should I slink back to the car? Should I—

The door swung open. My heart rate spiked until I could feel it in my throat, and for a second neither of us spoke. Simon looked like his usual unflappable self, but different at the same time. More casual. The times he'd been out of costume he'd been in his usual button-down shirts and crisp jeans. Simon wasn't a dress-down kind of guy.

But at home he was, apparently. At home he wore a faded gray University of Maryland T-shirt and a pair of well-past-broken-in jeans that sat low on his slim hips. This was not someone who had plans to go out, much less entertain visitors.

"Emily?" My gaze flew back up to his face. He'd obviously taken a shower after Faire like I had; his hair was still a little damp and fell over his brow. I'd seen him with that smoldery guyliner around his eyes so often that he looked oddly vulnerable now without it. The silver hoop still hung from one ear. He cocked an eyebrow, and my face flushed. I'd come to his door and then stood there staring without saying a word.

"Hey," I finally said, trying for a smile and mostly failing.

"Hi." He looked down at the bottle of rum I held in my arms. "You know I'm not actually a pirate, right?" But he stepped back from the doorway and waved me in.

"Oh, I bet he's in there somewhere," I said with an airiness I didn't feel as I walked past him and inside. His house looked . . . settled. Lived in. The front hallway was lined with what looked like thirty years' worth of rows of family photographs. But the kitchen gleamed with new appliances, and the old kitchen table only had one placemat, with an open laptop and a pile of paperwork on the other end. He'd been in the middle of something, paying bills maybe, and I'd interrupted his quiet Sunday night.

Simon walked past me into the kitchen, where he got two shot glasses down off a shelf. I opened the bottle of rum, and he poured us shots.

"So what are you doing here?" He slid one of the shot glasses across the kitchen counter to me.

Good question. I downed the shot in an effort to stall and shuddered at the bite of the alcohol. So many questions bubbled to the surface of my brain in answer to his. So many things I wanted to know. About him. About us. Was there even an us? Where could I possibly start?

Sensing none of my inner turmoil, he sipped from his shot glass, savoring the rum, keeping his eyes on me. He looked as placid as always, while the top of my head was about to fly off. How dare he kiss me like that and not give a shit about it afterward.

There was a good starting point. "You *kissed* me." I spat the words out, accused him.

"Ah." He set his glass down and fiddled with the cap on the rum bottle. "I did."

"More than once. You kissed me *today*."

He picked up his shot glass again and knocked back the rest of the rum before splashing in a little more. "I did. In character."

"What?"

"Your character likes my character. The pirate." He picked up the bottle of rum, sloshing the liquid in illustration. "You kissed me back, you know."

"You kissed me out of character too." I waved off his offer of a refill. I'd had half a beer at Jackson's and wanted to keep my head clear. "Last Saturday, when you were yelling at me for missing pub sing and moving some tables around."

He clucked his tongue before taking another sip of rum. "The tables were fine where they were."

"They're even better where they are now." I sucked in an annoyed breath. This was *not* what I had come here to talk about. "And then you kissed me." There. Back on topic. "That was *not* in character."

"You're right." He closed his eyes and dropped his head. "I'm sorry."

I blinked. "Sorry?" That was the last thing I'd expected to hear, and the word stung. I remembered our kiss, our real kiss. How he'd pulled away, tried to apologize. And I hadn't let him. I'd pulled him back and made him kiss me again, and he hadn't wanted to.

Oh, God. I'd misread everything. I wanted to get out of this kitchen, run out of his house and forget I'd ever met him. But, like poking at a bruise, I had a morbid desire to make it hurt more. "You're sorry you kissed me." Yep, that hurt worse. Nausea rose in my stomach. I couldn't look at him; it hurt too much. So I kept my eyes trained on the kitchen floor. On his bare feet, poking out from the bottoms of those old, frayed jeans.

"Yeah." His voice sounded like gravel, and his toes flexed against the floor. "I shouldn't have. And I really shouldn't have kissed you today at the chess match. That was a shitty thing to do. I thought it would be . . ." He sighed, and I still couldn't look at him. I examined his lower kitchen cabinets as he spoke. "It was for the bit, you know? When I'm . . . when I'm him it's okay to do that. Because it's not really me."

"So it's okay when it's fake. It's all been fake between us." I tried to force a laugh, but it came out as an embarrassing cross between a hiccup and a sob. The sound fell flat in the quiet kitchen. "Of course, I get it. I forgot, you think I'm just this stupid college dropout, so why would you . . ." I had to get out of there. I was equal parts enraged and mortified, I was about to cry, and I couldn't let him see. I took a deep, shaking breath and pushed all the emotion down, forcing a smile to my face instead. "Sorry to bother you. Keep the rum." I pushed off the counter and started for the front hallway. "Enjoy your night."

"Hey." I didn't see him move, but he'd crossed the room in an instant, catching my arm before I could leave. "No. This has nothing to do with you dropping out of . . . why would you think that?"

"That day I first told you," I shot back. I was barely holding it together, but if he wouldn't let me leave with dignity, I may as well let him have it. "At the bookstore? I told you I hadn't finished college and you looked at me like I was nothing."

"No." He didn't let go of my arm, but he softened his grip from grasping to holding. "That wasn't it at all. We were joking about Shakespeare and it was . . ." His expression gentled. "It was really nice. But then I saw your face when you said you hadn't finished school. You looked disappointed. In yourself. I hated that for you." His thumb stroked my arm while we talked, both soothing me and heating up my blood in a way that had nothing to do with anger.

"Then why?" I shook my head as I tried to reorder my thinking. All this time, I'd thought he'd looked down on me from day one. But this sounded more like empathy. "Why was it a mistake to kiss me?"

He dropped his hand, and now it was his turn to study the floor. "I . . . I can't imagine Mitch likes it much when I do." He cast a rueful smile at the linoleum. "That's why I'm sorry. Not for kissing you. And that's why I did it today. At the chess match, in front of everyone. Because we'd established these characters, and that story line. It was like a loophole. Just this once, I could kiss the girl I wanted and there wasn't a damn thing Mitch could do about it."

The girl I wanted . . . Those words sent a thrill through my chest. But they weren't enough. They were past tense. *Wanted*. Not *want*. "What does Mitch have to do with this? He sent me over here, you know. To see you." I took my phone out of my pocket and waved it at him. "How do you think I got your address?"

"He sent you . . ." Simon shook his head at the floor. He scrubbed a hand across his cheek, a gesture I had come to recognize after all this time knowing him. He was upset, at a loss. "Why would he do that?" His eyes snapped up to mine, and the intensity in them made me catch my breath. "Did he think it would sound better coming from you?"

"Did he think what would sound better?"

"Telling me to back off. To leave you alone."

"Why the hell would he do that?"

"Well, you and he . . ." His mouth snapped shut, and he suddenly looked lost. Not as lost as I felt, but he was catching up. "Aren't you and he . . . ?"

"No." But understanding started to shine through the cloud of my confusion. "No, we aren't."

"No," he repeated. He looked a little longingly at the rum bottle, and when he looked back at me the longing lingered in his eyes. "Then why has he been all over you, hugging you, asking you out?"

"As a friend. He's been . . ." I shrugged. "He's been trying to make me part of the group."

He narrowed his eyes. "And why were you talking about what was under his kilt?"

A surprised laugh spilled out of me. I'd forgotten about that. "Are you kidding? Every time you flip him over your shoulder the world can see he's wearing bike shorts."

A smile played around his mouth, and his exhale almost sounded like a laugh. "But then today, at the chess match. He was challenging me, acting like you and he . . ." He shook his head as realization hit. "He wasn't telling me to back off," he said. "He was telling me to fight for you." The tension eased out of his shoulders. "I've known that guy for more than twenty years, and this is the first time he's ever been subtle."

The thought of Mitch being subtle made me smile, but when Simon looked up at me the smile faded from my face. The air between us was charged with a kind of energy I'd never felt before as a silence settled over the kitchen. I slipped my phone back in my pocket, and my fingers brushed against the scrap of paper. The fortune. *Ask the right question.* We'd cleared a lot of air between us, but I hadn't obeyed the fortune. Not yet.

The deep breath I took didn't shake at all. I took a step closer to him, and his eyes sharpened like lasers as I approached. "Do you want to kiss me again?" Everything inside of me started singing when I said it, so yes. This was the question I needed to ask. "Not as Captain Blackthorne. Not kissing Emma." My voice was casual, conversational, like someone suggesting a lunch date. His eyes stayed fixed on me as I took one of his hands between both of mine and held on tight. "But you. Simon. And me. Emily."

"Yes." The word was pushed out on a shallow breath. But he didn't reach for me. He stood motionless and watched me move his hand, placing it on my waist like I was positioning us for a dance. He slid it around to my back, letting out a strangled sound when his fingertips met my bare skin. "Christ, Emily, you have no idea how much I want to . . ." He swallowed hard and didn't finish the sentence.

His hand was warm on the small of my back. He tightened his grip, and I followed the gentle pull until I was standing in his arms, his other hand curving around my shoulder. His T-shirt under my hands was as soft as it looked, and he sucked in a breath as I touched him. I felt the thump of his heart under my palm, and the speed and the intensity of it reassured me. I wasn't alone in this.

As I looked up at him I realized I wasn't nervous anymore. I didn't feel unsure. I stared up into his eyes, that kaleidoscope of brown and green and gold, and I had only one more question to ask.

"Will you kiss me again?"

"Yes."

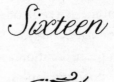

But Simon didn't kiss me. Not at first. His gaze roamed over my face, as if amazed that I was there in his arms. I pictured us standing here in his kitchen until the world ended around us, just staring. After somewhere between thirty seconds and an eternity he ran his hand down my arm and up over my shoulder again. I shivered under his touch as his journey continued, up the side of my neck to trace my jawline, catching some stray curls that had come loose from my hasty updo. He was taking his time, enjoying this, but if he didn't get on with it I was going to scream. He dipped his head down slowly and my breath froze in my chest. His exhalation was warm against my lips in that split second before he kissed me again.

He tasted like rum and heat. His mouth didn't press so much as caress, one small kiss after another as we got used to the feel and the taste of each other. I didn't remember reaching for him, but suddenly my hands were cradling his face, his beard rough against my palms, his groan vibrating against my lips. The small kisses became longer with each touch, each drag of his mouth on mine, and when his tongue grazed against mine those kisses turned electric. Tentative tasting became more intense exploring with tongues and lips and teeth, and sinking into his kiss was the easiest thing in the world. Breathing became something that happened to other people, and by the time we both gasped for air he'd pressed me against the kitchen counter, the edge of it hard against my lower back.

As we fought for breath, our eyes devoured each other, unable to look away. I'd known Simon for months now, and I'd seen different sides of him. Uptight rule-follower. Easygoing pirate. Both of those personas were stripped away now and I'd found a new Simon underneath. The real Simon. I liked him. A lot.

I snagged the collar of his T-shirt and tugged, and as he bent to obey me his smile was delicious against my mouth. I kissed him until that smile dissolved and he stooped a little, hooking his hands under the backs of my thighs and lifting me up against his body. If I wasn't already short of breath, the feel of him hard against my lower belly made stars swim in my vision. He boosted me up to sit on the kitchen counter. When he stepped between my legs my dress hiked up, and he followed the path with his hands, smoothing over my knees and flirting with where the skirt stopped about halfway up my thighs. His touch zinged through my whole body, setting my skin on fire and making my breasts swell against the cotton of my dress. At this new angle he had to tilt his head up to kiss me and I raked his hair back with my fingers. He kissed me like no one ever had before, like I was the only thing keeping him alive. I hooked my legs around his hips and pulled him more into me, wanting more of his heat, his strength.

His hands skimmed up my sides, teasing the edge of my halter dress where fabric met skin, never quite touching the spots that ached the most for his hands. But when he started to tug at the knot at the back of my neck a wave of cold washed over me, and I stopped him with my hands on his wrists.

"Wait."

He immediately let go of me and took a deep breath like he was waking up. "Sorry. Yeah." He blinked at me with slightly unfocused eyes. "You're right," he finally said on a shaky breath. "We're . . . this is moving too fast, isn't it?"

"No!" I grabbed for him, fisting a hand in his T-shirt as he started to step away from me. I already missed his body and wanted it back against mine. He let me pull him back until he stood between my legs again, but his eyes were wary. His hands went to the kitchen counter, not back on me where I wanted them. "That's not . . . that's not it."

He took my hand, threading our fingers together. "Then what is it? Are you okay?"

"Yeah, it's just . . ." I blew out a breath as old insecurities came flooding back. I was being stupid, but I couldn't help it. "You've seen me at Faire. Dressed like . . . well, dressed the way I'm dressed."

He nodded solemnly, though his eyes still sparked with want. "I have." If he was confused at the change in topic he didn't say.

"I need you to know I'm not . . . I mean it's obvious I don't have . . ." I gestured to my chest with my free hand. "The outfit is false advertising, okay?" My shoulders slumped a little. "I don't want you to be . . ."

Understanding broke across his face. "Disappointed?" He raised an eyebrow, and I caught my breath at the rush of heat that he sent through me. I struggled to stay on topic, but it was hard to concentrate when I wanted him touching me again.

"Yeah."

He stretched up on his toes to kiss my forehead, following it up with a kiss on my cheek, then my jaw. "You know that's ridiculous, right?"

"Not . . . not necessarily?" But his tongue was doing things to the skin just under my ear that made me lose the thread of the conversation.

"Seriously. Who the hell would tell you . . ." His mouth stilled on the side of my neck, then he sighed. "God damn it. I swear to God I'm going to find that ex of yours and punch him in the nose."

I shook my head. "Later." He was right. I was being ridiculous. The last comparison to Jake fell away as it became clear that the past had no place here. Besides, if I turned my head a little his mouth was *right there* and why wasn't I kissing him? I remedied that immediately, and from the sound Simon made he didn't mind at all. As his mouth took mine I reached for his hands and put them back on my body. He immediately curved one hand around my back, his fingers following the line of my backbone, while the other hand slid up my side then hesitated. I put my hand on his and steered it where I wanted it.

Simon broke the kiss, sucking in a breath when I closed his hand over my breast, and his other hand tightened on my back. "Fuck." He pressed his forehead to mine, his eyes riveted to my hand over his, guiding him, encouraging his touch, and he caught on quickly. He molded the fabric of my dress over my breast, learning its size, its weight, and how could I have ever felt uncertain about this? I'd never wanted anyone's hands on me more. My nipples tightened, hardening into almost painful peaks against the palm of his hand. His breathing deepened as my body reacted to him. "Christ, Emily." His mouth brushed against mine, almost compulsively. "You're perfect."

"Language," I chided with a voice I barely had. "You teach children with that mouth?"

He pulled away to look at me, his eyes dark and glassy with passion. "Oh, Emily." He made my name sound dangerous. There went his eyebrow again, and his lips kicked up with a wicked smile I didn't know he could make. "I do a lot of things with this mouth."

My throat went dry, heat surged through me, and I shivered anew. "Yeah." My voice was little more than a whisper. "I'm gonna need you to show me."

"Gladly." He kissed me again. Thoroughly. Hungrily.

"Mmm, okay, that's pretty good," I said when he was done. "What else you got?"

He laughed, and it was like the sun coming out. How many times had I seen him smile at Faire, and wanted that smile to be for me? Now it was, and it was almost too much to take.

"That sounds like a challenge." He tugged on my hand, helping me down from the counter. "The kitchen counter is nice and all," he said as he led me out of the kitchen. "I had it put in last year; still paying off that credit card." A wicked smile lit up his face. "But I have many, many more comfortable surfaces to choose from around here."

"Hmm. Well, I mean, I did just get here. The least you could do is give me a tour."

"I know exactly where to start."

We barely made it out of the kitchen before he pressed me against the wall in the hallway. We took plenty of breaks on the way up the stairs and to his bedroom at the end of the hall.

He didn't turn on the light. Instead, he drew me into his arms in a dark bedroom that smelled like him. I couldn't tell if it was soap or aftershave, but it was a clean, warm scent with an undertone of leather that had come to mean Simon. I wanted to bathe in it. I wanted his scent all over my skin, and when he reached for the ties at my neck I helped him push my dress down over my hips and onto the floor, leaving me in my bikini underwear and heeled sandals.

"No fair. You have on all these clothes." I fisted my hands in his T-shirt and pulled it up and over his head, and he let it drop behind him. "It's too dark in here," I said. "Turn on a light or something. I can't see you."

"Can't. I'd have to let go of you." He took my hands and put them on his chest, and damn. I knew he was in decent shape, what with all the stage fighting he did. A guy who flipped a brick wall like Mitch Malone twice a day wouldn't be a weakling. But knowing something intellectually and actually running my hands up a set of tight abs, to a muscled chest sprinkled with just enough hair to tickle my fingertips, was something else entirely. I forgot how to form words, so instead I stepped closer and let my mouth follow my hands.

He sighed from deep in his chest as my tongue started a tentative trail across his skin. He found the clip in my hair and pulled it out, spreading my hair out with his hands. I hooked my fingers in the belt loops in his jeans to hold him close as I let myself explore his throat with my lips, my tongue, my teeth.

"Emily . . ." His voice broke off with a hiss when I bit down gently on that place where his neck met his shoulder, and his hands tightened in my hair. I teased him with my tongue until he pulled my head away and kissed me again, his tongue invading with an urgency he'd never shown before. And then we were moving again. The backs of my knees hit the edge of his bed and

I sat down easily, putting a hand behind me for balance. I felt a smooth quilt under me; of course Simon was the kind of guy to make his bed every day.

I expected him to lay me back on the bed and, well, get on with things. I anticipated his weight pushing me down, his body stretched over mine. I didn't anticipate him sinking to his knees on the floor in front of me.

"I want you to know . . ." He slipped off my right sandal, and his hands lingered on the instep of my foot, traveling up my ankle, my calf, learning my shape. "I'm not a one-night-stand kind of guy." The other sandal thudded to the floor.

"You're not?" My breath shuddered. Would I ever be able to breathe normally again?

"No." His hair brushed against my skin, teasing, feather-like strokes as he turned his head to kiss his way up my leg. "Never have been. This means something. You mean something." His mouth on my skin sent me to the brink of insanity, but his words were a dart of sweet pain. How did he know the exact thing I needed to hear, and how did he know to say it to me now?

"I'm serious, Emily." His voice was hoarse, desperate, and he pulled away to look up at me. "If you want this . . . if we do this . . . I need for it to mean something to you too."

Tears clogged my throat and I cradled his face in my hands. My eyes had adjusted to the darkness of the room. A trickle of moonlight I hadn't noticed before fell across his face and I drank in his eyes drinking me in. I'd never seen anything in my life more beautiful than this man, on his knees in front of me in the moonlight.

I could see him well enough to see the vulnerability in his expression, the way he bit his lower lip as his eyes met mine squarely. His eyes reminded me of the vision I'd once had of him and me and a pirate ship at night, and the memory sent my blood racing. "I wouldn't be here if it didn't mean something." I leaned down, taking his mouth and biting that lip myself. "If you don't touch me," I said against his mouth, "and I mean right now, I'm gonna lose my goddamn mind."

His chuckle was low and dangerous. "Language." But he skimmed his hands down my sides before tugging my underwear over my hips and down my legs, and I kicked them away. He captured the kicking leg and placed a lingering kiss on my calf before slinging that leg over his shoulder.

I fell backward with a low moan, catching myself first on my hands, then my elbows as Simon's mouth moved up my leg, this time with purpose, to my knees and finally to my inner thigh. I knew what was coming, and I wasn't sure if I was ready for it.

The first stroke was with his fingers. The second was with his tongue. I collapsed flat on the bed as he got to work. I couldn't move. I couldn't breathe. Every nerve ending, everything that made up every molecule of me, was focused on Simon's mouth on my body. Nothing else mattered.

He kissed. He explored in slow, maddening licks. Fingertips dipped, stroked, discovered. He moved so slowly, so sweetly, that I didn't feel anything build, there was no anticipation, and I wasn't prepared for the orgasm that ripped through me. Before I was ready I was convulsing against his tongue and his fingers, gasping with breathless cries, fighting to roll my hips while he held me down with one hand and his mouth gave no mercy.

After what felt like a lifetime my body calmed, and Simon eased his grip on me. I stared up at the ceiling, which I could now see pretty well in the dark.

"Okay, I'm impressed," I told the ceiling. "You've got quite the mouth on you."

There was that chuckle again, and the bed dipped beside me as Simon crawled up to join me. Now thoroughly acquainted with the bottom half of my body, he seemed determined to do the same with the top, starting with my navel. He kissed a path up my sternum, licking his way to my breasts. If he had a problem with their size he didn't let it show. In fact, he gave them plenty of attention, enough to make my breath come out in whimpering sighs. I struggled to sit up, grasping for him, needing his mouth on mine again. He kissed me slow and deep, and I caught his moan in my mouth. I rolled into him, twining my legs around and between his, when—

"What the hell?" I pulled away and looked down. "Why are you still wearing pants?"

"It's not my fault." Simon leaned in to kiss my neck, and one of his hands moved south again, where I was still a little sensitive. "I got distracted."

"No, you don't." I squirmed out of his embrace and scrabbled at his jeans, popping the button and wrestling the zipper down. "Get these off." Our laughs combined as we got him naked. When he pulled me back into his arms there was finally nothing between us, and we both sighed together at the feel of nothing but skin against skin. His cock pressed against my lower stomach, hard and hot and impossible to ignore. I snaked a hand between our bodies to curl around him, and he hissed at the contact.

"Wait." His voice shook as I gave him a long, slow stroke. I ignored his plea and concentrated on learning the feel of him, heavy in my hand and slowly growing slick as I established a lazy rhythm. "Wait. God, Emily. Wait, please." He leaned away to fumble in his nightstand, and I grinned and nibbled on his shoulder. Revenge was fantastic.

"Very nice," I said in response to the rip of the condom wrapper. "I like a man who's prepared."

His laugh was harsh and desperate, and it made my smile widen. "Not even close. You have no idea how relieved I was that I had one in there. It's been a while."

"Yeah?" The thought warmed me, reinforced the feeling that this was right. I was where I was supposed to be.

"Yeah." The laughter was gone from his voice now, and my heart thudded as he reached for me again, this time with purpose. But instead of rolling me under him like I expected, he pulled me into him, both of us still on our sides, and hooked my leg over his hip. We were face to face, belly to belly, and he took my hand and brought it back to his cock. "Please." His voice was little more than breath now. His forehead was pressed to mine, and as I stroked him a sigh shuddered out of him. "Please."

I knew what he was asking for. I guided him, teasing the both of us with the tip of him stroking my clit. Then he hitched my leg higher on his hip and he rocked into me, just a little. A strangled sound that could have come from either of us broke the night. He withdrew and pushed into me again, then again, each time a little deeper until finally he was buried inside me, our hips flush against each other.

He didn't move at first. Instead his mouth sought out mine and I kissed him like I was trying to get even closer to him, pull him in deeper. He moved slowly, soft pulses like he couldn't bear to pull all the way out. I was fine with that. Now that we were connected I didn't want him to go away.

But not for long. As his breathing deepened his thrusts became more insistent, and I felt urgency rise in me again. Before long I rocked against him, meeting his passion with my own. His breath came in pants, hot in my ear. His hand was warm and sure at the small of my back, tilting my hips, changing the angle of his body in mine.

He was close. I could feel it in the way he moved, his rhythm stuttering. His hand fell from my back to my thigh, pulling it higher, tighter against him. Once my body was positioned like he wanted it he slid a hand between our bodies. "You can come again, love. I know you can." It wasn't a question. Not a request. It was a command, growled in my ear by a pirate, whose finger-tips stroked me in short, quick circles. Heat coursed through me and I gripped the back of his neck, my fingernails digging into his skin. He growled from deep in his chest, and the rumble of it sent shivers across my skin. When he stroked me harder I bowed against him, wanting to escape the overwhelming feel-ings and trying to get more of him at the same time.

Everything built again, fast, from where he stroked me, where he rocked against me, building higher and higher until I tight-ened and broke in his arms. I clung to him and cried out as waves crashed through me and I spasmed around him.

He stilled his movements as I came, and before I could catch my breath he pressed me under him into the bed. Too weak to hold on, I dropped my hands to lie on either side of my head and he reached for them, threading our fingers together and holding on tight. I tilted my hips up to take him in as deeply as I could. His mouth drank from mine greedily as he drove into me harder.

"I've wanted you for weeks, Emily . . . weeks." The words poured out of him between shuddering breaths and desperate thrusts. He dropped his head, his mouth on the side of my neck. "God . . . I've been trying to stay away from you, not touch you, not want you . . ." His eyes were closed and his words washed over me, spoken against my skin, and I gratefully let them soak in. "Then you show up here in that little dress, you make me crazy. Emily." My name was a hoarse cry torn from his throat, his hands tightened impossibly on mine. "You feel so . . . I don't know if I can . . ."

"It's okay." I wanted to hold him, but he was holding me down too tightly. So I canted my thighs up, clinging to him, and I kissed his neck, his jaw. "It's okay," I said into his ear. "Let go. I've got you." I found that silver hoop with my teeth and tugged on it a little, ran my tongue along the shell of his ear, biting, and he sucked in a breath like he was drowning. Then his body shuddered above mine, into mine, and we rode out his orgasm together.

He never did turn on the light that night, but I didn't mind. Everything I needed was easy to find in the dark.

Seventeen

The *first thing* I realized, as I blinked slowly awake the next morning, was that Simon was a cuddler. The second thing I realized was that I was too. We'd slept with our legs tangled together, and even in sleep he had one arm wrapped around me and his other hand buried in my hair, holding me to him.

At first I tried to pretend I was still asleep so I wouldn't have to move. I'd never felt this way in my life. Warm. Safe. Protected. No one had ever made me feel cherished the way Simon had during these last few hours.

I could get used to this.

Early-morning sunlight filtered in through the half-closed blinds that had let the moonlight in the night before. I stretched a little, and Simon's arms tightened around me in sleep while I let my mind wander. Monday morning. No bookstore. No Faire. That one beautiful, blissful day where I had nothing planned. The only thing on the agenda was keeping an eye on Caitlin, making sure she didn't burn the house down while April was at work . . .

Shit.

I exploded out of the bed, sheets flying, and scrambled for my dress.

"What . . . ?" Behind me, Simon struggled for wakefulness as I snatched my underwear off the floor.

"I have to go." I yanked on my underwear and shook out my dress, too flustered to worry about modesty. Or politeness. My phone thumped to the carpet and I scooped it up, punching in April's number while I pulled my dress on over my hips. "I'm sorry!" The apology was out of my mouth before April could even say hello. "I know, I'm late. I'll be there in a sec."

"There you are!" April sounded a little too casual for someone who'd been left in the lurch. "Are you okay? I just checked your room and . . . well, you're not there. Where the hell are you?"

"I know, I know." I glossed right over her questions. "I'm on my way now, though." I tucked the phone between my shoulder and ear so I could pull up the halter part of my dress and tie it around my neck. It was a little awkward, but I got it done. "Be there in about ten minutes. You won't be late to work, I promise."

"Nah."

I stopped short, one sandal on and one in my hand. "What do you mean, 'nah'? Are you calling in sick?"

"I mean I can do this. It's time I drove myself. We were talking about it last night, weren't we?"

"Yeah. But I was going to ride with you just in case. Be your backup."

"Just hang tight and keep your phone on. If I need you I'll call, okay?"

"Okay." I sank down to sit on the edge of the bed. "Okay. But . . . text me when you get there?"

"Of course I will. And then tonight you can fill me in on why you were out all night. Everything okay with you?"

"Me? Umm . . ." I looked over my shoulder at Simon, who was sitting up in bed with his arms crossed over his knees, his smile a mix between amused and perplexed. He met my eyes and raised an eyebrow, and I couldn't help but smile back. Looking at him brought back the warm/safe/cherished feeling I'd had when I woke up, and the worry in my gut melted away. "Yeah," I said both to my sister and to the man I'd spent the night with. "Everything is definitely okay."

I hung up and tossed my phone down onto the bed, and Simon reached across the blankets for my hand. "Are you sure about that? Those three minutes were a roller coaster."

"It's a long story. I'd need coffee before I could even begin to go into it." I toed off the one sandal I'd put on and flopped down on my back with a long sigh. "Sorry for the wake-up call."

He shook his head and brought my hand to his mouth. "It's no problem." He took his time, kissing the back of my hand, the tips of my fingers, and I started to squirm. Yeah, I could definitely get used to this. "But I do have coffee, if that helps. I also have eggs. Do you like omelets?"

I couldn't help the smile that broke over my face. "I love them."

In the kitchen, while the coffeemaker burbled, Simon cracked eggs in a bowl and got cheese and milk out of the fridge. He directed me to the cabinet with the coffee mugs and I poured the coffee. Pretty soon he was busy at the stove, so while the eggs and cheese sizzled together I took my cup of coffee and wandered out into the front hallway for some basic snooping around. The wall of family photographs was a good place to start.

Dear God, Simon was an adorable child. When Mitch had talked about the two of them growing up together, I'd pictured Mitch swinging from the monkey bars and hitting on the other first graders, while Simon was probably in a tiny starched shirt with immaculate hair, reading at the side of the playground. I wasn't too far off. Making my way down the wall of pictures was a sped-up journey through time: a dark-haired woman and her sandy-brown-haired husband, first with one dark-haired boy then two. While most of the early ones were posed, professional shots, there was the occasional candid, especially of the two brothers.

Even as a child Sean stood out. The older the boys got in the photos the more magnetic Sean appeared, with a smile that drew you in, made you want to be part of his orbit. I studied Simon's older brother in the most recent photos. I'd heard so much about him at this point that it was like coming face-to-face with a legend. The last pictures showed him thinner, with circles under his eyes, but his smile was as magnetic as ever. Just from looking at these photos I wanted to know him better. His death must have been devastating to this family.

But more than Sean's smile, the thing that stood out to me in this succession of photos was Simon's. In early photos he smiled with his whole face, the bright, broad grin of a happy child. But the older he got, the more the smile faded until it was the close-lipped half curve of the lips that looked like the Simon I knew. He didn't look unhappy in any of the pictures, just less exuberant. Like he knew Sean's smile was enough to light up a room on its own, and he didn't need to contribute to the wattage.

I didn't hear Simon approach, but his arms slid around me from behind, careful not to dislodge the coffee cup in my hands. He didn't speak; he seemed content to nestle my body into his until we were as close as we'd been when I woke up. I knew that I could release all of my tension and melt into his arms, and he would hold me up.

Instead I gestured with my coffee mug at the wall of family history. "So where are your parents?"

"In the basement. I let them out on holidays, if they behave." He squirmed away from the elbow I aimed at his stomach. His laugh was a low rush of breath in my ear and I remembered how he'd once chastised me for filling out a form incorrectly. Was this the same man?

"No," he said once I'd stopped threatening him. "They're in South Dakota right now, on their way out to the West Coast for the fall."

"South Dakota?" That made about as much sense as them being in the basement.

He nodded, resting his chin on my shoulder and looking at the pictures of his family. "It was hard on all of us when Sean died. My mother especially. Everything in this house, this town, reminded her of him, and it sent her into this downward spiral that . . . Some days she didn't get out of bed at all." His arms tightened around me and I laid one hand on his forearm, squeezing as much comfort into my touch as I could.

"One day my dad pulled into the driveway in this huge RV. He didn't talk to her about it beforehand, just went and bought the thing. I thought she was going to kill him. But she came around, and they started taking it out on the weekends. They took longer and longer trips, and before I knew it, my father had taken early retirement and they were off traveling the country."

I tilted my head up to look at him. "They just . . . left you?" I didn't like it. In the space of a few months, he went from being in a family to living alone? No, I didn't like it at all.

"I sure as hell wasn't going with them. Twenty-five years old and driving around the country with my parents in a big tin can? No, thank you." He smiled at the thought, but his smile was wistful and a little sad. "They send postcards, and come home in

December and stay for a few weeks through the holidays. Last Christmas, they gave me the deed to this house."

"Hell of a Christmas present." I raised my eyebrows, and he snorted in response.

"They said it was going to be mine eventually anyway." His gaze roamed over the pictures on the wall. "I was living in Baltimore when Sean first got sick, then I moved back here and got a substitute teaching job. I'd planned to help out with things for a year or two until he got better. I wasn't going to stay forever. But then Mr. McDaniels retired, and Willow Creek High needed an English teacher. Then I suddenly became a homeowner . . ." He shrugged. "Things just kind of happened. There's something comforting about living where you've always been. Everyone knows you. You're part of something." His eyes lingered on a picture of himself and his brother as teens. "Of course, that also means you're not allowed to change. I guess I'm going to be Sean's little brother forever."

Mitch had said something similar, but before I could say anything about it, Simon's face cleared, like the sun coming out from behind a cloud. "Come on, your eggs are getting cold." He dropped a kiss on my shoulder and took my hand. "You promised me a story, remember? It's your turn."

I let him lead me back to the kitchen, where he'd laid a second place mat on the table, and between forkfuls of a very good omelet, I filled Simon in on some of the details of April's accident. Well, not the accident itself, but its aftermath.

"So she doesn't drive at all?"

"Not since she got out of the hospital. She tried a couple times, but she freezes up when she's behind the wheel." I got up from the table to refill my coffee mug. "I mean, I don't blame her. T-boned at a major intersection? I think I'd see that every time I closed my eyes." I held up the carafe in invitation, but he shook his head, so I sat back down at the table across from him.

"Anyway, getting back to normal seems to be helping her. She went back to work recently, and her mood improved big-time. Maybe now that she's driving it'll be another step. But I'll feel better when I know she's made it there okay." I sipped from my mug and closed my eyes in appreciation. "You make excellent coffee. I'll be over every morning for this."

"Please do." His gaze lingered on mine, and I knew he wasn't just offering coffee. My smile widened, letting him know I'd be happy to take him up on that offer.

My phone buzzed on the table. April had sent a selfie of herself in her work parking lot, thumbs-up in front of her SUV. *Made it!* When I put the phone down it was like a weight fell off my shoulders. More importantly a veil had been lifted from my eyes. I replayed the last hour or so in my head and my heart sank. "I'm sorry. I've been an asshole."

He was surprised into a laugh. "What? Since when?"

"Since I didn't even say good morning."

"Oh." He raised his coffee mug at me in salute. "Well, good morning."

"No. Not like that." I got up and went to his side of the table, and he scooted his chair back a little so he could turn to me as I did. I ran a hand through his hair—this was a thing I got to do now—and bent to kiss him. Slowly. Softly. Thoroughly. "Good morning," I said through our kiss, pronouncing the words deliberately.

He smiled against my lips. "Good morning." He pulled me into his lap until I straddled both him and the kitchen chair. "Much better. I'll admit I was worried for a minute there." His fingers stroked slowly up my back, learning each ridge of my spine. "When you jumped out of bed and started throwing on your clothes before I'd even woken up, it was like you'd realized what a mistake you'd made."

I blinked. "Mistake?"

"You know. Sleeping with the enemy and all that." His voice was light, almost teasing, but his eyes had this edge to them I didn't like.

I cupped his cheek in my hand, watching the way his expression softened the more we touched. I wanted to crawl into him, become part of him so he would never feel alone again. But I didn't know how to tell him that without it sounding like the world's creepiest Valentine's card so instead I kissed him again, pouring everything I felt into it. I told him I couldn't even remember a time that I'd thought of him as the enemy. I told him how much it meant to have someone in my life now who wanted me for me, and not for what I could do for him.

He tasted like coffee, smooth and dark and rich, and I remembered something Chris had said once about Simon being an acquired taste. She was right. I was hooked.

Eighteen

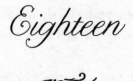

W hen I pulled into the driveway later that morning there
were two texts on my phone. One from Caitlin, telling
me she was riding her bike into town to meet some friends, and
a second from a number I didn't recognize.

Thanks for the rum.

Warmth spread in my chest, in time with the smile on my
face. I couldn't reply fast enough.

Thanks for the coffee.

I added Simon's number to my contacts and slipped my
phone into my pocket before I did something stupid like turn
around and go back to his house. But my head was too full of
confusion, and I was grateful the house was empty for the day.
April would come home tonight with a million questions, and

before she did I needed to figure out what to tell her. I needed to get my head around what had happened between Simon and me.

Now that I was home, those hours in Simon's house, in Simon's bed, seemed like a life apart, removed from the rest of the world. As I went back to my everyday routine, a low-level panic crept into my blood. He'd said he didn't want a one-night stand, but lots of guys said things like that, didn't they? Especially when they already had the girl naked and in their bed. Things could look awfully different by daylight. He'd seemed so sincere at breakfast, but when I'd left he hadn't mentioned seeing me again. That text hadn't exactly opened a door, either. Or was I expecting too much? I was way out of practice here.

By the time April and Caitlin were both home and dinner was on the table, it was safe to say my head was still a mess. So I did what I did best. Pushed down my feelings and focused on the people around me.

"So how do you feel?" I asked April. She hadn't said anything about her first day of driving since her accident.

"I'm okay." She reached for a piece of bread. "If you want to know the truth, I think I waited too long. I kept waiting to freak out and it never happened." She shrugged. "So honestly, the whole thing was kind of anticlimactic."

"I don't know, I think that's good. Boring is better than scary."

"True." She huffed out a laugh. "I think I can use some boring for a while. At least as far as I'm concerned. So let's talk about you instead."

I blinked innocently. "Me?"

"You. Did you get laid last night or what?"

I nearly spit my iced tea across the table. "April!" I jerked my head toward Caitlin, who looked at the both of us with wide eyes.

"Is that where you were?" Caitlin asked. "I thought you went somewhere after you took Mom to work."

"I am not talking about this now." I crossed my arms.

"Oh, yes, you are," April said. "Caitlin's not a child. Well, she is. You are," she told her. "Don't go thinking you can pull this kind of shit for a long, long time. Like maybe when you're in your thirties."

"No fair! Em isn't that old, and she gets to—"

"Have some more salad." I shoved the serving bowl at my niece.

But April wouldn't let it go, and turned back to me with bright eyes. "Did you pick up someone at Jackson's last night? That's where you went, right?"

"Yes. But no . . ." I sighed. "I went to Jackson's, but I didn't pick up someone. I . . ."

"Wait." April snapped her fingers and looked at Caitlin. "You said some guys were fighting over her at Faire? It's the hot coach, isn't it? The one that wears a kilt?"

I put down my fork. "Okay, these are Caitlin's teachers we're talking about here." April was pretty permissive in her parenting, but this was bordering on weird. Should Caitlin be here for this conversation?

"He's not my teacher." Caitlin shook her head and reached for her glass of milk. "I had Ms. Simmons for gym."

"See?" April said. "Not her teacher. So spill."

I sighed. I wasn't getting out of it. "No. It's not Mitch. It's . . . it's Simon." My skin buzzed just speaking his name. Damn, I had it bad.

April blinked, her expression blank. "Who?" But Caitlin gasped and dropped her fork.

"Seriously? You're going out with Mr. G?"

Technically I hadn't *gone out* with Simon; a hookup didn't count as a date. But I didn't correct Caitlin, because it was close enough.

April peered at me. "Then why don't you look happier about it? Do you like the guy?"

"I do." I had a flash of memory of straddling his lap at the kitchen table, sinking into his kiss, and I had to blow out a breath. "I really do."

"So what's the problem? When are you seeing him again?" She frowned when she took in my expression. "Oh. Okay. Caitlin, you're excused."

"But you said I could hear . . ."

"I lied. I need to talk to your aunt. If you go watch TV with the volume up, I'll do the dishes, but you better go now before I change my mind."

That did it. Caitlin was out of her seat faster than I'd ever seen her move. She paused by my chair on her way out. "If you're still going out with Mr. G when he's my English teacher, I'll get a better grade, right? Don't break up with him and screw up my GPA, okay?"

"Out!" April bellowed, and Cait was gone. She turned to me, her expression serious again. "Was this a onetime thing?"

I groaned. "I don't know. I'm not . . ." I stabbed at my salad, taking my frustration out on the lettuce. "I'm not good at this kind of thing."

"What do you mean? It's not like you've never been in a relationship before."

"Yeah, but look how well that went." I tossed down my fork. "I met Jake at a frat party when I was nineteen. We were drunk, we . . . you know." I shrugged. "We were just together after that. He never asked me out; I never accepted."

"So what's different now?"

"Nothing. Well, we weren't drunk, but . . ." I shook my head. "A month ago I hated the guy, and I thought he hated me. This is like a summer romance on steroids. What if he's done with me once Faire is over?" It was too soon for me to ask him for any promises, and it was certainly too soon for him to offer any. The uncertainty of it all gnawed at the pit of my stomach.

April chewed on her bottom lip. "Love is always a risk, isn't it? But here's a question for you: how does he make you feel?"

I thought about that. I thought about Simon and the word "love" and my heart felt buoyant. It must have shown on my face because April nodded.

"There you go," she said. "Okay, look at it this way. What if someone else came to you with this? What if I came to you with this? What would you tell me to do?"

I didn't even need to think. "I'd tell you to give it a chance. That this could be the real thing." I groaned and hid my face in my hands. Why was it so easy when it was someone else's problem? Why couldn't I give the same advice to myself?

"Exactly. Dummy. Give the guy a chance. Don't write him off, don't decide he's going to fuck it up before even letting him try. That's all I ask."

"Okay." But so much still seemed uncertain. How should I act when I saw him again? Would we make an announcement at the Saturday meeting? Start making out in the middle of town and see who noticed? Relationships were confusing.

Turned out, I didn't need to do anything.

"So." Chris had a Cheshire cat grin the moment I walked into the bookstore on Tuesday. "Anything you want to tell me about you and Simon?"

My mouth fell open, while my heart thrilled. Simon and me. There was a Simon and me. "How do you know already?"

She started unpacking her Tupperware containers of pastries she'd made at home on Monday, smile still firmly in place. "Nicole saw Stacey, who told her that she saw Mitch at Jackson's on Sunday night—"

"Stacey wasn't at Jackson's on Sunday. I was there."

Her smile widened. "You'd already left. Mitch told Stacey you were going over to Simon's to talk stuff out with him. Then I ran into Simon at the grocery store yesterday, and he looked happier than I've ever seen him." She shrugged. "I put it together myself, and just now you confirmed it."

I opened my mouth, closed it again. She was right, I had confirmed it. Good thing I'd never wanted to be a spy. I would have been terrible. "Fine. Yes, I went to visit Simon on Sunday night."

She raised her eyebrows. "And?"

And we banged the hell out of each other all night. I can still feel his lips on my skin, and I want more. I cleared my throat. "And we talked stuff out." I let my smile fill in the blanks, and Chris definitely got the message.

"I'm glad to hear it. I think he's been crushing on you for a while. He's a good person, and so are you. You both deserve to be happy."

"Thanks." I flushed at the compliment. "I mean, I don't know where this is going yet, but . . ." The smile wouldn't leave my face, though, and was this turning into a slumber party? I fully expected that in a half hour the first customer would come in and we'd be braiding each other's hair, still talking about boys. "So I take it everyone'll know by Saturday?" I stowed my bag under the cash register and helped Chris set up the café counter.

She'd made cookie bars, brownies, and lemon squares, and our supply of danishes from the local bakery had arrived. Everything was individually wrapped and ready to go. We were fully stocked.

"Welcome to Willow Creek." Chris arranged some of the baked goods into a little display under a domed glass lid and stowed the rest under the counter while I got the coffee and espresso machines up and running for the day. "News travels fast around here." She cast a glance my way. "Is that bad? Do you not want people to know about it? Are you two keeping it secret or something?"

"No. At least, I don't think so?" I thought about going to Faire on Saturday, seeing Simon again, and pretending this hadn't happened. His eyes looking through me as we got ready, not acknowledging the way we'd reached for each other in the middle of the night when sleep wasn't an option, the perfect way we fit together, the sounds he made when he was inside me. The sounds we both made. My heart trembled at the thought, and I knew I wouldn't be able to do it. He was a part of me now, and all I could do was hope I was a part of him too. "No," I said again, more definitively this time. "Hell, no. I'll send a group email to everyone in Faire if you want me to." Kids were on that mailing list, but what the hell.

Chris looked at me closely for a second, then smiled. "Good." I felt like I'd passed some kind of test. I got it. Simon was a lifelong resident of this town, and Willow Creek looked after its own. For all that I'd gotten involved around here, I was still the newcomer. She wanted to make sure Simon wasn't going to get hurt. So did I.

"Okay. New topic." I flipped open the notebook I kept under the counter near the cash register. "Book club. It's getting too late in the summer to do one before Labor Day. But if we decide on a book today, I can get an announcement out on social media, and hopefully get some interest, and the event itself can be sometime in late September."

Chris nodded. "Give everyone time to order books."

"Exactly." I tapped my pen on the page. "This will work, believe me."

"Oh, I do." She headed back to the front of the store again, and I followed. "Come on. While I'm thinking about it, let me show you how special orders work. You like all that online stuff, you'll pick it up quick."

As the lazy summer morning turned into a lazy summer day without a lot of foot traffic, Chris stood up and stretched.

"I've made an executive decision. I'm going home."

"What?" I looked at the clock. Not quite lunchtime. "It's way too early to close."

"I didn't say anything about closing. I said I was going home." She got her purse from under the front counter and rummaged for her keys. "You've covered the register plenty of times. You know what you're doing."

My instinct was to argue with her, but she was right. I did know what I was doing. Our midweek traffic was small enough that I could man both the cash register and the coffee counter with a minimum of trouble.

"Okay," I finally said. "I can handle it." She was probably taking advantage of having an employee while she could. I couldn't blame her for snatching a few hours off here and there.

The bell over the front door chimed, and I caught my breath as Simon walked in. After all this time, we hadn't interacted much outside of Faire. (Unless you counted one pretty significant interaction in his bedroom the night before last. I for one

counted the hell out of it.) He looked like a strange amalgama-
tion of his identities: the crisply ironed shirt and immaculate
jeans of Simon Graham, but with the longer hair and face-
framing beard of Captain Blackthorne. The juxtaposition was . . .
well, I squirmed a little and fought the urge to hop the counter
and wrinkle that shirt in the best possible way.

Simon stopped short inside the doorway when he saw me,
and Chris nudged me with her shoulder. "Now, I know for a fact
you can handle him." While my face flamed with mortification
and Simon's eyebrows knit in confusion, she snickered at her
own joke and walked out of the store with a wave. Simon held
the door for her, then turned back to me.

"Hey."

"Hey." I dropped my head to the counter and let the cool
glass soothe my forehead. "God, it's like working for my mother."

"What was that about?"

I shook my head as I stood back up. "She knows. Apparently,
the whole town does."

"Knows?" After a beat his expression cleared and his eyes
widened. "About us?"

"Yeah." I bit the inside of my cheek and waited for his reaction.

"Huh." He looked over his shoulder in the direction Chris
had gone, as if he could still see her. "Well, if Chris knows, that's
as good as taking an ad out in the paper." He tilted his head,
thinking. "Do people still do that?"

"Do what?"

"Take ads out in the paper. Do people still even read the paper?"

"I . . . I guess?" I was a little confused by the direction the
conversation had gone, but now that he mentioned it I was curious too. "I mean, my mother does. The Sunday paper has cou-

pons, you know." Coupons that she still clipped and sent once a week to April and me, inside greeting cards where the coupons fell out like oversized confetti when we opened them.

He considered that. "Seems like a dying thing, though. So will the idiom change? Should we start saying things like 'posting it online'?"

"'Create a banner ad'?" I suggested, leaning my elbows on the counter.

"See, I like that better." He mirrored my pose and he was close, so close to me that my heart pounded. I was no match for his smile. "Close to the original idiom, and it implies the same thing—spending money to make an announcement."

I allowed myself a second to be lost in his smile before I laughed. "Good God. Once an English teacher, always an English teacher."

"Guilty. I can't help it, I love language." He straightened up again, which brought him too far away. I missed him. "That's why I'm here, actually."

"Because you love language?" I gestured around. "Well, it is a bookstore."

"Because I'm an English teacher. I wanted to check on the summer reading inventory. Make sure kids are actually doing the reading."

"Or at least buying the books?" I tried not to let my disappointment show, since I thought he'd come to see me. Seeing him today had lit up things in me that I hadn't even realized were dark, and all my doubt had fallen away once he walked through the door. But now the dark came creeping back, like a cloud over the summer sun, and it chilled me just as much, because he wasn't here to see me. This was just business.

The display was relatively picked over, but there were a few copies of each book left. I straightened up the books left on the table. "Looks like you've got some slackers in your class this year. Unless they're putting it off till the end of the summer. I hope they're speed readers."

"No, this looks about right." He picked up the annotated *Pride and Prejudice* and flipped idly through it. "A lot of kids are moving over to e-book versions, especially of classics they can get cheap or even free. Or they get them out of the library." He put the book back down. "I order fewer books than I have students, and I still end up with too many. I'll assign it again in a few years, and Chris will sell them to a new group of kids."

I stared hard at the book display. "Recycle your assignments. Sure." I didn't want to talk about his students or their reading lists. But that seemed to be where we were.

"Hey." His voice dropped an octave, and when I looked up he was studying me with concern in his eyes. "What's the matter?"

I shrugged out of the hand he started to place on my arm. His touch was too confusing right now.

His face fell, but he didn't reach for me again; his hands went into his front pockets. "Come on, Emily. Talk to me."

Oh, God. I'd put that uncertain look on his face, and I hated myself for it. *Give the guy a chance*, April had said. Okay. I took a deep breath for courage. "I need to know how you want me to play this."

"Play what?" He looked flummoxed.

"This." I fluttered a hand in the space between the two of us. "I told you, Chris knows. The banner ad, remember? So how do you want me to act on Saturday? Just . . . same as ever?" I choked on those words, because that was the last thing I wanted. I wanted to be kissing him right now. But I soldiered on. "Because I can do that, if that's what you want. Go back to that. If you want." My breath came fast in my chest and I was repeating my-self, babbling like a robot starting to break down. But the thought of going back to the way things had been with Simon hurt more than I had thought possible.

"No. Hey . . ." He reached for my arm again but stopped him-self, his fingers flexing in the space between us. "Why would you think that? What did I do?"

"Nothing." This was terrible. He'd looked so happy the morn-ing before at his kitchen table, and I'd ruined it all. Could I fix this? I reached for him this time, and he let me take his hand. "This is all me. This is your town, you know? These are your people. And I . . ." I took a shaky breath as his thumb stroked lazy, soothing circles along the back of my hand. Even when I had hurt him he was trying to make me feel better. "I'm not very good at this."

"At what? Living in a town?"

I laughed weakly. "At relationships. At knowing when I'm in one."

The uncertainty on his face turned to even deeper confusion. "But you said you'd been with your ex a long time."

"Five years." I nodded. "But it was a drunken hookup that kind of became . . . comfortable. It wasn't like he ever asked me out."

"And neither did I." Understanding dawned on his face, and his confusion became horror. "Oh, Emily, I never meant . . . I don't want you to think . . ."

"No, it's okay!" After talking over each other, we both fell si-lent together. Finally Simon took a breath.

"Can we start over?" He tugged a little on my arm as he stepped closer, and we met in the middle. "Emily?"

"Hmm?" I could never get over how many colors were in his eyes. From a distance, they looked like a plain brown, almost dull, but up close they were a riot of color. He was my very own pointillist painting.

"Hi." I caught a flash of his smile as he bent to kiss me. His lips were warm and his kiss was sweet. Gentle. He only deepened the kiss a little while his hand slid into my hair and his other hand curved into the small of my back.

I smiled as he pulled away. "Hi."

"That's better." He cupped my cheek in his hand, his thumb tracing the curve of my cheekbone. "I've missed you since yesterday. Is that weird? Does that make me one of those stalker guys?"

"Only if you follow me home. Cut off a lock of my hair while I sleep. Something like that."

"I thought I'd save that for next weekend." He bent to kiss me again but swerved at the last second to brush his lips against my cheek instead. "I have a theory about you, Emily Parker."

"You do?"

"I do." Another kiss on my cheek, and then his teeth grazed my earlobe, and I shivered. "I don't think you've ever been wooed. Have you?" The words were a low whisper in my ear, and the shiver intensified.

"Wooed?" The word felt strange in my mouth.

"Wooed," he repeated, punctuating the word with a kiss on my other cheek. "Courted. Swept off your feet. Had someone show you how you make him feel."

"I . . . I can't say that I have." That was an understatement.

"Then brace yourself." He straightened up and backed away from me a step or two. "I'm going to woo your ass off."

Nineteen

D espite *his promise* to woo my ass off, the rest of the week went by without my feeling particularly wooed. Sure, Simon dropped by the bookstore a few more times, and he never left without giving me a kiss that made my toes tingle. And Friday night we went on an actual, proper date: flowers, dinner, a movie, the whole bit. Now that our bad first impressions of each other had been shattered, we had everything to talk about over dinner, and having Simon next to me in the dark of the movie theater, lightly stroking the side of my throat before trailing his fingertips down my arm to hold my hand, made me want to do things that had nothing to do with what was on the screen.

It was all lovely. But not particularly woo-ful. Still, as he led me up the walkway to my front door, I decided it didn't matter. He was making an effort, and I was more than happy to play along. So when he bent to kiss me good night I stretched up onto my toes, and his mouth took mine under the amber of the front porch light. A perfect kiss to end the night.

I smiled as he pulled away, more content than I'd felt in

years. I reached up to brush his hair off his forehead because I couldn't stop touching him quite yet. "Thank you."

He raised his eyebrows as he leaned into my touch. "If you're going to thank me every time I kiss you, it could get pretty repetitive."

I shook my head. "For tonight. This was wonderful. Consider me wooed."

"Oh." A knowing, slightly wicked smile tinged his mouth. "Oh, no. This wasn't wooing."

"It wasn't?"

"Nope." He bent to kiss me again, a quick punctuation on the evening before he left. "This was just a date. When I woo you, you'll know it."

The next morning at Faire he was scarce as we all got ready. I glimpsed him once across the tent, but he disappeared before I could get to him. While I sighed with frustration as Stacey and I started up the hill, I also had to laugh at myself. A few weeks ago, he was the last person I wanted to see. *Down, girl,* I told myself. *Maybe he's trying to be professional while we're at Faire. You can hold out till tonight.*

When we got to the tavern, there was a single red rose laid across the bar.

"What's this?" Stacey picked it up and twirled it by the stem. I recognized the rose—we all did. There was a vendor at the front of the grounds near the main gate. She sold flowers, mostly roses, as "favors." They could be given to knights before they charged into battle in the joust, or to your favorite fighter at the human chess match. (Mitch had been given his fair share of roses. Obviously.) Or they could be handed to your sweetheart as you strolled the Faire.

Janet shrugged as she adjusted her ponytail under her baseball cap. "It was here when I got here." She tucked her red volunteer shirt more securely into her shorts, and her smile rivaled Mona Lisa's. "There's a tag on it, though."

"Oh, I see it." Stacey caught the slip of paper between her fingers, and her smile became a grin. "Em-*ma!* It's for you!" She said my name in a singsong voice and dangled the long-stemmed rose at me until I snatched it from her. Sure enough, my name was on the tag. The handwriting was unfamiliar, but when I turned the tag over my heart skidded in my chest.

Let the wooing commence.

"That's from . . ." Stacey closed her mouth with a snap as I looked at her with rounded eyes, but I couldn't stop her grin. "I know who that's from!" The singsong hadn't left her voice. I should have been annoyed, but instead her grin was infectious. I tucked the rose behind my ear, threading the stem through my hair so the bloom nestled above my left ear. Red roses were kind of cliché, but they were cliché for a reason. Red was the color of love. Of passion. Of the heart. The heady fragrance of the flower enveloped me as I started my day, and it certainly ensured that Simon—or was it Captain Blackthorne now?—stayed in my thoughts. As wooing went, it was pretty effective. I couldn't wait to thank him.

I had no idea that was just the beginning.

Less than an hour after the front gate opened, a family came into the tavern. The couple were probably in their midthirties, along with a small girl dressed as a princess. We got a lot of patrons like that. Parents who wanted a drink but couldn't exactly leave their kid to wander around alone outside. It's not like we were a real bar, just a tent out in the woods. Hard to enforce an age policy at the door that way.

Stacey served the parents while I swept off the stray leaves that had accumulated on the tables overnight. I was almost finished when I realized the little girl had come closer and was now gazing up at me with big blue eyes.

"Good morrow, Your Highness." I gave her a low curtsy befitting her princess dress. She was adorable, all pink dress and blond ringlets. She couldn't have been more than six. "I hope you are enjoying the day. And may I say, that's a beautiful rose. I have one just like it, see?" I crouched down to show her the rose in my hair, since she was indeed holding a long-stemmed red rose from the flower seller at the front gate.

She reached up a small hand, and I ducked my head a little so she could touch the flower in my hair. She patted it gently, then examined the rose in her hand carefully. "Are you Emma?"

I froze. How did she . . . "Yes." I cleared my throat. "Yes, I . . . I am Emma."

She looked back at her parents, who were close enough to hear our conversation, and they nodded at her encouragingly. The little girl then extended the rose to me. "It's for you."

"Oh. No. No, thank you, milady." The last thing I wanted to do was take this little girl's flower. Kids were capricious. If I took it now, in five minutes she might be screaming for it again, and I didn't want to give the parents a headache like that. "I have one already, see? You should keep yours."

She shook her head, little blond ringlets dancing, and extended the rose to me more emphatically. "It's for you," she said again. "The pirate said so."

My jaw dropped, and for a moment I forgot how to speak. "The . . . pirate? What pirate?" What a stupid question.

"The pirate," she said, a little exasperated, as though repeating it would explain everything. "He said find Emma and give it to her. He told Mommy where to find you, but it was easy. He said you were a pretty girl with curly brown hair and a blue dress."

"Did he?" I pictured Simon, kneeling in front of this little girl, giving her a rose and asking her to be a delivery person, and my heart swelled. I looked from her to her parents, smiling in our direction, and back to the little princess again. "Well, I thank you." My hand shook only a little as I took the rose from her tiny fingers. "You did a wonderful job of finding me. I will be sure to tell him so when I see him." I touched the flower to the tip of my nose, automatically sniffing it even though I was already wearing one. Now I had two. As I stood up and bid the petite princess farewell I tucked it into the knot at the back of my neck and moved the first one back there to match it.

The third rose came from two giggling young women wearing corset tops and short skirts. They ordered what was probably their third round of hard ciders of the morning before presenting me with the long-stemmed red rose. The back of my head started to get pretty crowded, and when roses four and five arrived before midday, Stacey plucked the first three out of my hair and started fashioning a flower crown for me. By the time I had seven roses, the flower crown was pretty lush, not to mention heavy.

"Once you get a couple more it'll look perfect." She looked giddy at the prospect, and I turned to her in alarm.

"More? How many more are there going to be?" I peered at her while she giggled. "Did you know about this?"

She raised her hands in innocence. "I didn't. I promise I didn't. But you have to admit, it's pretty cool. Romantic." She looked toward the chess field with a thoughtful expression. "I had no idea the Captain had it in him."

"Hmm." And here came rose number eight, delivered by a Captain Jack Sparrow impersonator. He bestowed a kiss on my hand along with the rose, and I thanked him as prettily as I could, lamenting that his accent, not to mention his costume, was much better than mine. I was going to have to step up my game next year.

Next year? I stopped twirling the rose. Why was I planning next year already? Surely that was assuming too much. Counting on the future was the kind of thinking that got me hurt. Dumped on the way to a better life. I stomped down those ugly thoughts and brought my attention back to the present. Back to this silly number of roses arriving to me throughout the day, one at a time.

We were too busy in the afternoon to drop by the chess match, which must have derailed some of the rose delivery plans. Because once it was over, several of our fellow cast members dropped by the tavern, along with roses nine, ten, and eleven. By the end of the day the flower crown on top of my head made me look like a wood nymph, and there were more roses stuck at random into my hair and one was threaded through the laces of my bodice. Janet had left for the day, and Jamie had started to break down the bar when Mitch appeared, a smirk on his face and a rose in his hand.

"No." I held up a hand, as if that would stop him from coming any closer. It didn't. "No," I said again. "I don't need any more roses." I tried hard to sound annoyed, but I hadn't stopped smiling since I'd gotten the first rose that morning.

"Too bad, milady." Mitch actually bopped me on the nose with the rose he held. "I am here to escort you to pub sing."

I tried to wave him off. "I think I'll skip it today." I wanted to collect my niece and get home as soon as possible. One side effect to all of these roses was that Simon had been on my mind all day, a side effect enhanced by the fact that he hadn't come by the tavern once. It was so unlike him that all I could think about was getting home, showered, changed, and over to his place pronto. I needed to thank him properly for all these roses. And in this case, "properly" meant "naked."

Mitch laughed. "Nice try. You're not skipping anything." I had never been handed a rose so forcefully in my life, and by now I was an expert on being given flowers. He took my other hand and nestled it in the crook of his elbow. "I'm under orders." He half led, half dragged me to the front of the grounds, where most of the cast and the remaining patrons had gathered for pub sing. By the looks of things, it was winding down; most of the acts who participated had already performed, and a quintet of women singing in a cappella harmony was just finishing up.

No sooner had they left the stage than Simon, still in costume as Captain Blackthorne, hopped up and commanded the attention of everyone there. "I want to thank all of you for joining us here today at the Willow Creek Renaissance Faire." His authoritative voice traveled without the aid of a microphone, and when I looked at him I was amazed that this was the same man with the shy smile in all his family photographs. He was a completely different person in the costume and persona of a pirate. But the great thing for me was I now found both men equally compelling.

"It's been a lovely day," he continued. "The weather's been perfect, and we have all enjoyed having you. I would like to give my particular thanks to those of you still here who assisted me today on my quest.

"For those of you who weren't a part of it, let me explain it to you now. We have in our midst a woman named Emma. She is a tavern wench of great beauty, whose smile lights up the day like the sun, and the night like the moon. She has absolutely stolen my heart, but I do not mind in the least. In fact, if she would agree to keep my heart and take good care of it, I would never want it back."

My own heart pounded at this speech, while the logical side of my brain tried hard to parse it. Who was speaking here? Captain

Blackthorne, the pirate I'd been handfasted to at the beginning of Faire, and spent weeks bantering with in character? Or was this Simon, the mild-mannered English teacher, who had kissed me so sweetly in the bookstore a few days before? Or were they two halves of a whole, one living neatly inside the other?

"Recently, I learned something very important about my lovely Emma. Something tragic." He paused here for emphasis. "She told me she had never before been wooed." He pressed a dramatic hand to his heart. "Can you imagine something so terrible?"

Yes, I could. Nuclear war. Sad kittens. The rumored worldwide chocolate shortage. But for the sake of argument I kept my mouth shut and let him keep talking, even though my heart pounded and every cell of my body shook. I was not a center-of-attention kind of girl.

Which was too bad, apparently.

"So I made it my mission to woo the fair Emma. With the help of all of you, who delivered the signs of my affections to her all day long, so she might know she is constantly in my thoughts, and always will be. And now I ask you, my dear Emma!"

I almost dropped the rose I was holding, because he threw out an arm, gesturing to where I stood in the back, and all the patrons turned to look at me. It took a moment to realize I was muttering under my breath. "Oh, no. Oh no oh no oh no oh no . . ." The memory of my very public, very projectile-vomity stage fright from my college days was suddenly in the forefront of my mind. That would create the wrong impression here.

"Deep breaths, gorgeous." Mitch planted one huge hand square in the middle of my back and gave me a little shove, propelling me down the center aisle toward the stage, where my pirate awaited me. He hopped to the ground and met me toward the front of the aisle.

"I ask you, Emma." His voice was softer now, pitched lower, more for me and less for the world at large. He extended a hand to me and I didn't hesitate to take it. When his hand closed around mine, solid and sure, all my shaking stopped and the apprehension drained away even as he led me onto the stage. He wouldn't let me barf in front of all these people. With my hand in his, I felt safe. I was still aware of the audience, but the world that mattered had shrunk down to the two of us. "Would you say that you have been successfully wooed on this day?" The accent was Captain Blackthorne's, but the words, the voice, were all Simon.

His eyes smiled down into mine, and I knew I looked utterly ridiculous in my blue and white wench ensemble all but covered with red roses. But I also knew, as I smiled back at him, that I had never been so happy, and never felt so much a part of something in my life. Not only Simon, but the entire Faire around us, had become my home.

"Aye, sir." I stuck the rose I still carried behind his ear. "I have indeed been wooed."

His smile became a grin, then a laugh, and without any further warning he slid one arm around my back, the other around my shoulders, and he dipped me, as though we were the romantic finale of a black-and-white movie, and while my head spun from the change in equilibrium he kissed me, to the cheers of everyone. His mouth on mine did nothing to stop my head from spinning, but his hands were supportive and strong. He wouldn't let me fall.

Once he let me up again and we were off the stage, he drew me close into an embrace as the clapping died down. "Come over tonight," he said, softly enough so only I could hear him. "Wear the roses."

I shook my head. "I'm filthy. All covered in roses and Faire dirt. I should wash up first."

"No." He brushed his mouth against mine one more time before murmuring into my ear. "I can't wait that long. Come over now. I'll take care of you." When his voice was pitched that low I felt it deep in my chest, and there was no way I could say no.

It wasn't hard for me to arrange for Caitlin to get a ride home with one of her friends that night, so I drove straight to Simon's place. Upstairs in his bedroom he slid the flower crown off my head, then plucked the roses from my hair and my dress slowly, one at a time, letting each fall to the floor, to the bed. He spent an eternity taking my hair down, carefully leaving the pins on his bedside table, winding the loose strands of hair in his fingers as they were freed.

"I can't get enough of your hair," he murmured as he unlaced my bodice slowly, drawing the garment off my shoulders. My chemise slipped down over one shoulder and his mouth lingered on the skin that had been exposed. He took just as much care with the rest of the layers of my outfit, untying and unpinning, peeling fabric from me like removing petals from a flower. As I did the same for him, stripping away his clothes, he kept coming back to my hair, drawing it over my shoulders, teasing my skin with the ends of it. "The way it curls around my fingers like it's alive . . . I can't get enough of it, enough of you. I've never . . ." He sucked in a breath and didn't finish that sentence, choosing instead to kiss me deeply and lead me into the shower.

We spent an inordinate amount of time soaping each other up, removing every trace of dust and dirt from a day spent in the woods. I took full advantage of the opportunity to really explore him. He had a runner's body, lean and muscled. I stroked my hands down powerful thighs, kneading the muscles there, before I sank to my knees in front of him. I tilted my head up to watch the water sluice down his stomach, and his eyes burned down into mine as he watched me take him into my mouth. He let out a guttural sound and one hand cupped the back of my head, gripping my hair without pulling.

"Not fair," he gasped. "I'm supposed to be wooing you. This . . ." There was a dull thud as the back of his head hit the shower wall. "This is the other way around."

I didn't care, and I let him know with every lick that I was exactly where I wanted to be. We tested the limits of his house's hot water heater, and I was impressed with its capacity.

I should have known when Simon said he'd take care of me, he didn't mean it as innuendo. Well, not entirely. After our inordinately long shower he wrapped me in his bathrobe and started a load of laundry so my Faire outfit would be clean for the next day. We ordered takeout and enjoyed a cozy night in.

Later that night he got his revenge for the shower, alternating the teasing caress of an errant rose petal across my skin with a slow stroke of his tongue or a whisper of breath until my body quivered underneath his. My mouth searched blindly for him, kissing anything I could reach: cheek, chin, throat. I bit down on his shoulder and he gasped in a shock of indrawn breath. By the time he grabbed for a condom and then pushed inside of me, we were both beyond ready, and we rocked together mindlessly, racing for climax, surging together.

Afterward he took my mouth in a lazy, sated kiss that went on for days. "Now, my dear Emily," he said. "Now you can say you've been wooed."

Twenty

My *mind was* still full of roses when I went to work at the bookstore on Tuesday. Chris had asked me to take care of opening the shop on my own, so it was safe to say she had gotten into this whole having-an-employee thing. Little by little, over the weeks she had taught me almost everything there was to know about running the shop. After setting up the coffee counter and unlocking the front door, I got the front register ready to go. The morning progressed in what had become a comforting routine. A few people who worked downtown had started making a point of ducking in for a morning coffee and pastry. I thrilled inside every time; my idea had actually worked. Business wasn't exactly brisk, but I wasn't bored, either.

When Chris got in later that morning she gave me a knowing smile; roses were on her mind too.

"Nice weekend?" She sounded casual, almost disinterested. As if she hadn't seen me adorned with roses, being elaborately kissed in front of a crowd.

"Yeah." I kept my voice equally nonchalant as I finished making her vanilla latte. Her favorite. I knew that by now. "Pretty good."

Chris snickered and took a sip of her latte, closing her eyes with a smile. "You're getting pretty good. Are you sure you've never been a barista? Never put in time at a Starbucks?"

"Nope. I could make more money at a bar. But I have to say, this is a lot more fun."

"The coffee?"

"All of it." I gestured around, encompassing the entire store. "I've enjoyed helping you out, setting all of this up."

"This wouldn't exist without you. Well, the store would, obviously, since it's been here. But all this . . ."

"It wasn't much," I protested. "A few tables and chairs."

"And our new book club has its first meeting next month. And Nicole said a writers' group called over the weekend. They want to have meetings here. I know it doesn't seem like much, but I couldn't have done it on my own. Organizing it all." She tipped her cup at me in acknowledgment. "That's something you're very good at."

"Oh." The compliment flustered me, and I busied myself by wiping down the counter. "I don't know about that. I just . . . I get an idea in my head of how things could be, and if I can make them happen I do it. Doesn't seem like much."

"Well, it is. Stacey keeps saying she can't believe it's only your first year at Faire. You have everything so well organized at the tavern."

I laughed. "That's where my years at working in bars comes in handy. A bar is a bar, even if it's out in the woods." But I couldn't keep the smile off my face or the pink out of my cheeks. People had been talking about me. In a good way. That wasn't something I was used to.

As the day went on, Chris did whatever paperwork needed doing at the beginning of the week while I did, well, everything else. Unpacked the boxes of new books that were delivered on Monday, tidied up some shelves. Little indie bookstores didn't do a roaring business on a Tuesday at the tail end of summer, so we weren't exactly busy. After a while Chris looked up from her paperwork.

"You know Lauren, right?"

"Lauren Pollard? She's one of the kids, right?" Meaning, one of the kids in the cast. I was pretty sure Chris was talking about one of the dancers who came by the tavern a few times a day for water.

Chris nodded. "Nicole goes back to school at the end of August. I told Simon I wanted a high school student to help out this fall, and he suggested Lauren. She's going to come in on Friday. Do you think you could train her back here?"

"Sure." Even as I automatically agreed, my stomach dropped and my world stopped spinning. While we occasionally had a rush of customers, on the whole we were barely busy enough to keep the two of us from being bored. There was no need to hire reinforcements unless . . .

. . . Unless one of us was leaving.

Chris had been running this place on her own until I came along. Now she was hiring help. We hadn't talked about my plans past the summer, but I'd assumed I was sticking around. Although that wasn't fair, was it? Chris didn't know my plans had changed. All she knew was what I'd said at the beginning of Faire: that I was staying through the end of the summer. It wasn't fair to get upset that she was planning for a future with that in mind.

I could say something. I could say, "Don't hire Lauren. I want to stay." But old insecurities began flooding back, taking hold in my heart. What if she didn't want me? What if my usefulness to her was at an end? I'd started to think of Willow Creek as my home. But if I was being fired, maybe I needed to rethink that.

Not to mention Simon knew about the new employee. He knew Chris was replacing me. Maybe he was fine with me leaving at the end of the summer too.

It was a lot to consider, and I was still turning over these new revelations when Simon dropped by the shop. I didn't see him at first; I'd heard the door chime from the front while I tidied up the coffee counter and straightened up a nearby display. But I recognized the timbre of his voice, mixing with Chris's in conversation, and I thought about staying back here. Hiding. Curiosity won out, though, and I headed up front to say hello.

"I'm not sure if they should come back next year." Chris sighed. "Their shows didn't bring in very many patrons compared to others. And if they're talking about charging more next year, then maybe they're pricing themselves out of our Faire."

"I don't know." Simon's brow furrowed and his expression was serious as I came around the corner. "They've been part of the Faire for a long time, haven't they? They were one of the first acts Sean hired. I'd hate to start just changing things."

"This isn't a random change, Simon. And it's been three years. We should start mixing in some new talent. What do you think, Emily?" Chris turned her attention to me as she saw me approach. "Did you catch any of the jugglers' shows this summer?"

I stopped short. "We have jugglers?"

Chris snorted, and Simon's laugh was a short bark, an involuntary reaction. "Fair enough." I tried to parse his smile—was he glad to see me?—but my own distress melted away when I got a good look at him. He was impeccably dressed, as always, but he looked faded, wrung out. This wasn't the carefree figure who had wooed me on Saturday. This was a man with a lot on his mind and in desperate need of a vacation. Or at least a nap.

If Chris noticed his apparent weariness, she didn't comment on it. "I can't start planning next year yet. Let's get this summer over with first."

"Almost there," I said. Those words had become a familiar refrain lately. Mid-August in Willow Creek had brought blazing hot temperatures and a strange sense of both sadness and urgency. Even though we still had two weekends left, people started talking about Faire like it was over. Some people looked forward to next year even when this summer wasn't over yet, while others swore this was the last time they were getting involved. Maybe they'd sit out next year, those people said. Simon told me privately that the people who said that the most were usually the first ones back the next spring.

Chris nodded in agreement. "This second half of the summer always goes so fast."

"It does." But Simon's nod was businesslike. "But you know we have to start booking for next summer months in advance." He took his tablet out of his messenger bag. "If we're going to look at changing acts, that's going to be a lot more work. We should figure out—"

"We will." Chris channeled a little of her Queen persona, shutting Simon down. "Just not right now, okay?"

Simon blinked at the sharp tone in her voice, and to be honest so did I. "Sure. Okay." He didn't look happy about it, but he slid the tablet back into his bag. "We can get together after Faire is over and talk about it."

She smiled in relief. "That sounds perfect. Come by the house for dinner, maybe the week after Faire's over?"

Simon nodded, and I wondered what I'd be doing that week. Would I still be in Willow Creek at all? How much longer was April going to let me stay in her guest room when I was out of a job? But I didn't want to plan for any of that yet. So instead I tugged on Simon's hand, and he followed me to the back of the shop, where I ushered him to a table and pointed. "Sit. Coffee?"

"Yeah. Yeah, that would be great, thank you." He let his bag fall to the table as he dropped into a seat.

"Maybe Chris has a point." I poured him some coffee and added the amount of milk I knew he liked before bringing it to him. "Enjoy the last couple weeks of Faire. You don't need to worry about next year yet."

He took a too-long, too-fast gulp of coffee, wincing at the heat of it. "If I don't, no one else will." He blew across the surface of his mug. "It's up to me. It's always up to me."

I didn't like the tone of his voice, how hopeless it sounded. "But it's important, right?" I sat down next to him, my hand on his arm. "I mean, it's your brother's legacy. It's what you—"

"It's what I do." This was the least enthusiastic I'd ever heard him, and I had a feeling he didn't mean to show me this side of himself. A side that was more stuck with keeping things going than doing it because he wanted to. Had he let anyone else see it? Or did everyone think, like Mitch and like Chris, that he was perfectly content in this? Chris treated Faire as a hobby, while it took over Simon's life. Were they the only two who kept the whole thing running? Simon was terribly overworked if so.

There had to be a way to help him. But was it my place? A day before, I would have offered to help come up with a solution. But a day before, I thought I was making a home here, and I was still rattled from my conversation with Chris earlier, and knowing

Simon had had a hand in hiring my replacement. How many more things was I wrong about?

So instead I gave his arm a reassuring squeeze, and he shook his head as though he were waking up from his thoughts.

"Sorry, that's . . . well, it's not important now, is it?"

"If it's important to you, then . . ."

He waved a dismissive hand. "No, Chris is right. It can wait. I have better things to pay attention to for the next couple weeks." He brought my hand to his mouth for a kiss, and a smile lit up his eyes. This was a part of his pirate personality that had crossed over into his real life, and I couldn't complain. Although I'd never been with a guy who had been into hand kissing, with Simon it felt natural. But his words landed with a thud in the pit of my stomach. Would I really get only two more weeks with him? Part of me wanted to ask, get it all out in the open. What if that conversation went badly, though, and I ended up with no more weeks at all? Two was better than none. Right?

Simon didn't notice my inner turmoil. "The shop closes at six, right?"

I nodded. "I'm here for a few more hours. I can meet you later—"

"I can wait." He indicated the laptop bag on the table. "I've got some work I can get done."

"If you're sure . . ." I pushed back to my feet. "Let me know if you need more coffee, okay?"

As the afternoon went on, I split my time between the coffee counter and the front of the store, helping Chris whenever she needed it. She seemed to need it more than she usually did, teaching me about running the shop. It was interesting, since retail was new to me, but I didn't get why she wanted me to learn all this now when my time there was coming to an end. When she left around five I went around to the back to close down the coffee counter. I may have stopped at a certain table to run a hand through my favorite pirate's hair.

"Still here, huh?"

Simon looked up from his laptop and smiled at me. "Where would I go? I'm waiting for you."

"Not too bored?"

"Not at all. I've been busy . . ." He pointed at the screen, and I leaned over to take a look.

"What's this, online gaming? I didn't take you for a . . ." I squinted at the spreadsheet he had up. "That's a terrible game."

He laughed, ending with a cluck of his tongue. "It is. Planning ahead for the school year. I've been meaning to catch up on some paperwork. I may as well do it here." He reached for me, catching my hand in his and kissing my knuckles again. "I'm way behind this summer." He cocked an eyebrow in my direction, that look that made me want to start unbuttoning. "I've had other things on my mind these past few weeks, for some reason."

"Hmm. Can't imagine what." I tried to sound innocent, but mostly failed. "I'm closing up soon. We can get some dinner, if you want."

"I'd love that." One more kiss and he released my hand. While I cleaned out machines at the coffee counter, I caught my attention wandering back to Simon. Now that summer was ending his teacher persona was coming back; I could see it in the way he carried himself. Captain Blackthorne would be more apt to sprawl in a chair. But Simon's posture was more rigid; he sat up straight, frowning occasionally at his laptop before jotting something down in a notebook at his side.

"I can't believe the summer's almost over." I almost rolled my eyes at my pathetic attempt at small talk. Maybe I would mention the weather next.

"It went too fast." But his voice had turned grave, and I peeked over to see him frowning at his laptop.

"What's the matter?"

"The end of the summer is always a little weird." He sighed. "Summer's something I look forward to every year, you know . . . Faire. Being a pirate. But then in September I'm just me again." He could only hold my gaze for a moment before he glanced off to the side. "You didn't like that guy much, as I recall."

"I don't know." I couldn't stop my smile. "He's kind of grown on me." He looked back at me, and this time our gazes held. He smiled back, a small curve of his lips, but it was enough.

This kind of talk made me nervous. I wanted to ask him what he wanted from me. From us. Should we talk about whether this thing between us had a future? But then the bell over the front door chimed, and I had to get back to work. I hadn't expected a late-afternoon rush on a Tuesday of all days, but before I knew it I could close up for the night. I threw the bolt on the front door and flipped the Closed sign over. I needed to count down the cash drawer, but I also needed to see Simon. I'd left him alone much longer than I'd wanted to.

Flipping off half of the overhead lights as I went, I called his name as I reached that side of the shop. "Excuse me, sir, but we're closing . . ." My voice trailed off when I registered his table was empty. His laptop was still open but had gone dark, so he'd been away for a few minutes at least. His pen was tossed down on the open notebook, half a page filled with ridiculously neat block writing. One glance at the page, and I knew where he was.

Our classics section was small but well stocked with the basics. I found what I was looking for there in the semidarkness of the stacks. Simon leaned against the bookcase, elbow braced on a shelf, a slim volume open in his hands. I cleared my throat, and he looked up almost guiltily.

"Sorry, I got distracted. Closing up, though, right? I noticed it got darker in here."

"Picked up on that, huh?" I walked over to check out the book he was holding. It was hard to read upside down in the dim light. "What's that?"

"Shakespeare." He handed me the book. "I do a short unit on Shakespeare with my AP kids at the beginning of the year, and I was deciding which sonnet to talk about."

"Oooh, the sonnets. They don't get enough love." No wonder the volume was so thin. A *Complete Works*, on the other hand, could qualify as a murder weapon. I flipped through the pages before coming back to the page he was reading. "Sonnet 29? You like this one?"

"I do." An arm slid around my waist as he pulled me closer. He nestled me into him, my back against his chest. "It feels apropos for this summer."

"Really?" I tilted the book a little to catch more of the light, and read out loud, my voice a quiet murmur:

"When, in disgrace with fortune and men's eyes,
I all alone beweep my outcast state,
And trouble deaf heaven with my bootless cries,
And look upon myself, and curse my fate . . ."

"You have a good voice for Shakespeare." Simon's mouth was right next to my ear, and I turned a little to look at him over my shoulder.

"English major, remember? I've always loved the way Shakespeare sounds." I turned back to the book as he brushed a kiss on my temple. "So this is about you? Sounds like you had a shitty summer so far."

"I wasn't in a very good mood at the start of it, if you recall." He fiddled with a lock of my hair, one of several that had escaped from its clip during the day.

I did recall. He'd been in a pretty bad place. Lots of people had commented on it to me, but had I been the only one who had actually talked to him about it? Did the rest of this town take him for granted? "Yeah, but 'bootless cries'? 'Curse my fate'? Seems a little melodramatic."

"I'm a dramatic guy." I felt his smile against the side of my neck, and I kept reading.

"*Wishing me like to one more rich in hope,*
Featur'd like him, like him with friends possess'd . . ."

The lightbulb came on easily here. "Mitch." I shook my head. "I can't believe you were jealous of Mitch."

"Always have been. He's always been everything I'm not. He has an easy time talking to anyone. And look at the guy."

"Nah," I said. "I'd much rather look at you." A memory flitted across my brain of when I'd first met Simon and disliked everything about him. I dismissed it quickly. Stupid memory.

"*Desiring this man's art and that man's scope,*
With what I most enjoy contented least . . ."

"Faire's been my favorite thing. For years." He drew a deep breath. "But this summer was different. I didn't want to be there, didn't want to see you when you didn't even want to talk to me."

"You weren't exactly nice to me." I tried to defend myself.

"Then I started to get to know you better, but I thought you and Mitch were together and . . . yeah. I wasn't in a great place." His arms tightened around me when I read the next line:

"Yet in these thoughts myself almost despising . . ."

My throat closed and I choked on the last word. I didn't like to think of Simon hating himself. It was too awful to contemplate. I'd come a long way from thinking of him as the Ren Faire Killjoy.

"Haply I think on thee . . ." Simon took up the reading of the sonnet, but he didn't need the text in front of him. Show-off. Instead he mouthed the words against the nape of my neck, and they traveled on a murmur of breath, a deep rumble in his chest that I strained to hear.

"And then my state,
Like to the lark at break of day arising
From sullen earth, sings hymns at heaven's gate . . ."

He turned me in his arms; the small book tumbled to the floor as he guided my arms up to grip the shelf above my head. Simon's mouth plundered mine—there was that pirate again—and I arched into him. A shelf dug into my back, but with his hands trailing down my arms, across my collarbone, and down to my breasts, I didn't notice or care.

His mouth traveled down my throat, painting Shakespeare's words onto my collarbone with his tongue.

"For thy sweet love remember'd such wealth brings
That then I scorn to change my state with kings."

Another deep, drugging kiss, and he pulled away, but only far enough to lean his forehead against mine. "Emily." Color was high in his cheeks, his pupils wide and dark; he looked wild. He cupped my cheek, his thumb stroking my skin, and his eyes searched mine as though I had hidden the answer to something in them. "I—"

"Hush." Just like that day at the tavern, I didn't want him to talk. I didn't want to take the chance that he was starting to say goodbye. Instead I stretched up to kiss him again. If this was nothing more than a summer fling and I only had a few more weeks with this man, I was going to take full advantage of every moment. I would stockpile every touch, every kiss, for the day when I wasn't in his arms anymore. The summer wasn't over yet. We still had time.

Twenty-one

I*t didn't take* long for me to realize that my new "don't ask, don't tell" policy about my future in Willow Creek was a load of crap. Instead of being the best way to avoid heartache, it made everything worse. I went through my days with a sense of dread, and every time Chris asked me a question I almost flinched, expecting the hammer of unemployment to fall.

Worse, it affected my relationship with Simon. I'd told myself I was going to enjoy every minute with him. Instead I turned into a jittery mess, analyzing every text message for hidden meanings, worrying that every conversation was the beginning of the end.

By Friday morning I wasn't sure I could take much more. I certainly wasn't going to make it two weeks. Lauren Pollard showed up for training, which only heightened my anxiety as I showed her around the espresso machine and she made several failed lattes. The first three went down the sink, but the fourth looked promising. Good froth, color looked right. I took a cautious sip and let the taste bloom across my tongue like I was a coffee sommelier.

"That's your best one yet." I set the mug down but kept my fingers curved around the handle. "I think Chris may actually drink this one."

On the other side of the coffee counter Lauren let out a relieved sigh. "I had a good feeling about that one. I think I'm finally getting the hang of it!"

"I think you are too. Excellent job." I took the mug with me from the coffee counter to the front of the bookstore. Chris was at the front counter, and she raised her eyebrows as I approached.

"Better?"

"Much." I passed the mug to Chris. She took an appraising sip and nodded.

"And she's good with the hours we mentioned, right? Did you talk to her about that yet?"

"I did." The more we talked about the job—my job, Lauren's job now?—the more my anxiety spiked, and I reached around Chris for my purse. I needed gum. "Tuesdays and Thursdays after school until we close at six, and then a shift on the weekend. She seems like a responsible kid. I think it'll work."

"Oh, she is." Chris cradled the mug between her palms. "I've known Lauren's family since she was in diapers, and of course, she's grown up doing Faire."

"Of course." Chris knew Lauren better than I did. She was going into her junior year, and needed an after-school job to round out her college savings. Her being a Faire veteran certainly spoke to her work ethic. It hadn't hit me until recently that these kids were giving up a lot of their summers. When every weekend was spoken for from June to almost September, long vacations were impossible.

I could relate. Faire had been a grueling experience. Long days, uncomfortable clothes. But it had also been more fun than

I'd ever had in my life, and I'd made friends who had become family. Funny to think it had all started as an obligation I'd taken on for Caitlin's sake, another thing I needed to do while I took care of April. As the summer progressed, all those obligations had fallen away one by one. April had recovered and was back to her old life. She didn't need me. My obligation to Caitlin would end when Faire did. And as for the bookstore . . .

I dug into my purse and tried to focus on the positive. If I wasn't needed here anymore, I'd be free to go wherever I wanted. Away from here.

No. That wasn't a positive at all.

My pack of gum was in a small inside pocket, and as I took it out a scrap of paper came with it. A fortune, from a fortune cookie: *Ask the right question.*

I smoothed the paper out between my fingers as I remembered. I'd been scared that night, scared to ask the questions that had really mattered. But doing so had knocked me out of my stasis, both with my sister and with Simon. I needed to do that again. I needed to stop being afraid to stand up for myself. I needed to ask the questions that mattered, instead of waiting for life to happen to me.

"Chris, do you have a second?" I was still looking at the paper when I spoke, and I watched the writing shake a little between my fingers. But it was too late; the words were out of my mouth. I forced my gaze up to Chris, who looked at me with raised eyebrows.

"Sure," she said. "What's up?"

"I need to talk to you. About the fall." My voice trembled and I ran out of breath on the last word, but I must have gotten my point across because she nodded.

"Good. I need to talk to you too. How about I'll send Lauren on her way, and you can make us a couple of lattes?" She looked down at the mug in her hands and back up to me with a plaintive look. "Real ones?"

A nervous laugh escaped from my lips. "I can do that." While Chris escorted Lauren back to the front I pushed down my nerves and made a vanilla latte for each of us. The repetitive motion calmed me, and by the time I brought them over to the table by the window I felt almost normal again. This was good. Get it all out in the open, so I could start planning my future for real. I always did better when I had a plan.

Chris sat down across from me and lifted her mug, inhaling the steam. "Oh, that's more like it." She blew over the surface of her coffee before taking a sip. "So, what are you thinking about the fall?"

I drummed my fingernails on the side of my own mug and tried to figure out how to hurry along my own firing. I'd never done this before. *Ask the right question.* I focused on the fortune and sucked in a barely shaking breath. "How much longer are you going to need me working here? In the fall? Once Lauren starts?"

Her brow furrowed. "What do you mean?"

I tried to shrug, look unconcerned, but inside I wanted to scream. Why was she being so obtuse? Would she just fire me already? "I'm just trying to plan ahead. Figure out where I'm going next, that kind of thing. I mean, I've already trained my replacement." I glanced out the window so the hurt in my eyes didn't show. I should probably start packing tonight. I probably had stuff scattered all over April's house from my months of living there.

"What?" Her surprised, sharp tone made me turn back to Chris. Surprise widened her eyes. "You're leaving?"

My wide-eyed stare matched her own. "Maybe?"

Her shoulders slumped around a sigh. "I should have talked to you about this sooner. I figured with the way things were going, with your sister and your niece, not to mention Simon, you were planning to stick around. I guess I should have made sure before assuming anything."

"Well, I mean, nothing's set in stone . . ." Then I registered what she had said. "Talk to me about what?" This didn't sound like the kind of conversation that led to getting fired.

"About the future. Let me start from the beginning." She looked down into her mug. "This spring, my mother had a stroke, and—"

I gasped. "Chris! I'm so sorry! Is she okay? What can I . . . ?"

"Oh, she's fine," she rushed to assure me. "She's fine. She retired to Florida a few years back, and if there's one thing they're good at down there, it's taking care of old people. But assisted living facilities are so expensive, and I worry about her getting the right kind of care. So in September I'm going down to spend the winter with her in Florida. Then I'll bring her back with me in the spring when the weather's warm. That way she can stay in her house, and I can take better care of her."

"But . . ." I was definitely missing something. "How are you going to run the store from Florida?"

"I'm not. Well, I guess technically I am. I'll be a phone call away, or an email, or a text. But I was hoping you'd be able to take over for me while I'm gone."

"Take . . . over . . ." I was having a hard time making those words make sense in my brain. "So you're not firing me?"

Chris almost spat out her coffee. "No! Why would you think that?"

"But . . ." I gestured over to the coffee counter. "You had me train Lauren. You know, to help out in the fall. She'll be doing my job."

"Exactly. So you can do mine. Why do you think I hired Lauren? And started teaching you the accounting system and how to handle the online ordering?"

I took a sip of my latte because I didn't know what to say. Chris wasn't firing me. Simon hadn't been saying goodbye.

"So what do you think?"

"I think I've been a paranoid idiot for the past couple days."

Chris laughed. "About the job," she said. "Are you in?"

The future stretched out in front of me, suddenly clearer and brighter than it had seemed in a while. A full-time job. A town I liked. I let a slow smile spread over my face. "I'm in. Of course I'm in."

We spent the rest of the day hashing out the details of my new position—store manager, that sounded nice—and we determined I'd spend the next few days finding any shortcomings in my training so far. By now I pretty much knew the ins and outs of the place, and like she said, she'd be a phone call away. But I'd never been given responsibility on this kind of scale. I didn't want to screw it up.

But I wasn't going to screw it up. I could do this. I could help not only Chris, but myself as well. For once I wasn't compromising for someone else's benefit. My whole life had fallen into place over the course of one conversation. I had a job. A future. Family. And . . .

Now I started to grin. And I had Simon. Not only did I have a future, but we had a future.

I couldn't wait to tell him.

Thankfully I didn't have to wait long. Simon was due to meet me at the store after I closed up and we were walking to a nearby restaurant for dinner. It had to be an early night, of course, since we both had Faire the next day. His timing was perfect; he arrived as I was locking the door.

"Hey. You look . . ." After kissing me hello, he took in my appearance and broke into a smile. "You look happy."

"That's because I am happy." I wasn't surprised that my emotions showed on my face; I practically bubbled over with excitement. And relief. When I looked at him now, all the doubt I'd had for the past few days fell away. He hadn't gone behind my back to help Chris hire my replacement. How could I have doubted him? "I have so much to tell you." But I wasn't sure where to start. How much did he already know? Knowing this town, probably everything. I went with the obvious. "Lauren came in today for training."

"Oh, yeah! I'd forgotten about that. How did it go, will she work out?"

"It went great. She's going to work out fine." I nodded enthusiastically. I was doing everything enthusiastically right then, down to holding his hand. Our fingers were threaded together, and I swung our joined hands between us as we walked. I loved this. Walking down the street of what had become my town, holding hands with this man who, in such a short period of time, had come to mean so much.

"Well, if hiring a new employee makes you this happy, maybe Chris should have done it sooner." He looked down at me with amused delight.

"There's more," I said. "Since we have Lauren now, I got a promotion. I'm going to manage the store for Chris while she's away."

"Away?" Alarm lit up his eyes. "Where is Chris going?"

Oh, so he didn't know. I needed to back up. "Florida. She's going down to stay with her mother, help take care of her. Which means I'll be sticking around for the foreseeable future. So you're looking at the new manager of Read It & Weep."

"What?" He shook his head like he hadn't heard me right, a look of dismay spreading over his face.

"Don't worry," I said. "Her mother's okay. I mean, she has some medical issues, and I guess she needs more care now, which is why Chris is going down there, but—"

"Chris is leaving?" He stopped walking now. "She's . . . she's leaving?"

Something prickled at the back of my neck. I thought he'd been upset because of Chris's mother, that maybe he knew her. But that wasn't it. "Yes . . ." Did he not hear the part where I was staying?

Evidently not. "Okay, but is she coming back? Ever? Or is this a permanent thing?"

"Just for the winter." He looked so distressed I wanted to re-assure him, even though his reaction made no sense. I had no idea he and Chris were so close. Why hadn't she told him about all this, then? "She'll be back in the spring. I think they're going to be splitting their time between here and Florida from now on."

"Oh. Okay." He blew out a long breath, relief clearing his ex-pression. "So she'll be back in time for Faire." He nodded. "That's good."

A sick feeling bloomed in my chest and his hand was sud-denly too heavy to hold so I dropped it. "That's your takeaway here? With everything I just told you, your big worry is if Chris will be back in time to put on a big dress and play the Queen again next year?" He hadn't even registered that I was staying. Or if he had, it didn't rate a mention. Not while the topic of Faire was on the table.

"Sorry, but yeah. That was the first thing I thought of. Because . . ."

"Because that's what's important." I nodded, my head bobbing on the end of my neck like a toy. That sick feeling trickled its way down to my stomach, leaving cold in its wake. "Faire's what's important to you. Not Chris's mother's health. Not that I'm staying here in town, and we can . . ." I swiped an angry hand across my cheek; where had that tear come from? "That fucking Faire is all that matters." I'd been here before, in a relationship like this. Where I always came second. Where once again my worth was measured in what I could do for someone, not who I was.

"You really think . . ." His face hardened, his eyes sharpening. Despite the longer hair and the beard, he looked more and more like the Simon I had first met all those months ago. "After all this time, that's what you think of me?"

"Can you blame me? You sound like the guy I knew during rehearsals, telling me I wasn't taking anything seriously."

"Oh, great." His laugh was sardonic, and it stung. "We all know how much you hate that guy." He paced away from me a step or two, raking a hand through his hair. "I've got bad news, Emily. Summer's almost over. Pretty soon the pirate you like so much goes back into storage, and I have to be that asshole again."

"You're not . . ." I didn't finish the sentence, because, well, he *was* being that asshole. I tried again. "You don't have to be that asshole." Why did he think that one personality couldn't exist without the other? Couldn't he see that he was really the best parts of both personas? And that I wanted them both?

"Sure I do." He said the words casually, but his voice dripped with acid. "It's who I am. Mitch is the fun guy. Sean was the fun guy. That's the kind of guy you want, right? It's why you like me right now. I get to be fun, I get to *have* fun, for six weeks a year, when I'm running around the woods dressed like a pirate. But the rest of the time? I'm the serious one. The one who gets shit done. Everyone likes the result, but no one cares it's all on me to make it happen."

"Do you ever let anyone help you?" I wished we were back at the shop, because throwing a book at his head seemed like a really good idea. Where was that *Complete Works of Shakespeare* when I needed it? "Hell, Simon, you blew a gasket when I moved some tables around! You don't want Chris to fire some jugglers no one comes to see! It's all on your shoulders because you like it that way."

"So I should not do Faire anymore, let it die? That'd be a great 'fuck you' to my brother. For all his hard work."

"That's not what I'm saying and you know it." Everything was tinged with red, and I wanted to scream in frustration. "The problem is you can't let go of it, because if you do, someone might change something. And you can't have that. But here's the thing: you can do this Faire the same way every year, exactly the way your brother left it, and he'll still be gone. He's never coming back."

Simon sucked in a breath, the color high in his cheeks, his eyes bright. "You think I don't know that? Of course he's not coming back. No one's coming back!" By now we were openly yelling at each other in the street. Thankfully we were still in the business district, where most of the storefronts were darkened up and closed down for the night. "This Faire is all I have. My brother's dead. My parents left; they left me alone in that . . ." He bit back his words, his jaw clenching so hard a muscle jumped in his cheek. All my anger drained away when I saw the sadness in his eyes. The resignation. This may not be the life he wanted, but he didn't know how to live any differently.

You have me, I wanted to say, but it felt like an inadequate offering. Not to mention a presumptuous one. How was I supposed to fill the holes in his heart left by so much loss?

I couldn't, could I? He still hadn't even acknowledged I was going to be a permanent fixture of Willow Creek. He hadn't noticed because it wasn't important enough to him. Certainly not as important as Faire.

That was my answer. There was no way that I'd be enough. Like I hadn't been enough for Jake. Would I ever be enough for anyone?

Tears flooded my vision and I blinked them back hard. I couldn't let him see. This was my fault, after all. I'd fallen too hard and too fast, and he'd never promised me anything. No, this was all on me.

"I need to get home." My voice was gravelly and I cleared my throat hard, my head bent as I searched through my purse for my keys.

Simon stopped short. "No, come on. It's okay, let's go to dinner."

"I can't." My voice didn't even work that time. I made myself look at him, which was a mistake. He looked startled, confused. I wanted to comfort him. I needed to get away from him. "I can't," I said again. "I need to go home."

"Hey. Wait." He reached for me, but I shrugged him off and he dropped his hand. "Look, I'm sorry. Let's talk about this."

It was tempting. If any two people were good at talking, it was Simon and me. But the hollow feeling in my chest told me this couldn't be fixed with talking.

"You're so focused on the past it's all you can see. How can we have a future if all you keep doing is looking back?" I clutched my keys so hard they made divots in my palm. "I can't compete with a memory. I already spent five years being someone's lower priority. Being second best always. I can't . . ." I couldn't talk anymore. I suddenly felt bone-weary. *Tired.* I knew this feeling. I'd talked to April about this very thing not too long ago. What had she said then? *Stop fighting losing battles.* My big sister knew her stuff. I gave a shaking sigh. "I deserve better than that."

I turned to go, and he grabbed my arm. "Emma. Emma, wait."

I sucked in a breath as everything went white.

Emma. Not Emily.

Emma.

And there it was. The truth in one Freudian slip. I really was just a tavern wench to him after all. A cog in his Ren faire machine. My first impression of him had been proved right, and it broke my heart.

I slowly turned back to him. He looked as though he'd realized his mistake a moment too late, his face stricken, but he still held on to my arm like it was a lifeline. "Wait." His voice was quiet, desperate.

"Emma's gone." I didn't sound like myself. My voice was quiet, steady, and barely there. "Served her last fucking drink." I pulled back, and he let go of my arm. For a long moment we stared at each other, his eyes golden-green in the streetlight, wide and sad. But he didn't say a word as I walked down the block to my Jeep. He was still standing there on the sidewalk as I drove away.

Twenty-two

I *made it about* two blocks away from the downtown area before I had to pull over. I could barely see the road through my tears, I couldn't take a substantial breath, and my thoughts were going a mile a minute. I fumbled in my purse for my phone, and it took three tries for my shaking hands to send a coherent text to Stacey. She was still technically in charge of us wenches, after all. I can't come to Faire this weekend. I'm sorry.

The message went from "delivered" to "read" almost immediately, and five seconds later my phone started buzzing in my hand. Stacey wasn't one to put things off.

"Are you okay? What's the matter, are you sick?"

"No. No, I'm fine. I . . ." I was crying, apparently. It wasn't what I'd intended, but there I was in the front seat of my Jeep, ugly tears splashing all over my phone.

"Yeah, you sound fine. Where are you? What do you need?"

The concern in Stacey's voice, not to mention her immediate offer of help, made me want to cry even harder, but I sucked in a deep breath and got it together. "Really, I'm okay."

Her sigh was a loud rush of breath in my ear. "Oh, crap. What did he do?"

I hiccuped another sob. "What? Who?"

"Simon. Seriously, did he screw this up already?" She didn't give me a chance to answer. "Okay, I'm on my way to Jackson's now. Meet me there in ten minutes." Before I could argue she'd hung up. I tossed my phone in the passenger seat and swiped at my face, which was a hopeless mess. But she was waiting for me, so I put the Jeep in gear and drove to our hangout.

Jackson's looked like a completely different place on a Friday night. The lights were brighter, and it looked less like a dive bar and more like a knockoff of a national chain bar and grill. Half an hour, three orders of mozzarella sticks, a couple beers, and most of a pizza later, Stacey sat back in her seat in our booth. "Well," she said. "You're sure as hell not going to Faire this weekend. You don't need to deal with that crap."

Gratitude rushed through me and I sagged against the table. "You have no idea how glad I am to hear that." I took a sip of beer. "I thought everyone was going to hate me now."

"What, because I've known Simon longer?" She scoffed. "Please. Wenches before . . . well, something that refers to guys that rhymes with 'wenches.'" She grinned at me, and I managed a watery laugh. "Don't worry about it. And don't worry about Faire. The Maryland Renaissance Festival starts up this weekend too. Everyone who wants to go to a Renaissance faire is heading over to that side of the state. These last couple weekends are usually pretty slow. Besides, you have our volunteers whipped into such good shape we could probably both take the weekend off and no one would notice."

"Oh, yeah. Simon would love—" The thought had come so naturally that for a second there I'd forgotten what had happened between us. Making fun of Simon had become one of my favorite things to do this summer, second only to kissing him. Now, though . . . now we were nothing. How was I supposed to live in this town with him in it?

"Hey." Stacey reached across the table and laid a hand on my arm. "Quit thinking. It's going to be okay."

I nodded dully, then focused more clearly on her hand on my arm. "Your nails are all fancy." She wasn't one to get manicures, but tonight they were extravagant French tips. Not exactly period for Faire tomorrow, but like she said, if it wasn't as busy maybe no one would notice. But now I took in her entire appearance. Her hair fell in tousled blond curls, and even in this lighting I could tell she was rocking a perfect smoky eye. "You have plans tonight, don't you?" I narrowed my eyes as she took her hand back and looked a little guilty. "A *date*. Please tell me you didn't cancel to watch me cry in my beer."

She waved one of those perfectly manicured hands. "He can wait a little bit. Had to make sure you were okay." She peered at me. "Are you?"

"I am. Really." I was lying. I also wanted to know who her date was with. Mitch? No. He'd been out with me at Jackson's a couple weekends before, and she'd had "plans" then too. Besides, I could see Mitch now, leaning against the bar on the other side of Jackson's, a beer in his hand, talking to a cute little brunette.

I decided to let it go. This town had few enough secrets as it was; may as well let Stacey keep one if she had it. So instead I pushed Stacey out the door for her date, paid the check, and went home.

"Hey." April barely glanced up from the TV when I walked in, which was probably for the best. "You just missed Mom. She called to invite herself and Dad down for Thanksgiving. I think this is gonna be a downside to you and me living in the same town . . . whoa." Now she peered at me. "Are you okay? You look like hell."

"Thanks." I dropped down on the couch beside her. "I broke up with Simon." Speaking the words out loud for the first time made it real, the way it hadn't been before, and all the pizza-and-beer therapy I'd had with Stacey went out the window.

"What?" April grabbed for the remote, turning off the TV. "You were out on a date with him. What happened?"

"We never made it to dinner." I stared at our reflections in the blank television screen. She was right: I did look like hell. Shit, I was crying again. I blinked, and heavy tears hit my cheeks, followed by more, a steady stream of them now, and I waited as long as possible before trying to draw a breath, knowing it wouldn't be successful. I pressed my palms to my eyes, hard, as April's arms came around me.

"Do you want to talk about it?"

My head fell onto her shoulder. "No." But between sobs I told her what had happened between Simon and me: what we'd said, how we'd said it, down to the look in his eyes when I'd gotten in the Jeep and driven off. She didn't say anything. Instead, my sister held me and let me talk and cry until I ran out of both words and tears. It was ugly; I was going to owe her a new shirt, possibly a new couch, when all this was over.

"Do you want to know what I think?" Her voice was a quiet murmur in my ear. She was good at the comforting mom thing. Of course, she had fourteen years of experience at it.

I nodded against her shoulder and sat up. "I fucked up, didn't I?" I leaned forward, bracing my elbows on my knees. "I jumped down his throat for no reason, and I ruined everything." My eyes burned from crying and my cheeks were hot, but I deserved the pain. I looked longingly at my purse, which I had dropped by the door. "Could I apologize? Maybe I can go over to his house and—"

"No." The vehemence in April's voice made me close my mouth with a snap. "You don't go anywhere *near* him—are you kidding?" Her eyes blazed and I didn't dare argue. "You absolutely did the right thing, and I won't hear otherwise." I opened my mouth to answer, but she shushed me before I could say a word. She really was good at laying down the law. "You stood up for yourself. You put yourself first. I know it's hard, and I know it sucks. But if he can't put a relationship with you over keeping up that living shrine to his brother every damn summer, then he doesn't deserve you."

She was right. I knew she was right. It didn't mean I had to like it. "But shouldn't I help . . ."

"No. Not if it hurts you." Her voice was harsh, but her eyes were kind. "I know you want to." She looped some of my hair behind my ear. "You want to help everyone. But you need to help yourself for a change. Do what's right for you. Would you be happy with him like this?"

I had to think about it. It had only been a couple hours, and there was already a Simon-shaped hole in my heart. I rubbed absently at my chest where it ached. I'd do about anything to make that pain go away. But then I remembered how I'd felt when he'd brushed past my good news and focused on what had mattered to him. And what had mattered to him hadn't been me. As much as I hurt right now, I'd be trading one kind of pain for another.

"Why?" I finally asked, the word an embarrassing wail. "Why aren't I important to him? I thought he was . . . I thought he . . ." *Loved me.* But I was wrong. I wanted to cry again, but I was out of tears. Now I was tired. Numb. "I thought he was different." My voice was tiny, humiliated, and I almost didn't recognize it. I pressed my hands to my eyes again. "God, I'm an idiot."

"No, you're not." April's hand was on my back, rubbing in slow, soothing circles. "You picked two shitty guys in a row. It happens." She leaned over to the end table and grabbed a box of tissues. "Let me take care of you for once," she said while I yanked out tissues by the fistful and pressed them to my hot, tear-streaked face.

I hardly slept that night, my dreams filled with images of bright red roses disintegrating into dust, bottles of rum smashing on the floor into shards of broken glass. My subconscious took this breakup pretty literally. When I woke up, the sun was higher in the sky than I'd expected and the house was silent. I rolled over and looked at my phone. I'd overslept; the alarm had been turned off. On a regular Saturday I'd be in the woods, getting strapped into my costume right about now. Instead I slung my bathrobe around my shoulders and rubbed my swollen, aching eyes on the way to the kitchen for a cup of coffee. I didn't look at any mirrors. I didn't want to know.

April's SUV wasn't in the driveway, and she'd left me a half pot of coffee, the burner still on. I was most of the way through my first cup when she got back. She tilted her head and looked at me, twirling her keys around her finger.

"You know what today is?"

Was this a trick question? "Saturday?"

"It's the first Saturday you and I have had free. Completely free. Since . . . well, since you came here."

I thought about that. "I think you're right."

"Come on." She grabbed my arm and hauled me to my feet. "You're not going to sit around and watch Netflix and eat ice cream all day. Get in the shower."

"But I like ice cream . . ." My argument was ineffective as she manhandled me down the hall toward the bathroom.

"You'll like brunch better."

She was right. Brunch had mimosas. After we'd had our fill of waffles and orangey booze, our next stop was a salon for manicures, followed by pedicures. I could see what she was doing; the goal was to keep my mind off of everyone at Faire for the day, and for the most part she succeeded. It was nice to spend an afternoon picking out nail colors and wiggling my newly blue toes in my sandals instead of slumped on the couch while Netflix asked, *How many episodes of reality television are you planning on watching?*

Later, when April dropped me off at the house on her way to pick up Caitlin, my phone buzzed with a text. I smiled. Stacey. You alive?

I'm okay, I texted back. How was your date?

Three fire emojis popped up in response, followed by an eggplant and . . . were those water droplets? Oh, dear. I had no answer for that.

When April said she was going to take care of me, she meant it. She shuttled Caitlin back and forth from Faire all weekend so I wouldn't have to go anywhere near it. She fed me wine in the evenings in the hopes I would get sleepy, but the alcohol only made me giggly, then morose. But I was so thankful she was there, and it would have been a much, much worse weekend without her.

I was almost glad to go back to the bookstore on Tuesday. Rip off the Band-Aid, stand on that same sidewalk where I'd told Simon I didn't want to see him anymore. I took a deep breath and unlocked the door to the shop. This was my new life, after all. Just another Tuesday morning. It was an elaborate lie I told myself.

Chris was due in later that morning, and I couldn't stand the wait. It had to be common knowledge by now that Simon and I had broken up; people had found out we'd gotten together quickly enough, after all. What was she going to say? I was still the newcomer. All my friends here had been Simon's friends first. Had I lost not only my burgeoning relationship with Simon, but my new sense of community? Not to mention my new job?

I busied myself by hauling out the stepladder and dusting the tops of the bookshelves, and when the bell over the door chimed and Chris walked in, my heart climbed into my throat. Moment of truth time. I tossed down the dust rag and hopped to the floor. For a moment we looked at each other, then she stepped forward and enveloped me in a hug.

"Are you all right?"

I let my forehead fall on her shoulder as I hugged her back. "I think so." I straightened up and swiped at the tears stinging my eyes. I must have stirred up a lot of dust. "I take it word got around?"

Her nod was almost a shrug. "It was an interesting weekend." She didn't elaborate. I didn't ask her to. "You sure you're okay?"

"Yeah." I swiped at my eyes with the back of my hand. "I'm fine. It's not like we were together very long." My voice and my expression were light, casual even. I tried my best not to reveal that my heart was broken. "It was just a summer thing. A half-of-the-summer thing. We didn't work out. That's all." The words hurt to say out loud, as though there was a fist around my heart and each sentence made it clench tighter and tighter.

Chris looked at me like she knew I was lying, but thankfully she didn't call me on it. "You're really not coming back to Faire?"

"No. I can't . . ." I couldn't face Simon in his Captain Blackthorne persona. I couldn't pretend to be Emma, the wench in love with a pirate. I couldn't cheer on a chess match or let him kiss my hand with promises in his eyes, especially now that I knew for certain those promises weren't real. "I can't," I said again.

She gave my hand a squeeze. "Don't worry about it," she said. "Everything will work out the way it's supposed to."

I tried to keep that in mind all week as I kept myself busy and tried not to think about Simon. He certainly did his part; he didn't stop by the bookstore once, and my phone was silent when it came to his number. With no more Faire for me and Simon vanishing into thin air, it was like that part of the summer had never happened. I half expected to snap awake at any moment from a fever dream caused by binge-watching Shakespeare adaptations, back in my old apartment in Boston.

Chris was very kind and didn't bring up the crash and burn of my love life after that first morning, and for the most part I followed along. But something in the back of my mind kept bothering me, and by Thursday morning it wouldn't let me go. I had to say something.

"Are you still seeing Simon next week?" His name almost hurt to say out loud, but I pushed past it. "To talk about Faire next year?"

"That's the plan." Her face was so full of sympathy I had to turn away from her, look down at the armload of books I carried. "Don't worry. I won't ask him to drop by the store. I know you can't avoid him forever in a town this size, but I'm not going to . . ."

"No." I waved a hand. "That's fine. I mean, yes, thank you, I can't . . ." My breath started to shudder, and how long was I going to cry about this? I shoved the emotion down. "That's not why I was asking." I put down the books. I was going to shelve them, but multitasking was off the menu today. "Look, when you talk to him, about next year. He needs help."

Her brow furrowed. "Well, of course he needs help. That's why I help him plan . . ."

"More than that," I said. "I know he loves doing this Faire. It's his highest priority." Boy, did I ever know that. "But sometimes

I think . . . Chris, I think he's taking on too much. He's drowning in it."

"What?" She looked startled for a second, then shook her head. "No, he's fine. Faire's his thing. He's always a little burned out at the end of the summer."

"Faire isn't his thing. It was Sean's thing, and now Simon has to do it." My heart was pounding hard now. I felt like I was bringing up something I had no right to discuss. Chris had known Simon for years. Decades, even. I'd known him for a handful of months. But all I could see were Simon's eyes. How tired they'd looked. How trapped. If I truly was the only person who saw it, I needed to say something. "He's doing it the way Sean did it because he doesn't know what else to do. And he can't move on. He'll keep doing this Faire till he drops, and he'll be nothing more than Sean's little brother forever, carrying on what Sean wanted. But he needs to be his own person with his own life." I ran out of nerve and shrugged. "I don't know. I could be wrong. You probably know him better than I do. Just . . . could you ask him? Make sure he's really okay?"

Chris looked at me carefully, and I waited for her to tell me that it was none of my business. I had broken up with Simon; what right did I have to tell her how he felt? But instead she nodded, her face as kind as ever. "Of course. I'll talk to him, don't worry."

"Thanks." I picked up the books and went back to work, ignoring the tears that had dropped to my cheeks. I'd said what I needed to say. Maybe Simon and I weren't meant to be, but if saying something to Chris could help him in some way, it was worth it. Fixing things was what I did, after all.

A little after noon on Friday the bell over the door chimed, and I was surprised to see Stacey walk in, wearing her blue work scrubs and carrying a bag from the deli down the street.

"You haven't eaten, have you?"

"No." Unless you counted the three brownies I'd shoved in my face from the coffee counter. Chris was an excellent baker and I was still wallowing.

"That's what I thought." She unpacked sandwiches at one of the café tables while I grabbed some bottles of water for us. She'd brought me a Reuben, which she knew was my favorite. I thanked her and bit into it gratefully. My stomach growled in appreciation at the first bite of real food of the day. We ate in companionable silence for a little while, which was refreshing. Most conversation around me lately tended to be of the *how are you holding up* variety, and I'd run out of ways to answer that question.

After we'd finished, she started to gather up the lunch trash, but I slapped her hands away and started the cleanup myself.

"You should come out to Jackson's tonight."

I sucked in a breath. "I don't know. Do you think that's a good idea?"

"Yes. I think it's an excellent idea. Our night out last week got cut short, remember?"

I raised my eyebrows. "Because you had to go get laid."

She wrinkled her nose at me but didn't deny it. "And you were crying in your beer." I had to concede that point. "Seriously, let's go out. Simon won't be there. You know he likes to get his beauty sleep on Friday nights."

I started to smirk, but the mental image of Simon sleeping reminded me of his room. His bed. That warm quilt. His arms around me during the night, like I was something worth holding on to. Had he ever felt that way? Had I imagined it all? *Stop.* "Yeah," I said. "Maybe I will."

Of course, I changed my mind about fourteen times, back and forth as to whether or not I should meet up with Stacey for our night out. No matter what, Jackson's was the unofficial Faire hangout. Simon might not be there, and while Stacey had made it clear our friendship was still intact, I had no idea how everyone else would react to me.

But I'd also spent a good part of the week researching apartments and made appointments to look at some I could afford that were close to the bookstore. I was planning for my future in Willow Creek. This was going to be my town too, damn it, so if I wanted to meet my friend for happy hour I should be able to do so without fear of being run out on a rail.

I shouldn't have worried.

"Paaaaaarrrrrk!"

Mitch threw his arm around my neck in that weird, strangling hug he liked to do. It was like being attacked by a tree, but he only did it to the people he liked, so I smiled and leaned into it. "How you doing? I heard you had a shitty week."

Master of nuance, that guy. "I did. But this helps." I took the proffered tequila shot and tossed it back. Just one tonight. I needed to stay in control. I didn't want to end the night sobbing and singing bad karaoke. I pushed the shot glass back in Mitch's direction and looked around the bar.

"Don't worry, I already looked. He isn't here."

"I wasn't looking for him." But I smiled in thanks, which only widened as he passed me a beer. "Stacey was meeting me here; have you seen her?"

"Here I am! And here you are!" Stacey appeared as if by magic and practically tackled me in a hug from behind. "I'm so glad you made it!"

"Of course she did." Mitch turned back to the bar and signaled for a drink for Stacey. "Why wouldn't she want to hang out with us? We're awesome."

"I couldn't agree more." I took a sip of my beer and leaned happily against the bar. "So tell me everything. What did I miss last weekend?"

Mitch raised his eyebrows. "Really? I thought you were bitter about Faire."

"No, she's not!" Stacey nudged him. "She's bitter about pirates who act like dickheads."

"We certainly have one of those." He sighed, then brightened. "In that case, you will absolutely want to hear about Saturday's first chess match."

"I do? Why's that?"

He barked out a laugh. "It sucked."

"That's an understatement!" Stacey giggled around the mouth of her beer bottle. "I mean, you've been doing this fight, what, twice a day for almost two months now?"

Mitch snorted. "Not to mention the past three years."

My eyes widened. "What happened?"

"Simon fucked up all over the place, that's what happened. His timing was off; he couldn't get the punches to look even close to convincing. I pretty much had to dive over his shoulder like some kind of asshole." He shook his head. "He got it together for the rest of the weekend, but the boy was rough." He brightened. "It was pretty funny, though. I think someone videoed it—I need to ask around. But I told him last night when we . . ." He caught himself and looked up at me then, stricken.

"It's okay," I said, oddly touched that Mitch had so much concern for my feelings. "You're allowed to talk to the guy, you know."

"Yeah." He shook himself. "I mean, yeah, of course. I've known him for years. I talk to him plenty. That's normal."

I blinked. That was . . . vehement. "So . . . ?"

"Hmm?" He looked at me blankly.

"So you told him last night . . . ?"

"Oh, yeah. I told him he'd better get his shit together. We're going to meet tomorrow morning to run through the fight again, make sure he knows what the hell he's doing." He took another swig of beer. "Oh, hey, speaking of, you should come on Sunday."

"'Speaking of'? Speaking of what?" I looked down at my beer. I hadn't had much to drink, so why was it hard to follow Mitch's conversation tonight?

"Faire," he said quickly. "Speaking of Faire."

Stacey rolled her eyes. "We're always speaking of Faire, aren't we?"

"I'm not coming on Sunday." My heart started pounding at the thought of it. "I need a break from pirates and wenches for a little while. Maybe forever. No offense." I bumped Stacey's shoulder.

"No, I agree with Mitch," Stacey said. "You should come."

I leveled a look at her. "You were the one who said I didn't need to. I shouldn't have to 'deal with that crap,' remember?"

"Oh, no. Not to work it. Not in character. But as a patron."

"Yeah," Mitch said. "On Sunday."

"Sunday?" He seemed awfully insistent, but I couldn't figure out why. "Why not tomorrow?"

"Because Sunday's the last day," Stacey said. "It's . . . I dunno, it's always a little more fun. A little more silly. And besides, the vendors that are still there sometimes put stuff on sale, so you can maybe get a new corset or something."

"If I were planning to do Faire ever again."

She shrugged. "Never say never. If you're going to live here in Willow Creek, you're going to have something to do with Faire."

"Yeah, it's kind of a law." Mitch polished off his beer, then went to exchange the bottle for a new one.

I turned to Stacey. "You honestly think I should go?"

Stacey's nod was emphatic. "You should. Hey, see if April will come with you. Strength in numbers and all that. Might make you feel better."

I considered that. "You know, she hasn't come to Faire all summer."

"I don't think she's *ever* come to Faire." Stacey took a sip of her drink. "Maybe she should. She seems nice, but I don't think I've ever seen her out anywhere. I know she's a single mom, but she's still allowed to have fun, right?"

"You're not wrong." The more I thought about it, the more I liked the idea. Going with April sounded a lot less scary than going alone, and maybe it would be fun to go as a patron. See all the shows I'd been missing. Go to the joust, have a turkey leg.

"So come to Faire on Sunday," Stacey said. "Bring April and let's buy her a drink. I'd love to hang out with her."

I liked that idea too. April meeting my friends and becoming part of this little group. "Yeah," I said. "I'll talk to her."

But I didn't need to. Caitlin brought it up for me instead on Saturday night.

"You and Mom should come to Faire tomorrow." A freshly showered, home-from-Faire Caitlin shoved a forkful of lasagna into her mouth before I could caution her that it was too hot.

"You're gonna burn your . . . what? We should, huh?"

"Yeah." She sucked in some air around the bite of hot pasta, then drank half a glass of milk in two gulps. "It's the last day tomorrow. It's supposed to be fun."

"Yeah," I said. "I've heard that. Slow down. I didn't spend the afternoon making lasagna for you to make yourself sick eating it too fast."

Caitlin rolled her eyes, but cut a smaller bite.

"I don't know," April said from the other side of the table. "It could be fun."

"Really?" I looked at her askance. "I offered you free passes at the beginning of Faire, and you didn't want to go."

"Because of my leg."

I narrowed my eyes. "It wasn't because of your leg. You said it sounded like a boring way to spend a day."

"Maybe I changed my mind." A small smile played around her mouth. "I should probably see what my daughter's been up to all summer, don't you think? I'll bring some tomatoes, we can chuck them at Simon."

Caitlin snorted, and I had to laugh at this show of sisterly support. "That's okay." After a week apart, anger and indignation had started to fade, replaced mostly by a dull aching sadness. I missed Simon. But calling him would be useless. When it came down to Faire or me, I knew where his priorities lay. He was stuck in the past, and until he could move on, there was nothing there for me.

"So you're okay?" April asked.

"Yeah." I sighed the word, which made it pretty unconvincing. "I will be." Better.

"Good. Let's go objectify men in kilts tomorrow."

That brought a smile to my face. Mitch would be happy to oblige us, I was sure.

"Sure," I said. "Let's do it."

Twenty-three

I t *felt strange* to pull into the regular parking lot at Faire, where paying patrons parked. All these weeks I'd pulled into a dirt lot hidden off a side road, and Caitlin and I would forge our way in early-morning, watery sunlight to the Hollow. But this time we dropped Caitlin off, then killed time by caffeinating at a nearby coffee shop, where we fueled ourselves with coffee and bagels and stashed bottles of water in our bags before returning to Faire and parking in the front lot with the rest of the patrons.

The middle-aged volunteer working the ticket booth was named Nancy. I thought I'd seen her three times the whole summer and spoken to her once. Maybe twice. But her face lit up when she saw me, and she came around to give me a hug like we were old friends.

"Emily! So good to see you. And you must be April." She reached over to squeeze April's hand in an approximation of a handshake. "Your daughter has done such a great job this summer. You must be so proud."

"I am." April's voice sounded the way her bemused smile

looked. "I'm looking forward to seeing what she's been doing all summer."

"Well, you'll usually be able to find her near—oh, I guess Emily knows where she tends to be. You've been here long enough, haven't you?"

I nodded, because it was easier than explaining that I rarely left the tavern/chess field part of the grounds. But when I started digging in my purse for my wallet, Nancy waved that aside.

"You're not paying for your tickets, are you crazy? Go on inside, enjoy the day!" She gave us a little wink. "The last day is always a little different."

"Well." April looked over her shoulder at Nancy as we went inside the main gate. "She was nice."

"Nice how?" That could mean a lot of different things to April. Nice and nosy. Nice and overly friendly.

But this time April shrugged. "Just . . . nice."

"Welcome to Willow Creek," I said, even though she'd lived there for years. "Pretty much everyone is like that."

She started to respond, but we passed through the main gate and walked into another world.

I shouldn't have been awed by the sight of the Renaissance faire in full swing. But the sensory overload when you walked in was fantastic. Sunlight glowed through the bunting wound through branches above our heads. Near the front, a group of student cast members performed an intricate maypole dance to the accompaniment of prerecorded mandolin and flute. Vendors lined the lane where we walked, and every step showed me things I had never wanted in my life but suddenly needed to own. Leather-covered journals, flower crowns, handmade boots. One vendor had a booth shaped like a Romany-style wagon, selling crystals and tarot cards.

My heart squeezed at the sight of the rose seller, but I was able to hustle April past her booth quickly.

"What are we checking out first?" April brandished the map we'd been given at the front.

"I know exactly where to start." I didn't need the map for this. I led her down the lane, winding around the patrons and cast alike. The Celtic musicians had come back for the last weekend of Faire, and I could finally catch their show.

"Oh, good call," April murmured to me when the performers, a band called the Dueling Kilts, took the stage. Three men in kilts with acoustic instruments. One had long hair swirled up in a man bun, and another wore a devilish smile. It was like I'd tailor-made a show for her. For both of us. I hadn't even known that about these guys. All I'd known of their act were the bits I could hear from my station at the tavern, but I had to agree I'd made a very good call indeed. They didn't even need musical talent, really. We would have been happy standing there gazing at them.

Once the show ended and we'd each slipped a tip in the form of a couple folded bills into the waistband of a well-worn kilt, April consulted the map again. "I want to see your tavern."

"Oh." I froze. "No." I'd been so distracted by all the parts of Faire I hadn't seen that I'd forgotten about the parts of Faire that were as automatic to me as breathing. The tavern. The chess field. Simon. "No," I said again. "We can skip that part."

"No, we can't." She grabbed my arm and marched me along. "It's before noon on a Sunday, I just saw a hot guy in a kilt, and now I need a drink. Let's go get one."

She would not be denied, and as we rounded the familiar bend my skin began to prickle. By the time we reached the tavern I was one large, quivering nerve ending. My senses were on high alert, my eyes darting for a glimpse of a man all in black. I didn't know what I would do if I saw Simon. Punch him? Cry? Run away? All of the above?

But he was nowhere to be seen in the tavern, and after hugs from Stacey, Jamie, and the rest of the volunteers, followed by a round of drinks, I felt a lot calmer. Calm enough that by the time we strolled by the chess field a little while later my legs hardly shook at all. As we passed it the match was in full swing, and I kept my head turned away from it. I could do this. I could ignore him.

Actually, I couldn't see him. As much as I tried not to look, I caught myself scanning the field, more surprised by what I didn't see than by what I saw. I didn't see black leather or a hat with a large red feather. I slowed my steps as Mitch stalked to the center of the board to fight, both anticipating and dreading what was coming. Surely Simon would take the field with him. But no, Mitch's fight was with the Quarterstaff Kid instead.

I looked around for a wild moment, expecting Simon to pop out from behind a nearby tree or something. Where the hell was he? There was no way he'd shirk his responsibilities on the last day. Top priority in his life—he'd made that more than clear.

"What are we looking at . . . ooh, another kilt!" April paused for a moment to watch in appreciation as Mitch spun through the steps of the fight. I couldn't blame her; the man put on a good show. After spending so many weeks with Mitch's insane physique I had become immune, but now I saw the fight through my sister's eyes. A green plaid kilt swirling around muscular thighs was truly a sight to behold.

After Mitch disarmed the Quarterstaff Kid and sent him to the ground, ending the fight, we both shook ourselves and blinked at each other. "So you had no interest in that one, huh?"

"Mitch?" I snorted at the thought. That ship had sailed a long time ago. "No. He's just a friend."

"If you say so." She stole another look in his direction. "I'm just saying, I'd have been a lot more into sports in high school if the coach looked like that." She was quiet for another moment, then shook off the thought. "Food?" I pointed down the path and we set off.

A couple hours later we had split a massive smoked turkey leg, which was as awkward to eat as you might imagine, and had flower crowns in our hair. The ribbons from the crown floated down my back and trailed down to my elbows. We stopped again at the tavern so April could rest her leg. And get another glass of wine.

I still hadn't spotted Simon, which at first I'd been relieved about, but as the day wore on I became confused. And more than a little sad. Stacey and Mitch had been so insistent that I come today. Had they given Simon the heads-up so he could avoid running into me? I didn't like the thought of that. This Faire was Simon's home. He loved it more than anything. I shouldn't have come here if I made him this uncomfortable.

"Do you want to head home?" I didn't like the way April was rubbing her bad leg. But she waved off my concern.

"I'm fine. My stamina's not what it was before the accident."

"Seriously, we can go . . ."

"Nah." She put her leg up on the bench next to us. "I just need to slow down a little. Wine first. Then joust."

I still didn't feel great about dragging her all the way across the grounds to the jousting field, but she insisted she was fine and she could rest there while we watched. I couldn't argue with that, and deep down inside I really wanted to see the joust. I'd been looking forward to it all summer, and it was unlikely I'd be back to the Faire in the future.

"I can't believe I've never seen this!" I squirmed a little on the hard wooden bench. April crunched on a giant pickle she'd bought from a wandering vendor and grinned at me.

"You've had a busy summer. And this is clear on the other side of the grounds. I'd be surprised if you came over here much at all."

She had a point, and I was about to tell her so when knights on horseback cantered into the ring. It was late summer and pretty damn hot, and these men were in chain mail with tunics on top of that. The horses they rode were massive, almost Clydesdale in size, probably to support the weight of all that armor. They came thundering through the jousting field, and the pounding of their hooves resonated in my chest. I leaned forward with my elbows on my knees and watched, enraptured. The knights and horses worked together in breathtaking concert. Dirt flew under hooves. Lances crashed against one another and against shields. I knew this was all rehearsed—these guys did the show twice a day, like the human chess match actors—but those were still real horses hurtling toward each other at real speeds, and those lances looked like they'd hurt a lot if they struck someone by accident.

By the time it ended I sucked in a deep breath, as though I'd been afraid to breathe throughout half the show. I turned to April, who looked equally bowled over.

"Damn," she said. "Just . . . damn." She took a deep breath like I had, and turned to me with wide eyes. "This shit goes on every year, and I never knew. Huh."

"Not bad for a small town, huh?" I stood up to leave, and she followed.

"I guess." Her skepticism sounded a little forced, and I rolled my eyes. But she caught my eye and grinned, and I threw an arm around her shoulders in a quick hug.

"C'mon," I said. "Let's get out of here."

As I started to scoot down the row to the end of the bench and the exit, April caught my arm. "Let's go that way, it's closer."

I looked where she pointed, the other way down the row to the secondary exit. She was right; for some reason fewer people were heading in that direction. So I reversed course and followed her instead, around the ring of the jousting field and through the gate. We came out on the left side of the jousting field, near a small clearing, and my breathing stalled when I saw where we were.

April was right, I hadn't been on this side of the grounds much at all. Except for the first day of Faire. The handfasting. That day had been the beginning of everything between Simon and me. The first time he'd kissed me, even though it was staged. The first time I'd felt his hand around mine and felt safe. Protected. Like he was the one I was meant to be with. It had all been fake emotion, brought on by being in character and fancy words spoken while our hands had been bound together with a golden cord. But it had felt real, and more importantly, it had led to something real.

Something real that was now over. I cleared my throat hard and geared myself up to walk past the handfasting that was obviously getting ready to start now. I had no desire to be anywhere near it, so I kept my head down and my feet moving.

"What are those people doing there?" Of course April had to notice and ask me about it. I sighed inwardly. It wasn't her fault; I'd never told her about this part of my time at Faire. So I forced a smile and a casual tone of voice.

"Oh, it's this mushy thing, it's for couples, no big deal."

"It looks cute. Let's go see."

"April, no." But she would not be deterred. She hooked a hand around my elbow and practically dragged me over there. "No," I said again, squirming in a pathetic attempt to get away. "Why do you want to see happy couples? I'm still in the ice cream and brownies and booze phase of my breakup, you know. This could set me back weeks."

"Ah, the holy trinity of heartache." She grinned at me over her shoulder. "Shut up and come on."

There was a small crowd gathered for the handfasting, but it didn't look right. There were hardly any patrons. Two or three milled around on the fringes, but everyone who was actually in the clearing was a cast member in costume. But there weren't very many cast members, either. A scant handful, and I realized with a jolt I knew all of them. The Queen was there, of course, since she performed the ceremony. Every time I saw Chris in costume, it was hard to remember she was the same woman who wore her hair in a long braid and made killer lemon squares. Caitlin was next to her, like a good little lady-in-waiting; my niece caught my eye and grinned at me. Now I was suspicious. She looked like she was up to something.

"Ach, it's about time, lassie." And there was Mitch, with his exaggerated Scottish accent, bowing to April and me like we were in royal garb ourselves.

"About time?" I looked from him to April and back again. "What's he talking about?" But neither one of them answered. Instead, April propelled me forward with her hand on my arm, and when Mitch took my hand I followed along, a habit born of weeks of men reaching for my hand while in costume and me giving it freely. He dropped my hand as we reached the center of the clearing, and I stopped walking, barely noticing when Mitch stepped back.

There, in the center of the clearing, was Simon.

Not Captain Blackthorne.

Simon.

He wore jeans, a crisp light green cotton shirt open at the throat, and a sheepish expression. His hair was cut short like the first day we'd met, so he no longer had the shock of hair that hung over his brow, and those red burnishes the sun brought out were almost invisible in that closer crop. The face-framing beard was gone too, not to mention the smudges of eyeliner he had sported most of the summer. No leather. No hat. No earring. All traces of the pirate had gone. All that was left was . . .

"Simon?" I could only stare at him. He looked so different. He looked like that serious, judgmental dickhead I'd met on day one, who told me I'd filled my form out wrong. Except that man had worn a disdainful expression. This man was just the opposite. He looked at me as though I were the only thing that mattered.

"Emily." His gaze roamed over my face as though he hadn't seen me in weeks, but he didn't move toward me. I remembered I was mad at him, that we'd broken up, but I was so stunned to see him completely stripped of his pirate persona, that none of that seemed to matter. Not when he was looking at me like that.

"But Faire's not over." I gestured at his outfit, as though I were imparting new information he had missed. "You weren't at the chess match today." Also vital intel he probably didn't know.

He nodded slowly, solemnly. "You're right."

"But . . ." Too many thoughts were in my head at once, and they all wanted out at the same time. "Why aren't you in costume?" He'd told me how precious those days he spent as a pirate were to him. Why had he cut that time short?

"I'm proving a point." Now he moved toward me, just a step,

his eyes still on me. "You gave me a lot to think about, you know, last week. And you were right."

"I was?"

"You were." He took another step toward me. "About a lot of things. But the most important thing is that my brother is gone. Nothing I do will bring him back."

"Oh." I sucked in a little air through my teeth. That hadn't been the nicest thing I'd ever said. "I'm sorry. I was—"

"Completely right. You made me see how much I've been stuck in this loop. Sean died, but I'm the one who became a ghost. Micromanaging this Faire, not letting anyone breathe, including myself. And the worst thing, the absolute worst thing I did that night, Emily, was make you think you didn't matter. That you weren't good enough. That a Renaissance faire—that anything—was more important than you. I'm so sorry, Emily. No one should make you feel like that." He didn't reach for my hand, although I wanted him to more than anything. "I did a lot of thinking over the past few days, and I'm stepping back from Faire."

"What? No." I shook my head. "You can't quit Faire." I looked around guiltily at our friends who were gathered around us. "He's not quitting Faire," I told them. Chris pressed her lips together to hide her smile.

"I didn't say I was quitting," he said. "I'm stepping back. Letting more people help out. Mitch, for example, is excited to take over some of the organization next year."

"Okay. I didn't say I was 'excited,'" Mitch said from behind me. I could practically hear the air quotes. "I said I'd help out. What exactly do I have to do?"

Someone shushed him; it sounded like April. "Be quiet, Kilty." Definitely April.

"The point is," Simon continued as though Mitch hadn't interrupted, "it's time to let other people be in charge. I can honor my brother more by letting go of the past and living my own life. And Emily . . ." He was so close now, his eyes searching mine, and I was as caught in his gaze as I ever was. "The only thing I'm sure I want in that new life is you." He took my hand, and our fingers threaded together instinctively. I held on tightly because, despite everything, I'd missed him so much. "Everything that makes up my life—my job, my house, even Faire—I didn't choose any of it. I didn't get a chance to." He pitched his voice low now; his words were for me alone. "They all happened, were passed on to me as something to take over. And I took them over because I thought I should. But then you came along, Emily, and you weren't a *should*. You were a *want*. Being with you was the first thing I wanted, the first thing I chose for myself, in years. And I fucked it up so completely that night."

"No." My heart ached for him, for his past, for those obligations that had been heaped on his shoulders. Our fight seemed insignificant in comparison.

"Yes." But Simon wouldn't let me put myself second this time. "I did. I put all those *shoulds* ahead of you, and I deserved it when you walked away from me. But you still told Chris I needed help. You knew what I needed when I didn't even know what to ask for. I hoped that meant there was still part of you that cared. That I could get a second chance to tell you how much you mean to me. Not for what you can do for me, or for Faire. But for who you are. And for who I am when I'm with you."

"But . . ." This close, his clean scent surrounding me, it was hard to think. "Are you sure about this? I know how much you love Faire."

"I do." He nodded in agreement. "I love Faire. But I don't need Faire. I need you, Emily." He reached for me then, his palms cupping my face. "I love you."

I caught my breath at his words, my throat closing in a sob. My heart was so full I was sure my love shone in my eyes, but in case he couldn't tell I whispered the words back to him. "I love you, Simon."

He closed his eyes, and relief smoothed across his features. Then he cleared his throat. "So . . ." He reached into his back pocket and pulled out a length of golden cord.

I let out a choked laugh. "We did that already, remember? I think it was good for a year and a day. We've got a while till that expires."

"No." He shook his head. "I mean, you're right. We were bound once before, but it was fake. It doesn't count. I want you to understand everything I feel for you is real. Will you start this new life with me, for a year and a day? Not as Captain Blackthorne and Emma. But as you and me. Simon and Emily."

The words were an echo of what I'd said in his kitchen that night, when I'd come to his house with a bottle of rum to proposition a pirate. What he offered me now was ten times better. A new start. A real start. I drew in a shuddering breath and reached for the cord. We each held on to an end of it, winding the golden cord in our fingers, letting it connect us. But that wasn't the ceremony, and my mind went blank. "I don't remember what we're supposed to do."

"I know this part." Caitlin suddenly appeared between us and took the cord away. "You have to join hands." Her accent had slipped, but whatever. It was the end of Faire and this was an unorthodox handfasting. She took my hand and placed it in Simon's. His hand closed around mine, and we both let out a small sigh of relief. I remembered the first time we'd done this, how I'd felt a sense of peace. That peace was back. For good this time.

Then Chris spoke, in her lovely lilting voice as Queen. "Groom and Bride, I bid you look into each other's eyes. Will you honor and respect one another and seek to never break that honor?"

Groom and bride. I'd been horrified when she'd said those words at the beginning of the summer. Now the peacefulness expanded. This wasn't a wedding, not even close, but it was the beginning of something very real. Very right. I looked up at Simon and as he looked down at me I could see the same reflected in his eyes.

"Yes." I answered the Queen's question but addressed Simon as I did so. He did the same.

"And so the first binding is made." Cait followed directions, wrapping the cord loosely around our joined hands.

"Will you share each other's pain, and seek to ease it?"

"Always," he said immediately, but I was too full of emotion to speak. His hand squeezed mine, and I squeezed back. *I'm here,* I wanted to say. *I'll always be here.*

"And so the second binding is made." This second loop brought our hands tighter together.

"Will you share the burdens of each, so your spirits may grow in this union?"

At our murmured assent, the cord was looped around a third time.

"Simon and Emily." I blinked up at Chris, surprised to hear our names being used. She dropped a wink at me. "As your hands are bound together now, so your lives and spirits are joined in a union of love and trust. Above you are the stars and below you is the earth. Like the stars, your love should be a constant source of light, and like the earth, a firm foundation from which to grow."

I couldn't think of a better way to start a relationship.

Simon pulled his hand free from mine, only to reach for me with both hands and finally kiss me the way I'd wanted him to ever since I first saw him in this clearing. His kiss felt different; I'd never kissed him when he was clean-shaven. But his lips were warm, and his mouth tasted like home. His arms around me, his body against mine, felt like home. I curled a hand around the back of his head, his close-cropped hair slipping between my fingers, and held him to me. He exhaled a long breath into the crook of my neck. I *love* you, he mouthed against my skin, and I held him tighter. We were both home.

When we drew apart we were mostly alone. The rest of the group had started to disperse, giving us a little privacy by heading up to the front for the final pub sing. April walked ahead with Caitlin, but she looked over her shoulder at me. She sent me a wink and I crinkled my nose at her. Had everyone in my life been in on this?

Simon brought my hand to his mouth as we walked, reassuring himself that I was there. That I wasn't going anywhere. "I'll need you to distract me next summer at Faire, you know. So I don't try micromanaging everything."

"Hmmm. I bet I can think of some ways." Next summer seemed so far off. But I couldn't imagine being anywhere else. My roots had definitely started to take hold. "Is it okay if I don't want to be a wench next year?"

He shrugged. "Sure."

"What about a pirate?" I wiggled my eyebrows suggestively. "Does the Captain need a first mate?"

That earned me a laugh, and my heart thrilled. Simon didn't hand out laughs freely. "Very possibly."

"Oh! I know!" I grinned up at him. "I can be Shakespeare."

His laugh vanished, followed by a scowl, but his eyes still shone in amusement. "No. You can't. Shakespeare wrote Shakespeare."

"But what if he didn't?" I poked him in the side. "What if it was *Wilhelmina* Shakespeare?"

"No." More insistent this time, he dragged me to the side of the path until my back rested against a tree. "It wasn't." His lips grazed mine, a kiss for each word. "Shakespeare. Wrote. Shakespeare."

He had his Teacher Voice on again, but when I looked up into his golden-green eyes I recognized the glimmer in them. The pirate was still in there. Those two parts of his personality weren't as disparate as he thought they were.

I kissed him again and decided not to argue. I had a year and a day. I could talk him into it.

Epilogue

One Year and One Day Later

I *was not able* to talk him into it.

While Simon had relinquished control of many aspects of Faire, he remained firm on the topic of faux Shakespeares, no matter how many times I brought it up. Some stupid crap about not wanting to fill the kids' heads with conspiracy theories before they went to college. Fine. Instead, I spent part of the spring recruiting high school students from Simon's English classes, along with a few drama kids. We gathered on Wednesday afternoons at the bookstore, where we read *Romeo and Juliet* together and had roundtable discussions about themes, context, and the best way to bring the words to life. Then we put together a selection of scenes from the play, which they performed on one of the stages at Faire that summer. Caitlin abandoned her fancy lady-in-waiting dress and joined us; she made an excellent Nurse.

The rising seniors in the group had already decided that, even without a show to put on, we would continue the Shakespeare readings in the fall as a kind of book club. We picked *Twelfth Night* to read next, and I ordered copies, which the kids agreed to buy from me instead of downloading elsewhere. Even though Cait was only a junior she was very much part of the group, and already looking forward to smugly sharing her knowledge of the play since she'd already read it.

Although my official job at Faire was "Keep Simon From Twitching Too Much Because Things Were Changing," I was more involved than ever. In addition to directing the kids through their *Romeo and Juliet* scenes, I found myself in charge of the wenches, a job Stacey was happy to give up. It was an easy task, now that I had some advance notice and prep time. Over the winter I talked to the manager of Jackson's, and the bar agreed to sponsor the taverns at the Faire. Yes, *taverns*, plural. I proposed a second tent near the food vendors, since plenty of people would want beer to go with their turkey legs, and once we set it up it quickly became much busier than the tent I had worked the summer before. Waitresses from Jackson's volunteered a day or two at a time, some in busty corsets and some in red T-shirts, and everything ran much more smoothly with professional servers in place. There were no more jokes about beer being forgotten.

Stacey and I were still dressed as tavern wenches, but we were able to roam, floating from one tavern to the other, stopping to curtsy to other characters, engaging in conversation, and all in all having much more fun than we'd had the summer before. I spent a lot of time on the sidelines of a certain chess match, catching kisses from my black-clad pirate. Those leather pants were just as compelling the second summer as they had been the first.

I was proud of Simon. He had a hard time when we first started making changes, but as others made suggestions and we put them in place, he started to understand Sean's impact in his community wouldn't be erased. He even made the biggest suggestion of all: cutting the run of Faire from six weeks to four. I'd mentioned to him what Stacey had said to me about those last two, hottest weeks of the summer being the least busy, and after we spent an evening crunching the numbers at his kitchen table, he realized we were right. Those two extra weeks were like a weight lifted from the whole town. Families with kids in Faire could take vacations at the end of summer; we could hire fewer acts over the course of Faire, which meant more money retained for the schools.

Over the winter I'd found a small apartment on the edge of the downtown area, so I finally got out of April's guest room. Simon had made some noises about me moving in with him, but I loved being close enough to walk to work. Besides, I couldn't picture living in his parents' house, a feeling that only intensified when they came back to town for Christmas and I met them. They were wonderful people—though I retained a little resentment toward them for leaving Simon alone in his grief—but I felt like more of a guest at the Graham home than ever, and I didn't see that changing if I moved my stuff in there. He didn't push, which I appreciated, and we alternated time between our two places. I kept a toothbrush at his house, and he kept one at my apartment.

With Faire over again and the rest of August stretched out lazily before us, I went back to work. Chris and I alternated days at the bookstore for the rest of the summer to give us both a break. Simon dropped by sometimes to work on his laptop in the café, and if we made out in the classics section more than once after closing, the books never said anything.

So life had settled into a nice routine by late August, about two weeks after Faire had ended. I was at the bookstore on a Monday, even though it was closed, catching up on online orders, ordering the books for April's next book club meeting, and other miscellaneous paperwork. I looked up in surprise when the door chimed, but it was Chris, letting herself in with her key.

"You're not supposed to be here," I said. "Aren't you taking your mom to the doctor today?"

"Already did. Everything's good, and she's cleared to go back to Florida in October. Knowing Mom, she'll be packed up in a week." She moved past me to the back room.

"She loves it down there, huh?" I grinned at the spreadsheet I was working on, giving it only half my attention.

Chris groaned. She was not a fan of Florida. "Goddamn hot, buggy state with giant alligators waiting to eat your face. I don't know what she sees in it."

I snorted, and the door chimed again. I turned in surprise; Chris must have left the door unlocked. "I'm sorry, we're not open . . . oh, hey." I smiled to see Simon. Now that Faire was over he'd shaved off his beard, but I'd talked him into keeping his hair longer. Though truthfully, it hadn't taken much convincing. He liked the way I ran my fingers through it.

That wasn't the only piece of the pirate he'd retained going into the fall. The silver hoop earring stayed in his ear, even though his pirate days were over for the year. He'd have to take it out during the week at school, of course, but otherwise that small piece of jewelry seemed to be a touchstone for him, reminding him that Simon the English Teacher could have a little swagger too, could smile a little more freely. Captain Blackthorne the Pirate didn't need to hoard it all.

"Hey." He leaned across the counter, and I did the same on the other side to collect a quick kiss. "Any news on the summer reading front?"

I shook my head. "Not really. One or two. Your kids are worse than last year."

He sighed. "Oh, well. I don't care anyway. Come here."

"What?" A startled laugh escaped me. "What do you mean you don't care?"

He didn't answer me. Instead he held out his hand, and instinctively I took it. "Come here," he said again. "I need to talk to Chris."

"She's in the back room." But he tugged on my hand, and I had no choice but to follow him out from behind the counter and into the back room.

"Your Majesty?" Simon's voice carried through the back room of the store, and I looked at him in startled confusion. It was a good ten months before Chris was Her Majesty again.

Chris poked her head from around a shelving unit, smiling when she saw the both of us. "Simon, hi! I didn't know you were here." She didn't sound convincing, and I was immediately suspicious. "What can I do for you?"

He cleared his throat. "Your Majesty," he said again, his voice formal but not his accented Faire voice, "it has been a year and a day since you bound me to this woman. We have come before you today so I may declare my intentions."

"A year and a day? What are you . . . oh." My eyes went round. The handfasting. It had been on the last day of Faire last year, which would have been a year ago yesterday. With the new Faire schedule I'd lost track, but Simon had remembered.

If Chris was surprised by this, she didn't let it show. "By all means, then, continue. I daresay you don't need me around for the actual declaring, though." She bustled past us, her purse looped over her shoulder.

I turned and watched her leave the back room and head for the front of the shop. A few seconds later the door chimed, followed by the thunk of the key turning in the lock. "That was weird," I said, turning back to Simon. "What was that all . . ."

But he wasn't there. I blinked at the empty space where he'd been standing a moment before, then looked down to where he knelt in front of me. A small square box in his hand. My eyes went even bigger and all the breath left my body. "Simon, what . . ."

"Shush, I'm declaring my intentions." He smiled up at me, but that smile trembled. He held out his hand again and I took it without hesitation, even though my hands were shaking. Everything was shaking.

"Okay," I said, my voice faint and not terribly steady. "What are your intentions?"

"Well," he said. "I have four."

"Four? Seems like a lot."

He narrowed his eyes but didn't lose his smile. "Are you going to argue with me about my intentions?"

I hiccuped a nervous laugh. "Sorry. Please continue."

"Thank you." He cleared his throat. "My first intention is to sell the house. I told Mom and Dad they have until Halloween to decide what they want to keep before it goes on the market."

"What? Simon, that's fantastic!" All of my nervousness drained out of me at this news. I'd wanted to suggest this for months. I'd hated the way his parents had foisted it on him, but hadn't wanted to overstep.

"Yeah." He acknowledged my outburst with a smile. "It turns

out they didn't think I'd want to live in it forever. They gave it to me as a nest egg. So I could sell it and . . . well, that leads me to my second intention."

"Okay. Second intention. Go."

"My second intention is to choose a new house, which I hope you'll help me with, since my third intention is for us to live there together."

"Both very good intentions. I like these a lot." I couldn't believe how calm I sounded when my brain was zinging with energy. "What's number four?"

"Number four is the best one. The most important one. My fourth intention . . ." He swallowed hard, and his smile faltered. I knew what was coming now, and wanted to reassure him even as everything inside me shook with emotion. "My fourth intention is to marry you, Emily. Let me show you every day that you are the most important person in my life." He drew a slow, shaking breath. "Those are my intentions. Do you approve of them? Will you marry me?"

I couldn't answer. I wasn't sure if my voice even worked. So instead I dropped to my knees, and the ring box fell with a thud to the floor behind me as our arms came around each other. I pulled his mouth down to mine. "Yes," I whispered. I tasted tears that could have been his but were probably mine.

The back room wasn't as sexy as the classics section, but I soon discovered it would do in a pinch.

Acknowledgments

Writing is a solitary endeavor, yet the process of bringing a book to life takes the help of so many people.

All the love and thanks to my brilliant agent, Taylor Haggerty, who just rolled with it when I said, "Hey, how about a story with Ren faire pirates and Shakespeare jokes?" You've been my rock during all the publishing madness; I truly wouldn't be here without you.

I can't believe how lucky I am to have found a publishing home at Berkley. From the first phone call with Kerry Donovan, I knew we were on the same wavelength, and I'm so happy we got to work together on this book. It's been so much fun! Everyone at Berkley has been so welcoming and supportive, including Sarah Blumenstock, Jessica Mangicaro, and Jessica Brock, and I can't thank you enough for all your hard work. Sorry about all the vests. (No, I'm not.)

I'm so thankful for my extraordinarily talented critique partners, Vivien Jackson and Gwynne Jackson (no relation) (that I know of). You are two of the most brilliant writers I know;

thank you for reading messy first drafts and helping me bounce ideas. This book wouldn't exist without you. Viv, keep writing that SIC because I need it; and Gwynne, I MISS YOUR FACE.

Annette Christie, you were so kind to read an early draft, and your suggestions increased the swoon level by at least twenty-five percent. You are a genius and I'm forever grateful.

Where would I be without my Bs? Nowhere. Brighton Walsh, Helen Hoang, Ellis Leigh, Anniston Jory, Melissa Marino, Suzanne Baltsar, Laura Elizabeth, Esher Hogan, and Elizabeth Leis Newman, you girls provide all the inspiration, laughter, encouragement, Chicago Mix popcorn, and face masks that I need. I love love love you all.

Additional thanks to the VLC group chat—ReLynn, Helen, Ash, Courtney, Jenny, and Trysh especially, for the love, the pics, the GIFs . . . London Fogs all around. #ICan't

ReLynn Vaughn, thank you especially for the GIFs. You know the ones. You are the best enabler.

Many thanks to Brenda Drake and the Pitch Wars community, especially my mentor, Brighton Walsh, who taught me everything I know about structuring a novel, and also traumatized me with pictures involving Pringles cans. I can't thank you enough, B. The class of 2016 Pitch Wars mentees (Go Raptors!) is a wonderful, supportive group of people and I'm lucky to be one of them. Meet you in the sprantenhausen!

Shout-out to the volunteers, cast, and crew of the Lady of the Lakes Renaissance Faire. Whether I'm a volunteer or a patron, Faire is one of the highlights of my year, and writing this book let me hang out there a little longer. It's been an honor to be a pub wench in your ranks. Special thanks to Michael and Jennifer Dempsey for sharing your stories.

When I asked for beta readers for this book, I hoped one or two people might read it and give me their thoughts. I was amazed and grateful for the deluge of feedback. Thank you, thank you to Kate Clayborn, Elisabeth Lane, Helen Hoang, Re-Lynn Vaughn, Trysh Thompson, Ian Barnes, Rosiee Thor, Adele Buck, Haley Kral, and JR Yates for your time and efforts. You helped make this a better story.

Joining Romance Writers of America was the best decision I made when it was time to take my writing seriously. I'm so grateful to have a local chapter, Central Florida Romance Writers, who have been so supportive and encouraging along the way. Thank you all.

Writing friends are integral, but non-writing friends are just as vital. Amanda Bond and Julie Dietz, thanks for understanding when deadlines had me bailing on nights out, but just as importantly thanks for sometimes dragging me out from behind the computer for wine walks and movie nights! Hate chicken is on me. Mandy Lantigua and TraMi Willey, you Stupid Terminators, I love you.

Finally, I have to thank my husband, Morgan Lee. Occasionally he likes to burst into my office when I'm writing a super-emotional scene to tell me about something funny he found on Facebook, and sometimes he likes to encourage me by saying, "Is that book done yet?" and "You're not getting paid by the hour to write that book, you know." But he has always believed in me, and never blinked an eye when I went to retreats and conferences that we couldn't afford so I could improve my craft. I've never seen anyone as happy as he was the moment I told him I sold a novel. Thank you for having my back, honey. I love you.

S*imon turned his* attention to me, and his brows drew together. "Are you sure about that necklace, Stacey?" His voice was pitched low since he'd dropped the accent and his character. "It seems a little . . . elaborate for a tavern wench."

My fist closed around the pendant, the dragonfly's wings digging into my palm. "Perhaps it's time for a change, then, Captain." I kept my voice light, almost teasing, so neither of them could see my irritation.

"She has a point," Emily said. "The taverns are mostly run by volunteers now. Maybe Stacey and I can be different characters next summer."

"Perhaps." Simon shifted from one foot to the other as his Faire accent crept back. He didn't like change, especially when it came to Faire. But Emily looped her arm through his, bringing his focus to her, and the smile returned to his face. "Perhaps," he said again. Fully back in character, his voice was pure pirate, and he bussed Emily's temple. "For now, though, I'm due on the chess field. Would you lasses care to join me?"

"The last human chess match of the year? I wouldn't miss it." Emily's devotion was adorable, especially since the chess match was as choreographed as the joust we'd just watched. Twice a day, Captain Blackthorne fought against Marcus MacGregor, a giant of a man wearing little more than a kilt and knee-high boots and carrying a massive sword. And twice a day, Captain Blackthorne lost said fight. But Emily still cheered him on, every time.

I shook my head. "I'll walk around a bit more, if you'll forgive me." I was too restless. The last thing I wanted to do was stand still and watch a show I'd seen so many times I could probably perform it myself.

Emily peered at me with shrewd eyes. "Everything all right?"

"Yes, yes." I waved her off. "I'd simply like to take in the scenery a little while longer."

"Of course." She squeezed my arm in goodbye as Simon doffed his hat and gave me a friendly bow. "Meet you at pub sing, then."

I had to laugh at that. Emily never made it up front for the farewell show of the day. But hope sprang eternal.

Alone now, I stowed my old necklace in my belt pouch, tied the green silk cord around my neck, and set off down the lane again, my long skirts kicking up dust. I took the long way around the perimeter of the site where we held Faire every year.

It was midafternoon and the sun was still high in the sky, but it felt like the sun was setting on the summer. Many of the shows had finished, but I passed a children's magic show that was halfway through its set, and I stopped to listen to the magician's patter for a few moments. Multicolored banners hung from the trees, catching the sunlight as they blew gently in the breeze. A couple of kids ran past me, headed for the lemonade stand. The sound of a tin whistle floated from somewhere nearby.

I ducked inside a booth displaying hand-tooled leather items, inhaling the heady scent. I'd walked by this booth several times but had never explored its contents. Inside, the wire-mesh walls were lined with leather goods—vambraces and belt pouches, as well as modern-day accessories like belts and wallets.

"All handmade," the attendant said, not bothering with a fake accent. She was my age, dressed in low-key peasant garb: a long, dark green skirt and a loose chemise, pulled in with a leather waist cincher.

"Do you make all this?" I touched a soft blue backpack made of buttery leather that hung on the end of one display.

"My husband and I do, yes." She bent down to scoop up a small toddler in a long chemise. Even the kids dressed period here at Faire. She turned to greet another patron who had ventured out of the sun and into the cool shade of the booth. But before she walked away she looked over her shoulder. "Anything you like, let me know. You'll get the Rennie discount: Thirty percent off."

"Oh. Thanks." A warm feeling went through me at her words. Not at the discount, but at what it represented. She considered me one of them: one of the crew. With as much effort as I put into this Faire each summer, I'd never considered myself on the same level as the performers and the vendors who came through every year. They had their own culture, almost their own language, and I was on the outside looking in. After today these woods would be empty, while all the acts and vendors around me moved on to the next Faire, and it was a sharp pain to the heart. Like life was moving on, and I was being left behind. Sometimes I wished I was the one packing up and moving on. Sometimes I was tired of standing still.

I blew out a long breath. The Renaissance faire had been my

happy place since I was eighteen, and I didn't like the way I was feeling now. Had I outgrown the Faire? Or had it outgrown me?

I took one more glance back at the blue backpack before making my way out of the booth. One necklace wasn't enough retail therapy to keep this melancholy at bay. Thirty percent off . . . I was going to have to come back for that.

I continued to wander the lanes with no conscious destination in mind, when my feet brought me to the Marlowe Stage. The Dueling Kilts' last set was about to begin. Perfect timing. I slipped into the back of the crowd, between a couple of costumed vendors, right as the guys took the stage.

The Dueling Kilts were a trio of brothers who played Irish standards, mixed with slightly naughty drinking songs, all on a hand drum, guitar, and fiddle. Their instruments were acoustic, their kilts hit just at the knee, and they were very, very easy on the eyes. My eyes strayed, as they usually did, to Dex MacLean. His red kilt was shot through with just enough dark green to keep him from looking like a stoplight, but it was still bright enough to draw attention. As though his powerful legs weren't doing that well enough on their own.

His broad shoulders strained against his off-white linen shirt, and he stomped one booted foot in time with the music he played. He shook his long dark hair out of his eyes as he turned to his compatriots, and his smile made something thud in my chest. Dex MacLean had been my favorite part of Faire for the past two summers. The man had a body like a Hemsworth, and I'd explored about every inch of it last summer. Just like he'd explored mine. He'd been clear from the start, of course. No strings. Just sex. I was fine with that. I wasn't looking to settle down anytime soon, and I didn't like Dex for his conversation.

Again, body like a Hemsworth. What kind of fool would I be to pass that up?

This summer had been different. He'd lost his phone over the winter, along with my number, so my initial texts had gone unanswered. We'd snatched a night or two together, and he'd still been fan-damn-tastic at it. But he hadn't asked for my number again, and I didn't volunteer it.

So now I watched Dex play this last show on this last day of Faire with a curious mix of satisfaction, smugness, and regret. *I've had that*, the smug-and-satisfied side of my brain said. *But why hadn't I gone back for more?* I pushed down the latter thought, opting instead to appreciate what—and whom—I'd done.

Next to me, one of the vendors sighed. I recognized her; she sold tarot cards and crystals out of a booth shaped like a traveling wagon. She leaned over to the woman next to her. "So much pretty on one stage."

Her companion nodded. "Should be illegal, those legs. Thank God for kilts."

The tarot card seller sighed again. "Too bad he's such a manwhore."

"Really." I raised my eyebrows in her direction, and the two women turned to me with conspiratorial grins. There was that feeling again, of being a Faire insider, with access to the best gossip.

"Oh yeah." She leaned a little closer to me, and I did the same, like she was about to share a secret. "I'm pretty sure he's got a girl at every Faire."

"I'm sure he does," the other vendor said. "Wonder who it is here." She glanced around the audience as though she could identify Dex's Willow Creek hookup by some kind of secret symbol.

I bit hard on the inside of my cheek. If he was discreet enough to not blab about it, then I would be too.

"No idea," I said, pleased at how noncommittal my voice sounded.

"Lucky girl, though. I bet she had a hell of a summer." The tarot vendor snickered, and I forced myself to do the same, though my laugh was a little hollow.

At the end of the song the two women slipped back out of the crowd and back to their booths. As the next song started, there was a touch on my elbow.

"Good morrow, milady Beatrice."

My attention slid away from Dex and to a different MacLean altogether. Daniel, Dex's cousin, managed the Dueling Kilts. "Well met, good sir." I bobbed a quick curtsy, still in character. Then I dropped the accent. "Faire's about over, you know. You can call me Stacey now."

Daniel huffed out a laugh. "New necklace?"

My hand went to the dragonfly around my neck, the silver warm now from laying against my skin. "It is," I confirmed. "Just picked it up this afternoon."

He nodded. "Looks nice." His eyes lingered for just a second, then he turned his attention back to his cousins on the stage. Not for the first time, I contemplated the MacLean DNA. Dex and Daniel were both tall, but that was where the resemblance ended. Dex was dark, solid, and strong-muscled, a man who looked like he was about to rock your world in a dangerous way. Daniel was lean and fair, with bottle-green eyes and more of a swimmer's build than a bodybuilder's. His red hair was partially hidden under the black baseball cap he always wore. He looked less like he was about to rock your world and more like he knew exactly how you took your coffee and would bring it to you in bed. While the Kilts played the Faire, Daniel stuck around to man their merchandising booth. It didn't seem like enough to keep him busy, but maybe Dex and the others required that much supervision.

Daniel was a comfortable, easy presence, even though I was pretty sure he knew all about Dex and me. Especially since I'd run into Daniel at the hotel ice machine at two in the morning. There'd been no explaining that away.

Sure enough. "You . . . Um." Daniel cleared his throat, and I glanced over. His eyes were still on the stage. "You know about Dex, right?"

I blinked. "Well, I'm familiar with him." Very familiar, but he probably didn't need details.

He shook his head and leaned a shoulder against a tree, hands shoved into the front pockets of his jeans. "I mean, you know he's . . ." He sighed and turned those green eyes my way. "You know he's kind of a player, right?"

"A wench at every Faire?" I raised my eyebrow, and his laugh in response was more of a snort. "I'd heard that." I sighed a dramatic sigh and looked back at the stage. "Guess I'm not special."

I'd meant that as sarcasm, but Daniel didn't respond. I turned my head, expecting a knowing smirk on his face, but instead a flush crept up the back of his neck as he studied the ground. "I didn't say . . ." He cleared his throat and tried again. "I don't mean that you . . . I mean you're . . ." Finally he sighed in exasperation and looked up at me again. "I just don't want you to get hurt, that's all."

Oh. That. I waved an unconcerned hand. "Don't worry. I'm a big girl. I can handle it." I cast around for something else to talk about. Anything. "So. Off to the next one, right? Are you going to the Maryland Ren Fest? I think everyone hits that one next."

He nodded. "Yep. Very different than smaller ones like this."

"Sure." I pressed my lips together. "I bet you're glad to see the back end of Willow Creek." I looked hard at the stage. I loved this Faire. I loved this town. But that didn't mean that everyone did.

"Not at all." If Daniel had picked up on my reaction he didn't say anything. When I glanced back to him he was looking at the stage too, not at me. "This is one of my favorite stops every year. It's a nice town."

And just like that, my lick of defensive anger dissolved, and relief swept through me like a cool breeze. "Yeah. I think so too."

Onstage, the Dueling Kilts finished their set, and Dex lifted his chin in my direction. I'd already raised my hand in a wave when I caught Daniel doing an identical chin-raise in response. Ah. I turned the awkward half-wave into a too-casual check of my hair. Of course. Wench at every Faire. And Dex was done with both me and the Willow Creek Faire.

I shook off the sting of disappointment. There were only a few minutes left in this year's Faire now, and I was going to wring every possible moment out of it. These weeks in the woods were so much more fun, so much more interesting, than my real life. After all, I lived in a small town. Not a lot changed in Willow Creek.

Yeah. Famous last words.

Photo by Morgan H. Lee

Jen DeLuca was born and raised near Richmond, Virginia, but now lives in Central Florida with her husband and a houseful of rescue pets. She loves latte-flavored lattes, Hokies football, and the Oxford comma. *Well Met* is her first novel, inspired by her time volunteering as a pub wench with her local Renaissance faire.

CONNECT ONLINE

jendeluca.com
facebook.com/jendelucabooks
twitter.com/jaydee_ell

Ready to find
your next great read?

Let us help.

Visit prh.com/nextread

Penguin
Random
House